# Praise for
# Nicci French

"Fabulous, unsettling, and riveting."
—Louise Penny

"Complex. . . . Intriguing. . . . Truly unique."
—Tami Hoag

"Searing. . . . In the rich vein of Kate Atkinson."
—Joseph Finder

"Unforgettable. Psychological dynamite."
—Alan Bradley

# THE
# LYING
# ROOM

# THE
# LYING
# ROOM

# NICCI FRENCH

*WM*

WILLIAM MORROW
*An Imprint of* HarperCollins*Publishers*

THE LYING ROOM. Copyright © 2019 by Joined-Up Writing. All rights reserved. Printed in the United States of America. No part of this book may be used or reproduced in any manner whatsoever without written permission except in the case of brief quotations embodied in critical articles and reviews. For information, address HarperCollins Publishers, 195 Broadway, New York, NY 10007.

HarperCollins books may be purchased for educational, business, or sales promotional use. For information, please email the Special Markets Department at SPsales@harpercollins.com.

Published as *The Lying Room* in the United Kingdom in 2019 by Simon & Schuster.

FIRST U.S. EDITION

Library of Congress Cataloging-in-Publication Data has been applied for.

ISBN 978-0-06-267672-6
ISBN 978-0-06-267673-3 (library hardcover edition)

19 20 21 22 23   LSC   10 9 8 7 6 5 4 3 2 1

*To the wonderful Sarah Ballard,*
*our guide and friend*

Therefore I lie with her,
and she with me

SHAKESPEARE, SONNET 138

# 1

# THE ASSIGNATION

When Neve pulled up the blinds, the kitchen sprang into life like a theatre set, empty and waiting for the familiar show to begin. She looked around: it was all a bit threadbare, the skirting boards scuffed and that crack running down the wall. She and Fletcher had been meaning to do something about it for years. There were wine stains on the table and a couple of cigarette burns, cobwebs drifting high up among the lights. Dinner from last night hadn't been properly cleared away. There were dirty plates on the surface next to the sink and the milk had been left out. Last night: she let the memory pulse through her and then she pushed it away. Not now. Not here.

The clock said it was ten past seven. She filled a glass with water and drank it slowly, tied her dressing gown more firmly, took a deep breath and turned to face the room. The door opened on cue.

'Morning,' she said cheerfully to her eldest son.

Rory blinked, mumbled something, bobbing his head. He was wearing blue jeans, a blue tee shirt and a blue jumper. He had her Irish paleness and he was going to be tall, as she was: in the last year, he had grown by four inches, like a piece of elastic being stretched to the point of snapping. Sometimes Neve thought she could almost see him growing, his limbs elongating, his feet large and flat, his bony face exhausted.

'You're very matching,' she said. She wanted to put an arm round him but she restrained herself; he had started to dislike being touched; hugging him had become a stiff, awkward business. He would soon be eleven. Next year he would be at secondary school and in uniform.

He sat at the table and she put a packet of cornflakes and a bowl in front of him and got the milk from the fridge. He only ever ate cornflakes for breakfast, and now he tipped a rustling heap of them into the bowl and covered it with a pool of milk. He pulled a book towards him and opened it. From upstairs came the sound of raised voices, a lavatory flushing, a door banging. With a jolt, she remembered the clothes she had flung into the washing machine last night and hurriedly pulled them out, into the clothes basket.

The clock said seven-fifteen.

'Morning,' Neve said again, still cheery. One of her jobs had always been to crank up the day, get them all going.

It was Fletcher entering this time, his hair damp from

the shower and his beard newly trimmed. He barely looked at her, staring abstractedly out into the garden instead. She was grateful for that.

'Tea?' he asked.

She didn't need to answer. She always had tea in the morning. Fletcher always had coffee. It was his job to make them and empty the dishwasher and put out the rubbish. It was her job to get breakfast down the children and make their packed lunches.

She shook oats into a saucepan and added milk and a tiny pinch of salt, put it on the hob to heat. She did it all without thinking. Connor had porridge with golden syrup on top every morning. Fletcher had toast and marmalade.

Fletcher poured water onto the teabags, then went to the stairs and shouted, 'Connor! Breakfast!'

Dreamily, Neve stirred the porridge, feeling it thicken against the spoon. Her body felt soft and boneless. In the garden the autumn light was thick. She put one thumb against her lower lip and for a brief moment closed her eyes.

She heard, dimly, that Fletcher was saying something just behind her and looked round.

'What are your plans today?' He put a mug of tea in front of her.

'I thought I'd go to the allotment. Make the most of my new free time.'

To be outside, she thought with a rush of relief, there in the coolness of the morning, sinking a spade into the earth, pulling up weeds, getting tired and dirty, blisters on her hands and soil under her nails and not thinking of anything. A few weeks ago, she had taken the plunge and gone half-time at work. She knew that in almost every way it was a foolish decision. She had always been the main earner and they needed the money more than ever. Mabel was about to go to university. Meanwhile, everything from the boiler to the roof seemed to be decaying in its own way. The gutters needed replacing and there was damp in the little room behind the kitchen. She would sometimes tot up figures, trying to make the sums come out differently, discussing it with Fletcher in a matter-of-fact way that wouldn't make him feel diminished. 'It's just the way it's turned out,' she would say.

One evening a few months ago, after she had biked home from work through the pouring rain and was making supper, still in her yellow cycling jacket with soaking trousers and squelching shoes and water dripping from her hair, she had thought: *I can't go on like this. I've had enough.* Enough of always being in a hurry, always a bit behind, always feeling there was something she'd forgotten; enough of feeling close to tears in meetings or of waking in the night with her head full of unfinished tasks and, behind everything, standing over her like a dark wall, the perpetual, relentless, bone-thinning anxiety about Mabel. Going part-time, working only three and a half days a week, was an experiment in carving out a space – just a small space – for herself so that she didn't go quite mad. *And look how that turned out*, she thought.

Fletcher was emptying the dishwasher. She was rummaging in the fridge for something for the boys' packed lunches. Now Connor was in the room, solid and round-faced and bristle-headed and loud, everything done emphatically while his skinny elder brother bent over a book about insects. Neve looked at her sons and her husband and for a moment they all seemed like wind-up figures, going through the motions of the morning, as they did every morning, in the routine built up over the years without even noticing, each with their allotted parts.

*I can see you.* The phrase fell through her mind like a smooth, round stone, so clear that for a moment she thought it had been said out loud and stared around her. Fletcher was slicing toast, frowning in concentration, the tip of his tongue on his upper lip. Or had it been: *I* can see *you*?

She unwrapped a block of cheese. How was it possible to feel so tired and so awake at the same time, so wretched and so exultant? Normal, be normal, she instructed herself.

'Did you sleep OK?' she asked Fletcher.

'Fine. I didn't even wake when you came in. What time was it?'

'I don't know. Not too late. But you were dead to the world.' She picked up her tea and took a large, hot gulp.

'After midnight,' said a voice, cold and sharp as a blade.

'Mabel! You're up early.'

Mabel stood in the doorway. She was wearing a

short, brown-and-black checked dress, ribbed tights, smart little ankle boots. Her brown hair, which left to itself fell in cloudy curls, was tied in tight plaits and perhaps because of this her face seemed thinner than usual.

'I've been awake for hours,' she said. 'Maybe I haven't even slept. Maybe I was awake all night. Don't do that!' She glared at Connor, who was digging his hand into the cereal packet and now scooped out a handful to push it into his mouth. He glared back at her; his mouth was too full to answer. 'Anyway,' she continued to Neve. 'I heard you come in. After midnight.'

'No wonder I'm tired,' Neve said brightly. Perhaps too brightly. She had a sudden longing for a cigarette, though it had been years since she last smoked, unless surreptitious cigarettes at parties counted. She had given up when she had children. Stopped smoking, stopped drinking, stopped dancing till dawn and eating fish and chips for breakfast, stopped spending days wandering round markets with her gang of friends or taking off for an unplanned weekend by the sea with Fletcher because, well, why not? It wasn't that she regretted these things because even now – or especially now, when she was putting it all at risk – she loved her life, her children, her husband. But why does no one tell you, she wondered, how *hard* it is? Except of course they do tell you and you don't believe them. You think you can do it differently, cost free, carefree.

Mabel sat herself down at the table and Fletcher put a mug of ginger and lemon tea in front of her. Mabel always drank herbal tea at breakfast and if things were going well, she would eat some fruit, one blueberry at a time, one segment of a tangerine, with all the white pith pulled delicately off. No fruit this morning. Neve tried not to watch her. She seemed to have spent years watching her daughter and trying not to watch her, of always being on guard, heart like a bruise and throat clogged with dread but trying to behave as if everything was all right. In eight days, she told herself, Mabel would be gone – and what would she do then? Who would she be without her?

'How was Tamsin?' asked Fletcher.

'Oh, you know. Still angry. She got a bit drunk,' Neve said, busily spreading butter on slices of bread now. 'I didn't like to leave her.'

Fletcher turned the radio on for the seven-thirty news and sat down with his toast and marmalade. He was looking at something on his phone, intent. Connor was saying something about football after school. Rory was levering himself from his chair, still reading his book, all bones and sharp wrists. He needed new clothes; he needed hearty soup and collard greens and sticky toffee pudding. Mabel was taking tiny sips of her tea, her eyes watchful over the rim of her mug, her neat plaits framing her mutinous face.

There was a screech of a chair as Connor sprang to his feet and at the same time the ping of a text from Neve's mobile that was lying on the table amid all the debris of breakfast, in full view.

She turned to look and then laid a hand flat over it.

'Go and clean your teeth,' she said to Connor. 'You

don't want to be late again. Then you need to feed the guinea pig.' She knew he wouldn't.

She scooped the phone up and slid it into her dressing-gown pocket.

Mabel slid from her chair. 'I'm off,' she said.

'You're going out?'

'Is that a problem?'

'Where?' It was out of her mouth before she could stop herself, but since when had words become so treacherous? 'I mean, it's a bit early. Quiet, Connor, I can't hear myself speak. Teeth! Now!'

'A bit early for what?'

'I don't know. Don't take any notice of me. I'm tired. I'll see you later. If you're around. Are you in for supper?'

'I don't know.'

Mabel put her mug down and left the room. The front door opened and then closed. She had always been good at sudden exits.

'You do look a bit washed out,' said Fletcher. 'And your bruise is turning yellow.'

Neve put up a hand to touch her cheek, which felt puffy and sore. A few days ago, cycling home in the dark, someone had pushed her off her bike, or stumbled into her path – maybe a drunk man, or a person angry with the world. She had flown in eerie slow motion through the air, thinking, *this is going to hurt,* and landed in a heap on the road. Her cheek had been badly grazed and her jeans ripped.

She looked at her husband: his collar-length dark hair

and his neat beard; his round glasses and behind them, sad, brown, watchful eyes. There were little creases on his face she hadn't noticed before and the beginnings of a cold sore at one side of his mouth. He had a glum, morning air to him. In her pocket, the phone was alive, thrumming.

'I'll be fine. Early night.' She remembered something. 'You know that we're going to Renata's birthday tomorrow evening?'

'Is it an early evening thing?'

'More of a party.'

Fletcher groaned.

'We're out the day after tomorrow as well,' Neve continued.

'What do you mean?' said Fletcher.

'There's a kind of college reunion. Jackie something organised it, and Tamsin.'

'Jackie who?'

Neve thought for a moment.

'I can't remember. Yes. Cornfield. Jackie Cornfield. You must remember her.'

'Vaguely. But why do we need to meet her for a drink?'

'Because that's what old college friends do. Not just her – us lot, and other people as well.'

'This is going to be the week from hell.' He stood up. 'I'm going to see someone about a job. I'll be back later.'

Neve allowed herself a moment's thought about her husband. Maybe that was why he was in a sour mood. Fletcher was an illustrator. Or at least that was what he answered when people asked what his job was. But the money he earned mainly came from his painting and decorating jobs. It was work he despised. He hated not earning money and he hated earning it. Sometimes, when he had no work on, he would sit all day in the small room they'd made into his studio and Neve knew he didn't even make a mark on the paper, and he knew that she knew. Sometimes, Mabel would be sitting in her room as well, or lying in her bed, the covers pulled over her. On those days, Neve always made an extra effort to fill the house with cheerful things: putting on music, turning all the lights on, baking cakes or biscuits, playing cards with the boys or being roundly beaten at computer games. It was like there was a button at the back of her neck: press it, and she would spring into cheerful-mother mode.

'I didn't know. I hope it goes well.' She put one hand on his shoulder. They were almost the same height: shoulder to shoulder and eye to eye. Rory was going to be tall too and it was too early to tell with Connor. But Mabel was small and slight: their changeling child.

Fletcher picked up his jacket and left. Neve shooed Connor up the stairs, shouting instructions after him. Then she was alone in the kitchen again, the air stilling around her. She took her mobile from her pocket and keyed in the password. The text appeared on the screen: *I'm free until midday. Come as soon as you can.* There was no caller ID but it didn't matter. There was only one person who could have sent it.

\*

She put the breakfast things into the dishwasher, wiped the crumbs off the table and hung out the few clothes in the garden, the wind fluttering through the bright skirt and the white shirt whose top two buttons were missing. Then she finished making the packed lunches: sandwiches – cheese and tomato for Rory, cheese without tomato for Connor, an apple each and an oat biscuit. It was pretty uninspired but she'd forgotten to stock up yesterday. Yesterday: like a dream; or like the only thing that was real and everything else seemed thin and vague. She chopped a nectarine into a bowl and spooned yoghurt over the top and sat down to eat it with another mug of tea, while upstairs she could hear water running and an object being dropped heavily on to the floor. But she couldn't face a mouthful.

At half past eight Neve saw Rory and Connor out of the door and watched them as they walked up the road, side by side but in their different worlds: Rory had earphones in and his shoulders were hunched together, his hands in his pocket. Connor looked small and robust beside him, and he walked erratically, slowing down then speeding up, swinging his backpack from one shoulder to the other.

At last she was alone. She went upstairs and took off her dressing gown, looking once more at the message on her phone and then turning it face down on the bed. She had a shower so hot that the water felt like needles on her skin, soaping her body all over, washing her hair and for once making the effort to blow-dry it rather than just rub it roughly with a towel. She cleaned her

11

teeth for longer than usual, watching her face in the mirror as she did so. Fletcher was right. The bruise was turning yellow, which gave her a jaundiced, unhealthy air. In two weeks' time, she would be forty-six. Next year, she and Fletcher would celebrate their twentieth wedding anniversary. They had been so young and in such a hurry then, so sure of each other and their life ahead. Now there were tiny silver threads in her dark hair: no one else had noticed them yet. There were little lines gathering on her face. At night, lying in bed beside Fletcher, she sometimes had hot flushes that made her whole body heavy and oppressive, like she was drowning in the rising flood of herself.

She should go to the allotment but she wasn't going to. She knew that one day, probably one day soon, she was going to regret this. Part of her, the part that watched and judged, already did.

She rubbed lotion into her body, cream on her face. She put on black knickers and a new black bra, snipping off the price tag, feeling slightly sick with longing, with danger, with guilt, with freedom, with being a stranger to herself. She pulled on skinny black jeans and her beloved, scuffed ankle boots, and then rummaged through her drawers till she found a jersey that was pale grey, soft against her skin. Small silver earrings. A beaten-up leather jacket that she had owned almost all her adult life. A bright scarf. No make-up: the first few times she'd worn some, but those days were over. She put perfume on her wrists and behind her ears, a dry, musky, night-time fragrance. It wasn't even nine o' clock but time had folded up on itself. She slid her bangle over her wrist.

Key. Mobile. Wallet. She put her new leather backpack over her shoulders. She wasn't used to it yet; it was too glossy and had too many complicated sections, so she kept losing things in it. Her old one had lasted more than fifteen years, until it had been stolen from under her nose when she was at lunch with Renata and Tamsin. She lifted her bike down from its hook in the hall and wheeled it on to the pavement, mounted and swung out into the cool bright morning, heart lifting like a bird in flight. Away.

She had cycled the route from Clapton into town and from town back to Clapton so often that it sometimes felt almost invisible. She'd done it on hot summer nights in shorts and a tee shirt. She'd done it in driving rain with hands so numb that she could barely shift the gears. She'd cycled to business meetings, to Christmas parties and birthday parties and leaving parties. She'd cycled to markets and to shops and to funeral homes. She'd cycled when she was so tired that she almost fell asleep in the saddle and she'd cycled on bright sunny winter mornings when she felt awake to every glimmer of light, every ripple of sound. She'd cycled sober, she'd cycled stoned, she'd cycled drunk and on one startling occasion had decided to get off the bike when she had the distinct impression that the passing cars were talking to her.

She passed the corner of Hackney Downs.

Two men walked past carrying tennis rackets. People were pushing buggies. And she was cycling into town to commit adultery, having also committed adultery the previous evening.

Through London Fields, little children running around, dogs running after sticks.

Yesterday, she had cycled home in the darkness with no lights in a fog of wine and aching pleasure and guilt. It had been after midnight, as Mabel had sourly reminded her, when she'd opened the door softly, taken off her shoes and tiptoed up the stairs. In the bathroom, listening out for any sound, she'd hastily taken her clothes off and then crept downstairs again in the darkness, put them in the washing machine, switched it on.

Last night had been a sort of farewell: he was going to a conference for several days. This morning was unexpected; clearly he had found a few extra hours. It had been so long since someone had wanted her like that, urgently, every minute counting.

At the canal, she joined all the other cyclists in their gleaming helmets and high-visibility jackets heading into the busy centre.

Last night, when she'd got into bed beside Fletcher in the darkness, felt him shift his position and heard a mutter from him out of his sleep, she'd wondered how could he not know. How could he not sense it, even in his deep sleep? It felt like she was giving off an electric charge, sparks that would jab and sting at anybody near her. She had always thought that if one of them had an affair, the betrayal would explode their marriage, blowing the life they had painstakingly constructed over the years into glinting, jagged pieces. Yet she had betrayed Fletcher, day after day, and nothing had happened. He still slept peacefully beside her at night and rose with her in the morning; the boys went off to school and returned; Mabel still perplexed the family with her restless moods, swinging between charm and rage; Neve still managed the chaos of the house, went to work, saw her friends, paid the bills. Life continued in its tracks. Perhaps, she thought, it would be like a building that is demolished, holding its shape after the button is pushed, only gradually losing its outline, wavering, folding in on itself with a roar.

Pedalling along the towpath, Neve tried to think clearly, if only to avoid steering into the canal. She had seen that happen once to someone else. She wasn't sure whether the man had been pushed or whether he had swerved to avoid someone or whether he had just been inattentive and missed a curve. But she witnessed the aftermath: a man in a suit, knee-deep in the water, one hand clutching his bike, one hand on the bank. She'd stopped with several other people to pull him and his bike up on to the land. He kept apologising. Everyone said it didn't matter, but he kept saying sorry, to someone, for something. She mostly remembered being surprised at how shallow the water was, just a couple of feet. She'd always thought it was deeper.

Leaving the canal, she cycled through the smart little streets behind the Angel and crossed City Road down past Sadler's Wells and on to Theobalds Road. A glimpse of the huge plane trees of Gray's Inn. A throb of anticipation, and the shivery feeling that nobody, apart from him, knew where she was. In the last few weeks she had travelled into another country, a country where everything felt different, where the rules no longer applied. She understood with absolute clarity that what she was doing was wrong. She was deceiving Fletcher but she wasn't going to deceive herself.

She had to concentrate as she went past Red Lion Square, lorries and buses and building works and fumes that made her cough. At the lights, she waited next to a cyclist delivering sandwiches, and as the lorry behind them revved its engine, they exchanged dismayed glances: the nightmare of High Holborn. The lights changed and a taxi swung across, almost hitting her, and then she was across Kingsway at last. She pulled on to the pavement, got off and wheeled the bike down Drury Lane, where she locked it to a post. She checked her reflection in the window of a sandwich bar.

The anonymous brick building in the small side street must have been a warehouse once but now, like everything else, it had been converted into apartments. Neve punched in the code and walked up the stairs. She took out her purse, easing the key out from where it was discreetly stowed behind a credit card, opened the door and stepped inside.

'Hey,' she called.

There was no answer.

'Saul.'

No answer. Perhaps he had stepped out to buy

something like coffee or milk. It was half past nine. She took off her jacket and hung it on a hook by the front door.

She walked along the little corridor and into the living room and suddenly there was too much to take in, like she had been blinded by the light or deafened by an explosion and then punched at the same time. She stepped back away from it until she felt the wall behind her, holding her up.

He was lying on his back and he was dead. Somehow she'd never even known the meaning of being dead until she'd seen those open eyes. They weren't staring eyes. They were just things now, open and exposed. His mouth was also gaping open, as if in vast, unending surprise.

His head was framed by a pool of blood, dark red, smooth. His face looked dead but every bit of his body looked dead as well. His arms and legs were splayed in unnatural positions. His right elbow was caught under his body, which made his hand stick up. It was as if he was halfway through the process of turning over. It looked uncomfortable and Neve felt an impulse to make him comfortable, to pull the arm free, like when they had been entangled in bed together, sweating, out of breath and she helped him ease his hand from under her bare back.

The front of his grey suit had ridden up, exposing his belt and the lower part of his white shirt. One of his knees was slightly raised and a sock was visible, an improbably garish red and yellow. She knew those socks. Once they had stumbled into bed blindly and passionately and unthinkingly and afterwards, lying across him, she had peeled them off, belatedly, and he had laughed.

She looked around the room. At the far end, away from the street, was a small dining table. One of the chairs was lying on its side and she thought she could see what had happened. He had stood on the chair for something – to hang a picture? To change a light bulb? – and had slipped and fallen heavily, catching the edge of the table, tried to raise himself, failed and fallen back and bled to death.

Just for a moment she had the thought: what a terrible, stupid way to die. Then she saw something else, lying on the floor, but not within his reach. It was closer to her, near the street side of the room. It was a hammer, a big one. The handle was bound in blue vinyl; the shaft was silvery steel. But the head was dark, wet. She leaned down to look more closely. It was clearly blood. She stepped towards the body and almost immediately recoiled. The far side of his head, the side she hadn't been able to see, wasn't properly there. It was caved in. It was a dark mush. She could make out the fragments of bone.

As she raised herself up, she felt a swirling dizziness, as if she might fall over or be sick. She took a few slow breaths to steady herself.

She looked at the hammer and she looked back at the body. At Saul's body. It was hard to think. It felt impossible to make sense of anything, but one thought slowly emerged and hardened and took shape. This was a murder. Saul had been murdered. She turned the sentence around in her head: someone had murdered Saul. He had texted her – what was it? An hour ago? More like two hours. And in that time he had been murdered.

She took out her phone ready to dial 999. She had never found it so hard to dial a number before. Her fingers were trembling over the keys and then she stopped, looking back at the table. It still had the remnants of the dinner from the night before, the dinner they had eaten together. Plates, cutlery, a half-empty salad bowl. But no wine bottle and no wine glasses. She didn't need to look for them, she knew where they were. She walked back and along the corridor where they had staggered last night, entangled in each other, clutching the glasses and the half-full bottle, and she opened the bedroom door and was hit by the smell of perfume, her perfume, and other smells, the smells of bodies.

The bed was unmade. There was a glass on each side of the bed. The empty bottle was lying on the carpet.

There was a little chair in the corner and, for the first time since she had entered the flat, she sat down and made herself think: not about herself, not even about Saul, who she had loved, or been in love with at least, and who was dead and she would never see again or hold again. No. She thought about Mabel, about her terrible last years, everything that she'd come through. She'd been such an eager little girl, optimistic and vulnerable, but in her teenage years that had changed; the house had slowly darkened and dread had gripped the family. Perhaps it had been because of the drugs; perhaps because of the boy she had lost her heart to in that agony of first love; perhaps just because she was a teenager and full of turbulence and longing. As Neve stood there, her phone in her hand, she remembered those times: Mabel crouched in the corner of her room, her knees drawn up under her chin, vomit on the floor beside her, staring at Neve with dull eyes. Mabel not coming home. Mabel coming home at dawn, lipstick smeared across her face and her clothes ripped. Mabel in hospital on that awful night, tubes in her arm, her face almost yellow. There had been days when Neve and Fletcher had thought she wouldn't survive. Every time the phone rang Neve's heart would thump wildly. But she had. What would happen when she discovered that her mother had been having an affair, that her beloved father had been betrayed? Would everything unravel, the life that had been so painstakingly stitched back together?

Neve stood up and walked through and looked at Saul lying on the floor.

He was dead. He had been murdered. But it wasn't about her or them. That was irrelevant to whatever it was that had happened here. She looked at her watch, understanding that she needed to make up her mind and then she needed to act. The blinds on the windows facing the street were closed. Nobody could see in from the office across the street.

She decided.

First things first. In the bedroom, she pulled the

20

sheets off the bed, the cover off the duvet and rolled them up. She fetched the towels from the bathroom (they were still damp from last night). She fetched the little hand towel from the second lavatory. She pushed them into the washing machine in the little kitchen. Was there anything else? She couldn't think of anything. She put it on a quick wash: twenty-eight minutes.

She slid off her bangle and put it on the surface near the sink, then found some kitchen gloves under the sink and pulled them on. She took a series of trips between the table and the kitchen, loading the plates and glasses into the dishwasher. She'd cleared the table and all the surfaces. Was there anything she'd forgotten? Again she walked around the flat. In the bathroom was a glass with the two toothbrushes in. It was so stupid, but suddenly she couldn't remember which was the one she had brought, so she took them both.

She closed the dishwasher and put it on the shortest wash: thirty-four minutes. The larger items, the salad bowl, a saucepan, serving spoons, were in the sink. She scrubbed them thoroughly and laid them out to dry.

This was only the beginning.

She pulled the black plastic bag out of the kitchen swing bin. It was about a quarter full. She tossed the two toothbrushes into it. Then, standing there in the kitchen with a dull ache that started in her chest and spread up into her throat, her ears, her head, like a low hum of pain, she made herself think. She had to do this systematically, room by room, making sure she didn't miss anything. She had to remove every single trace of herself. Saul was dead but Mabel was alive. She had to hold on to that.

She took a second plastic bag from under the sink for the things she would take away and started where it was easiest: the bathroom. Taking off her soft jumper, she laid it in the hall with the vague sense that she mustn't spread fibres around. In the medicine cabinet, there was a packet of condoms: she dropped it into the bin bag. Her hand cream, her migraine tablets and the little round bottle of perfume: she'd keep those. She slid the cotton-wool balls and the half bottle of shampoo standing on the side of the bath into the bin bag. The stub left over from the candle they'd lit, lying in the warm water together in the guttering light, and she blinked away the image. Later, that would be for later. Not now. Bin bag.

She sprayed detergent into the tub and scrubbed it thoroughly and even sprayed underneath it. Wiped the taps. Threw away the nail brush and the soap, just in case. Sprayed and scrubbed the sink. What had she touched? She tried to remember. Had she put a hand on the little mirror where now she saw her face and was startled by the pale severity of her expression, the puffy bruise, and the ghastly absurdity of the new black bra? She sprayed the glass till she was only a misty blur.

Next, the bedroom. She took the two bags in there and for a moment stood, quite slack and dismayed. Was she really doing this? She reached under the blind and opened the windows wide. This room needed wind blowing through it, to get rid of the smells of the night before. There was a tumbler on the floor by her side of the bed – as though they had sides of the bed, she thought, and been a settled thing, a couple. She took the tumbler to the kitchen, washed it and put it on the draining board, then returned to the bedroom. First, she looked under the bed. There was a tissue, an old train ticket, a receipt for a takeaway they'd had a week ago, a pen without its top. Into the bin bag.

Every new object set off a small, sharp hit of memory. Neve felt like her body was being jabbed, over and over. By his side of the bed was a postcard she'd given him of a Modigliani painting she'd always loved; she hadn't written anything on it. They didn't write to each other. Why would they? They had seen each other most days, walking past each other, pretending not to notice, looking in the other direction. How did nobody realise? She would keep the card. And the lip gloss, the deodorant, a pair of tights. From the wardrobe, where a few of Saul's shirts hung alongside one good suit, she found a favourite tee shirt that she had no memory of wearing there but which needed to return home. She knelt to make sure nothing had rolled under the chest of drawers and as she did so heard a faint sound. She didn't move, didn't breathe. Her whole body was locked in terror: someone was in the flat, moving softly around. But the sound died and she understood with a loosening rush of relief that it was simply the wind blowing through the open window and shifting the blind. She returned to her hunt. She was sure she had left some underwear here, but although she looked everywhere, in each drawer, under pillows, even under the mattress, she couldn't find it.

In the kitchen, the dishwasher had seven minutes left to run and the washing machine two. Neve stared at the little red light in impatience, willing it to go faster, watching the tangled sheets and towels coil past in the round window. The machine gave a small judder. One minute. She put away the saucepan, the salad bowl and serving spoons. When would he be missed? When would someone come looking for him? Just thinking of a knock at the door made her break out in a prickling sweat.

The washing machine gave a bright ping and she pulled the door open, hauled out the wet sheets and towels and crammed them into the dryer, turning the dial and hearing it chug into motion. She thought of her own clothes from last night billowing on the line at home.

She spotted her bike lights on the hall windowsill, next to a trophy Saul had been given just last week for 'innovation in management'. It was a modernist block of rough stone with his name engraved into it. He'd said the only place it could go was in the lavatory, but it hadn't even got that far. She picked up the bike lights and dropped them into the bag.

Now for the living room. He was in there. He. Saul. Saul was in there with his mashed-in head and his empty eyes, but she still had to do it. She took a deep, heaving breath and entered. At first, she tried not to look, but somehow that made it worse. She could feel him there, this dark mass of blood and body, solid and cooling. Suddenly she wanted to touch him, but she mustn't touch him, not in rubber gloves like a professional, handling the body; and not without gloves like she was his intimate, leaving her prints on his skin. She gazed down at him, at the body that used to be him, and for a brief moment let another version of the story play in her mind: Saul opening the door in this grey suit and white shirt, taking her hand, drawing her in, closing the door, giving her that smile and then not smiling anymore. They had both known what harm they were doing – and Neve wasn't someone who did harm, not like that. She was the wife, the mother, the worker, the friend, with silver threads in her hair and lines gathering on her face.

At last she turned away. There was a drawing she'd done here, when she was telling Saul what she grew in the allotment. She'd made little sketches of the vegetables as she talked, pencilled doodles of courgettes, squash, garlic, green beans, chard, beetroot. She screwed the paper into a ball and dropped it in the rubbish bag. A book of short stories by women that she'd left here and would take home with her. The drier was rumbling in the kitchen. She moved around the room, around the body, picking things up, leafing through books, looking under cushions on the sofa. She glanced at the stack of work-related things on the table, folders, invoices stapled together, brochures that Redfern had produced, then left them.

With a flash of memory, she remembered the poem

she'd written out for him, because he'd pressed her
for a memento he could carry around with him. He
had been half serious and half ironic, ardent and performing being ardent, so that even in the first shock of
passion she'd thought to herself, *he's done this before.*
She never asked him. It didn't matter. Laughing, she
had written out the only poem she knew by heart, the
one she performed when tipsy at parties. 'Jenny kiss'd
me when we met,/Jumping from the chair she sat in ...'
Jenny was Neve's middle name so she had always felt
the poem belonged to her. Where was it now?

She went into the hall and found his overcoat and his
wallet. The rubber gloves made it hard to search but she
didn't dare take them off so she rifled clumsily through
all the contents until she was sure there was no poem.
Then she had a terrible thought: perhaps it was on him,
in his pockets. Returning to the room, she knelt beside
the body, half squinting so as not to clearly see the
wound, and made herself pat at his pockets, then put
her hands into them, first of his jacket and then on his
trousers. His body shifted under her tentative hands.
Was he already getting cold? Were his limbs stiffening
and his blood congealing? No poem. Maybe it was at
his home, tucked into some secret place. The police
would find it and show it to his wife and to people at
work, asking: *do you recognise this handwriting?* Or
perhaps it was in the drawer of his desk at work. And
they'd find it there as well, and everyone she worked
with would know. And then Fletcher would know. And
then ...

She stood up. Perhaps he hadn't kept it.

Another thought. His mobile. Where was it? She gazed around wildly. This flat was just a little pied-à-terre for him to stay in when he was working late or starting early, with few objects in it: a shelf of books, some work folders that were stacked on the side, a fridge with not much food, a freezer containing ice cubes, a change of clothes. At Neve's house, it was easy to lose things because of the layers of clutter that had built up over the decades, but here it was hard. Neve understood that she wasn't thinking clearly at all but was behaving like a drunk person trying to remember how to be sober. At the thought, terror pumped through her. Her movements became jerky and her hands were trembling. She could hear her blood thundering in her ears. She had been wandering around sluggishly, but she had to get out of here. She had to get out of here quickly. Every second counted. What did she have left to do? The washing. Yes. She practically ran into the kitchen and opened the drier. The bedding was still damp and she gave a little whimper as she turned the dial for ten more minutes.

The dishwasher. She opened it and pulled out the plates, the cutlery, the mugs. There was a crash as she dropped a glass. She picked up the shards and could feel one cutting in through the rubber of the glove and into her thumb. She swept up the rest and put them in the bin bag.

What was she forgetting? The kitchen looked spotless but she was suddenly convinced there was a mistake somewhere, so large she wasn't seeing it. She went back into the living room and looked down at Saul, as if he was the mistake. His face was beginning to change, to darken. She felt that she couldn't bear it, and yet there she was doing what she was doing.

Back in the kitchen, she took the laundry out of the washing machine: still a bit damp, but it would have to do. It took her far too long to put the cover on to the duvet, which became unmanageable and got twisted up and lumpy.

At last it was done. She peeled off the gloves, put them into the bin bag, which she knotted together. Saul had told her that in this area rubbish was collected every day of the year, even on Christmas Day. She was about to open the door when she realised she was still only wearing her bra and she almost laughed – or maybe she was almost sick, on the wooden floor of the disinfected flat where the smell of perfume and sex had been overlaid by that of detergent and bleach. She pulled on her jersey, then her jacket and scarf. She'd cut her thumb on the glass and she sucked at it, thinking how easy it would be to smear blood on the door as she left. Her hands didn't seem to belong to her and her face was tight and rubbery, like a mask had been pressed over it. She pushed the door open a few inches, waited for any sound, stepped out on to the landing and closed the door.

She was assailed once again by the feeling that she'd left something vital behind and stood motionless, one leg forward. The feeling wouldn't go away. She opened up the little letter box and peered through but saw nothing. She got the key out again, managed to get the door open without dropping it, and went back inside. On the kitchen floor was the plastic bag with all her things in it: she'd nearly left it there, with perfume, book, tee shirt, tights. She picked it up and thrust it deep into her leather backpack, then went and took a last look at Saul. It seemed like his body was shrinking, or the room was getting larger. Had he once been Saul? She gazed at him as he receded.

'Goodbye,' she said out loud, but her voice sounded tinny and artificial. The flat was full of noises, rustles and creaks and the bang of a pipe. The air stirred around her. Her skin prickled, but when she turned round, no one was there.

Out on the pavement, Neve tried to jog away from the building, the bin bag banging against her, but her legs felt boneless and her breath was coming in painful gasps, as if the air was thin and she couldn't suck enough into her lungs. She slowed, tried to walk calmly and look normal. The sun was in her eyes and nothing was real. That little room she'd left wasn't real, but a set where violent death had been staged. The scene in front of her, that wavered and lost its outline in the golden light, wasn't real. Her affair with Saul was just the fever dream of a woman in her forties who had grown weary of the slog of family life.

She left the bin bag outside a Turkish restaurant, in a pile of other identical bags. What now? She looked at her watch: twenty to eleven. For a moment she couldn't think where she'd left her bike. Drury Lane, that was it. So she made her way there, walking very slowly, in her new underwater world. As she mounted it, she suddenly thought of the CCTV cameras that people are always saying you can't get away from. Perhaps she'd already been filmed and soon detectives would be looking at grainy images of her going into the building at just before half past nine and leaving at shortly after ten-thirty, and all of this would have been for nothing. She pulled her scarf over the lower part of her face and cycled away, wobbling in and out of stationary cars, half blind.

On the canal towpath, she braked and got off her bike. The thought of simply heading home was unbearable, for what would she do amid the shabby clutter of family life? Fletcher might be there, or Mabel, or both, and she'd have to behave as though nothing had happened, stutter out her lines and act being herself. She wasn't ready. The thought came to her, with the dull thud of truth, that she would never get over this. If she had just had an affair, a mid-life fling, she could have come out on the other side, guilty but intact. Gradually life would have resumed its old shape around her. A day would have come when the memory lost its dangerous edges until at last it was just a blurred soft thing in her mind, shuffled in with all the other memories. But this changed everything, made it more solid and more dangerous. What had been an affair had become a death. A murder.

There was a little café on the water and Neve locked her bike to the racks beside it and went inside. The only other occupant was a young woman with a rope of brown hair coiling down nearly to her waist and a buggy in front of her. For one crazy moment, she had the thought that the baby was Mabel; things were sliding impossibly together. It looked like Mabel used to: small and bald, with a curious expression on its round face. She had been such a placid baby, such a settled and enigmatic toddler. Fletcher and Neve used to congratulate themselves on the job they had done as parents.

She asked for an Earl Grey tea and took it to the seat by the long, low window. A burly man with a deep scowl on his face very slowly jogged past. She wrapped both her hands round the mug for the comfort of it and took a small, hot sip. The sludge in her chest eased a bit. She stared at the world outside but wasn't really seeing it.

Neve had met Saul nine months ago, when the large, successful company he managed took over the tiny, failing company she and her three friends had founded when they were in their late twenties and not long out of art school. His company was called 'Redfern Publishing'; theirs 'Sans Serif'. They used to design and typeset pamphlets; chap books; books that had tiny print runs but were beautiful objects with thick rough pages, carefully selected fonts and marbled inside covers; posters for music festivals and poetry readings. At Redfern, they still dealt with some of their old customers but they also designed conference brochures and trade magazines.

Gary said that they had thought they could conquer the world, but the world had conquered them. Actually it had been a relief to finally admit that their exhausting glory days were over and they could be employees at last, with regular pay, working hours and a pension.

Neve felt she should have remembered her first meeting with Saul. It should have been something strange or romantic or funny. But there had been so much else going on. She and Fletcher were just getting to the end of that awful two years with Mabel, watching their daughter fall apart and then trying to put her together. They had more or less put her together, or, really, she had put herself together, but it still felt she might unravel at any moment.

And there was all the business of moving offices, from a ramshackle place just off Seven Sisters Road to a bright sparkling space next to the Old Street roundabout. There was the emotional baggage, of course, but most of all there was real baggage, years and years of stuff that they'd accumulated: cabinets full of letters and documents and original designs and pieces of artwork. Some of it was beautiful and really deserved to be framed, some of it was financial documentation that needed to be preserved, some of it was a sentimental reminder of old times and a great deal of it was rubbish. The problem was deciding which was which. It felt like they weren't just being taken over. They were leaving home and moving house and having a nervous breakdown at the same time.

Meanwhile, Saul was just one of the suits. Before

the move, Neve and her three friends had had many meetings where someone in a suit or some people in suits talked through issues with them, lectured them, rebuked them, instructed them. Saul must have been there sometimes, but it was all a blur and she couldn't actually remember which ones were him and which ones weren't him.

Once they were installed in the Old Street offices, he was just one of the people they'd see around, like the disapproving woman in the office next to theirs or the various men and women at the front desk or at the coffee machine.

But as she gulped at her tea, burning her mouth as a way of shocking herself back to life, she couldn't stop herself thinking of him that first proper time. She was alone in the office, working late, when she heard a voice behind her.

'You should go home.'

Neve looked around; he was leaning in the doorway. 'Is that an order?'

He stepped inside. 'I've always thought you can get everything done by six,' he said.

For the first time, she looked at him properly. He was tall, with short dark hair touched with silver and a very light grey suit that had a sheen to it. She remembered thinking that he was so not her type. She'd always gone for the outsiders, the lost, the tormented. Saul did not look like any of those. Nice eyes, though. Grey-blue, slightly amused. Sitting in the café, she thought of those eyes staring up at the ceiling.

'When we first started,' she said to Saul, 'when we had a big project, we'd sometimes work right through, the whole night. At three or four in the morning, someone would go out and buy bagels and we'd eat them and drink coffee and just carry on working.'

He gave a smile and leaned against the desk opposite her. 'When you first started,' he said. 'So what happened?'

'We got older, got married, had children; well, I had children anyway. Some of the magic goes out of working late if you have to arrange a babysitter. And the idea becomes a bit tiring and you don't really feel like a bagel in the middle of the night.'

'And yet you're here,' he said.

'My husband's at home. Don't worry. I'll turn the lights off when I leave.'

He turned to go and then stopped and looked at her again. 'I used to do that too,' he said. 'I don't mean work. I'd never work all night. That's insane. But when I was at college, I remember going to parties and doing stuff and afterwards I'd get back to my room at seven or eight in the morning and go to breakfast and have a fairly normal day. If I had a time machine, I'd go back to myself and say, enjoy this while you can, because when you're fifty – actually I'm not yet fifty, that's next year, but even so – when you're fifty you won't be able to do this.'

'The worst bit,' said Neve, 'is that at fifty, you won't even *want* to do it.'

'Stop,' he said. 'That's enough gloomy observations about being old. By the way, you can't turn them off.'

'Turn what off?'

'The lights. When you leave. It's all done centrally. It's some rule I never quite understood.'

Neve thought of his words now, talking of when he would be fifty, an age he would never reach.

It wasn't much, looking back on it, that meeting, but from then on they nodded at each other in the lift or if they passed in the corridor. When the other people in the office criticised him in the way they criticised everybody and everything at Redfern, she didn't join in.

She bought another mug of tea.

How could this have happened? Who could have done this to him?

A week or two later, she was coming out of the office and found herself in the lift with him and they started talking.

'I'm surprised to see you at this time,' he said. 'When I think of you, I think of bagels at three in the morning. I just can't help it.'

Neve was surprised by the idea of his thinking about her at all, but as they emerged on to the pavement, he suggested going for a drink. He immediately held up his hand.

'Before you answer,' he said. 'I'm going to say that this is not about work. I won't be talking about business plans. I won't be asking you to evaluate your colleagues. It's not a secret interview.'

'All right,' she said.

What did she remember about that first drink together? She remembered the bottle of wine on the table. He looked at the menu and said that if they were going to have more than a glass then it was cheaper to get a bottle. Even so, it felt like giving in to something. What did they talk about? She could only remember what they didn't talk about. They didn't talk about work. They didn't talk about children and the difficulty of having teenagers. Neve knew he was married and he knew she was married but they didn't talk about it. He didn't say his wife didn't understand him. They didn't talk about getting older and putting on weight and going grey and becoming invisible. They just talked. It was easy. Nice.

Now, sitting at that table with his body on that floor a mile or so away, Neve remembered that evening almost like a silent movie. His smile. His surprisingly smooth, hairless hands. Almost delicate. She remembered his alert look. She didn't remember what she said but she remembered him nodding, paying attention, laughing. She didn't remember what he said either, only that as he spoke he had lifted his hands eloquently and looked at her, properly looked at her. And perhaps it was then that she had understood that she had been starved of that intimate, urgent sense of being looked at, noticed, recognised – or perhaps that came later.

The only bit of conversation she remembered was afterwards, when they left the bar and he accompanied her to where she had locked up her bike.

'I had to see that you really had one,' he said. 'That it's not an imaginary bike.'

'I really do have one.'

'Where's your helmet?'

'I don't have one of those.'

'Why?'

'Because I don't want to.'

'Why?'

'I want to feel free.'

'Free and brain-damaged?' he said.

'They don't necessarily go together.'

Brain-damaged. Brain-damaged. At that moment, he may have pictured her, sprawled on her bike under a lorry or a bus. And now she could picture him.

'We should do this again,' he said.

'All right.'

Another of the things Neve remembered from that evening is that he didn't crowd her. He sat opposite her, didn't press himself against her, didn't lean over her. He didn't touch her arm or put his hand on hers.

But, after she had unfastened her bike and was holding the D-lock in her hand, he kissed her goodbye, first on one cheek and then the next. And then – somehow this wasn't initiated by him or by her but by both of them – they kissed on the lips, at first softly, then more urgently. She opened her lips. He tasted of the wine they had drunk together. Neve didn't feel twenty-five again, but fifteen, with everything in front of her. It had been so shockingly intimate that she felt faint. They moved apart and looked at each other, a little dazed.

'Fucking hell,' she said.

'I don't,' he began. 'I don't usually do this.'

Even then, Neve was certain that wasn't true but she didn't mind. He was just trying to be polite.

She didn't remember anything specifically about what happened when she got home. Perhaps Rory was reading and Connor was playing football in the tiny garden, banging the ball into fragile shrubs and ploughing up the grass into muddy runnels. She probably cooked dinner. Maybe she had an argument with Mabel. She couldn't even remember if Mabel had been there. Fletcher would most likely have been in his room. They would have all eaten together – something they'd always done even during the worst times.

Afterwards, perhaps they looked at something on TV, one of the series they watched as a family, or perhaps they played cards, or maybe everyone retreated to their own spaces, Rory to read, Connor to play a computer game, Mabel to do whatever Mabel did in her room: brood and stare at her pale face in the mirror and huddle under her bedclothes and cry. Sometimes the house felt happy and full of light and comfort, and sometimes, no matter what Neve did, it was heavy with gloom. She and Fletcher would have gone to bed together. Did they have sex? They still did fairly regularly, even after all these years and his bouts of depression and Mabel's more flamboyant, even lethal, form of despair. They had tried to keep holding on to each other, despite the temptation to turn away from each other because of the pain. But she couldn't remember that night.

The one thing she really remembered about that

evening at home was lying in bed in the dark with Fletcher breathing softly beside her. She thought to herself: what happened? There in the dark she had a completely vivid memory of the feel of Saul's lips, the unfamiliar taste of him. She thought about it and her reaction to it as if it had been someone else.

*He's going to ask me*, she thought. *And yes*, she thought. *Yes, I will.*

Neve finished that second mug of tea. She knew she mustn't think about Saul like this, stepping back into the past. She would drive herself insane. Besides, there was so much else to think about. This morning's text; that was one thing. Wasn't that text as potentially incriminating as leaving some trace in the flat? It occurred to her that it was the first text she'd ever received from him; she had never phoned him and she hadn't even known he had her mobile number. She pulled out her phone, clicked on it and then deleted it. But what did that mean? Was a deleted text really deleted? Wasn't everything kept somewhere? Wasn't everything recoverable? She did a search: *are deleted texts really deleted?*

It turned out there was good news and bad news. When you synchronise your phone with your computer, the deletion becomes permanent. The bad news was that, so far as she could understand it, it might or might not be kept by the phone company. She thought about the text. It didn't refer to the flat specifically. Or to her. Or to him.

But wouldn't the text also be on his phone? So where was the phone? The obvious answer was that whoever had killed Saul had taken it. But what for? What would they do with it? As long as the phone wasn't found, the message wouldn't connect her to the flat and to Saul.

She realised that she was already thinking like a criminal.

It was nearly one when Neve arrived home. She opened the door and stepped inside, preparing her reason for not having gone to the allotment after all and her expression of normality. But the house was quiet. She took off her jacket, then went up the stairs, as quietly as possible. Fletcher's work room was on the second floor but she could see from where she stood that the door was shut which meant he was in there, working away at something, or not working away at it. Good. She went into the bedroom, took her clothes off, put on ancient jeans, a tee shirt and a flannel shirt: allotment clothes. She went downstairs again and put her trousers and jumper into the washing machine. Again. She took all the things she'd taken from the flat – the perfume, the book, the bike lights, the tee shirt and tights – back in their proper places, still creeping round the house like a thief. Later, she would have a long, hot bath and wash her hair once more. It was like the morning was sticking to her, invisible clues all over her body, smears and prints and fibres and lies.

At last, she called hello up the stairs in a cheerful voice. Put the kettle on. Went into the garden, past the pile of glass frames that had been there for months now, waiting to be made into a greenhouse. Fed the poor guinea pig and filled its water bottle, pushed a handful of clean straw into the hutch. It peered out looking concerned, and gave its canary squeak.

She brought in the washing. Made tea – more tea. The thought of food made her stomach heave.

Her mobile rang in her pocket, making her start. It was her mother, asking what Rory would like for his birthday.

'Oh, I don't know. Let me think,' said Neve.

'How about one of those little microscopes. He likes science, doesn't he?'

'That's a nice idea.'

'Your father thinks binoculars would be better.'

'Both sound nice.'

'Anyway, let me know.'

Fletcher came down the stairs and greeted her, running his hand through his hair. He looked tired and a bit defeated, in one of his gloomy moods. Neve's heart lurched with pity and tenderness. She put her hand on his shoulder briefly and he glanced at her and moved away. She asked him about the meeting that morning and he shrugged: just a job, like other jobs.

He was peering into the fridge for something to eat. She needed to go to the shops, needed to fill the fridge, buy flowers, fill the house with solace.

'How was the allotment?' he asked.

She said it had been just what she needed and that next time she'd bring back lots of vegetables: beans and onions and beetroot and some of the autumn raspberries. She tried to imagine she had been there after all, sinking her hands into loamy soil. She told him it had been good to be outside on such a perfect September day. 'Days like this are a gift,' she said to him, her voice coming from somewhere very far away.

Then she stopped speaking abruptly because the words were unlocking something dangerous and vastly sad in her. Saul was dead. Of course, she had seen him dead, a corpse, an object on the floor with his nice suit ruffled up and his blue-grey eyes empty. But she hadn't understood it or felt it, or let herself know what it meant. Everything was over for him, every gift of a day. He had a son, though he hadn't talked much about him. He had a wife. She was pretty sure his mother was still alive. He had friends. Work colleagues. He had a whole intricate world, of which she was just a tiny secret corner. But someone had smashed a hammer into his skull and everything had stopped: all his hopes and plans; all his lightness, his sureness, his laughter, the elegant lift of his hands in a gesture of surrender or surprise.

'Are you all right?' she heard Fletcher asking.

'Why wouldn't I be?'

The afternoon passed in a blur. She went to the shops up the road and found herself in a trance by the yoghurts, with people rushing past her purposefully, pushing their trolleys like battering rams. An old man by the fruit and veg pointed to the pale, pitted oranges and said that it reminded him of being in Malaga with his wife, who'd died a year ago and now they'd never go to Spain again. His eyes filled with tears and so did hers.

She bought too much food and then flowers from the florist across the road and trudged back home, the carrier bags digging into her fingers. There was a hollow in her stomach. She didn't know if she felt hungry or nauseous.

She made a lemon cake. The sift of flour and the sun yellow as a yolk and low in the sky now. She told herself that this day would end.

Rory came home, entering the house quietly as though he wasn't quite sure if he belonged there.

Mabel came home. Neve heard her going upstairs and having a long shower, then going into her room. When she came downstairs an hour or so later, she was wearing a pair of black leggings, a baggy yellow jersey and knitted slippers, and her hair was loose round her face. There was a purple smudge under each eye, like someone had pressed a large thumb there. Her lips were pale and cracked. She looked slightly ill and about nine years old.

She watched Neve lift the cake out of the oven and test it with a skewer to see if it was done, then turn it out on to a cooling rack. She watched her wash up dishes and mop surfaces. Neve felt her daughter's eyes following her around the room and she suddenly felt trapped. She thought: *I could run away, right now, out of the house, up the hill, wind in my hair, no one looking at me, alone, unencumbered, unashamed, free.*

*Free*, she heard herself saying to Saul. And he had kissed her.

Suddenly, disastrously, under Mabel's gimlet gaze, she felt that first throb of unexpected desire return. For a second, she was back there, with him, and everything about to begin.

'I'm going to fetch Connor from football,' she said to Mabel.

And then they were all together in one place. Her family, her little tribe. She stood in the kitchen making a vegetable lasagne, because it was comfort food and because it took quite a long time to prepare and she needed that, and she listened to the sounds of the house. Connor pounding up and down the stairs and Fletcher's heavy trudge, music playing from Mabel's bedroom, the phone ringing and being answered, someone at the door with a delivery, an argument breaking out and then just as suddenly stopping, her mobile vibrating in her pocket, but it was only Renata and she couldn't bring herself to talk to her, to anyone. And sometimes she felt calm and sometimes she felt cold and slow and ghastly, stony with terror.

They ate together. Neve lit candles and put flowers on the table, and she opened a bottle of red wine and poured some for her, Fletcher and Mabel, taking a small dizzying sip, feeling her mind tip sideways. She tried to remember how she usually behaved, asking herself what Neve would do. She looked from face to face and smiled and leaned towards them. She asked about their days. Talked about the book she was reading – it was about trees, and how they communicated with each other. Talked about items she'd heard on the news. Rory picked out the mushrooms and laid them on the rim of his plate. He was rapt with attention when she described the underground network of trees; his thin face glowed.

Mabel didn't talk at all and she barely ate. She crouched forward in her chair, her hair falling over her face. Her wrists were bony, little hollows beneath the thumb joints. Her fingernails were bitten right down. Neve reminded her that they had a date to go shopping for all the things she would need for university and Mabel dug her fork into her heap of lasagne and said, 'If I still want to go,' in a low, ominous voice. Fletcher's face contorted at her words, but they'd learned their lesson about moments like this and nobody said anything. They sat in silence until Neve stood up to clear away the plates and Fletcher joined her, running water into the sink and rolling up his sleeves. His face was heavy with distress, there was a soft slump of his shoulders, but she could feel Mabel's eyes on her so didn't touch him on his hand as she wanted, to remind him they were still in this together.

Later – after she and Fletcher had cleared up, after she'd read to Connor, sitting on the edge of his bed and seeing his flushed, clean face turn drowsy and the eyelids flicker, after Rory had shown her his latest cartoon drawings, after she'd sat in front of her computer looking through news items and finding nothing about Saul – she lay in bed beside Fletcher. They both turned off their bedside lights and settled themselves in their night-time positions, shifting to get comfortable, twitching the duvet and arranging their pillows just so. Neve thought of all the times they'd done this over the years, getting into this bed together. She should be able to remember the first time they'd spent the whole night with each other, but couldn't. Twenty years of nights. Twenty years of making love, having sex, reading books beside each other, arguing and making up, talking in the dark; of children crying from another room and one or the other rising and going to them, or of a child sliding their warm bodies between them; twenty years of lying beside each other in their separate dreamlands. At first Fletcher lay on his back, his forearm over his eyes, and she lay on her side, facing away from him towards the window, willing him not to touch her. Because she couldn't. Not tonight. He turned so they were back to back. After a few minutes, his breathing changed and she knew he was asleep.

But Neve couldn't sleep. She had longed for the day to be over and the night to come, sealing her up in its darkness and quiet, but now that it was here, she felt like she was lying on a high ledge and if she let myself relax she'd plunge over it. She didn't even dare close her eyes. Thoughts whirled about in her mind like dry leaves, weightless but tormenting. She hadn't put the last load of washing on. She hadn't bought butter or vegetable stock or sachets of washing liquid. She needed to talk to Connor's teacher. She needed to make an appointment with the doctor. She needed to arrange a weekend for her and Fletcher to visit his parents. They kept asking him. It was Rory's birthday soon, just a few days after hers, and she hadn't bought him anything yet and why was he so quiet? Was he quiet for the same reason that Connor was loud: because of these last years with Mabel? She reminded herself that the allotment really did need tending. And the guinea pig's hutch needed clearing out. Those pictures needed hanging in the kitchen. The boiler needed fixing or replacing. She should dig out old pots and pans and cutlery for Mabel to take with her – and did Mabel really mean that she might not go after all? Tomorrow she had to go to work; surely everyone would know by then. Had she closed the window in the bedroom before she left, and did it matter? His body would be cold now. Stiff. She hadn't called Renata back. And she had been unfaithful and Saul was dead. She was in love with a dead man, wretched with guilt and hopeless with sorrow and desire for a dead man, while her husband gently snored beside her.

She was sure she would never sleep, but she must have done because she woke with a lurch of horror, sweat on her forehead and between her breasts and on her back, her breath coming in painful rasps as if she'd been drowning and was now lunging to the surface to gulp mouthfuls of air.

Her bangle. She'd left her bangle in Saul's flat. She'd

taken it off when she put on the rubber gloves and laid it on the work surface. And she hadn't put it on again. She could see it now: a crooked silver circle, lying in full view.

She almost moaned out loud. She could hardly have left anything worse behind. It wasn't any old bangle. It was like her signature. She didn't wear much jewellery, but she wore that almost every time she went out. Everyone would recognise it: the police only had to show it to her friends at work, and they'd say, 'Sure, it's Neve's.' Anyway, it was unique: Fletcher had told her very proudly when he presented it to her on her fortieth birthday that it was handmade by a designer in Hackney whose tiny workshop he'd visited. No piece was the same. She might as well have written a message in lipstick on the bathroom mirror: *Neve was here.*

What should she do? She lay in the darkness, Fletcher warm beside her, and had a sudden impulse to wake him up and tell him everything and feel the relief of giving up. But there was Mabel, always Mabel, their precarious daughter. She couldn't give up. She had to go back there. She had to go back there right now. She twisted to look at the time on the radio: it was a quarter to three.

She slipped from the bed. Fletcher gave a single snort, like he was laughing, and pulled the duvet closer. He was still fast asleep. She didn't want to risk pulling drawers open, so crept out of the room, stopping on the landing for a few seconds to listen. Connor and Rory slept on the second floor but Mabel was on the same floor as Neve and Fletcher, in a room overlooking the garden. The house creaked, its old pipes whined. Nothing else. She tiptoed down the stairs. She took the clothes she'd worn to Saul's flat out of the washing machine and put them on. There were no socks; she pushed her bare feet into her walking boots that were in the shoe rack by the front door, then took her leather jacket from the hook, picked up her keys that were on the ledge. She checked her wallet was there then slung her backpack over her shoulders, switched on the bike lights and pushed the bike out on to the pavement, closing the door behind her and wincing at the sharp click that it made. With a stab of panic, she thought she might have left the front-door keys inside but she patted her pockets and felt them.

She avoided the canal, which at night always felt eerie, and pedalled as fast as she could along roads that were mostly deserted. A few cars went past and a fox ambled along the middle of the road as though he owned it. The night was cool and windless; the clarity of the day had gone and clouds hid the stars. Neve kept thinking about Fletcher waking and finding she wasn't there. Or Connor might have one of his nightmares and rush into the room demanding to be comforted.

She locked the bike, turned off its lights, walked towards the entrance half expecting police to spring at her from all directions with flashlights and batons and voices booming at her through megaphones. But it was quite deserted and she entered the security number by the light of the street lamp and stepped inside, ran up the stairs whose lights came on automatically and for one moment made her stop in alarm. Before she got to the top she took her backpack from her shoulders, removing her wallet. Behind that door, Saul lay dead. She wouldn't even go into the living room, just dash into the kitchen, snatch up the bangle, be gone.

She opened her wallet and slid her finger in to fish out the key. She gave a gasp. It wasn't there. She didn't understand. She knelt on the floor and shook everything out, which wasn't much because the wallet was new as well as the backpack, and she didn't have all the credit cards and cash and various membership cards and a few business cards that used to fill her old one. She pushed her hands into all the pockets of her trousers, her jacket. She pushed her hands into the various intricate pockets of her backpack.

She tried to remember everything she'd done: she was certain that when she'd used the key to get in, she'd replaced it in her wallet. But then – oh God – then she'd taken it out again to go back inside. What had she done with it? She strained to remember but couldn't. Had she left it in the flat, beside the bangle? She wanted to weep; she wanted to curl up in a little ball there in the hallway, a mirror image of the body inside.

She put everything back in the wallet with fat, useless fingers, and stood up. She peered through the little letter box. Then she put her backpack on and went down the stairs, on to the empty street. Unlocked her bike, turned on the lights, cycled back home. She lifted the bike on to its bracket, took off her jacket and hung it on the hook, took off her walking boots and put them back on the rack. She went into the kitchen, removed all her clothes and bundled them back into the washing machine. Naked, she crept up the stairs, wincing at the ominous creaks, past Mabel's closed door and into their room. In the dim light, she could make out Fletcher's humped shape and hear the steady rumble of him breathing. She climbed into bed and wrapped her arms around herself and waited for morning.

# 2

# THE BIRTHDAY PARTY

As Neve crammed the final plate into the dishwasher, so tightly that it probably wouldn't wash properly, she stopped and – just for a moment – didn't know where she was. She'd got up, showered, got dressed, exchanged words of some kind with Fletcher, supervised the breakfast, made the packed lunches, shepherded the boys out of the door and somehow done it all in a sort of trance, with her mind on other things.

She blinked and looked around. Fletcher was sitting at the table with his coffee, reading a magazine. Mabel hadn't appeared yet.

She was thinking about the bangle. She saw it when she closed her eyes. She saw it when she opened her eyes. She could feel its absence around her wrist. At every moment, whether she was standing under the shower or spreading butter on bread or asking the boys about the day ahead, she was picturing it lying next to the sink. Fletcher said something about an article he was reading and he might has well have been speaking in a foreign language.

She needed to get out of here. She couldn't bear it for another second.

'I've got to go to work,' she said. 'I need to get in early.'

Fletcher looked up at her. 'You remember the party?'

Party? She had forgotten the party. But now she remembered. Renata. She'd called Neve yesterday and Neve hadn't called back. Birthday. Fuck.

'Yes, yes, of course.'

'Have we got her anything?' Fletcher said.

'Could you do that today if you've not got anything on? A book or something.'

'You're so much better at things like that.'

'I'm going to be a bit busy.'

'She's your friend, really. You know the sort of thing she likes.'

Any other day this could have been the beginning of an argument. Not today.

'I'll try to get something,' she said.

'If you can't, just let me know.'

'Don't worry.'

Fletcher was right about this. He was really terrible at buying presents. He had a strange knack of buying people either what they already had or what they couldn't possibly want. Nothing in between.

Out in the hallway, getting ready to leave, she found her backpack and rummaged inside for her purse.

She felt the familiar bric-a-brac, and then her fingers brushed something right deep down, in one of the unnecessary little side compartments. Was it possible? She pulled it out. There in the palm of her hand was the key to the flat.

She took a few deep breaths and had several thoughts at the same time. The first was a sense of gratitude that flooded through her like she'd never felt in her life. She thanked everything conceivable: providence, the universe, God, though even at the time she could see that it was a strange sort of deity that looked out for people who tampered with murder scenes.

Then she felt another emotion, one of alarm. She thought about those times when she was on her bike and started making mistakes: didn't notice a car turning left in front of her, then hit a pothole because she hadn't been looking properly at the road surface. On a day like that she always knew that something was slightly askew. It might not be much, perhaps a late night, or she was distracted by worries about one of the children. But when this happened, she tried to tell herself that this was the day when there was a big accident waiting to happen and she'd have to concentrate extra hard to avoid it.

This wasn't just about a bad night's sleep. She had found the body of her lover and though she had felt she was functioning, she wasn't. She must be in a state of shock. She had tried to eradicate every trace of herself from the flat and she'd left her bangle there, like a calling card. She'd lost the key even though it was in her bag all the time. She thought she'd looked for it every-where. Calm down, she told herself. Take it slowly.

'What was that?' said Fletcher's voice, coming from the kitchen.

She didn't realise she'd said the words out loud. That was another sign of madness: talking to yourself.

'Nothing. I was just going. See you later.'

She set off on her bike in a frenzy, went through a red light on Dalston Lane and almost collided with a van. It screamed to a halt and she ended up leaning against the front bumper with a fiery face screaming silent obscen-ities at her through his windscreen. She made a gesture of apology and set off more slowly and carefully. Her cheek throbbed with the memory of falling.

It was infuriating. It felt like every traffic light from Hackney to Holborn turned red as she approached. She tried not to ask painful questions: what if the body had been found? What if somebody saw her coming out of the flat? And the fact that she was trying not to ask them meant she thought about them the whole way.

Once again, she left her bike round the corner. There was no point in hovering in the street until it was supposedly safe. How would she know? Loitering outside, looking anxiously around, would be one way of being remembered. So she walked straight up to the street door keeping her head down in case an invisible camera was watching her, tapped in the code, went up the stairs, met nobody on the way, and let herself into the flat.

She had thought that she wouldn't need to look at

the body again. She could just walk to the kitchen, grab the bangle and leave. But she had a terrible, vertiginous desire to go and see it again, to establish that it hadn't all been a terrible dream. She didn't give into it. She walked straight into the kitchen.

The bangle wasn't there.

She couldn't believe it. Its absence was like a hole in reality. She had been so sure. As she entered the kitchen, she had almost been stretching her hand out to pick it up. She closed her eyes. The memory of pulling the bangle off was so clear she could virtually feel it as it passed over her hand. Could it have been in the bathroom rather than the kitchen? She started to run but then heard her shoes clattering on the floor. If anyone was at home in the flat beneath, they would now have heard that someone was here. She stopped and walked as gently as she could to the bathroom. No, it wasn't there either.

She told herself to think. She could have put the bangle in a pocket. She felt in her jacket; of course it wasn't there, she'd already known that. The jeans she'd worn were at home. She'd check them later. But she'd already looked there, and anyway, surely they were too tight for a bangle.

Or she might have picked it up and put it down somewhere else in the flat. Where? She had been into every room in the flat, every cupboard, every drawer. She checked the surfaces first, then the bedside tables and under the bed. She started opening drawers but realised that was ridiculous. She walked along the corridor looking at the windowsills and then into the living room. And there he was.

He was lying in the same position but he looked different. His eyes were cloudy now. His face was discoloured and blotchy and swollen. He looked like he had been beaten up. But she knew that the change was actually caused by what was happening inside his dead body. There was a smell also, very slightly sweet but in a bad way. She made herself breathe only through her mouth and not look at him, edging around him. She went back to the bathroom just to check she hadn't missed it the first time. No. It really wasn't there. Perhaps she had put it in the bin bag. It was possible. If she had done that, it would be fine. It would disappear with the rest of the rubbish.

Another possibility was that she had taken it with her without realising it. That would be fine too. Just so long as it wasn't in the flat.

But what if it *was* in the flat? Could it be somewhere completely obvious and she just wasn't seeing it? She knew that every minute she stayed there increased the possibility that something would go wrong. She needed to go. She took a tissue and wiped the few things she had touched, handles on doors and drawers.

She was about to leave – she had raised her hand to open the front door – when she stopped. There was something odd about the flat. What was it? She thought and thought. She walked back to the living room. Suddenly she realised. It wasn't what was there. It was what wasn't there. The hammer. The blood-stained hammer that had killed Saul was gone. Someone else had been here. With a flash of horror, she wondered if they could still be here. No. She had been into every room.

She was utterly confused but somehow it felt even more urgent to leave. Using the tissue, she opened the door and stepped out of the flat. Immediately she heard footsteps. At first she couldn't tell where they were coming from. She moved her head around. They were coming from upstairs. As quietly as she could, she stepped back into the flat and pushed the door almost closed but not so far that it clicked shut. She waited, holding her breath, and heard the steps get louder, pass right in front of the door and continue down the stairs. It felt like an age until the street door opened and slammed shut. She stepped to the window and saw a man in a suit cross the road and disappear round the corner.

She left the flat once more, closed the door and got out of the building without seeing anybody. She walked back to her bike and unlocked it but didn't get on. She needed to think. Somebody took the hammer away. It could only be the killer. He – or she – must have suddenly thought that it was too risky to leave it. Did that mean that the killer also took the bangle? What possible reason could there be for that? She tried to think of other explanations. It was possible that she had taken the bangle without noticing *and* the killer had come back for the hammer. But she couldn't think clearly. Her heart was beating too fast, she was breathing too quickly.

Then she thought of something else: Saul's body, lying on the floor, and what was happening to it in that flat with its central heating. She knew she had done a bad thing, finding the body and acting only to protect herself and her family. But it was still possible to do a right thing, or at least a part of a right thing. She could report it. But how?

The obvious answer was to call from a phone box, if it was thirty years ago. She couldn't remember when she had last used one but she knew that some still existed. She got out her phone and searched for phone boxes nearby. Russell Square.

It took less than five minutes to get there. She locked up the bike and felt horribly conspicuous opening the door and stepping inside. It felt like any passer-by would be looking at her wondering what she was doing and remembering her. There was a notice next to the phone saying that emergency calls were free. That was something. She pulled her hand inside her sleeve, lifted the phone up and dialled 999. She assumed that calls were recorded, so took the tissue and put in front of her mouth.

'What service?' said the voice.

'There's a dead body.'

'Name, please.'

Neve slowly said the address and then replaced the receiver. She stepped out of the phone box with a feeling that now it really was going to start.

She stood and looked around Russell Square. There were people sitting on the benches, even a few brave people sitting on the damp grass with their morning coffees. Over the previous twenty-four hours, whatever she had been saying, whatever she had been doing, Neve had been thinking of that body on the floor. She was the only person who knew. She corrected herself. No, there was one other person.

Now, the woman she had just told would tell someone who would tell someone else. A car would be dispatched. Perhaps it was already on its way. They'd knock at the door and there'd be no answer. What did they do when that happens? Do they call a locksmith? Do they use a battering ram? Then they would find him.

What Neve really felt like doing was going home and getting into bed and pulling the cover over her head and not coming out until all of this was over. Couldn't she pretend to be ill? She seriously considered that for a moment, but quickly saw what would happen. Saul would be found dead. It would emerge that Neve Connolly had been away from the office on the day the murder was reported, claiming unconvincingly to be ill. Hiding under the duvet would be no protection at all.

There was no getting away from it. She would have to get on with her life and behave the way an innocent person would behave. The fact that she *was* innocent – innocent at least of the murder – was no help at all.

She got on her bike and headed back east, wobbling between buses and lorries. She stopped at lights and noticed on the pavement a white bike locked to a railing as a memorial to a cyclist who had died at that spot. Ghosts everywhere. In a flash, she imagined herself in an accident here, a car hitting her, an ambulance arriving, and she would have to explain why she was here, why she was approaching work from the wrong direction. It would be almost as bad as being caught in the flat. The thought hit her with a jolt of adrenaline, clearing her head as she cycled back along Theobalds Road and Clerkenwell Road and then turned off, just before the Old Street roundabout.

She locked the bike up. She felt like she was going to walk onstage playing the part of herself. What did she normally do? She bought a coffee in the café along the street because that was what she usually did. Should she buy coffee for the rest of the office? No, that would be too memorable. What was crucial was that nobody said, 'She seemed diffcrent that morning, as if something were on her mind.'

She got in the lift with a couple of people she didn't know and got out on the fourth floor, which was entirely occupied by Redfern Publishers. Most of it was open-plan – ranks of desks and computers and waist-high partitions – but there were large glass-walled rooms round the edge, one of which had been allocated to Neve and her friends when they moved here. They had imported some of their old things from Sans Serif, and Renata had insisted on putting some of their tatty posters up on the glass walls and bringing their old mugs with them. It was as if they were pretending nothing had changed, thought Neve. Gary in particular rarely ventured out of their room or made an effort to get on with the rest of his colleagues.

To get to her office, Neve would have to walk past Saul's office and then the office of his assistant, Katie. What was so difficult about that? As she passed Katie's office she glanced through the door and saw it was empty. She was just feeling a sense of relief when she saw Katie coming towards her at the far end of the corridor, business-like in dark grey, walking briskly. Neve tried to compose her expression into something impassive.

'Yes?' Katie stopped in front of her, blocking her way.

'What?' said Neve.

'You looked like you were about to say something.'

Neve tried to think of the sort of thing she might normally be expected to say. 'I was wondering if Saul was in today.'

Katie's eyebrows shot up. 'Didn't you get the email? He's at a conference today and tomorrow. So he won't be back till after the weekend.'

'Yes, sorry, I forgot.'

'But you could call him. Have you got his mobile number?'

'It's all right,' said Neve. 'It's not important.'

'Or is it something I can deal with?'

'Don't worry. I'll talk to him when he gets back.'

She walked past Katie towards her own office, and stood in the doorway to look in. Renata and Gary were already sitting at their desks. During the move, they had bagged the good desks, next to the window. It wasn't the most beautiful view in the world: the permanently traffic-clogged roundabout and the bombastic apartment buildings beyond, but at least it was light.

'Morning,' she said.

The two of them looked up. Neve had known them so long – twenty-five years, a quarter of a century – that she barely saw them anymore. They had become a part of her landscape. Now, in her stressed state, she glimpsed them as if she were seeing them for the first time. Renata's curly hair that was the colour of horse chestnuts and used to fall past her shoulders was cut short and streaked with grey; her large, dark eyes were framed with little wrinkles. She was wearing a colourful, patterned sweater, the sleeves pulled up to her elbows. She was still lovely, thought Neve, with her small, soft body and her smooth skin and her expressive face. Gary was leaning over his computer screen. His hair was entirely grey and his beard was just a beard, not a fashion accessory like the men just up the road in Hoxton and Shoreditch. He was wearing a baggy, fawn-coloured shirt. Both of them seemed dressed in a style designed to tell the world: we're not corporate, we're different from everyone else, we don't really belong here.

'She didn't do it,' said Gary to Renata.

'No.'

'What?' asked Neve.

'We had a bet on. That you'd come in singing.'

'What?'

'It's what you always do when one of us has a

birthday,' said Gary. 'You come in singing "Happy Birthday".'

Yes, thought Neve with a stab of guilt, she did. And she usually brought flowers or a tin of biscuits, even a cake she'd baked.

'Happy birthday,' she said, walking over and kissing the top of Renata's head, smelling the nicotine and the limey shampoo she'd used for as long as Neve could remember. 'Sorry I didn't sing. It's been one of those mornings.'

Neither of them asked what she meant, because they knew – or thought they did. She meant Mabel, she meant Fletcher; she meant last-minute homework and lunch boxes and PE kits and bills and leaking pipes and a lost wallet and a puncture and the guinea pig to attend to – oh fuck, the guinea pig, thought Neve. She hadn't fed it.

'No worries. It's not a very distinguished birthday,' said Renata. 'You can sing tonight instead.'

Tonight: the party, the little speech she had promised to make, the present.

'Of course.' She nodded energetically several times, made herself stop nodding.

'You'll arrive early, won't you?'

'I'll try. Anyway, you always worry about parties until they start and then you have a great time.'

'You mean I drink too much.'

'You drink just the right amount. Where's Tamsin?'

'She's having a shower,' said Gary. 'This running can't be good for her. She came in looking like she'd finished a marathon.'

'It's therapy,' said Renata. 'At least that's what she says. What about you?' She looked at Neve. 'Is cycling therapy?'

'I don't know about that. It's quite stressful.'

'Your bruise is turning yellow.'

'I know.' She wished people would stop saying that.

'Are you sure you weren't in a fight?' asked Gary.

'Quite sure.' Neve put her coffee down on her desk.

'Hey,' said a voice behind her.

Neve turned round. It was Tamsin, damp hair tied back, a flushed face, denim skirt and a cotton shirt half tucked in and trainers. Again, she had the eerie sense that she was seeing her friend clearly for the first time in years: the weight she'd put on (and was now trying to run off), the frown marks, the way she chewed her lip when she was anxious. It seemed such a short while ago that they'd been young and reckless and full of a radical optimism. Neve had a sudden memory, so vivid she could almost have been back there, of the four of them sitting in the cemetery just near this office one lunchtime, eating cherries and spitting the pips and laughing. She couldn't remember what they'd been laughing about but she could remember the feeling of it, carefree and joyous. For a moment, she felt bewildered.

Suddenly Tamsin's expression changed. 'Fucking hell,' she said.

Neve had knocked her coffee over. It had gone everywhere, across her papers and a file and book and it had even splashed across the keyboard of her computer. They all rushed across, making such efforts to be helpful that they pushed her out of the way. Gary picked her papers out of the pool of coffee. Renata ripped some sheets off a kitchen roll and started wiping the surface.

'Did any get on the computer?' asked Tamsin.

'I don't know,' said Neve. She wanted to cry. No, she wanted to howl and shout and let the strange and ghastly feeling that was burrowing its way through her guts out into the open. She bit her lip. 'I think it splashed a bit.'

'I know this is irritating to say,' Tamsin continued, 'but you need to keep liquid away from computers. It's the one thing that just utterly destroys them. I know it's not much comfort now, but it might be a wake-up call.'

Neve stopped herself from saying that, yes, Tamsin was being irritating. Things were going badly enough already. She swallowed hard and thanked them all and said they should all just get back to their desks and carry on with the work they were doing.

What they were doing was preparing a brochure for a pharmaceutical conference. It wasn't the sort of job they were used to. Gary had complained about the whole idea from the outset.

'In the old days we would have been standing outside the conference with placards, not doing their propaganda for them.'

Renata had tried to soothe matters by saying that they needed to show that they were team players but Tamsin had taken Gary's side.

'What's next?' she'd asked. 'Arms dealers? Tobacco?'

Neve had tried to stay out of these arguments. Saul was part of the management and she didn't want to take sides either for or against him. When Tamsin had called on her to give an opinion she just said that the issue wasn't worth discussing. This was a job they had to do and that was that. It also happened to be true, as even Gary grumpily admitted.

He contemplated Neve's computer. 'Actually, it wouldn't be such a bad idea.'

'What?'

'If we accidentally' – he made scare quotes with his fingers – 'spilt coffee on a few strategic computers in the building. That might ease our hurt feelings.'

Renata shook her head. 'Is it going to ease your hurt feelings to get us all fired? Or arrested?'

'It's fine,' Neve said. 'I was stupid. You get back to work and I'll clean it up.'

She found a box of tissues and wiped her desk and shook coffee off the papers on the desk. None of them seemed particularly important. When she was finished, she sat for a moment and stared at the screen of her computer, then she looked around at her colleagues. It was like a bomb was set to go off and everybody's life was going to be changed by it and she was the only person who knew. Almost the only person.

Tamsin was talking loudly on the phone. 'And then he only went and . . .' She realised that everybody could hear what she was saying and her voice dropped to a murmur. Neve assumed it wasn't a work call. Gary was hammering on his keyboard as if it was a manual typewriter. Renata was just staring at her screen. Neve thought of the old days, in their old rackety office. Usually you could tell what people were doing. You could see them sketching, designing pages, marking up copy. Now everyone was bent over their computers; they could have been accountants or they could have been poets.

Neve could barely force herself even to look at her screen or at the papers on her desk. She looked through her email, deleting the offers of car insurance and wealth from Nigeria and Eastern Europe. All the time she thought of what was happening in Covent Garden and she wondered how they would learn the news. The police would alert the family. But would they alert his place of work? And if so, who would they alert? Would they contact the CEO? Neve couldn't even remember his name. He was Canadian and had only been appointed a few months earlier. Saul's wife might reach out to someone in the company, most likely Katie.

Saul had avoided talking to Neve about his wife. Even so, she knew she was called Bernice and she knew things about her that she didn't think she had a right to know. She had once been introduced to her at some office function, when they had first joined Redfern, but that was all.

Renata had met her once or twice. She had got talking to her at a company event. She described her as glamorous, a bit brisk, chilly, looking over her shoulder for someone more important. Gary had never met her and he had had little to do with Saul since the takeover.

He was angry about what had happened to their company and contemptuous of the people who now had power over them. He projected much of that anger on to Saul and the other suits. Neve had spent an evening with him a few weeks ago when he'd drunk about three drinks for every one of hers. As the drinks had gone down, he had become increasingly lacerating about everything, including himself. He should have resigned as soon as this takeover started being talked about. In fact, he should have left years ago and formed his own company. He should have gone freelance, like Fletcher did. Now there was a man of integrity. Nobody told Fletcher what to do. Nobody told Fletcher what time to turn up in an office. (Neve thought to herself that this was part of Fletcher's problem, but she didn't say it aloud.)

Neve could remember particular things Gary had said when the alcohol was really kicking in.

'You can tell a lot about this country,' he said, jabbing his finger at Neve in a way that made her move backwards, 'by what men like Saul Stevenson have done to men like me.'

Remembering that, with a sickening lurch, Neve started to think about something she had tried to avoid. Who could have done this to Saul? Gary disliked Saul. He more than disliked him. For Gary, he was a symbol of everything that had gone wrong with his life, of everything that had stopped him from being the person he had wanted to be. But could he possibly have killed him? Neve tried to imagine a scenario in which the two of them might have met and got into an argument that turned violent and Gary had struck out at Saul and perhaps he'd fallen and hit his head and so it was almost an accident.

But it was a laughable idea. Even Tamsin, even Renata, would be more likely to get into a fist fight than skinny, anxious Gary. And this meeting that supposedly turned nasty – why would Saul meet Gary in his flat? And if it were Gary who initiated it, why would he turn up at the flat when Saul was supposed to be at a conference? And if all that had happened, why would Gary be bad-mouthing Saul in the office, drawing attention to his hostility? And then she remembered the hammer.

Neve told herself to stop thinking about that. It was a distraction. At some point, today or even tomorrow, everybody would know. She needed to prepare herself. She needed to act the way people acted when something completely unexpected happened, something shocking. She tried to think about how she would have behaved if she hadn't known about it in advance. Would she have cried? Sworn? Laughed in the nervous way people do at funerals? She had never been good at acting, even in school plays. She must be glacially calm. That was often the way people reacted to terrible news. Yes, that's what she would do. Be mute, expressionless.

She resumed typing an email when she sensed someone was near her. She looked up. Gary was leaning on the side of her desk, slightly too close, with a large, odd smile on his thin face. She suddenly felt tired and she looked away. This all felt too hard.

'I'm sorry. I'm in the middle of something.'

Gary spoke as if he hadn't heard her. 'Do you know this friend of mine, Jill Blaine? I knew her at college.'

'I think I've met her. Why are you grinning at me like that?' His smile was wobbling and changing; it looked like there was a live creature in the middle of his face.

'I don't know. I can't stop myself. It's not funny.' He swallowed; she saw his Adam's apple rise and fall convulsively. 'It's a complete coincidence, but a few years ago she worked with Bernice Stevenson. It was on a magazine. Actually that doesn't matter. But they became quite close. You know that Bernice Stevenson is Saul's wife?'

Neve felt a ringing in her ears; everything went blurry so that she had to rub her eyes. She felt a strong feeling of nausea. This was it. This was it. It was happening now. She thought of that moment when you put your hand in boiling water and the pain hasn't arrived yet but you know it's coming.

'Yes, I know,' she managed to say.

'I just talked to her. I mean Jill. And she just got off the phone with Bernice.' He paused for a moment and when he spoke it was in a puzzled tone, not believing what he was saying. 'He's dead. Saul died.'

There was a pause. Neve's mind suddenly went blank. She didn't know what to do, what to say. She wished she could see what Tamsin and Renata were doing and she could copy them but Gary was in the way so she couldn't. She gripped her desk with both hands as though to keep herself in place.

'My God,' she said. It didn't feel enough. 'Who would do that?'

'What do you mean?'

Neve felt a flash of horror and shame at her stupidity. The very first thing she had said and she had given herself away.

'What happened?' she asked. 'Are you sure?'

'Dead?' said Tamsin. 'Fucking hell. Did he have a heart attack? He's too young.'

'I don't know,' said Gary. 'I don't think so. Jill said everyone at the house was crying. But there were police there. That doesn't sound like a heart attack.'

'It must have been an accident.' Tamsin looked at Gary. 'Or was it you? Were you sticking pins into a doll?'

Gary looked at her. His smile faded. 'That's not funny.'

'What?' said Tamsin. 'Are you pretending to like him now?'

'Stop.' Neve found her voice at last. 'A person has died. Someone we know.'

Then they heard a sob and looked round. Tears were running down Renata's face and she was wiping them with her sleeve.

'Sorry,' she said. 'I'm being stupid. I can't stop myself. Oh dear.'

Neve walked over to Renata and put her arms round her. She could feel the squash of her breasts and the soft tickle of her hair.

'You're just reacting the way we all should.'

'You seem pretty calm,' said Tamsin.

'I'm just in shock,' Neve said. 'Like all of us.'

For several minutes they were the only ones who knew. Outside their office the rest of the company went on as normal, staring at computer screens, talking on phones, drinking coffee out of cardboard cups, staring into space. And then everything changed: all of a sudden, groups were forming, people standing up and walking across to other desks. It was as though the place had been brought alive, Neve could see the same look on several faces, a kind of avid excitement. But other people were crying: Saul's assistant Katie was openly sobbing and several colleagues clustered around her, pushing glasses of water and handfuls of tissues towards her.

'Come on,' said Tamsin. She stood up and opened the door. Her shirt was still only half tucked in.

'Where are you going?' asked Gary.

'We shouldn't just stay in here, as if we weren't part of this.'

'We aren't part of it.'

'Yes, Gary, we are.'

They went into the hubbub together and it was like being at a party. Voices rose and fell, people made animated gestures, leaned towards each other, put hands over mouths, cartoonishly distressed. Neve looked from face to face. She saw mouths open and shut, eyes blink. *Saul*, she thought, *this is about you, but you're not here. You're the great absence. What would you make of it?* She had a sudden vision of him, raising his eyebrows at her across the room, that ironic smile.

No one knew the cause of death yet. Someone said to her, passing on fresh information as if they owned it, that he had been found at his flat, not at his family home. Neve felt her mind skitter. Would she have known about the flat? Did other people know? She had never understood how intricate and delicate the act of communication was, how many cues and contexts there were. She'd taken it all for granted but now she'd lost her grip on all the unwritten rules. She had no idea how to speak. If she opened her mouth, perhaps the truth would vomit out.

'Flat?' she managed.

That's what she would do. If she had to say anything, she would simply repeat what others said.

She removed herself from the huddle of people and went towards the door. No one saw her go.

She walked to Bunhill Cemetery, where all those years ago the four of them had eaten their bag of cherries. That must have been in June, she thought, or even July – cherries always come later than you think. Of course she'd been here many times since. She would wheel her bike through it on the way to work or come with sandwiches in the lunch hour. It was a small, crowded space – the religious dissenters had been buried in tightly packed rows, their stones tipped towards each other, as if the dead made up a community, still in conversation. John Bunyan was here, and William Blake, on whose memorial stone Gary sometimes laid wild flowers he picked from the verge on his way in. 'What would William Blake think?' Gary had asked about some Redfern proposal. 'William Blake died in fucking poverty,' Tamsin had responded.

Neve sat on the grass beneath one of the great plane trees whose leaves were turning coppery. She closed her eyes. She tried to breathe normally; it was as if she had forgotten how to do that too. In and out. She felt the banging of her heart, like something trying to escape. Saul had been killed, and she had removed evidence – evidence of their affair at least – and then someone else had gone in after her and removed even more. The hammer. Maybe other things.

She let herself remember his dead body. The hardening of it when she went the second time. What would he look like now? Was he even a 'he' any longer, or an 'it', a corpse? She imagined him lying on a slab now, in the cold and the glare of lights. Pathologists turning him, examining him, prodding his limbs, his chest, moving his head from side to side, forcing open his mouth, slicing through his soft skin.

'I have to see you,' he had said, the morning after that first kiss, stopping by her desk, asking her into his own office as if it was the most ordinary thing in the world, speaking to her in plain sight, everyone could see them through the glass walls, not touching her, not even the graze of a hand against hers, not smiling at her. Just: 'I have to see you.' She had nodded. No use pretending: this was going to happen.

'Will you come to my flat?' he asked.

'When?'

'Now. I'll leave at once. Follow in, say, half an hour.'

She told Tamsin, Renata and Gary there was an emergency at home and they nodded, barely noticing. They were all used to each other's emergencies, and anyway, Neve usually worked harder than the rest of them, arriving earlier, leaving later, dependable. She sent a message to Fletcher saying she might be a bit late; there was an emergency at work. She added that Connor had swimming after school and needed picking up. She cycled to the address Saul had given her. There was sun on her face, she could feel it now, and a warm wind. She was young again, the years and the burdens falling away until her body was light and rippling with desire.

Nothing mattered except this. A door opening. Blinds pulled down. Silence except for the traffic outside. Clothes taken off, garment by garment. Barely touching each other, holding back, waiting until at last the waiting was over and it felt to Neve, that first time in the flat, that she had been dying of thirst in the desert for a long time but she hadn't even known it until Saul had kissed her.

'I've never done this before,' she said afterwards, lying together in a knot of sheets. Then she added into the pulse of silence, 'You don't have to say anything.'

'All right.'

'Why me?'

'Don't be so modest.'

'I'm not.'

He looked at her then, frowning slightly. At last he said, 'I don't know, Neve.'

'Oh.' But she felt oddly elated at his answer.

'I'm not good with words,' he said, which was a lie. He was very good with words; he always knew how to turn them to his advantage. 'I'm smitten.'

'Smitten will do,' Neve said. 'For the time being.' Turning towards him, drawing him closer. That first time, when she let the world go hang.

She opened her eyes to the gravestones and autumn trees. Her mobile was giving a succession of pings and she pulled it out of her pocket. It was Tamsin: *Come back!* Then: *He was killed!!!!* Then Gary: *The police are coming to the office. Where are you?*

*On my way*, she sent. She stood up, brushed the grass and dry leaves off her clothes and steadied herself. *Now you're for it*, she thought.

Detective Chief Inspector Alastair Hitching was tall and solid, with the heft of someone who worked out. Neve guessed he was probably about her age but it was hard to tell because he was completely bald which made him oddly ageless. His pale skull shone under the strip lighting as he walked through the office. He wore a dark grey suit and a white shirt and his black shoes were polished.

'He looks like an undertaker,' said Tamsin, staring through the glass.

'He's nothing like an undertaker. He's like a boxing manager,' said Gary.

Neve didn't say anything. She thought he looked like a detective.

He spent a lot of time in Katie's office. A couple of uniformed officers were making their way round the floor. He didn't get to see them until after three, when he came into their room with a young woman whose hair was tied back so tightly it stretched the corners of her eyes. She didn't utter a single word during the meeting, just wrote things down with a pen that scratched on the paper. The tip of her tongue rested on her upper lip. DCI Hitching put out a broad hand to the four of them in turn. Neve saw Renata wince at his grip. When it came to her, she made herself look at him in the eye and give a slight, polite smile. He held her hand longer than she would have liked and looked at her in a way that scared her. Perhaps he already knew everything, she thought. She saw that there was actually a faint prickle of stubble on the sides of his scalp: he must shave his head each morning. He made a short statement, saying he just wanted to ask some preliminary questions. Informally. Neve found it hard to concentrate on what he was saying.

They introduced themselves, though he seemed to know who they were already.

'Irish?' he said, in response to Neve.

'Kind of. My parents came over from Cork when they were in their twenties. I've always lived in London.'

'Nice place, Cork,' he said. His voice was low and surprisingly soft; he had a slight northern accent.

'I don't really know it.'

'You can see whales along that coast,' he went on. 'If the mist clears for long enough.'

Hitching balanced his solid body on the corner of a desk and looked around him.

'You're new here,' he said to them. It wasn't a question. 'Keep yourselves to yourselves.'

'Is that what they say?' asked Gary. He looked so small and ragged next to the bullet-headed detective that Neve felt a rush of affection for him.

'Did you have much to do with Mr Stevenson?'

'No,' said Tamsin.

'No,' said Renata.

'Why would we?' asked Gary. 'He was management and we're just the underlings.'

The beam of Hitching's attention settled on him. Neve watched as Gary's face started to flush.

'No,' she said quietly, just so Hitching would turn away from Gary. 'We didn't have much to do with him. But we're very sorry.' Her voice was calm. 'Do you . . .' She made her way through the sentence carefully, testing each word before she uttered it. 'Do you have any idea yet of how he died?'

Hitching smiled suddenly, and his face was transformed by the creases that radiated out from his eyes. Neve didn't know if he looked more or less alarming. 'I can't talk about that.'

'But he was killed?' asked Renata. 'That's what everyone is saying.'

'That's why I'm here.' His dark eyes swept over all of them.

Afterwards, Neve could barely remember what he had asked and what they had answered. It was quite brief and formulaic; he was just trying to get a feel of things, he said, his eyes flicking from face to face. He was asking everyone in the company the same basic questions: their relationship to the deceased, the time they last saw him, their routine at the office, whether they had noticed anything odd in Mr Stevenson's behaviour recently.

'Oh, and your whereabouts at the time of his death,' he added, casually, like it was an afterthought.

'We don't know when he died,' Tamsin said.

'In general terms. Where were you between Tuesday evening and Wednesday mid-afternoon?'

One by one, they answered. Renata said she had been at home with her husband on the Tuesday evening.

'It's just us at the moment. My son is on a gap year.'

'And yesterday?'

She told Hitching that she'd come to work, arriving shortly after nine.

Gary had gone to a movie with friends the evening before, then to the pub. He'd returned home at about half past eleven.

'Do you live with anyone?' asked Hitching.

'My partner Jane.' Gary looked away from the detective. 'She was in bed when I got in but she woke up when I came to bed. And she was there next morning before I left for work.'

What Gary didn't say was that Jane, who he had lived with for fourteen years, had MS, which had deteriorated considerably over the past five years. Gary looked after her devotedly. He was a neurotic and sometimes bitter man, but with Jane he was sweet natured and patient, almost motherly. They hadn't been able to have children. Neve didn't know if they had wanted to and he never said, although when her own children were smaller she used to catch him looking at them and wondered if she detected a kind of longing.

'I was alone,' Tamsin said it defiantly. 'No one waiting up for me or seeing me off in the morning!'

Hitching turned to her, waiting.

'My husband left me six months ago,' she continued. 'So I live by myself now.'

'I'm sorry.'

'I'm better off without him. Good luck to her.'

'Right,' he said, with another faint smile. 'I get it.'

'Anyway,' said Tamsin. 'That has nothing to do with anything. On Tuesday, I went to the swimming pool on my way home from work. I had steamed cauliflower with yoghurt and tahini for supper. I talked to my mother on the phone. I went to bed early and I ran to work the next morning. Eight miles in under an hour.' She looked at Hitching's face. 'I'm getting fit,' she said. 'Post-break-up fit. New me. Too much information?'

'You can never have too much information,' he said. He turned to Neve. 'What about you?'

Neve remembered she had told Fletcher and Mabel that she was with Tamsin. Another mistake.

'Just an ordinary evening at home. With my husband, Fletcher. And my three children.'

'And the following day.'

The memory of that following morning flashed upon her. She hesitated, as if she couldn't quite remember, then said: 'I went to the allotment. I've quite recently gone half-time and yesterday was my day off. I left at about nine and came back home at lunchtime. I was there for the rest of the day except for a visit to the shops up the road for food. And to the florist. Fletcher was there – he works from home mostly.'

Hitching nodded. 'Thank you. As I say, this is just routine stuff. We might come back to you but for the time being, that's it. You can get back to work.' He smiled, looking through the glass. 'Not that it looks like much work is being done out there.' He stood up to leave, then seemed to remember something. 'You'll probably need to give individual statements.'

'Why?' said Gary. 'Is something wrong?'

'You mean, apart from someone in your office being murdered?'

'I wondered if there was a problem with something we'd said.'

Hitching shook his head.

'It's just form-filling,' he said. 'The bane of my life. There is one thing, though. Have any of you been to Mr Stevenson's flat?'

'You mean in the last few days?' said Renata.

'I mean ever,' said Hitching.

'No,' said Gary.

'No,' said Tamsin.

'No,' said Renata.

In those few seconds, Neve's mind became icily clear. She knew that even as they were speaking there were experts examining the flat, searching for any kind of trace: hairs, fibres, fingerprints. She had spent hours cleaning out the flat but it would only take one mistake, one thread.

'I have,' she said.

Hitching showed a flicker of interest. 'When was this?'

She gave what was supposed to be a casual sort of shrug. 'I don't know. A week or two ago, I think.'

'Why did you go there?'

'He asked me to drop a package off.'

'Was anyone else there?'

'No. It was all very quick.' An idea occurred to her. 'He was having a coffee so he poured a cup for me and we chatted and I left.' She thought that would cover her if they found a fingerprint on a mug or somewhere in the kitchen.

Hitching took a little notebook from his pocket and wrote in it. 'What was his mood?'

'I don't remember anything special,' she said. 'Anyway, I've seen him – *we've* seen him – in the office since then.'

'Of course,' said Hitching, closing his notebook and putting it in his pocket. 'It looks like I'm done here. Shortly my colleague will come and take your fingerprints and do a swab for DNA.'

'Why?' asked Gary.

'Just routine. Do you object?'

'Of course I object,' he answered. 'I know what my rights are. I can refuse.'

Hitching smiled. 'That's true. If you want to refuse, you can.'

'Gary,' said Neve, touching him on the shoulder. 'It's all right. They're just doing their job.'

'How many times have I heard that?' said Gary. 'They were just doing their job.'

He was squaring up for an argument, but Hitching seemed unbothered. He turned to Neve.

'That's a nasty bruise you've got.'

'A bike accident,' said Neve. She waited for him to say that it was turning yellow.

The others drifted back to their desks but Hitching remained, standing beside Neve. She wasn't sure whether to pretend that she had work she needed to get on with.

'One more question,' he said to her.

She felt a wave of unease. Had she made a mistake? It must be so obvious that she was concealing something. This was his job. He must be able to see it in her eyes.

'What?'

'I was wondering what you grow in your allotment?'

'Oh, right,' she said in relief. 'All sorts. Mostly vegetables – potatoes, onions, green beans and broad beans, chard, garlic. But I have a redcurrant bush and a blackcurrant bush as well. And late-autumn raspberries.'

'Isn't this the time of year when you have to pick it all?'

'Yes.' Neve thought of her little, neglected patch. She had to go there soon or everything would rot.

'Nice,' he said. 'I've been wondering whether I should try and get one.'

'You might have to wait quite a long time. It was years before ours became available.'

'I'm a patient man,' he said and he nodded at the four of them once more, then strolled out.

Neve waited for a few minutes, then went to the Ladies. She shut herself into a cubicle, locked the door. She leaned over the bowl and vomited in several spasms. Then she washed her face and rinsed out her mouth. When she returned to the office, she found a pack of mints in the drawer of her desk and put one in her mouth. Tamsin came across to her.

'I didn't know you'd been to Saul's flat,' she said.

'It wasn't worth mentioning,' said Neve.

'It seems quite a big thing to ask you to bring a package from the office across town.'

'It's not exactly across town,' said Neve, wishing Tamsin would just stop but feeling unable to stop her. 'It's a few minutes from here by bike.'

'But why didn't he ask Katie?'

'I don't know,' said Neve. 'Look, it didn't seem important at the time and now I can't even remember what it was.'

'The thing is,' said Tamsin, 'I was always surprised they took all of us to work here. I've been waiting for them to let one or two or all of us go. So I suppose if someone goes to Saul Stevenson's flat and doesn't mention it, I become a bit paranoid.'

'There's nothing to be paranoid about,' said Neve.

'I mean, we're like family, aren't we? None of us would take sides with the company against us, would we?'

'It was nothing like that.'

In the end, Gary had his fingerprints taken and obediently opened his mouth for the DNA swab along with everybody else in the office, although he continued muttering darkly about a surveillance society. As Neve was finally leaving, Renata approached her.

'It's an insane day to have a party,' she said. 'I should probably cancel it.'

'It's your birthday,' said Neve.

'That's another reason to cancel it. Getting older is nothing to celebrate.'

'It'll be good,' said Neve, not believing it.

When she arrived home and got off her bike, she saw there was a commotion at the front door of her house. She could only gradually make out what was going on. A gangly young man in jeans and a white tee shirt was struggling with something, which she noticed was a large armchair jammed at an oblique angle into the doorway. He looked round and saw her.

'There's no way through,' he said.

'Who are you?' said Neve.

'I'm Robbie,' said the young man. 'We met at Mabel's party.'

Mabel's party. Neve remembered that summer night as a combination of a witches' Sabbath and the world turned upside down. It had been a night of throbbing music, exotic smells and a tide of young people that came in and then finally, as the dawn was breaking, went out, leaving a trail of smashed glass and sticky floors and damp carpets behind. She had no memory of Robbie.

'What's this?' Neve said, pointing at the chair.

'I was getting rid of it,' said Robbie.

'But she's about to go to university,' said Neve.

'It can go in my room,' said a voice from behind the chair.

'It'll fill your room,' said Neve. 'And you won't even be there.'

Neve had had visions of disposing of some of the clutter in Mabel's room. In its disorder, it had some-times seemed like an emblem of what was going on in her daughter's head.

'I think the door might need to come off,' said Robbie.

'It's a front door,' said Neve. 'You can't just remove it.'

'I'll put it back.'

'I don't mean that. I think the door has a special kind of hinge for security. But you can do what you want. I just need to get inside.'

'It's a bit stuck at the moment,' said Robbie.

'If you can just pull it out,' said Neve, trying to keep her voice calm. She had an impulse to shout at Robbie and drag him out of the way by his straggly beard, but she knew that it wasn't really about the chair, irritating as it was.

He pulled the chair backwards and tipped it slightly so that Neve could squeeze through. Mabel looked at her mother sourly.

'It would have been easier to push it in than pull it back out,' she said.

'Is Fletcher here?' Neve asked.

'If he was here, he'd be down here helping us, wouldn't he?' said Mabel.

'Oh,' said Neve. 'Did he say when he would be back?'

'I was joking. He's up in his office like he always is when there's something to be done.'

'Don't be mean, Mabel.'

'How was your day?' said Mabel. There was an unsettling note in her voice, challenging.

'Strange,' said Neve. 'There's something I need to tell you.'

'So tell me.'

'Later. When you've dealt with the chair.' Neve looked at it. The idea of it in the house gave her a headache. 'Have you thought of taking the legs off?'

Neve left Mabel and Robbie examining the legs. She walked straight up the stairs and knocked on Fletcher's door. There was a murmur from inside and she opened the door and stepped in. The sight of Fletcher's study often provoked a twinge of envy in her. It was the one beautiful room in the house, facing east across their garden and over to the gardens of the next road along. It was almost like looking out on a park. The room itself was dominated by Fletcher's drawing board and the retro movie posters on the walls, and the shelves of catalogues and art books. Fletcher himself was seated in the old leather armchair with his laptop.

'How was your day?' said Neve, just as Mabel had asked her.

'I saw a couple of people.'

'What about?'

'Projects.'

On any other day, Neve might have probed a little more deeply. 'Couple of people' and 'projects' sounded like Fletcher's code for 'nobody' and 'nothing'. But not today.

'Something's happened,' she said.

And she told Fletcher about the day's events. It required fierce concentration: she was informing her husband about the death of her lover, but she had to tell the story as though it didn't affect her a great deal. She must seem upset but not too upset and she must only know what they had all learned in the office. She tried to speak calmly through the dread that was gathering around her as she looked at Fletcher's face.

When it was over, there was complete silence. He just looked blankly at her.

'Say something,' said Neve. 'Please.' It was like a sob. She put her hand over her mouth, terrified she would let something else escape.

'Like what?'

'Like how awful it is. How sad. How shocking.'

Fletcher looked at her thoughtfully. 'All right,' he said. 'It's awful. And very shocking.'

'This is someone at my work,' she said. 'You met him.'

'I met him once. At that party just after you moved into the new offices. It was for about one minute and he mainly talked to you not me.'

Neve didn't want to continue this conversation. There was something indecent about her talking to Fletcher about Saul. It felt like lying even when she wasn't lying directly.

'Can you tell the kids?'

'Why?'

'I can't bear to talk about it anymore,' she said.

He shrugged. 'I will if you want.'

'Thanks. We need to leave soon,' she said.

'What?'

'Renata's birthday party.'

'Oh fuck, that's right. Do we have to go?'

'Yes, we have to go. We don't have to stay long.'

'But isn't it inappropriate? With Saul having died?'

'We didn't really know him.'

'Have you bought her anything?' said Fletcher.

'I asked you to. This morning. Remember?'

'Did you?'

'Yes. Didn't I?'

'No. I think you said you'd do it. Can't you get something out of your store?' said Fletcher.

Neve kept a box full of possible gifts in case of emergency. But a series of birthdays and unexpected events had gradually emptied it and when Neve went up to her bedroom and pulled it out of the cupboard, all she found was a man's belt and a tee shirt that was at least three sizes too large. She looked around desperately and then had an idea. She took a hardback novel from the shelf. She had been given it for her last birthday by Fletcher's sister. It had won a prize and was highly regarded. Neve had meant to read it but as yet she had not even opened it. She examined it from every angle. It looked completely new. She checked to see if Fletcher's sister had ruined everything by writing in it but fortunately she hadn't.

Suddenly she heard a crash followed by the sound of something breaking. She ran out on to the landing. Robbie and Mabel had got the chair inside the house and were now pushing it up the stairs. It was teetering on the edge of the bannister. Neve could see behind them a framed photograph that had been knocked off the wall and was lying on the hall floor surrounded by broken glass.

'I'll clear it up later,' said Mabel. Her face was flickering with rage as she looked at Neve.

'Stop,' said Neve.

'I can't stop,' said Robbie's voice, from underneath the chair, further down the stairs, where he was holding it up.

Neve shouted at Fletcher, who emerged reluctantly. Neve managed to squeeze under the chair and then position herself next to Robbie, pushing it upwards while Fletcher dragged it from in front. They tipped it round the corner and reached Mabel's doorway. However they twisted the chair, it was just a centimetre larger than the gap.

'This time you really are going to have to take the door off the hinges,' said Neve.

'Can you help?' Mabel hissed to her mother.

'I can,' said Fletcher.

'Fletcher can't help,' said Neve. 'He's going to a party with me.'

Renata opened her front door wearing a tight-fitting purple dress and was swathed in a feather boa and clutching a glass of wine. Neve handed her the present, which she had wrapped in brown paper that Renata greedily ripped off. She looked at the book with the bleary attention of someone who was already a little drunk.

'Isn't this the one that won a prize?'

'I haven't actually read it,' said Neve. 'But it's meant to be very good.'

'I'll read it,' said Renata. 'I need to improve my mind. Go through, go through. Mingle.'

Fletcher stayed talking with Renata while Neve walked past people she didn't know and poured herself a glass of white wine in the kitchen. She briefly got into conversation with a man who said he was a neighbour of Renata and Charlie's and that in the last ten years he had earned more from the appreciation in value of his house than he'd earned from his salary.

'What about that?' he said, and then Neve noticed Gary standing just outside the kitchen door in the back garden. She excused herself and walked over to join him. He was smoking a cigarette.

'You OK?' she said.

Gary gave a slow smile and kissed her on her cheek.

'Can we make a deal?' he said.

'What kind of a deal?'

'Since I've been here, I've had three people come up to me and ask if I worked for the company where someone was just murdered. It's like I've got a tiny, tiny bit of celebrity and they want some of it.'

'So what was the deal you were talking about?'

'Shall we just take it as read that we're sad and shocked and not dine out on it.'

Neve took a sip of her drink. 'That's all very well. But he was murdered. It's going to be a big thing.'

Gary made a dismissive gesture with his cigarette.

'He was probably killed by a burglar,' he said. 'Or a jealous lover. It'll be cleared up quickly.' He looked over Neve's shoulder and pulled a face. 'Someone's not in a good mood.'

Neve looked round. Renata's husband, Charlie, was coming through the kitchen, collecting empty glasses and putting them in the sink. He was behaving as if the party was ending rather than beginning. Gary boisterously waved him across. Charlie frowned.

'Have you seen Renata?'

'She let me in,' said Neve. 'She seemed to be having a good time. She might be having a cigarette in the garden.'

'Could you do me a favour?' Charlie asked.

'What?'

'Could you keep an eye on her and make sure she doesn't drink too much?'

'You mean in general?' said Gary cheerfully.

'Tonight. At this party.'

'It's her birthday,' said Neve.

'And I don't want her to spoil it.'

For the next hour, Neve drifted around the party and people talked to her or at her animatedly: about their children's education, about Brexit, about the generally terrible state of the world. Several people had heard about the murder. Neve just nodded and murmured and people seemed satisfied. People kept topping her glass up and she was feeling quite blurry when Renata staggered into her and put her arm around her, almost dragging her down.

'What did he mean?' Renata said.

'What did who mean?'

'About the flat? About who had been to the flat? And you'd been to the flat. Why did you go to the flat?'

'We'll have a proper talk about this tomorrow,' said Neve, looking round, a little desperately. She saw Charlie on the other side of the room. She had an idea. She detached herself from Renata and walked across towards him, tapping her glass as she did so and calling for quiet. The hum of the party stopped. She gave a cough.

'Hi, everybody. My name is Neve. I'm an old friend of Renata's. We all want to wish her a happy birthday but first I'm sure that her husband, Charlie, will want to propose a toast.'

She looked across at Charlie and saw his pale, round, unsmiling face and at that exact moment realised that she had also had too much to drink. But it was too late. Everyone had turned and was looking expectantly at him and he was looking at her with an expression that was difficult to read except that it clearly did not represent gratitude.

'Well,' he said. 'Well.' And he cleared his throat.

'Someone get him a drink,' said a voice.

'I'll do it.'

That was Renata's voice, coming from behind Neve. Neve didn't dare move or look round or say anything. She was just looking at Charlie with a sort of creeping horror. Then she heard a sound. A terrible sound, starting with a cry and turning into a smashing clinking tumble. Now she looked round. Renata was sprawled on the ground and as she had fallen, she had clearly grabbed at the tablecloth. The tablecloth on which the glasses and bottles had been standing. And she had brought them down with her. She had screamed as she fell but now she was laughing. Neve looked round at Charlie. He was not laughing. He turned and left the room.

Neve and Fletcher were silent on the Uber ride back from the party. Neve was aware that she was more drunk than Fletcher. Perhaps Fletcher wasn't drunk at all. He was certainly in a bad mood. As they entered their house and stepped into darkness, Neve put her finger to her lips.

'They're probably all asleep,' she said.

'You don't know anything about being quiet,' said Fletcher in a murmur. 'You usually wake me when you tiptoe in late at night.'

Neve so hoped that wasn't true. Fletcher started to climb the stairs and she followed him, stepping with exaggerated care. She didn't feel particularly in control over her movements, especially in the dark. The house seemed to be rotating, very slowly, around her. She reached the top of the stairs. The grey shape of Fletcher's back moved in front of her. Suddenly, in the darkness, there was a sound of banging and tumbling and a shout. It came from slightly beneath her, down on the floor.

'Fuck,' said Fletcher's voice. 'Fuck. Fuck.'

She looked into the darkness and saw the dim shape of something ahead of her, something that Fletcher had fallen over. It was the armchair still stuck in Mabel's doorway.

# 3

# THE REUNION

The chair was still there the next morning when Neve clambered out of bed, with a heavy head and dry mouth, and went on to the landing. She stooped to look under it into Mabel's room. The thick curtains were closed but the little lamp next to the bed was on, casting a dim circle of light on to a scene of utter chaos. It was as if a team of burglars had run in and turned everything over in the effort to find some missing object. Clothes lay in drifts on the floor and hung from the open drawers of the chest, among them several things that belonged to Neve. There were books in teetering columns, splitting folders of papers and multiple towels (Mabel rarely used a towel more than once); in one corner a rickety pile of shoes, a tangle of chargers, a wastepaper basket overflowing with rubbish, an empty wine bottle, several crushed cans and on the window six or seven mugs. And there, almost hidden from view by the chair, Neve

97

saw Mabel herself. She was crouched near the wardrobe and was scrabbling through a bulging bin bag, tossing things behind her. The sight reminded Neve of something and after a few seconds she realised what: the scrappy terrier they'd had when she was a child, who used to love digging in their small garden, earth spraying out in all directions. It was an oddly unsettling sight and made even more so when Mabel suddenly paused in what she was doing and looked up. She stared straight at her mother; her face was round as a button and her lips bloodless. Neither of them spoke. Neve straightened up and went down the stairs.

For once, the staff all arrived early at the Redfern offices. Nobody wanted to miss out on anything, even if it was only rumour and guesswork. There was no pretence that anyone was working. People stood in groups, drinking coffee, gesturing, busy with their expert opinions on the life and times of Saul Stevenson. Murder had made them neighbourly. They asked each other how they were, what they'd heard, put arms around virtual strangers. Doors to the glass-partitioned rooms stood open and people walked in and out without knocking. A woman called Ellie wandered around with an enormous tin of shortbread biscuits she'd brought in. 'Terrible, isn't it?' she murmured with each biscuit she handed out.

Neve and her friends found themselves part of things in a way they had never been before. Even Gary was drawn into an animated huddle by the coffee machine, where he stood for a while, visibly uncomfortable but unable to extricate himself. At the centre of the hubbub was Saul's assistant Katie, who looked like she had barely slept and who moved slowly in a daze. Yesterday she had wept but this morning she was dry eyed, her mouth a thin straight line. She had worked with Saul for years and Saul had referred to her as his 'dragon': orderly, stern, plain speaking and loyal. Neve looked at her nervously: it suddenly seemed impossible that Katie didn't know about Saul's personal life, about Neve herself.

At last, with the arrival of Bob who was from senior management, people started to drift reluctantly back to their desks. Neve, sitting in their small space, looked at her friends and suddenly saw what an odd little group they made. Gary looked scrawny and drab, with his fuzzy, untrimmed beard and his favourite grey jumper that the moths had feasted on. Tamsin hadn't run in that morning, but had gone for swim in the London Fields Lido instead; her hair was still wet and she had tied it back in a high, lopsided ponytail. There was a pencil stuck behind one of her ears, and she had a dark smudge on one cheek. And Renata – well, Renata was clearly suffering the after-effects of the night before. Her coppery hair was a dishevelled halo, her normal brightness was smudged and grimy, and she kept groaning under her breath, pressing her slender fingers against her eyelids. She was wearing a shapeless jumpsuit and when she stood up to make herself more coffee, she looked like a worn rag doll.

When she caught Neve's eye, she grimaced. 'I feel like crap. Your turn next.'

'My turn?'

'Your birthday. Two weeks' time, right?'

'Oh, that. I'm going to go to bed early with a mug of tea.'

She needed to think about Rory's birthday though, which was a few days after hers. Mabel would be gone by then – unless she meant what she had said about not going. Neve thought of her angry face staring up at her from the floor. An ill wind was blowing through everything, she thought.

The phone on her desk rang loudly. Renata grunted in pain.

'Hello?' Neve said.

'Is that Neve Connolly?' It was a woman's voice, clipped and middle-class.

'It is. How can I help you?'

'This is Bernice Stevenson.'

For one ghastly moment, Neve could only sit in silence. *She knows*, she thought. *She knows about me.*

'Hello,' she managed at last. Then she managed to pull herself together. 'I'm very sorry for your loss,' she said. She glanced wildly at the others; no one seemed to have noticed that her world was caving in. They bent over their screens, oblivious.

'I know this is out of the blue,' Bernice was saying. 'But I'd like to speak to you.'

'Of course,' said Neve. *Get it over with*, she was thinking.

'I mean, in person.'

'Oh. But I don't—'

'I'm a few minutes away from you,' Bernice continued. 'In a café called Roundabout.'

'I know it.'

'I'm downstairs.'

Neve hung up. When she stood, her legs felt like water. She made an aimless gesture. 'I've got to just go.'

'Sorry?' Tamsin's eyebrows shot up.

'Something to attend to,' said Neve absurdly. She never used words like *attend to*.

'Trouble?' asked Renata sympathetically. She meant with Mabel.

Neve made an indeterminate noise in the back of her throat. 'Back soon,' she said as she picked up her old jacket.

She went to the Ladies, and stood in front of the long, speckled mirror. Her battered old jacket, her scuffed shoes, her face tired and bare of make-up, her hair that could do with a cut. She knew that Bernice was thin and elegant and glossy. *Soignée*, that was the word. But she – and she leaned towards the glass so her breath was misting it, scrutinising her little wrinkles and blemishes – she was workaday, practical, not glamorous; decidedly not classy. She wore flat shoes, bought her clothes from market stores and vintage shops, and rode a bike.

Suddenly Neve felt ashamed of herself. Saul was dead and his widow – the woman she had wronged – was downstairs waiting to speak to her and she was worrying about what she looked like. She washed her face and her hands, looking at the ring on the wedding finger. It hadn't been expensive and over the years had got a bit bent so it was hard to remove. She remembered Fletcher, in the register office, pushing it over her knuckle and his face working slightly – on the verge of laughter or tears, or maybe both. So long ago, thought Neve; so much water under the bridge. Why had no one warned them how hard it would be?

Neve bought herself a flat white and carried it downstairs to where Bernice was sitting on the sofa in the corner with a glass of mint tea in front of her. She hadn't touched it. She looked composed and impregnable – and of course, that was probably the point. Her hands were folded in her lap, her legs were crossed. Her dark gold hair was arranged in a prefect coil. Her face was like a beautiful mask: shaped eyebrows, smooth skin, glossy lips. Neve, looking at her from the foot of the stairs, thought how strange it was that the morning after her husband had been found murdered, Bernice Stevenson had carefully applied her make-up, done her hair and put studs in her ears. Even her dark blue jeans looked like they'd been freshly ironed – and who irons jeans, thought Neve, especially the day after you discover your husband has been murdered.

She knew that Bernice used to be an assistant editor on a woman's magazine but several years ago had given up work. Saul had once referred to 'ladies who lunch' and Neve had rounded on him: 'I hate it when men say things like that.'

'Like what?'

'You'll be telling me soon that she doesn't understand you.'

He hadn't done that. But he had told Neve that Bernice had once said, in the middle of their love-making, 'Remember we have to put the recycling out tomorrow morning.' Neve wondered if that was really true or whether it was a way of Saul feeling better about himself. And if was true, she didn't want to know it. She wished she hadn't talked to Saul about Fletcher's depression, like she was making an excuse for her infidelity. She felt shabby and underhand and ashamed. But perhaps it would all be out in the open in a few moments, and then what?

She walked towards Bernice, not smiling and trying to meet her gaze. Should she shake her hand?

'Neve.' Bernice didn't smile either.

'I'm so very sorry about your husband.'

Up close, Neve saw Bernice was older than she looked from a distance, little marks above her mouth, a looseness in her skin, and she felt an unwelcome surge of pity for her. She sat on the other end of the sofa and took a sip of her coffee before putting it on the table.

'You must have been surprised to hear from me,' said Bernice.

'Well—' Neve began but Bernice interrupted her.

'My husband is found murdered and I ring up

someone I don't know. That must seem very strange to you. Why would I do that?'

Neve waited. Her throat ached and her eyes were sore. Every part of her felt tight to the point of breaking and flying apart. *Get it over with*, she thought. It would be a relief really to be done with this.

'I'm going mad in a way,' said Bernice.

'You're allowed to be a bit mad,' said Neve. 'With what you're going through.'

'No, I mean really. This morning when the postman came, I started telling him what had happened and then I saw this look in his eyes. I could see he wanted to get away. Well of course he did. He had mail to deliver. He had a life to get on with. I feel like I'm going to be stopping strangers in the street and telling them that my husband has been murdered. It's like I have to keep unloading it.'

'You can unload on me,' said Neve weakly, but was Bernice just looking for a sympathetic ear?

'We have a son, you know,' Bernice said. She had very blue eyes, Neve saw. Thin lips. A straight nose. Everything about her was drawn with a clean line.

'I didn't know,' said Neve, untruthfully. 'It's awful,' she added hopelessly.

'He's seventeen. I had him quite late.' She looked down at her hands lying so calmly in her lap. 'I am several years older than Saul. We thought we couldn't have children; we'd tried for years and we'd pretty much given up by the time I got pregnant. It was a gift.' She lifted her eyes to Neve's face as she said this.

Neve tried to stop herself from flinching in shame.

Listening to Saul's wife telling her about her marriage felt indecent.

'Do you have children?' asked Bernice.

'Three.' Neve picked up her mug of coffee. Her hands were trembling slightly as she carried it to her mouth.

'Then you'll know how a mother feels.'

What did she mean? Protective, oppressed, adoring, exhausted, alert, tender, exultant, despairing, invisible, like a lioness, like an old rag, eaten alive ...? She set her mug down.

'Why did you want to see me?' she said.

Bernice blinked and touched her cheek as if she were rubbing away a tear.

'I know that Saul was having an affair.'

'Oh.' So here it came at last. Neve sat up straighter.

'You don't seem surprised.'

'I don't know,' said Neve. 'I mean – I just don't know what to say.'

'With someone in the office. Staying late, spending nights in the flat, having several mobiles on the go, buying me flowers. How stupid do men think we are?'

Neve's mind was working furiously, but like a wheel spinning round and round, unable to grip on to anything. Did Bernice know or did she not know?

'Who?' she heard herself ask.

'That's the question. I have my suspicions but I want to be certain before I make any accusations.'

'I still don't understand.'

'You don't understand why I'm telling you this?'

'No.'

There was a silence. It was all Neve could do not to hurl herself into it and confess.

'I couldn't ask Katie – Katie is very loyal to Saul. She doesn't like me because I'm his wife. Was. She wouldn't tell me anything. And people like Bob, well ...' She shrugged her shoulders dismissively. 'Men stick together. Only women know what women go through.' Her eyes glittered; Neve couldn't tell if it was with rage or tears. 'I'm not saying there weren't problems in our marriage. Saul wasn't a saint.' She gave a bitter laugh. 'You're quite new at Redfern, aren't you?'

'Yes.'

'I met you at one of the parties, didn't I?'

'I think so. Just to say hello.'

'You were wearing a long skirt in bright colours that was ripped all along the hem.'

'Was I?' Neve had had that skirt for about twenty years; it was coming apart at the seams but she couldn't bring herself to throw it away.

'I pointed it out to Saul and he laughed and said that was typical of you.'

'Oh.'

'So was he?'

'Sorry?'

'Was he having an affair? Did everyone in the office know he was having an affair? Was everyone laughing at me behind my back?'

'No. I mean, I don't know, of course. But if he was, well, if he was, nobody knew. At least, not as far as I'm aware. Not that they'd tell me. I mean, I'm on the outside and I'm not really part of things, but there was nothing, no sign of ...' Neve felt she was tying herself in knots. 'Nobody was laughing at you,' she said wretchedly.

Bernice leaned forward. 'How are you supposed to mourn for someone who humiliated you?'

'I don't know. I'm sorry.'

'I'm not sad. Not yet. I haven't shed a single tear. I suppose that will all come later. I'm angry.'

'With Saul?'

'He's dead. It's much easier to be angry with the living, don't you think?'

'Perhaps,' said Neve. She hesitated. 'What do the police say?'

'They're being quite mysterious. But that detective with the bald head, have you met him?'

'We all have.'

'He doesn't miss a thing. He'll find out.'

'Good.' Her voice was thin and scratchy.

'Apparently whoever killed Saul did a huge clean-up of the flat. There are things that seem to be missing.'

'So it was a burglar?'

'No. Nothing valuable.'

Neve nodded. Her head was suddenly aching.

Bernice uncrossed her legs and stood up in one easy movement, picking up the jacket that had been folded beside her on the sofa. She was tall, perhaps as tall as Neve herself. 'You can be my lookout,' she said, and for the first time she smiled, as if they were both in on a joke together. 'A bit late perhaps, but better late than never.'

*

Neve watched her go up the stairs and then she leaned forward and put her head in her hands. What had just happened? Was Bernice really asking for her help or had she been telling Neve that she knew? For a long while, she sat like that, with the hum of voices in the background. Then a text pinged on her mobile and she sat up and took it from her pocket. It was from Mabel. *Time?* was all it said. Neve frowned, not knowing what that meant.

She knew she should go back to the office, but she needed a few minutes to collect herself. She went upstairs and ordered another flat white, then sat at a table near the window, looking out at the street. A stout, bearded man in a yellow skirt walked past and Neve felt a rush of affection for her city.

She sipped her coffee slowly, making it last, and thought of what Bernice had said. The police knew there'd been a clean-up and things removed, but how did they know, what did they know? Of course, she had removed things herself, but then so had someone else. She frowned, trying to hold in her mind how the flat had been when she and Saul had been there, how it had been when she had found his body, how it had been when she had returned the following morning. She reached into her little rucksack, pulled out a pen and started jotting a list of what she had taken down on the paper napkin in front of her.

*Toothbrushes* × 2
*Hand cream*
*Migraine tablets*

*Lip gloss*
*Perfume*
*Shampoo*
*Postcard*
*Tee shirt*
*A sketch of vegetables*

As she wrote, it was like she was back there, moving stealthily round the flat while Saul's body lay in the living room. She looked at the list: it meant nothing. Nobody would be able to tell those things had been removed – although perhaps they would think it odd that there was no toothbrush or shampoo in the flat. More important were the things she had been unable to find. She wrote them down:

*Poem*
*Underwear*
*Saul's mobile*

Then underneath, in block capitals, she wrote:

BANGLE

She stared at the word and underlined it, then added:

HAMMER

She underlined that word twice.

*

109

'Hello, Neve,' said a voice behind her and she jolted, rattling the table, sending a teaspoon skimming on to the floor. DCI Hitching was standing in front of her, tall as a door. Neve snatched up the paper napkin and blew her nose loudly into it and then crumpled it into a ball.

'Cold?' he asked sympathetically.

She nodded her head violently, several times, then pushed the napkin into her pocket.

'I saw you through the window,' he said. 'I thought I could join you for a chat.'

'I need to get back to work,' she said.

'Just a few minutes won't hurt.'

He lowered himself into the chair opposite her. They were so close she could see the flecks in his irises. He had hairy wrists and eyes like sloes.

'I had to get away from the office for a bit,' she said.

'I know how oppressive it can get. People act strangely at times like this.'

'Yes.'

'Not you though.' He was looking at her in a way that made her skin crawl with dread. 'I admire the way you remain so . . .' He paused for a beat. 'Equable.'

'Equable?' said Neve. 'I'm not exactly sure what that means but I don't think it applies to me.'

'Calm,' said Hitching. 'Calm and balanced. That's why, when I saw you sitting here looking pensive, I thought I'd join you. It's always useful to think things through with someone sane and rational.'

'Then I might not be the right person for you.'

He smiled. 'You mean you're not sane and rational?'

'You should see me in the morning,' said Neve. 'I've got three children.'

'I feel your pain,' said Hitching. 'I've got two myself. Can I get you a coffee or a tea?'

'I'm fine. I've already had two coffees.'

'Tea then.'

'No thank you,' she was saying but Hitching had already left the table. He returned with a tray and small pots of tea. He handed one to Neve and poured himself a cup from the other one.

'Cinnamon and camomile,' he said. 'The woman said it would help me relax. I could do with a bit of that.'

'Can I make a comment?' said Neve, who disliked herbal teas.

'Of course.'

'You said you were just walking down the street and happened to see me through the window. That sounds a bit strange.'

Hitching took a sip of his tea and looked cheerful.

'By "strange" you mean unlikely.'

'I didn't mean exactly that.'

'No, you're quite right. That's clever of you, Neve. Is it all right if I call you Neve?' Neve nodded. 'I was in the building talking to a couple of your colleagues. You were one of the people I wanted to see. I went into your office and they said you had gone out suddenly. But then when I left, I did happen to walk past this building and catch sight of you. Lucky for me. Doubly lucky. This place is a discovery.'

'Yes, it's nice.'

'Good place for a meeting,' he said. 'Were you having a meeting?'

Neve was tempted just to say yes and nothing more but she thought that if Hitching found out about Bernice later it might seem strange. Suspicious, even.

'I was talking to Bernice Stevenson. That's Saul Stevenson's wife. I suppose I need to say his widow now.'

Hitching looked visibly surprised. 'Is she a friend of yours?'

'I've only met her once. She rang me and said she wanted to meet.'

'Why?'

'I think she needed someone to talk to.'

Hitching looked at her with a new interest. 'Yes, that makes sense. You seem like someone people might confide in.'

'She just wanted to talk.'

'What did she say?'

Again, Neve found herself at a loss. Bernice had really only said one thing and it was not a thing that Neve wanted to put in the mind of the detective in charge of the operation. But no doubt he would be talking to Bernice and he'd ask her why she had talked to Neve. So she had no choice.

'She suspected that her husband had been having an affair.'

'Why?'

'She just suspected it.'

'And why did she come into town to say it to you?'

112

Neve wondered if it was possible that Hitching himself suspected the same thing. Was he trying to get her to lie about something he knew the truth about? She needed to be careful.

'Sometimes people find it easier to say these things to strangers. Or virtual strangers. But this is probably something you should take up with her.'

'Did she seem angry?'

'She seemed like someone whose husband had been murdered.'

Hitching seemed to be considering this carefully. He took a notebook from his pocket and wrote something in it that Neve couldn't see.

'If you have an idea,' he said, 'you should always write it down. You think you'll remember it but you won't.'

Neve was curious about what idea Hitching might have had but she didn't think it right to ask.

'You went to his flat to drop something off,' Hitching continued. 'Do you know what it was?'

'I don't remember.'

'Do you remember anything?'

'I'm sorry. It wasn't something I thought about.'

'Was it big? Small?'

Neve felt a twinge of alarm. That was the sort of thing you would remember. She needed to think of something convincing but not too precise.

'I think he wanted some papers or files. They were in a package, or a large envelope, on his desk.'

'So we're talking about the size of an A4-sized envelope?'

'That sounds right.'

'Or bigger?'

'Yes, maybe.'

'Bulky?'

'I don't remember. I could fit it in my backpack. Why are you asking this?'

Hitching looked around, as if checking whether anyone was in earshot. Only one other table was occupied, a young man sitting in the far corner, tapping on the keyboard of his laptop. Even so, Hitching leaned across the table and spoke in a quieter voice.

'I've seen a number of murder scenes. I've seen them in the street and next to a canal and in parks and in houses and flats and bedsits. But I've never seen one like this one.'

'In what way?'

'We're having a press conference this afternoon, but I can give you a sneak preview. Your colleague was subjected to a violent assault. I won't give you the details. It might put you off your tea. But that's nothing out of the ordinary. What was strange was the condition of the flat. I've seen attempts to cover things up but this was on a different level. The flat was scrubbed clean and I mean really scrubbed. Everything was in its place. Even the bins were emptied. We did a search of all the bins in the area.'

Neve felt a sudden rush of alarm so severe that she thought it would show in her face. She had to ask. She couldn't stop herself.

'Did you find anything?'

He shook his head. 'I made an interesting discovery. In that area they collect the rubbish every day. I wish they did that round where I live.'

'What's so strange about that? So the killer got rid of the evidence.'

'Yes, but it seems like a strange combination. A frenzied attack followed by a systematic cleaning of the flat that must have taken hours.'

'I'm sorry, inspector,' said Neve.

'Please, call me Alastair.'

'Alastair. I don't know why you're telling me this.'

'I was working my way around to that. It's probably not important, but there was something else about the crime scene that was a little odd.'

'What?'

'As I said, the flat looked like it had been scoured clean. But there was a stack of files on the table. They were personnel files. Three of them. Tamsin Olivia Brodal, Renata Searle and Gary Peter Baldwin. The three people you share an office with.'

Neve looked down at her hands. She couldn't trust herself to speak.

'Can you think of any reason why Stevenson would have had those files on his desk? I mean those files in particular. I take it that there are dozens of people in your company.'

'I've no idea.'

'But what would be your assumption?'

'Our company has recently been taken over and incorporated into Redfern. I suppose that—' Neve stopped herself and gave a cough. She had been about to say 'Saul'. What did the others call him: Saul or Mr Stevenson? 'Mr Stevenson was probably carrying out some kind of assessment.'

'Do you mean he might have been thinking about making people redundant?'

'I suppose it's possible. We weren't sure if they'd keep all of us. Or any of us.'

'Then why wasn't your file there?'

'What?'

'Stevenson had the files of the three people you work with, but not you. No Neve Jennifer Connolly to be found.'

*Jenny kiss'd me when we met*, thought Neve. Her face was burning. *Jumping from the chair she sat in.* She saw Saul's face, his smile. He was suddenly in the room with her.

'Oh,' she managed to say.

'Why not?'

Neve reached for her tea and took a gulp, partly to calm herself, partly to give herself time to think. She hoped there was no giveaway tremor.

'How could I know that?'

'There are plenty of ways you could have known. Stevenson might have told you that your job was safe. He might have had a higher regard for you than for your colleagues. Or something else. Which is why I asked the question.'

'I've just moved to working part-time, so I have recently renegotiated my contract. I suppose it also means that the company would save less money by getting rid of me.'

'So you think he was considering firing one or more of your colleagues?'

'I was just thinking aloud,' said Neve. 'Which I shouldn't have done. I've got no reason to know anything about what was being planned.'

'But you just said that Stevenson was carrying out some kind of assessment.'

'I don't know what I said. I was just speculating when I thought we were having a casual chat and then it suddenly turned into an interview and I feel you're reading too much into what I'm saying.'

Hitching smiled. 'An interview? It's nothing like that. If this were an interview we would be sitting in a room with a recorder and someone else present and it would all be terribly formal. I'm going to be quite frank with you, I don't know what to think about any of this. Usually, when you arrive at the scene of most murders, it's bloody obvious what happened. This is different. I'm still at the stage of asking questions as a way of discovering what I should be asking questions about.'

'That sounds confusing,' said Neve. 'I'm sorry I've not been any help.'

'That's not true,' said Hitching. 'You've been more help than anyone else I've talked to.'

'Oh, that's good,' said Neve, not thinking it was good in any way. 'How do you mean I've been helpful?'

'In several ways. For example, when Bernice Stevenson gave a statement to one of my clever young colleagues, she didn't mention that she suspected her husband had been having an affair.'

Neve suddenly regretted mentioning it herself. 'I feel I've betrayed her,' she said.

'You've told the truth,' said Hitching. 'And don't worry. I'll be very discreet. But if she tells you anything else, I hope you'll let me know.'

'I'm sure she won't.'

'And this business of the files.'

'I don't see how that can be relevant.'

'I'm just interested why he should ask you to bring over the files on your colleagues.'

Neve had the alarming sense that she had incriminated herself by describing something that hadn't even taken place.

'I dropped that packet off weeks ago,' she said a little desperately. 'They probably weren't those files you found.'

Hitching looked thoughtful. 'You're probably right,' he said.

'Right? In what way? I didn't say anything.'

'Your file isn't in the office either, with all the others. It's disappeared.'

'Well,' said Neve. 'I don't know where it is.'

'It's strange though.'

'Is it? I suppose it is.'

'His assistant thinks it's strange.'

Neve thought of Katie's stern face, the way her eyes rested on Neve.

'And the other thing that's strange is that according

to his wife and his colleagues, he was going to a conference that morning. Why was he in the flat at all?'

'I don't know,' said Neve. She was about to come up
with some possible reason but bit down on the words.

'There's always a problem with investigations like
this. You find some interesting piece of information
and you construct a theory around it and it stops you
thinking about anything else.'

'What sort of theory?' asked Neve warily.

'That's the problem. I've been talking to you for
half an hour and I've already got two theories. Theory
number one: Stevenson was having an affair.'

'*May* have been having an affair.'

'All right. *May* have been having an affair. That
would explain why he was at the flat, wouldn't it?'
He smiled at her. 'Then you've got the possibility of
a spurned lover or a jealous lover's partner. And then
there's theory number two: Stevenson was about to
make a person or persons unknown redundant.'

'*May* have been about to,' said Neve. 'And surely you
don't kill someone who *might* be about to make you
redundant, do you?'

Hitching shook his head.

'The last murder I dealt with was over a drug deal
that wouldn't have bought you a cappuccino. So, it
could be theory one or it could be theory two but it
can't be both. And it could be neither.'

Neve looked down at her cup. It was empty.

'Your friend Renata, she seemed to have a bit of a
hangover,' said Hitching sympathetically.

'It was her birthday yesterday.'

'She mentioned that. And you're having a birthday quite soon, I gather.'

Neve gazed at him. Why had Renata told him that and what did her birthday have to do with anything? Was this some weird game he was playing? And then she had an eerie sensation, like she was underwater and a piece of debris was falling slowly towards her from the shipwreck above. For a moment she sat quite still, trying to work out what it was and then the memory thudded into her and she gave an audible grunt.

'Are you all right?' asked Hitching.

'Yes,' she managed to say, but she wasn't.

Her birthday was in two weeks' time. And – oh fuck, fuck, fuck – Saul had bought her a present. As clear as if he was in the room with her now, she heard his voice: *You just wait. So you'll never forget me.*

'Heartburn?' asked Hitching, leaning forward. So solid, so close. She could smell him.

'What? No.'

But her heart was burning, was thudding, and her face was clammy with fear. Saul had bought something for her and it was going to be delivered to the flat. He said it would be delivered to the flat in plenty of time for the day itself. Would it be addressed to her or to him? Would it have her name on it? Would Hitching, looking at it, know at once that it was meant for Neve Connolly? It would arrive this week or next. She felt dizzy.

Hitching was saying something. She narrowed her eyes and his face came into focus. He was watching her closely.

'I'm sorry,' she said, 'I should probably, you know ... And you must have more important things to do.'

'Of course, of course,' Hitching said. 'I should be the one saying sorry. I just wish all my interviews were as enjoyable as this. And as helpful. Not that this was an interview, as I said.'

They walked out of the tea shop together and stood facing each other on the pavement. Neve suddenly thought of her first proper meeting with Saul. Hitching wasn't going to do something awful like kiss her on both cheeks, was he? He held out his large hand and she shook it.

As she walked back to the office, she tried to reach beyond the thick dread.

What had that meeting really been about?

'Have you remembered tonight?' asked Tamsin.

'Tonight?'

'You've forgotten, haven't you?' Tamsin sounded injured.

'Look at her face.' Gary grinned. 'She's definitely forgotten.'

'I'm sorry. There's so much going on. What about tonight?'

'Neve! The reunion.'

Neve's heart sank. A group of friends from university days were gathering in a pub in Hackney and she really,

really didn't want to go. She hadn't wanted to go in the first place: after all, as she'd said to Tamsin, there was a good reason she had lost touch with almost everyone who was going to be there. But Tamsin, raw from the collapse of her marriage, was trying to make an effort to be sociable, and had begged her to come with her to lend support.

'You're not going to pull out?' asked Tamsin suspiciously.

'No, I'm not going to pull out. I won't come for long though. I'm quite tired from last night.'

'Don't remind me,' said Renata. 'I'm a dead woman walking.'

'But did you have a good time?'

'You mean, before I disgraced myself? Probably. I don't think it was worth it though. The things I remember are bad enough. I really don't want to know what happened during the gaps.'

'How's Charlie?' asked Neve, remembering the expression on his face as Renata had toppled over.

'Charlie is Charlie. Very disapproving. He never gets drunk. He never does things that he's going to be embarrassed by later. All very dignified.' She wrinkled up her face. 'I don't like getting older,' she said plaintively. 'I don't like being in my forties. My *late forties*. I looked in the mirror this morning and I barely recognised myself, all puffy-faced and squinty-eyed.'

'That's the hangover,' said Gary.

'I thought I'd get wiser.' Renata suddenly looked like a child, her pretty face woebegone. 'I thought I'd be calm and, well, happy. Happy!' Her voice rang out. 'And now all this with Saul,' she said miserably.

Neve was about to say something when her mobile let out a bright ping and then another; she pulled it from her pocket. It was Mabel again: *What time are we meeting?* read the first, and the second: *Half an hour????*

'Oh no,' she said. 'I'm supposed to be doing some shopping with Mabel. I forgot that too.'

'What kind of shopping?' asked Renata, who was wiping her eyes with her sleeves, smudging her mascara.

'Stuff for university. You know – mugs, spoons, things for her room.' She had imagined a relaxed hour or so with Mabel, mother and daughter bonding over teapots and duvet covers and woks – did people still have woks? 'I can't go,' she said, sitting down heavily, fatigue rolling over her so that she thought if she closed her eyes she could go to sleep right there and escape from the nightmare. 'I just can't.'

'Of course you can,' said Gary. 'You never take lunch breaks normally and it's important. Mabel's leaving home.'

'I suppose you're right.' Neve heaved herself out of her chair. She felt impossibly heavy and at the same time felt she might float away. 'Bad timing. I won't be more than an hour. If Bob asks, tell him I've just popped out. I'll make up for it. I'll work late.'

'No, you won't,' said Tamsin. 'Reunion, remember.'

'I'll work late tomorrow, then.'

123

'Don't be daft,' said Renata, giving her a small push. 'Go and have a nice time with your daughter.'

The nice time started badly. The chain came off her bike and got hopelessly kinked. Neve had to turn the bicycle upside down on the pavement to get it back on and by the time she'd finished, her hands were covered in oil, and so were her jeans. She thought of Bernice that morning, so impossibly elegant, and smoothed her hair back from her face, remembering too late that now her face would be oily as well.

'I've been here for ten minutes,' said Mabel, standing over her as she locked her bike to a metal signpost outside the department store. 'What's that on your face?'

'Oil.'

If Neve wasn't looking her best, neither was Mabel. She seemed to have lost weight overnight, although perhaps her platform boots made her look thinner while her over-large backpack, worn high, gave her a hunched appearance. Her face was pale and peaky and her hair was scraped back into a tight knot. She had a faint trail of spots running along her jawline. Her clothes – black ripped jeans, black long-sleeve tee shirt, black hoodie – weren't particularly clean and she looked malnourished and neglected. Neve wondered if she'd started taking drugs again – or maybe she was playing the part of someone who was taking drugs. She was a chameleon, always taking on the colour of her moods and her surroundings, always dressing up to play a part. It was impossible to tell what was real and

124

what was theatrical and self-invented, or how far Mabel distinguished between them. This had been a problem through all the farcical family therapy sessions they had had over the past years.

Certainly, she was not in a good mood. She glittered with a malevolent energy, was unable to keep still.

'How's the great clear-out going?' asked Neve. She hated her bright tone, hated the way that – even when her world was crumbling under her feet and a chasm opening up – she wrenched herself into the familiar role. She was the hoper, the believer, the holder-together. 'Is the chair out of the door?'

Mabel turned to her, standing on the balls on her feet and moving her head from side to side. 'No,' she said.

'I'll have a go when I get home.'

'Don't bother.'

'It can't just stay there.'

'Why?'

'It's your bedroom.' Mabel didn't just shut her bedroom door, she locked it.

'But I won't be in it.' She caught the expression on Neve's face and added: 'Or maybe I won't be.'

'Anyway, let's go and look at what you need,' said Neve, stepping into the revolving doors.

It took Mabel ten minutes to decide on a kettle. She hated all of the mugs. She said she didn't need any pans. When she spun round angrily, her backpack swept three tumblers off the shelf and they shattered on the floor. An assistant came towards them with a forgiving look on her face and made a big fuss of sweeping up the shards while Mabel twitched and scowled.

'How about a toasted sandwich maker?' asked Neve.

'You're joking.'

'What's wrong with them?'

'Everyone has sandwich makers.'

Neve picked a cafetière off the shelf and held it out.

'I don't drink coffee. Remember?'

'You'll want to make coffee for other people.'

'You want me to be sociable.'

'Of course I do.'

Mabel muttered something under her breath, then picked up a collection of wooden spoons. 'I'll take these.'

'Good.'

'And this.' She selected a long, sharp knife in its plastic sheath.

Neve had an uneasy feeling, looking at her daughter holding the blade in front of her. 'Shall we look at teapots?'

'I don't care.'

'About teapots?'

'Fuck teapots. I don't care. I don't care what we buy. I don't care if I have a toaster or a chopping board or a milk pan or matching pillowcases or lined notebooks or . . .' She gazed wildly around her. 'A laundry basket, or a bedside lamp. I don't care. It's all crap. Do you hear?'

'I hear.' Neve pushed away all of the fears that were crowding in on her and tried to concentrate on her daughter, who was wound so tight with anxiety and rage it seemed she might splinter into a thousand pieces. 'Let's leave this. It's the wrong time. We can do it another day – or just buy you things when we get there and see what you need.' She held up a hand. 'If you decide to go. And we can talk about that as well, but not now. Now we're going to have something to eat and a mug of tea and I'll go back to work. All right?'

'I'm not hungry.'

'Just a mug of tea then.'

'It's so hot and bright in here. It makes me want to break things.'

'I know. Here. Come with me.'

Neve put her arm around Mabel's bony shoulders and led her out of the store, on to the main road, down a side street, into a little café. She pulled back a chair for her and then slid into the seat opposite. She ordered a pot of China tea, lemon on the side, wondering how many mugs of coffee and tea she had drunk today. It occurred to her that she had had nothing to eat since she couldn't remember when but the thought of food made her stomach churn.

Mabel glanced at her, then lowered her head into her hands.

'Mum?' she said, almost inaudible. It had been years since she had called Neve that. Was she crying? Neve wanted to touch her, hold her, wipe tears from her daughter's small, grubby face, but she stopped herself.

'I'm here. Talk to me.'

Mabel lifted her head and straightened up. The

expression on her face hardened so that she looked almost spiteful. 'Why would I want to talk to *you*?' she said. 'Why in the wide world?'

Actually, thought Neve, stepping into the lift, pressing the button for the fourth floor, she didn't care anymore: she was too tired, too stupefied with all the deceit and all the fear. She saw herself in the lift's cruel mirror: her bruised face was strained and she had a smear of oil on each cheekbone. That wasn't the woman Saul had fallen for. Saul, she thought. He would be lying in the morgue now, on one of those metal trays.

They had never spent a night together, the clock had always been ticking. But once, lying in bed together after making love, he had fallen asleep. One of his arms had been over her body and their legs were tangled together. Neve had lain there for half an hour or more watching him as he slept: the way his mouth was very slightly open, the way he looked serious like he never did when awake. He seemed younger and more innocent in sleep, his face smoother, all the lines wiped away. She followed the smallest changes in his expression. He was so familiar and yet so mysterious, a stranger who had come into her life and who she knew would go out again. He stirred and opened his eyes to see her watching him, and he smiled at her – such a smile. She wouldn't forget. In spite of the shame, the guilt, the terror and the ghastly mess of it all, she would never forget.

The lift doors opened and she was face to face with Katie.

'Hello,' she said, startled.

'Neve.' Katie nodded. 'Good. I want to ask you something.'

'Of course.'

'In my office, if you don't mind. It's like a fish bowl in here.'

Neve followed Katie into her room, which was adjacent to the one that used to be Saul's.

'Apparently,' said Katie after she had closed the door, 'you've been saying that Saul was having an affair.'

'No!'

'That's what I've heard.'

'You've heard wrong.'

'You're new here.'

'I don't see what—'

'Everything was fine until you and your colleagues arrived.'

'I don't understand what you're saying.'

'It seems very simple. There are rumours flying around the place that Saul was having a fling with someone in the office. What do you say to that?'

Neve thought she might hoot with laughter. 'I don't know,' she said. 'I mean, as you pointed out, I'm new here. I don't know what goes on. I certainly haven't been saying any such thing.' She paused, then added: 'His wife thinks he was.'

'Bernice?'

'Yes.'

'So she knew?'

Neve had the feeling of stumbling around in thick

fog, things looming up at her. 'You mean, you knew Saul was having an affair, but you didn't know his wife knew?'

Katie shook her head. 'You'd be surprised what I know,' she said. 'Not much escapes me.'

'I should get to work.'

'He might be dead,' said Katie. 'But I can still protect him.'

'Good luck with that.'

Only Renata and Tamsin were at their computers. Neve sat at her desk and pulled up the files she'd been working on. She propped her chin in her hand and stared at the images without really seeing them. Little motes floated in front of her eyes. She was so drained that it was all she could do to keep from falling asleep on her keyboard, but into her tired mind spun sharp pieces of dread. Saul had bought her a present that would be delivered to the flat in the next few days. Bernice knew of an affair and suspected someone in particular – who? Katie also knew of an affair, and had implied she knew who it was with. Mabel was on the downward slope again, jittery and frantic and full of rage. Other things too: her bangle, which had disappeared. The hammer, which had also disappeared. Her personnel folder, which hadn't been with Gary, Tamsin and Renata's and wasn't here at Redfern. Nothing made sense. And then there was the detective, Hitching. She didn't like the way he looked at her. It gave her the creepy sense that he knew something.

'How was Mabel?' asked Renata.

'Not great. We didn't actually buy anything. I don't even know if she'll go.' She looked across at Renata and thought of telling the two of them everything: the affair, the cover-up, the feeling of terror that was engulfing her. The urge to confess and unburden herself was so strong that her throat was thick with it. She was about to speak, but Tamsin got in first.

'Gary is in a terrible state,' she said.

'Oh God, why? Jane?'

'No, or not primarily. It's money.'

'What about money?'

'He's just told me that he's up to his ears in debt.'

'I had no idea.'

'He thought we would get more when we joined Redfern. Because of that, in the year before the takeover he borrowed quite a lot. For his wife, he says. And then of course he got far less than he expected and couldn't repay the loan, which is getting bigger every day.'

Neve remembered how angry Gary had been with Saul and the whole management team: 'Not just taken over but taken in,' he kept saying.

'We have to help.'

'Of course,' said Renata. 'But how? Have you got any savings?'

'I've got nothing.'

'Exactly the same as me and Tamsin.'

'No, I've less than nothing,' said Tamsin. 'The divorce wiped me out. I tried to get a second mortgage but was turned down. At least I don't have children to worry about.'

'But we're all rich really,' said Neve. 'We might not have cash, but we've got houses that have tripled, quadrupled, or more, in value since we bought them. We're all millionaires.'

Tamsin snorted.

'We are,' insisted Neve. 'Me and Fletcher couldn't buy a shoebox on our income, but I bet our house is worth well over a million pounds and through nothing we've done. We were just the lucky generation. Except Gary never bought his own house. He didn't want to be part of the capitalist system.'

'So he's properly fucked,' said Tamsin gloomily.

'Sssh.'

Gary was crossing the office. His beard was straggly and his glasses were smeared. Watching him, Neve remembered when they first met as students. He'd been like an elf or a faun, small and quick and full of mischief. Now he just looked defeated. What had happened to him, to them all? And what was going to happen? She gave a long, slow shiver.

'I just spoke to Terry in Accounts,' said Gary when he came in. 'And he just spoke to Bob. And Bob told him that he thinks the police have no leads at all.'

'It's only day three,' said Tamsin.

'It's *already* day three,' said Gary.

Neve bent over her keyboard. If they had no leads, that was because she – and someone else – had removed all the evidence. She couldn't put it back again, but she had to work out what it meant.

A thought came to her. Saul was meant to be at a

conference. He had gone to the flat secretly and told her to join him there. Who knew apart from her that he would be there? The obvious answer to that was: nobody. The thought of it was like the cracked tooth that she couldn't stop probing with her tongue.

She tried to put it out of her mind and get some work done, though she was almost unconscious of what she was doing. Although no time seemed to have passed, it was suddenly half past three. She had promised to collect the boys from school. She got up and started to gather her things.

'So we'll see you later,' said Tamsin.

'What?' said Neve.

'You know,' said Tamsin. 'It'll be fun.'

'I'll definitely look in.'

'That sounds like a way of saying you might not come at all.'

The thought of not going at all felt attractive but Neve had promised that she'd be there. As she walked away, she heard a voice behind her. Renata had followed her.

'You will be there, won't you?' she said.

'Why do people keep asking me that?'

'I need to talk to you about something. It's important.'

Neve didn't like the sound of that. 'If it's important, we can talk now,' she said.

'It's a bit complicated,' said Renata. 'I'll need a drink and some privacy.' Her tone was light but she looked serious. 'As long as you'll be there.'

There was really no need for Neve to collect the boys

from school. Rory was eleven. Next year he'd be at a school with people who were old enough to vote. Even so, Neve quite liked the old familiar process of chatting with the other parents out on the pavement, sharing gossip, complaining about teachers. In the past year the conversations had become more complicated as the different choices for secondary school were revealed and debated and defended and argued about. On this day all that was irrelevant because she arrived late and Rory and Connor were at the gate of the playground with other children of parents who had failed to arrive. Connor was with his friend Elias, and Rory stood apart, his hands pushed into his pockets.

'I'm so sorry,' Neve said, preventing herself from reaching out and touching him. She hated being late for her children. And she hated seeing Rory at school, always on the outside of things, trying to pretend he didn't care – or maybe he really didn't care. Fletcher always told her that she was too anxious about him and she knew he was right. But how do you stop yourself, she thought. Those weeks and months of lying awake in the small hours, heart thundering and the taste of dread in her mouth, thinking about Mabel.

'You don't need to collect us at all,' said Rory.

'I like to.'

Elias's mother Sarah came up the hill, half running and half walking, arriving breathless, though she still managed to look neat. Her dark-brown hair lay in a coil at the back of her neck, her suit and jacket were well cut, her make-up discreet.

'Am I late again?'

'You're always late,' said Elias, scowling. 'And then you always ask if you're late again.' He kicked a stone. 'As if it's the first time.'

Sarah gave a hurt laugh then turned to Neve. 'Doesn't it make you feel horribly guilty?'

'Guilty?'

'Being a working mother.'

'Oh that. Yes. Of course.'

'Guilty at work because you've got to rush off home, guilty at home because you've got to rush off to work. Those phone calls from school when your child's ill or had an accident and you've got to go and collect them. My friend says I should never say I'm leaving work because of anything to do with the children – anything else is better, she says. But you've got three children and you've managed. You always seem so calm and sensible.'

Neve managed to laugh. 'That's not how it feels. Anyway, Fletcher works from home and that makes the biggest difference. I'm lucky. Really, I've just muddled through, like the rest of us. Did my best, which is often not quite good enough. Tried not to punish myself too much.' She aimed for a smile: two frazzled women against the world. 'Anyway, it's not as if we have a choice.'

'No,' Sarah agreed. 'Damn right we don't.' She was a single mother. Neve and Fletcher often had Elias over to give her a break.

They set off down the hill together, Neve wheeling

her bike, Connor and Elias ahead and bumping heavily against each other, laughing. Rory trailed just behind.

'Bye,' said Sarah at the corner.

As they entered the house and the boys ran upstairs, Neve remembered something.

'Has Whisky been fed?'

'How would we know?' said Connor as he disappeared into his room.

Neve wanted to shout after them: because when you asked for a guinea pig, you said that you would feed him and clean the hutch and Fletcher and I wouldn't have to do anything at all. But she didn't. Instead she got the box of pet food from the scullery, then went through to the kitchen, opened the fridge and tore off some leaves of lettuce and spinach and kale. She went out to the garden and opened the hutch, filled the bowl and scattered the leaves, and shut it again. Whisky emerged from his little refuge and chomped silently on the leaves.

Whisky. The name had been chosen by Connor. She wasn't sure why. It wasn't as if he was even whisky-coloured. He was a dirty sort of white with large black patches. She stood watching him as he ate. She had been feeling sorry for him but he looked contented enough. In fact, enviably contented. A life of living in warm straw gnawing fresh salad leaves seemed preferable to her own life. She opened the door of the hutch again and scratched him gently on the top of his head. He continued eating and paid no attention. She went back into the house.

For the first time, she thought of the evening ahead

of her. About once a year one or other of the old group of college friends organised a get-together. Sometimes it was a party but sometimes – like tonight – it was just a drink in a pub. Neve assumed this meant not many people were coming. That was good. She wasn't in the mood for a big occasion. It would also mean it wouldn't go on too long.

Back inside, she went straight into the bathroom and locked the door. She ran a deep bath and as she sank down into it she tried to ignore the sounds of the house, the raised voices, someone dropping a heavy object. She submerged herself entirely and for a moment she was in a silent world, just the sound of her heartbeat. She could stay here, she thought, adding hot water every so often, watching the skin on her fingers shrivel, just a body in water.

Someone rapped at the door. She sighed and hauled herself out of the tub, wrapped herself in a towel, opened the door.

'Something's burning,' she called out.

'Just toast,' Rory called back.

She dressed in loose-fitting trousers and an over-sized, rust-coloured sweater. She wanted to be comfortable, unsexy, invisible. She tried to avoid the mirror: she didn't want to meet her own gaze. But some things couldn't be avoided. She went up to Mabel's room. The chair was finally gone, although there were scratches and gouges on the wall outside and the door was slightly askew on its hinges. Neve knocked. There was some sort of human sound from inside, which she took as an invitation to open the door. The blinds were pulled down and the room was dark.

'Is it all right if I put the light on?' she said.

'I'd rather you didn't,' said Mabel's voice.

'Are you just lying the dark?'

'What's it look like?'

'It doesn't look like anything. It's dark. That's why I'm asking.'

'I'm doing yoga.'

'Really?'

'Of course I'm not doing bloody yoga.'

'All right,' said Neve. 'A couple of things. In case you're worried, I've fed Whisky.'

'I wasn't worried.'

'And I just wanted to remind you that Fletcher and I are going out to meet some people.'

'Again?'

'It's just an early evening drink. We shouldn't be late. Perhaps you and the boys could make some supper together.'

'Like what?'

There followed a complicated discussion between Neve and the voice coming out of the dark about what was in the fridge and what was in the cupboards and how it might be assembled. After it was finished, Neve thought of the fourth person in the family who hadn't fed Whisky. She walked across and knocked at Fletcher's door.

'Can I come in?'

'I'll come out.'

Neve felt an odd resentment as she always did when he said that. It was as if there was some secret that she would violate by penetrating his sanctum, as if he had someone in there with him. He opened the door and looked out.

'All right?' said Neve.

'All right what?'

'The drinks. At the pub.'

'You go,' he said. 'I'd rather just stay in.'

'I think you should come.'

'Why?'

'Because it's good for you to get out of the house. And because I'd like it.'

'All right,' said Fletcher. 'You go ahead. I'll join you later.'

'Don't be too long,' she said.

It was only a short bike ride. The Urban Fox was on Kingsland Road, an old pub that had been renamed and refurbished so that it looked older and more traditional than the previous version that had been all flowery wallpaper and strip lighting. Now it was bare bricks and floorboards and second-hand tables and chairs. When Neve stepped inside, it was empty except for Tamsin, Renata and Gary sitting at a table in the corner. There were open bottles of red and white wine and plates of cheese and smoked meat. Neve poured herself a glass of red wine.

'I thought this was a college reunion,' she said. 'Not a reunion of the office I've just left.

'Aren't you happy to see us?' said Gary. 'Anyway, if you're not, you can just blame Tamsin. It was her idea.'

'I'm not blaming anybody,' said Neve.

'It wasn't exactly my idea,' said Tamsin. 'Remember Jackie Cornfield?'

'Of course,' said Neve. 'God, it's been ages since I last saw her. She's one of the few people who actually stayed in Newcastle, isn't she?'

'That's right. I think she's had a bad time recently and she's trying to reconnect with people she'd lost touch with.'

'Oh lord,' said Gary.

'I think it's nice,' said Tamsin. 'So I'm supplying you three grumpy people, and she's contacted some others. I don't actually know who's going to turn up.'

'It's not exactly the old gang,' said Renata. 'I hardly knew her.'

'Of course you knew her and she's fun,' said Tamsin. 'Or at least she used to be fun. But then we all used to be fun and then we got old.'

'So where is she?' asked Neve. But she had scarcely finished talking when there was a cry of greeting and she looked around. Jackie Cornfield was not so much entering the room as erupting into it. Neve saw her as if in flashes, long wavy hair with streaks of green, purple dress, coloured beads. There was so much of her, it took a moment for Neve to see that there was someone with her, slightly hanging back, a man in a brown moleskin suit, and a dark burnt-red shirt, with a bulky case. He had almost-red hair, high cheekbones, slightly

140

jug ears, and he looked half amused, half embarrassed by the scene in front of him.

They all looked at each other the way they always looked at each other on occasions like this, all noting how much the other people had aged and then promptly denying it.

'You all of you look completely fantastic,' said Jackie. 'None of you have changed *at all*.'

'Tell that to my hair,' said Gary.

Everybody stood up and moved around the table to hug Jackie.

'It's been a long time,' Neve said to Jackie, and she looked at the man. 'So is this your—' She stopped. That was always a rather hard sentence to complete.

Jackie laughed loudly and put her arm round the man, who looked a little sheepish.

'You think we'd make a nice couple? Sweet. Don't you recognise Will? Will Ziegler? Just off the train from Bristol.'

Neve looked again and she did indeed recognise someone who had been in her year at college and who she had known quite well, back in the day.

'I'm an idiot,' she said.

He smiled. 'We're all idiots,' he said. 'And we're idiots who're getting old.'

'All right, don't rub it in,' said Renata. 'I'm feeling frail enough as it is.'

Neve looked at them both. Jackie she remembered vividly: she had always seemed larger than life, more brightly coloured than other people, louder, more demonstrative. But she had vaguer memories of Will, just that he'd been there, in those heady days when everything seemed possible. She smiled at them both.

Tamsin put her arm through Will's and led him round to the other side of the table, his bag tipping a chair over as they went.

'I feel like the country bumpkin,' he said. 'It's been years since I was in London.'

Gary fetched an extra chair. Jackie sat next to Neve. Renata ordered two more bottles of wine. She seemed to have recovered from last night's hangover.

There was an immediate flurry of conversation. Jackie talked about her work for the probation service.

'It's grim,' she said, with a laugh. 'You wouldn't believe the things I hear and see. It's hard to keep optimistic, but you have to, don't you?' She made an expansive gesture that almost hit Will in the face.

She had got married, had children, got divorced. 'The old story,' she said brightly.

Will lived in a village just outside Bristol with his wife, Karen, and two rescue dogs. 'No kids,' he said. 'It didn't happen.'

'Wasn't Karen a friend of that Alison Ferrimore?' asked Tamsin.

'Alison with the eyes of different colours?' said Renata. 'I remember! Whatever happened to her? She played the oboe.'

'The saxophone.'

Neve looked at Will's slightly crestfallen face as the

subject so quickly veered away from him, down the twists and turns of memory lane.

'What do you do?' she asked him.

He looked pleased. 'It's hard to explain.'

'Try.'

'I've got a company that deals with things like data.' He looked at their expressions. 'I said it was hard to explain.'

'Sounds like management consultancy,' said Gary suspiciously.

'It's more about logistics, infrastructure.'

'And you run the company?'

Will shrugged. 'We're a team really. It's been a hard slog to get to where we are now.'

'At least one of us has been successful,' said Gary. 'Maybe you could give us all jobs.'

'Well,' began Will, his face flushing slightly. 'If you—'

'He's joking,' said Neve, putting a hand on his arm.

'And you four have always worked together,' said Jackie. 'It must be nice. You always were a tight-knit group.' She sounded wistful.

Then she leaned in closer. 'But I heard that you and Fletcher ...' She stopped, looked sympathetically at Neve.

'What about us?'

'Were having troubles.'

'Me and Fletcher?'

'I must have misunderstood.'

'Who told you that?'

'I think Tamsin said you were going through a very rough patch. I shouldn't have said anything. Me and my big mouth.'

Neve gave a sigh. Tamsin must have been referring to everything that had happened with Mabel. She wished she wouldn't.

'We're fine,' she said.

Looking at Jackie and Will, people she hadn't seen for – what was it? – twenty years, they looked almost like ghosts of their younger selves. Neve remembered dancing with Will once in a dim and crowded hall; he'd been a terrible dancer, shuffling and self-conscious, his feet too big. And then there was Jackie, who had been funny and reckless. She remembered her drinking and smoking and singing loudly at parties. Then she looked round at Renata and Tamsin and Gary. Objectively they were middle-aged now, with wrinkles and grey hair and saggy skin and were generally battered by life, but still, for her, they remained the age they had been when she first met them, young, hopeful, heedless.

She felt a nudge and looked round. It was Renata.

'I'm going out for a cigarette,' Renata said.

'All right.'

'Do you want to come along?'

'I don't smoke. Since like fifteen years ago.'

Renata leaned in closer and spoke in a hiss. 'I know that. I mean that I want to have a word.'

Feeling slightly awkward, Neve got up and followed Renata out on to the pavement. They stood in a little designated smoking area to one side, where the pavement was littered with cigarette butts. Renata took a cigarette out and lit it and took several short drags on it.

'Well?' said Neve.

'I don't know what to do,' said Renata.

'In what way?'

She sucked on the cigarette almost desperately. 'I need to start smoking e-cigarettes,' she said. 'They're meant to be just as good.'

'Renata, what's this about?'

'I don't know how to say this.' She paused for a moment. 'You remember back in May when we first moved into the office and there was an event for us to meet people in the new company.'

'Vaguely.'

'I was terrified so I remember dressing up with an insane effort and being incredibly friendly with everyone and drinking a lot. I got into a long conversation with Saul. I talked about all of us, how we'd been friends since we were teenagers. I remember him saying he envied that. Anyway, none of that's relevant. What I'm really saying is that about two hours later I was in bed with him in his flat in Covent Garden.'

She looked at her cigarette and stubbed it out on the little brass container attached to the wall and lit another one. Neve looked at Renata, looked at her fingers as she handled the cigarette and the matches with the expertise of thirty years. It reminded her of being on a boat and staring at the horizon as a way of stopping yourself being sick.

'You probably expect me to say it was because I was having a bad time with Charlie and I wanted someone who really desired me.'

'I don't really—' Neve began but Renata spoke over her.

'It wasn't really like that. Things were just the way that they always are, whatever that means. I just drifted into it and I let it continue for a few weeks, a couple of months really.' She looked at Neve with what was almost a puzzled expression. 'It was kind of intense. The sex was amazing. And of course I got emotional about it all.'

Neve wanted to stop her but she didn't trust herself to speak.

'I knew it wasn't going to lead to anything and I think that was part of the attraction for him and I felt pretty awful about it really. It was almost a relief when he broke it off, though it was distressing as well.'

'When was that?' Neve managed to say.

'A couple of months ago, I suppose.'

That made sense, Neve thought to herself.

'He said stuff about his wife,' Renata continued. 'It was the first time he'd talked about her. What I really think is that he'd met somebody else. Somebody more exciting.'

'Why do you think that?'

'I just do. Does it matter why?'

'No,' said Neve. 'No. Of course not.'

'The real reason I'm talking about this is that I lied to the police.'

'What do you mean?'

'You heard me. I said I'd never been to the flat.' Renata looked at Neve with an urgent expression. 'So what do I do? That's a crime, isn't it, lying to the police. Do you think I should own up to it or continue with my lying and make the crime even worse?' Neve still didn't reply. She couldn't find the words. 'I don't know what they'd do if I told them. Would they tell Charlie? That would just wreck everything.'

Neve tried to think of what to say. There seemed nothing good to add. If Renata told the police about her affair with Saul and, worse, that she suspected that he was having an affair with someone else, surely they would look for that person. They would wonder why that person hadn't come forward. But she couldn't ask Renata to lie to the police to protect her.

'I'm sure they'd be discreet,' she began slowly. She took a breath. 'I'm not an expert but I know that lying to the police is a crime. It might be better if you tell them than they find out in some other way.'

'But maybe they wouldn't find out,' said Renata. 'And it couldn't have any relevance to Saul dying, could it?'

Neve thought. 'I suppose not,' she said. 'No.'

Renata stubbed out the second cigarette and then looked at Neve intently.

'You're such a good friend,' she said. 'You're the one person I knew I could tell and you would just listen and not judge and be calm. This means so much to me.'

That did it for Neve. 'If you tell the police,' she said, 'it'll be very painful. And it would mean Charlie would

147

almost certainly have to know. But in the end you might feel better about yourself. And it's the right thing to do.'

Renata came forward and hugged Neve who tried to reciprocate as best as she could but her arms didn't seem to function properly. As they moved towards the entrance of the pub, Neve saw Fletcher walking down the pavement towards them. He came forward and kissed Renata on both cheeks.

'Neve joined me while I was having a cigarette.'

'I hope you're not getting her addicted again.'

'Not much chance of that.'

Renata went inside and left Fletcher and Neve outside on the pavement.

'Thanks for coming,' said Neve.

Fletcher shrugged and then looked at Neve more closely. 'Are you all right?'

'I'm fine.'

'Tough day?'

'It's a strange time.'

Neve found it a relief to go inside and join the others at the table and lose herself in the general conversation to which she didn't have to contribute much. Several more people had turned up and there was an air of slightly anxious cheeriness. Fletcher went to the other side of the table and quickly got into conversation with Tamsin, Jackie and Will. They looked as if they were having a better time than she was. But then nobody, she thought, could be having a worse time.

She answered questions, asked them, laughed when everyone else did. She looked at Renata's expressive face, her cloud of hair, her dancing hands. Renata and Saul; Saul and Renata. She watched Renata hug everyone goodbye, pick up her jacket and leave the pub.

Her mobile gave a bright ping and she pulled it from her pocket. It was Mabel asking when they'd be back because she had plans for the evening.

*Soon*, she keyed in and pressed 'send' then went and squeezed herself in beside Fletcher.

'We need to go soon,' she said in a low voice. 'Mabel's going out.'

Fletcher looked round at her. 'Already?'

'It's nearly nine.'

'I'll go back if you want to stay longer.'

'No. I'm tired. It's fine.'

She stood up and put on her jacket, fishing in her pocket for her bike lights.

'You're going already?' asked Tamsin. Her cheeks were flushed and her hair was coming unravelled.

'I have to take over from Mabel.' She looked round the assembled group, speaking to everyone, lifting her hand in a gesture of farewell. 'It's been lovely. Great.'

Jackie Cornfield stood up and gave her a vast, perfumed hug. 'Let's meet *soon*,' she said. 'Just you and me.'

Neve nodded several times, her head bouncing up and down.

Will Ziegler stood up and kissed her, first on one cheek and then the other. He smelled of moss and wood.

'Very good to see you again after all these years. I would have recognised you anywhere.'

149

Neve nodded once more. Something was about to happen to her, she thought. She needed to leave.

Fletcher was on his feet as well, shaking hands. He was making an effort, she thought, but she wished he'd chosen another night for it. And then she heard him say:

'I tell you what. Why don't you three' – he meant Jackie, Will and Tamsin she realised – 'come and have a meal with us tomorrow night? For old time's sake.'

'But—' Neve began.

'That would be *wonderful*,' said Jackie. 'Are you sure it's OK at such short notice?'

Neve pulled at Fletcher's sleeve. 'I think we might be busy tomorrow night,' she hissed.

'No. Definitely not,' Fletcher replied.

'I think we are.'

He took his phone from his pocket and pulled up the electronic diary and opened it. 'Look. I've put all our dates in.'

'And Will's probably going back to Bristol,' said Neve.

'I only got here a couple of hours ago,' said Will. 'I'm staying with a friend for a few days, doing a bit of business here. But look, it's probably the wrong night. We'll find another time.'

'Nonsense,' said Fletcher. He was looking pleased with himself. 'We'd love to have you for dinner.'

'Great,' said Tamsin. 'It would be a relief to get out. People stop inviting you when you're not part of a couple.'

'Settled then,' said Fletcher. Good. Come at about eight.'

*

Outside, it had started to rain, a blustery, discomforting drizzle. Neve turned to Fletcher.

'Why did you do that?'

'What?'

'You know.'

Fletcher looked puzzled in a way that made Neve want to punch him in the face.

'You're always saying I don't make enough effort to be sociable. You go on at me to invite people round, go out and see people – and as soon as I do that, you don't like it. I can't win.'

'It's the wrong night.'

'It's Saturday night. Anyway, you sound like me. You always say that the right time is now.'

'We went to Renata's party on Thursday, then this thing tonight.'

'It's only nine.' He peered at her. 'You do look tired though. And you were out past midnight on Tuesday as well, seeing Tamsin.' She nodded miserably at the repeated lie. 'You just need an early night and you can have a lie-in tomorrow. It'll be fine. We can't un-invite them.'

'I guess not.' She unlocked her bike.

'What were you talking to Renata about? She looked upset.' He paused a beat then added, 'So did you actually.'

'Oh, you know. Life. I'll see you at home. I'll put the kettle on.'

She biked against the wind and growing rain, which came at her in waves. She didn't want to think; she wanted to drink a mug of tea and climb into bed and pull the covers over her head. She didn't want to dream; she wanted everything to be wiped away from her consciousness, for a while at least.

Renata was going to tell the police. It was the right thing to do. Neve thought about it over and over. She had to as well. She had to tell the truth before her lies were discovered. The thought of the present that Saul had ordered for her and which at any moment would be arriving at the flat stabbed at her. She had to tell Fletcher and then she had to go and see Hitching and confess everything, pull her whole life down on top of her.

Mabel was waiting for her, already pulling on the coat that Neve had given her on her last birthday. She was wearing high platform boots, a short leather skirt and lots of make-up. It was like a mask over her face.

'Everything OK?' asked Neve.

'We had pasta and I got beaten at various computer games and now Connor's asleep on the sofa and Rory's in his room with a book.'

Mabel was good with her brothers. Even at her lowest, when she seemed like a snarling animal in pain, she would pull herself out of misery to act the elder sister.

'Thank you,' said Neve. 'I hope we haven't kept you waiting.'

'It's OK.'

'Where are you off to?' She said it casually, as if she didn't really want to know.

Mabel shot her a sideways glance. 'Just to see a couple of friends,' she said.

'Enjoy it.' Neve wasn't going to say anything else; she absolutely wasn't. She turned to go into the kitchen. 'Take care,' she said.

'Neve.'

'Yes. Sorry. Just—'

But Mabel was gone.

Neve went into the kitchen to fill the kettle and turn it on, and then into the living room where Connor was curled up asleep in his pyjamas. She thought of letting Fletcher do it when he came home, but then leaned down and heaved him to his feet, half carried and half led him up the first stairs, then the second, into his room. She lowered him on his bed and pulled the covers over him. Teeth could wait till the morning. She leaned forward and kissed the top of his bristly head. He smelled of clean sweat. His eyelids fluttered and for a moment he smiled at her, then turned on his side and was asleep again.

She knocked on Rory's door and put her head round it.

'All right evening?' she asked.

He murmured something without lifting his head from his book. She closed the door and made her way downstairs. She was cold and soaking and tired to the bone. Her legs felt like they were filled with cement. Don't think, she told herself, don't remember. Don't look back and don't look forward.

She was on the second flight of stairs, on her way to the kitchen to make tea, when an alarm played from

Mabel's room. She halted. Mabel had an alarm clock that the boys had given to her at Christmas, which had moving feet and which lurched itself off the bedside table and on to the bed if Mabel didn't switch if off in time. It also had a tone that got louder and louder and didn't stop. It had been like a family joke. Mabel had in the past regularly slept through all the phone alarms that she set to go off every five minutes. But it made a terrible noise and she often forgot to set it anyway, or set it for some random time. Like now. Neve looked at her watch: twenty-five past nine at night.

The alarm sounded again. Soon it would wake Connor. Then it would wake up the entire neighbour-hood. She trudged back up the stairs and hesitated outside Mabel's room, then pushed open the door on to darkness. There was a strange smell in here, a bit foetid, and something else as well. She tried not to think what that might be: this was Mabel's sanctum. When she turned on the light, the room sprang into visibility, and it was like suddenly finding herself in an alternative reality: Mabel's chaotic university prepara-tions, Mabel's war zone, Mabel's self-harm, the inside of Mabel's head.

The chair was inside the room, separated from its legs that lay under the window, one of them broken. In the wild disorder, it was at first hard to pick out spe-cific objects: she saw soft piles of clothes and a tangle of metal and wood hangers, split bin bags, a rolled-up rug standing crookedly on end against the wall with Mabel's old teddy perched on top – and then she saw with a lurch of terror that Mabel had cut into the bear's soft middle so that its fabric innards were spilling out. The alarm rang again, getting louder.

Dry-mouthed, Neve moved further into the room. Her foot slid on something shiny and she looked down. There were dozens of photos on the floor and she realised that Mabel had ripped apart the family albums and scattered dozens, no hundreds, of photographs everywhere. She'd taken down all the pictures and posters from her walls and leaned them against her bed, except for one poster that she'd ripped into large pieces. A segment of face stared up at Neve, an eye as big as a hand.

The alarm rang again, insistent, like a drill inside Neve's skull, and she picked her way through the debris towards the clock but before she reached it, it took a few lurching steps across the little table and slithered into the folds of Mabel's duvet. Neve pulled the covers back and took hold of the clock, which rattled and shook in her hands. It had a yellow, smiley face. Rise and shine. It rang again.

Neve didn't turn it off. She was staring at something poking out from the cover. She put out one hand and lifted up her bangle.

She didn't know how long she stood there, holding it. The alarm clock shrilled once more and she heard Rory's voice calling: 'Mum? Mum, can you turn it off?'

She pushed the bangle over her wrist and fumbled with the little button at the back of the clock until the noise stopped. Then she lunged across the room, feeling things crack and splinter underfoot, shut the door and locked it. She fell to her knees and started to scrabble through the pile-up of things on the floor, ripping open bin bags and plunging her hand deep inside, delving into soft heaps of clothes, yanking open drawers. She worked in a silence that was broken only by the slight gasp of her breath.

At last she found it, wrapped in a blue velvet shirt at the bottom of a plastic shopping bag. She unrolled the shirt. Her fingers felt fat and useless. And there it was. The hammer.

The front door opened and then shut.

'Hello,' Fletcher called.

Neve sprang to her feet with the hammer, looking around her wildly. She grabbed a damp towel from Mabel's floor and wrapped it up, and then gathered up a few random clothes and added them to the bundle.

'Neve?' Fletcher again.

She unlocked the door and opened it. 'On my way,' she called back.

She made her way downstairs, clutching the bundle. Fletcher was taking off his coat in the hall.

'Hi,' he said. His hair was plastered to his skull and his glasses were steamed up but he looked more cheerful than he had done for days. 'That was a good evening, wasn't it?'

'I'll make tea,' said Neve. 'And put these things in the wash.'

She went into the kitchen. What now? She heard

Fletcher coming down the hall and she opened the back door and went into the garden. When she opened the hutch, she heard Whisky give a faint squeak. She laid the bundle on the wet ground, unwrapped the hammer and pushed it deep inside the pile of hay. She closed the hutch and went back inside.

# 4

# THE DINNER PARTY

Neve lay in bed in what felt like a fever of racing thoughts, flashes of sleep and a nightmare from which she woke up in a shock, the slow sense of where she was and then more of the torment in her brain.

Mabel had the bangle. Mabel had the hammer. Mabel had the hammer. Mable had the bangle.

It felt like the words were being shouted at her. It felt like they were flashing on a screen. They deafened her and they dazzled her. What could it mean? How could she have got them? Her mind was full of questions. Did someone give them to her? Did she get them herself? What had she *done* with the hammer? Her mind felt choked with the horror of it. And then back into the deranged dreams and the night passed in a muddled blur.

She didn't so much wake as find herself staring at the ceiling as the daylight slowly moved across it.

She reached for her watch. Ten past seven. She felt a sudden shock at having slept but then remembered it was Saturday. No school. The day when everyone slept in. Fletcher was next to her in the bed, breathing softly in and out.

Neve got up carefully, trying not to wake him, and walked round to his side of the bed to switch off the radio alarm. She picked out her clothes – old canvas trousers and a rough shirt – and carried them into the bathroom. She showered quickly, hoping she wouldn't wake anyone in the house, dressed and padded downstairs, softly like a burglar, a shoe in each hand.

She made coffee and toast and sat at the table. Normally she might have walked out and bought a newspaper and read it with her breakfast. She might have listened to the radio. This morning she just drank her coffee and took one bite of the toast, which tasted like old leather, and stared into space. She had two mugs of coffee and threw the toast in the bin. She thought of the people sleeping in the house and then she thought of Whisky in his hutch out in the garden.

The hammer.

She went out into the garden where a light drizzle was falling and picked a handful of dandelion leaves from the lawn, which was in bad need of mowing. She opened the door of the hutch and threw them in. Whisky emerged from the inside of the hutch and began to munch on them. She reached past him and retrieved the hammer from under the straw. She walked back into the kitchen and laid it on the table.

What should she do?

Her immediate thought was to dispose of it. Surely that would be easy. She could put it into a litter bin or throw it into some bushes in a park or into a canal. It felt wrong, of course, but she had done so much destruction of evidence. Why not just do a little more? But this was the actual object that was used to kill Saul. Maybe, just maybe, it might be needed. After all, the murderer was still out there. She stared at it. Mabel had taken it. And Mabel had kept it. Why? How? Her mind was a blur. She couldn't make any sense of it; she didn't want to.

The front-door bell rang.

It was probably the postman. As she got up to answer, the bell rang again. People would be waking up, she thought. She looked at the hammer. What if Mabel came down? She slipped it into her shoulder bag.

She opened the front door and it wasn't the postman.

'Mr Hitching,' she said awkwardly. 'I mean, inspector.'

'It's the weekend,' he said with a smile. 'I'm Alastair, remember.'

And indeed he was dressed for the weekend, but even his off-duty clothes had a formality about them, as if they'd been bought from the leisurewear section of a catalogue. He was dressed in pale chinos and a brown suede zip-up jacket and slip-on leather shoes.

Neve looked at her watch.

'It's not even nine o'clock,' she said. 'And it's Saturday.'

'I know, I know,' said Hitching. 'Can I come in? I don't want to disturb a family breakfast.'

'Nobody else is up,' said Neve and led him through to the kitchen.

While she made a fresh pot of coffee, Hitching sat down at the table. Her shoulder bag was on the table in front of him and he pushed it to one side, out of his way. Neve flinched. Wouldn't he feel how heavy it was?'

'I was meant to be out on the golf course,' he said. 'Have you ever played golf?'

'No,' said Neve.

'Don't like the idea of it?'

'Not particularly.'

'A good walk ruined,' said Hitching cheerfully. 'According to Mark Twain. It's always Mark Twain, isn't it? He probably didn't really say it. But somebody said it.'

Neve sat down opposite him and poured coffee out for both of them. 'I was about to go to my allotment,' she said. 'I've been neglecting it a bit.'

'Nice,' said Hitching. 'It's what English people do on Saturday morning. Dig the allotment, play golf, wash the car.'

'And yet you're working,' said Neve slightly sharply and then immediately regretted it.

'Murder inquiries tend to get in the way of weekends. Ask the wife. Anyway, something came up,' said Hitching.

Neve slowly took a sip of her coffee. She felt that it

would be natural to ask what it was but she wasn't sure she wanted to know.

'Sometimes it feels a bit unfair,' said Hitching. 'For want of anything better to do, you start investigating the victim. You know, for motives. Why someone might have wanted to kill them.'

Neve still didn't reply.

'I spoke to his colleagues. They talk about him being reliable, sensible, charming. People liked him. Of course, he was involved in the acquisition of your company. That must have ruffled a few feathers. But basically he seems to have been a straightforward, honest guy.' He paused and took a gulp of his coffee. 'I mean in his business life.'

Neve couldn't bear it anymore.

'I'm really sorry,' she said. 'I don't understand why you're here.'

He smiled again. 'You know, it's funny,' he said. 'Whoever I see, they keep saying, talk to Neve Connolly, she'll know. She's the one people talk to, she's the one people confide in.'

'I don't know why people would say that.'

'Your friend, Renata Searle, said that about you. She said you were like her conscience.'

'When did she say that?'

Hitching lifted up his left hand to look at his watch. He needed to pull his shirt slightly up his wrist to see it.

'Oh, about forty-five minutes ago.'

'You mean this morning?'

'She called up last night and came in first thing this

morning. It turns out that aspects of her statement were incomplete. To put it mildly.'

Neve felt strangely calm. 'Yes,' she said. 'I know.'

'I know you know,' said Hitching. 'You told her to come forward.'

'I didn't exactly tell her.'

'It was good advice,' said Hitching. 'Very good.'

'Is she in trouble?'

He sniffed. 'That remains to be seen. Perverting the course of justice is a serious offence. Judges don't like it. They don't like it at all. Something about attacking the basis of the system, that sort of thing. But she did herself a favour by owning up. Of course, it raises as many questions as it answers.'

They heard footsteps and looked around. Mabel pelted into the kitchen. She was in her pyjama trousers and a ripped tee shirt; she looked like a bony little child. For a moment, Neve felt unable to say anything at all.

'I'm Alastair,' said Hitching.

'He's a detective,' said Neve quickly. Maybe too quickly, she thought. 'This is Mabel. My daughter.'

'Is it about the murder?' said Mabel. 'It is, isn't it?'

'I just popped in for a chat,' said Hitching.

Mabel sat down at the table. Her face looked so pale that there was almost a green-blue tinge to it, and her lips were bloodless.

'Would you like some breakfast?' Neve asked.

'No, thanks.'

'Or some tea?'

'No, thanks.'

They sat for a moment in silence.

'Mabel is about to go to university. Next week.'

'It must be a busy time,' said Hitching.

'Of course,' said Neve. 'There's all sorts of things to do.'

There was another pause that Neve could feel as if it were toothache, the sort of toothache that spreads right through your head.

'We've been spending lots of time together,' said Mabel. 'Haven't we?' She turned towards Neve and stretched her mouth into a smile. Her pupils were huge. Neve wondered if she was on something.

'Yes,' she said.

'Going shopping. Things like that. It's as if we're catching up.'

'I wouldn't put it like that,' said Neve faintly. 'Although we have been spending time together.'

'We've even been working together on the allotment,' continued Mabel, speaking slowly and deliberately. She hesitated. 'Digging,' she added. 'Watering.' Neve stared at her but she continued addressing her remarks to Hitching. 'We went there first thing on Wednesday, almost before it was light, and worked there for hours and hours. Together.'

Shut up, Neve said silently, frantically to her daughter. Shut up. Don't answer a question that he hasn't even asked.

'Really?' said Hitching. 'That's good to hear.' He smiled again. 'Your mother was saying that she'd been neglecting the allotment. So it's nice to know that you're both tackling it.'

'There's still lots to do,' said Mabel. 'I mean, we did what we could. That Wednesday morning.'

Neve couldn't remember when Mabel had last been to the allotment. A year ago at least, and then it was just to pick some blackcurrants. If Hitching asked any question about it, anything at all, Mabel wouldn't be able to answer.

He stood up. 'You'll miss each other. Still, she'll be back before you know it.'

Neve stood up as well, hoping this would encourage him to get out of the house as soon as possible.

'Where's the allotment?' he asked her.

'Upper Clapton, by Springfield Park. It only takes about ten minutes to walk there, quicker if I bike.'

'I know it. Lovely spot. I'll accompany you part of the way: it will do me good to get a bit of fresh air.'

'What about your car?' asked Neve wildly.

'I parked several streets away. Thought I should stretch my legs.'

'I might pop into the shops on the way.'

'No worries,' he said cheerfully. He looked across at Mabel. 'Are you joining your mother later?'

Mabel looked puzzled.

'What with spending so much time with her,' Hitching continued.

'Not today.'

'Tell me,' he said, leaning towards Mabel, smiling. 'On the allotment, what do—?'

'I've got to go now,' said Neve. 'Or not at all.'

'Of course. I'm keeping you from your morning. Won't you need your bag if you're going to the shops?'

'My bag. Of course. Yes.'

He picked it up. She held out her hand for it.

'I can carry it for you,' he said. 'It's rather heavy.'

She tried to smile.

'It's fine. I'll take it. I just need to check some-thing – collect something – before we go. If you just give it here.'

She tugged the bag from his grip and it swung and bumped sharply against her leg. She imagined it tipping, the hammer falling to the floor between the three of them. Out of the corner of her eye, she could see Mabel gnawing at her nails. She practically ran out of the kitchen into the damp little scullery off to one side, pulling the door shut behind her. She stared around then plunged the hammer into the bag full of tangled wires from old appliances that she kept mean-ing to sort out.

'Sorry,' she said, going back into the kitchen.

'I've been asking Mabel about slugs,' said Hitching.

'Slugs?'

'The curse of all gardeners,' said Hitching. 'Them, and ground elder of course.'

'Ground elder,' repeated Mabel, as if it was a for-eign language.

'I should go,' said Neve.

The door swung open and Fletcher stood there, owlishly blinking. Behind him was Connor, just in underpants, pushing something chocolatey into his mouth.

'I slept too late,' Fletcher said. 'You should have woken me.'

'This is Inspector Hitching,' Neve told him. 'He's in charge of the investigation into Saul Stevenson's murder. Connor, what on earth are you eating?'

'Did you know Mr Stevenson?' asked Hitching.

'No.'

'A Twix,' said Connor indistinctly. He stared curiously up at Hitching.

'Then don't. Now, DCI Hitching's just going and I'm off to the allotment.'

'Are you a gardener too?' Hitching asked Fletcher. He seemed in no hurry to leave.

'No, that's just Neve.'

'And Mabel,' said Hitching.

'Mabel? Keen on gardening? First I've heard of it.'

'Yes,' said Mabel loudly and shrilly. 'Of course I am.' She gathered her knees up so she was coiled tightly in her chair. 'All that fresh air. Nature.'

She held up her hands with their bitten nails in a gesture that Neve imagined was meant to be one of joy. Fletcher looked dazed and Connor chomped loudly.

'Bye,' said Neve. She actually placed her hand in the small of Hitching's back and gave him a sharp push towards the door.

'So,' said Hitching as they walked down the road together. 'You've been keeping secrets from me.'

'I'm sorry?'

'Your friend Renata and her affair.'

'I didn't know until yesterday.' It was a relief to be saying something that was true.

'Really?'

'Really.'

'I would understand if you felt that you couldn't betray her confidence.'

'But I didn't know.'

'Not even a suspicion? She's your close friend, after all.'

'Not even a suspicion.'

'Funny how good people can be at keeping secrets. You'd think she would have had to have told someone.'

'Not me.'

'What about her husband?'

'Charlie? She definitely didn't tell Charlie.'

'But did he suspect?'

Neve remembered the look on Charlie's face at Renata's dreadful party.

'I don't think so. Will he have to find out?'

Hitching stroked the top of his bald head. 'That depends,' he said. 'It would have been much easier if she'd come clean at once. Secrets,' he ruminated, looking ahead, walking with long strides. 'They're dangerous things, don't you agree?'

Neve nodded. She thought of Saul's body, she thought of the great clean-up she'd done. She thought of Saul's present to her that was on its way to the flat.

Then she thought of the hammer – and of Mabel's pinched and chalky face.

'Yes,' she agreed. 'They are.'

They reached a junction and Hitching paused. 'Well,' he said cheerfully. 'Much as I'd like to come and see your allotment, this is where we part company. For the time being.'

Neve watched him walk away, and only when she could no longer see him did she let herself breathe normally. She wanted to sit down somewhere and put her head in her hands. Or lie down. She imagined curling up on the pavement, eyes shut.

What now? Was she really going to the allotment? The day stretched ahead of her, ugly and full of ambushes. She pictured Mabel's demolished room, her sour and terrified face. She turned round and walked rapidly back to the house.

'Hello,' said Fletcher, looking up from his coffee and the newspaper. 'I thought you were going to the allotment.'

'I was. I am. Where's Mabel?'

'In her room I think. Why?'

'Never mind.'

Neve ran up the stairs and banged on Mabel's door. 'What?'

'It's me. I want to talk to you.'

Rory joined Neve on the landing. 'I've got a headache,' he said.

'I'm so sorry. Mabel!'

'Go away.'

'I'll get you some paracetamol in a second, Rory. Hang on a second.' She left her son on the landing and went into her room, took the bangle from the bedside table, and returned to rap on the door once more.

'Go away. I'm busy.'

'You're coming with me to the allotment, Mabel.'

'I'm fucking not.'

'Open the door now.'

The door swung open and Mabel glared out of the dank gloom. Neve held up the bangle. 'Come on,' she said. 'I'll give you five minutes to get dressed.'

They left the house in silence. Mabel had pulled on some ancient jeans that were ripped at both knees and a baggy yellow sweatshirt with frayed cuffs. She hadn't brushed her hair and her skin looked pasty. She looked, Neve thought, like someone who'd been sleeping rough.

Neve had no idea where to begin. She felt entirely without a core, her mind lurching between all the possible meanings of her discovery.

'Mabel.' Her voice came out scratchy. 'I found the bangle in your room. And I found the hammer.'

Mabel whirled around. 'So?' she said. She looked almost triumphant.

'Why were they there?'

'Mother, mother,' said Mabel with a malicious playfulness that made Neve flinch. 'What do you think?'

What did Neve think? Looking at Mabel now, with her face full of hatred and fear, she could imagine her

170

bringing that hammer down on Saul's head. 'I don't know,' she replied simply.

'*I* know,' Mabel said. 'I know *everything*.'

'What do you mean?'

'*Everything*.' She looked wild now, and her face, which a few minutes ago had seemed like the face of a child, suddenly looked old and spiteful.

'Mabel, listen. You have to tell me why the bangle and hammer were in your room. I have to know.'

'No. You listen. Everyone thinks you're so wonderful. My friends say I'm lucky to have a mother like you. They have no idea that you're just a lying slut.'

'Please. Tell me what you've done.'

'What *I've* done. That's a laugh. I've known about you for ages. You thought you were being so clever but it was obvious. So I followed you. I saw you go into the place. I *saw* you.' She was breathless and there was spittle on her chin. 'You said you were with Tamsin or Renata or whatever. How could you? What about Dad? What about us? You're our *mother*.'

'Mabel.' Neve spoke sharply, trying to get hold of her daughter's attention. 'I know you're angry with me and probably hate me right now—'

'Fucking right I do.'

'I know what I've done has been damaging and wrong—'

'Then *why*? You're nearly fifty, for fuck's sake?'

Yes, thought Neve, she was not so far off fifty. She had a husband who was more or less unemployed and on and off depressed; a job that had ground her down;

financial worries. And she had a daughter who for years had turned her life inside out and upside down. She thought of saying, *it was because of you*. But of course she didn't, and of course that wasn't true, or not the only truth. And yet there had been times when she'd thought she would go mad with grief and anxiety, and her affair with Saul had been like a gulp of fresh water, reminding her that she still had a self, a sliver of life that belonged only to her. And even now, in the middle of this ruin, she had a small flash of memory: Saul smiling at her, holding out his hand. She could feel the pressure of his warm fingers.

'You disgust me,' Mabel was saying. 'You're disgusting.'

'Stop.' Neve held up her hand. A woman ran past them, her beautiful face glistening with sweat. Neve waited for her to be out of earshot before speaking. 'We must talk about all this. But before anything else, I need to know what you've done.'

'You're just trying to make this about me, but it's about you. You cheated on Dad.'

'Yes. But this has to wait.'

'Over and over again.'

Neve nodded.

'Who loves you and has never done anything to hurt you.'

Neve didn't reply to that.

'Didn't you mind about him?'

'Of course I minded.'

'Not enough to stop you, though.'

'No.'

'Were you so besotted?'

Neve wasn't sure how she was still standing, keeping her eyes on Mabel's.

'It was fresh and new,' she said. 'An adventure, perhaps.'

'Mid-life crisis.' Mabel's voice was ugly with sarcasm. 'I thought that's what men were supposed to get.'

Neve wasn't able to reply to that.

'Does Dad know?'

'No.'

'Are you certain?'

'All I can tell you is that I've tried to keep it secret.'

'Creeping around at night like a thief. Yes. I know. And if I knew . . .' She trailed off.

'I don't think Fletcher knows.'

'Or suspects?'

'I don't think so.' She didn't add that Fletcher had stopped looking at her, seeing her, attending to her. If he didn't know, it was because he no longer noticed her. Mabel said he loved her – but did he?

'Do you still love him?'

'These are things I should be talking to Fletcher about, not you. Not like this, as though I'm on trial.'

'You don't then.'

'I do love him. But it's difficult.'

'What does that mean?'

'Marriage is difficult.'

'Blah blah. Poor you. Are you ashamed of yourself?'

'Of course.'

'Good. I'm ashamed of you as well.'

'Now we've established that we're both ashamed of me, can we get back to what happened? You had the hammer. You went there.'

'So did you.'

'Yes,' said Neve.

'You got a text from him and you went.'

'Yes.'

'And so did I.'

'Mabel, what did you do there?'

'Why are you asking me? You fucked another man. I saw you go in. I was there.'

'Where?' Neve remembered being in the flat, hearing sounds, the tingle in her spine. Had Mabel been there all along, waiting for her to leave so she could take away the hammer? Neve couldn't keep her thoughts in order.

'I saw you coming out with your bin bag, looking like a criminal.' Her voice cracked. 'And you are a criminal.'

'I didn't want them to find out,' said Neve, lamely.

'You deserve to be caught and sent to prison because you've ruined everything. Everything in the world. And I'm a criminal too and it's all your fault. And I hate you and I'll never forgive you. I want to die.'

'Are you telling me . . .' Neve could barely bring herself to utter the words. 'That you killed him?'

'I'm not telling you anything.'

Mabel suddenly turned from her and broke into a shuffling run, head down. Neve ran after her, caught up with her, put a hand on her shoulder to bring her to a halt. They were near the park now. Ahead she could see the allotments spread out in a crazy patchwork.

'Talk to me,' she said.

'You're mad,' said Mabel. 'You look so ordinary, but you're mad. And you're trying to send me mad as well. You're supposed to be protecting me, not protecting yourself. Isn't that what mothers do?'

'I want to protect you. What did you do? Why were you there? You can tell me anything,' said Neve. 'Literally anything.'

'Says the woman who's had this dirty little secret for weeks and weeks.'

'Obviously you went into the flat after me, to take away the hammer and bangle. Did you go in before me as well?'

Mabel lifted her head and stared at her mother. For a moment, they both stood frozen on the pavement.

'I know what you're doing,' said Mabel at last. 'You lie and you lie. Your whole life's a great fat lie. Now this.'

'Mabel, my darling—'

'Shut up. Shut the fuck up. I can't.' She put her hand to her temples and bent forward. 'What have you done to us all?' she said.

Neve took her by the elbow and steered her into the park. The river lay ahead of them. She sat Mabel down on a bench, whose little metal plaque memorialised a woman called Kitty, who used to love this place.

\*

They never did make it to the allotment. Neve waited while Mabel rocked back and forth on the bench with her hands clutching her belly, occasionally wiping her snotty face with her grubby sleeve. At last she sat up on the bench and turned towards Neve.

'Aren't you going to ask me?'

'What?'

'If I'm going to tell Fletcher.'

'Are you?'

'No,' said Mabel. 'It would destroy him. You're strong and you've got loads of friends but he hasn't. He'd just go to pieces without you. Which is why what you've done is so monstrous.'

Neve stared out across the park to the allotments and imagined her patch, choked with weeds, bolting cabbage, rotting marrows, and the fruit rotting on the bushes.

'I still don't know what happened in that flat,' she said.

'You want me to say it out loud? OK. Let's get this charade over with. It wasn't me,' said Mabel. 'I was doing it for you. Satisfied?'

Neve looked at her steadily and Mabel held her gaze for a few seconds and then looked away. It was all she was going to get from her daughter.

'In which case,' she said, 'I should go to the police.'

'You can't.'

'Why?'

'Then Fletcher would know about everything.'

'I'll just have to live with that.'

'You can't. If the police find out I took things away, I'll be in trouble. My life will be ruined.'

'They won't find out.'

'So you'll be lying to them all over again?'

'I think I need to speak to a lawyer,' said Neve.

As they walked slowly home, Mabel said, 'One last question.'

'Go on.'

'Did you love him?'

Neve looked at her daughter, small and thin, with a grubby tear-streaked face, shadows under her eyes, bitten nails.

'No,' she said, turning her face away, seeing Saul opening the door and pulling her inside, out of the crush of the world. 'No, I didn't.'

*Yes*, she had said, brimming over with joy and betrayal. *Yes I do.*

Less than an hour later, Neve was sitting in the living room of the one friend she had from school who had become seriously rich and was still her friend. Amanda Fitzgibbon was a lawyer and her husband Rudi was a lawyer. Mandy was a solicitor, but not the kind that arranged the sale of your house or drew up your will for you. Not unless your will involved setting up trusts and foundations. And Rudi did a sort of law in the City of London that Neve had never quite understood. But she did understand what it had bought them.

They lived in Hackney, just ten minutes' cycle ride for Neve, but it felt like a world away. It was a large Georgian house with high ceilings and large windows and an impossibly big garden that backed on to other impossibly big gardens. The ground-floor rooms were full of mirrors and huge soft sofas and oak floors. Sometimes it felt like the sort of life she had always dreamed of and she had found herself being envious. But she had also spent many evenings in that house with a glass of wine, clutching Mandy's hand while the tears rolled down her face because Mandy's problems with her two daughters had been even worse than Neve's problems with Mabel. At least until now.

Out of her work clothes, in a light blue sweater, jeans and espadrilles, Mandy looked almost like any other of Neve's friends, but everything about her from her dirty blond hair to the bracelet around her wrist added a little tweak that signalled money, discreetly spent. Neve, meanwhile, was still in her allotment clothes: grubby trousers, ancient shirt, scuffed walking boots. The two of them sat on one of the sofas with a mug of coffee each and a cafetière and a plate of ginger oat biscuits that – infuriatingly – Mandy had baked herself.

She already knew about the murder but Neve filled her in on the details that hadn't been in the newspaper.

'I feel a bit bad about this,' said Neve. 'I've got this cousin who's a doctor and friends are always phoning him up on Sunday morning saying that their child has an earache and what should they do about it. Here you are on Saturday with the smell of baking and a nice day outside and I'm talking about work stuff.'

'You didn't do it, did you?' said Mandy.

'What?'

'It. The murder.'

'Of course I didn't do it.'

Mandy laughed. 'I was only joking. However, if you did do it, go and confess. You'll feel better.'

'But as it happens, I didn't,' said Neve.

'I'm glad to hear it. And by the way, don't feel guilty. I've spent the last couple of days working on the most boring merger in the history of the universe. It's nice to hear about some good old-fashioned criminal activity.'

She looked at Neve and her expression changed.

'I'm so sorry,' she said. 'We're talking about a colleague of yours. It must be awful for you. So what can I help you with?'

Neve took a deep breath and told Mandy about Renata, about her misleading the police and then owning up. As she talked, she looked at Mandy's face. By the time she had finished, Mandy looked like a different person. Suddenly Neve saw her in her office, doing a real job.

'So she came to her senses,' said Mandy.

'That's one way of looking at it.'

'It's the only way of looking at it.'

'But won't she get into trouble?'

Mandy shook her head. 'Obviously she's committed an offence, but I imagine the police will just be grateful she's come forward.'

There was a pause and Mandy looked at Neve with renewed interest. 'Is that the question you wanted to ask?' she said.

Neve hesitated. She had so many thoughts, so many questions, but she found it difficult to say them aloud.

'I forgot to mention that Renata told me about it last night. I think that talking to me was a part of why she went to the police.'

'Then you did her a great favour,' said Mandy.

Neve paused once more. 'Can I put a hypothetical question to you?'

Mandy gave a slow smile but Neve didn't find it reassuring. It was the smile of someone who knows something about you that they're not meant to know. 'Hang on,' she said. 'I think I know this one. Is it the one that starts with: "I'm asking for a friend"?'

Neve tried to smile back. 'This isn't about me. Renata told me that she had been to the murder scene days before, maybe even weeks. She'd been there several times because she and Saul had a brief affair. But what if that wasn't quite the whole truth? What if she had been there just after the murder?'

'You mean, if she was still lying about it?'

'More than that. If she had been there just after the murder and she had cleared up a bit.'

'Why would she have done that?' Mandy asked slowly.

'To clear away the traces of their affair.'

'Did she tell you that?'

'I think it would be best to treat it as hypothetical,' said Neve.

Now Mandy thought for a long time. She didn't seem to be finding it funny anymore. She reached for the cafetière and refilled her mug and took a sip. She pulled a face. It had gone cold.

'If you ask a lawyer for legal advice . . .' she began.

'Which I'm not doing.'

'All right,' said Mandy, 'but when – hypothetically –' she raised an ironic eyebrow as she said that, 'someone asks a lawyer for advice, the lawyer will generally tell them to obey the law.' She turned and looked at Neve with an almost fierce expression. 'Perverting the course of justice is really serious. Disposing of evidence is a particularly serious way of perverting the course of justice.'

'What do you mean by serious?'

'I'm not a criminal lawyer,' said Mandy. 'But I know criminal lawyers. The maximum sentence for perverting the course of justice is life imprisonment.'

'What?' said Neve, startled.

'Yes, but nobody ever gets that. So far as I know, the range is something like six months to three years. If your hypothetical friend did the sort of thing you described, then I am pretty certain that she – or he – would be in prison for closer to the three year end of that range.'

'But would they get sympathetic treatment for coming forward?'

'Three years would be the sympathetic treatment.'

Neve didn't reply immediately. She was thinking about Mabel and her dull-voiced denial of murder. What if it wasn't just about perverting the course of justice? For a moment, she felt cold, as if autumn had suddenly turned to winter as she sat there. She knew there must be lots of questions to ask but she couldn't quite think of any of them just then. She didn't even want to meet Mandy's eye.

'Wait,' said Mandy suddenly.

'What?'

Mandy got up and walked out of the room. Neve heard a clinking sound and then Mandy came back into the room holding a bottle of white wine and two large glasses.

'It's a bit early in the day for me,' said Neve.

'You're going to need this,' said Mandy. 'Come with me.'

At the far end of the living room was a door that opened on to a wrought-iron spiral staircase that led down into the garden. Neve followed Mandy down the steps. At the bottom there was a section of the garden paved in beautifully weathered Portland stone. Neve recognised the stone because she had seen it in a builder's yard once when she was planning her own garden and then had seen the price. Mandy twisted off the screw top and poured wine into the two glasses and then put the bottle down on to a table that also looked expensive. Everything in the garden looked expensive. Even the flowers. Neve took a sip of the wine. It tasted expensive as well.

'Nice,' she said.

'I'm not an expert,' said Mandy.

'You mean about this wine?'

'Well, I'm not actually an expert on the wine, but that's not what I meant. I'm not an expert on criminal law. It's funny. When I was first studying law I had this idea that I'd be sitting in police interview rooms telling my client to say "no comment". It never quite worked out that way. What I actually do is sit in an office going through the small print so that rich people can minimise their tax burden and defer earnings. I've never even been in a police cell.' She took a sip of her wine and then looked at the glass. 'You're right. It is rather nice.'

'I'm sorry,' said Neve. 'I've taken up too much of your time.'

'You're going to take up just a little bit more of it. First, I want to say that a part of me is hoping that this hypothetical person of yours really is hypothetical and you've come round here for a philosophical discussion. But that doesn't seem very likely. I don't know whether we're talking about your friend Renata or a friend of Renata's or a different friend of yours.' Mandy took another sip of wine. When she next spoke it was with a care and deliberation that felt quite different from anything she had said before. 'Or about someone else.'

Neve started to say something but Mandy held her free hand up to silence her.

'As I said,' Mandy continued, 'I'm no expert on criminal law. There is such a thing as client privilege but I'm not sure that it would apply to you and me talking in this garden. I think the most helpful thing would be if I think aloud in general terms and you don't say anything at all.'

Neve was startled. She had always thought of Mandy in connection with elegant clothes and interior designers and foreign holidays. She had never imagined her talking like this.

'First things first,' Mandy said. 'There's something boring about getting legal advice from a lawyer. A lawyer will tell you what the law is and to obey it. What I would tell' – she paused very slightly, indicating a certain irony – 'your hypothetical friend is to go to see a lawyer – not me, a real criminal solicitor, and I could suggest names – tell them everything and come forward. It won't be much fun but it's a bit late for fun. If I were going to be really pompous, I would say that what your hypothetical friend has done is also not just illegal but wrong. There's been a murder and if you tamper with the scene of the crime you're helping the murderer.'

Neve looked around the garden. At the far end there was a bird feeder on a stand. A bird was clinging to it. It was streaked with bright yellow. A goldfinch. Mandy even had beautiful birds in her beautiful plot of land.

'Can I ask one question?' she said.

Mandy frowned.

'It's a general question,' Neve continued. 'It's not about this specific case.'

'What?'

Neve pondered how to phrase this. 'If someone had tampered with a crime scene because they had very particular, personal reasons for tampering with it, reasons that had nothing to do with the crime, and then they came forward—' Neve stopped. She had almost got lost in her own sentence. She had to gather her thoughts. 'If she, or someone, had done all that, and came forward, would it be possible to keep the circumstances private?'

'You mean reasons why this person had tampered with the scene?'

'Yes.'

Mandy gave a mirthless little laugh.

'Is this person a child?'

'No.'

'Was this person working for the security services?'

Neve managed a wan smile at that. 'No.'

'Is the person under a current court order protecting their identity?'

'No.'

Mandy thought for a moment. 'Is there any issue of sexual assault?'

'No.'

'Then the answer is no. If there are court proceedings, then you have to assume that everything will come out.'

Neve put her glass down very carefully on the table. 'Thank you, Mandy, you've been very kind.'

'You don't look very happy about it.'

'I'm not very happy.' She shivered. It suddenly felt cold in the garden. She turned to go but Mandy put out a hand to stop her.

'There's something I haven't said. Remember when Chris left me?'

Neve did remember. Mandy's first husband walked out on her less than a year after their marriage. Mandy had fallen apart. Neve remembered hours with her on the phone, long walks, sitting together in silence.

'You were very kind to me,' said Mandy.

'Well, of course,' said Neve. 'We all wanted to help.'

Mandy gestured at her surroundings. 'I sometimes feel I need all of this just to prop me up. I couldn't talk to my mother, but you were like my mother should have been.'

They walked to the front door together. Before Neve stepped outside, Mandy put her arms round her.

'Tell your hypothetical friend that the thing about being outside the law is that you're outside the law. That can be a very dangerous place.'

Neve nodded. 'If she existed, I'd tell her that.'

Cycling home, she heard her mobile ring and she stopped to answer it. It was Fletcher.

'How about if you make the main course and I'll do the pudding?' he said without preamble. 'I thought I'd make my showstopper cheesecake.'

The dinner, thought Neve. The bloody dinner he'd arranged last night.

'OK,' she said.

'What are you going to cook?'

'I haven't thought about it.'

'I'm taking Connor to his football soon, so you'll have to do the shopping.'

'Right.'

'I'll text you the list of ingredients,' Fletcher said. 'I'll need to have them a few hours in advance. It's quite fiddly.'

'Right.'

'Will you cook fish or meat or neither?'

'I don't know.'

'Because you'll need to pick up some wine.'

'I won't be able to carry everything, and we've got loads of wine at home.'

'What about a starter?'

'What about it?'

'Maybe you could do your smoky aubergine thing.'

'Baba ganoush.'

'And those spicy nuts you make are nice.'

'I'll see you later.'

Neve put her mobile back in her pocket and propped her bike up on the wall, behind which stood a Georgian house. She could see a grand piano through its downstairs window. She sat on the edge of the pavement, put her head in the bowl of her hands and closed her eyes. Just for one minute, she told herself – until the feeling of sickness and dizziness faded a bit. She couldn't remember when she had last had a proper meal, or a proper night's sleep. She went over her conversation with Mandy in her head, remembering the stern and concerned expression on her friend's face, and then she let herself think about all that had passed with Mabel. The autumn sun was warm on the nape of her neck. She could just go on sitting here and let the disaster unfold far away from her. She heard a text ping on her phone. That would be Fletcher's list of ingredients, she thought dully.

'Are you all right?' said a voice.

She looked up to find a very old, very tiny woman staring down at her. Her face was like a wrinkled onion and her hat, which looked more like a tea cosy, only exaggerated the likeness. She was bundled up in a voluminous grey coat.

'Yes,' said Neve, struggling to get up.

'Do you have somewhere to go?' Her eyes were blue chips buried in the creases of her face.

Did she think Neve was homeless? Neve tried to smile at her but she wasn't sure it came out right because the old woman continued to look at her with something like pity.

She took hold of her bike. 'Just a dizzy spell,' she said and pedalled away.

Neve pushed a trolley along the supermarket aisles. She consulted the list of ingredients Fletcher needed for his raspberry and white chocolate cheesecake. It was very rich and her stomach churned at the thought of it. What should she make? She gazed helplessly about her, feeling the slow thud of a headache starting. She had no idea what Jackie and Will ate. Mabel might join them – her heart sank at the thought – and she was a vegetarian, sometimes a vegan. Tamsin was on a high protein, low-carb diet. Rory mostly ate pasta and rice and cornflakes.

Her mobile rang. It was her mother: Neve hadn't told her whether Rory would like the microscope or the binoculars. And had Neve heard from her brother? Her mother said Neve should seem him more often. Neve thought of mentioning that he lived in Seattle but said nothing.

She ended the call. It rang again, almost immediately. She didn't recognise the number on the phone.

'Hello?' she said.

'It's Bernice Stevenson here.'

'Hello, Bernice.' Her heart started to bump uncomfortably.

'I'm in town,' said Bernice. 'I've been talking to the detective again – the tall, bald one.'

'Oh,' said Neve. She could think of nothing else to say.

'He told me things.' A pause. Bernice's voice was high and clipped. 'About Saul's private life.'

Neve suddenly felt like the lighting was flickering. Things blurred and swam in front of her. She gripped hold of the supermarket trolley.

'Can I see you?' said Bernice.

'You mean – now?'

'Where are you?'

'I'm in a supermarket.'

'Which one?'

'In Islington.'

'Which one?'

Neve gave her the details.

'I know it seems strange,' said Bernice. 'But I really need to talk to you about this.'

Neve felt that it was time to say that, yes, it really was very strange and maybe Bernice should be talking to her actual friends or to a counsellor, anyone but her. But the phone had gone dead and it was too late. Neve stood stranded next to the vegetables. She picked up a butternut squash and then loaded a paper bag with vine tomatoes. What had Fletcher told her to make? Baba ganoush, that was it. She put three glossy aubergines into the trolley. Garlic. Her phone rang again, this time from home.

It was Rory. 'When are you coming back?' he said.

'Soon.'

'Can we do something together?'

Neve picked up a piece of ginger that was as large as a knobbly hand.

'I tell you what,' she said. 'Will you help me make dinner?' Of all the three children, Rory was the one who liked to cook.

'That's good,' he said, and ended the call without saying goodbye.

Pomegranate, she thought, and gazed around her. A woman in black trousers and a suede jacket was clicking towards her in her neat, shiny shoes. A complicated bag hung from her shoulder, thick with studs and metal clasps.

'Neve,' said Bernice. Her lipstick was orange. She looked ill. 'You probably think I'm disturbed. Or completely friendless.'

'I don't think either of those things.'

'I haven't cried yet. Not a single tear. It's like I'm frozen inside.'

'These things take time,' said Neve.

'I don't think I believe it yet.'

'It's very hard.' She put a large bunch of fresh coriander into the trolley. How much self-hatred could she survive?

'I was right,' said Bernice. 'Saul was having an

affair. Or affairs. The detective told me, though I knew anyway.'

'I'm very sorry.'

'What are you buying?'

'I'm having people for dinner. Something with squash,' she said. 'Maybe I'll do some marinated fish as well. And then salads . . .' Her sentence petered out. She gathered up a few bags of salad leaves and two avocados.

'Saul's favourite meal was roast lamb. I don't eat meat though.' She gave a strange, twisted smile. 'I don't eat much of anything really. I've been on a diet since I was about fifteen. Not got to let go of ourselves, have we?'

Neve started pushing the trolley, Bernice walking beside with her. Saul had made her a wild mushroom risotto once. Another time they'd eaten blue cheese on crackers lying in bed together. The crumbs had got everywhere. She put three limes into the trolley and two packs of raspberries.

'I used to think,' said Bernice, 'that if Saul was unfaithful I'd leave him. Just like that.' She snapped her fingers. Her nails were painted crimson, but the varnish was chipped. 'But it's never that simple.'

'No,' said Neve, trundling the trolley into the next aisle and keeping her eyes fixed straight ahead.

'Bit by bit, we become people we don't want to be,' said Bernice.

Neve put yoghurt into the trolley, and then eggs.

'I'm going to go to my GP just to make sure I haven't caught anything,' said Bernice. 'Because we sometimes still, you know, made love. Men are very different from women, don't you think? They can compartmentalise.'

Neve picked out a tub of double cream.

'Although it wasn't very often. I didn't really feel like it anymore. Maybe that happens to most women when they get older. What do you think?'

Neve didn't answer.

'What's odd,' Bernice continued, 'is that the last time we made love was actually the morning Saul died.'

They had arrived at the shelves of fish. Neve stared hard at the selection, squinting, trying to pretend she wasn't hearing what she was hearing. Plaice, she thought. Or Haddock. Grey mullet. Who bloody cares?

'He had to get an early train to London so the radio alarm went off before seven, but he brought me tea in bed – he always brought me tea in bed. And we had some stupid argument.' Bernice gave an angry sniff. 'About a fundraising dinner I'd said we'd go to and he didn't want to. And then, I don't know why really, we were suddenly kissing each other and he was pulling off his clothes.'

Bernice looked at Neve and half smiled. Neve tried to half smile back. She had forgotten the butter.

'And it was better than in ages,' said Bernice. 'The radio was still on and I dimly remember hearing the half-past-seven news, and it was only when Saul's phone alarm went off downstairs at twenty to eight that he realised he was running late for his eight o'clock train and he charged around the room pulling his clothes on like he was in some kind of farce and then he ran out of the door. I never saw him again.'

Neve murmured something meaningless.

'Does it make it better?' asked Bernice. 'He was having an affair – or had been having. The detective said it was over but I don't believe that. I think whoever it was who confessed about their affair was still lying. That's what I told the detective. Anyway, the point is that Saul was unfaithful to me, but perhaps he still loved me, in his own way. Still desired me. Does that make it better? Or worse?'

'Better, surely.' Neve made herself say. She took a deep breath. 'But did you still love him?'

'There's a question. I have no idea. Now perhaps I never will. But the thing is, I don't know what to do now. With my life, I mean.' She put her hand next to Neve's on the trolley handle, as if she needed to lean on something. 'I don't know,' she repeated.

They moved off together. Neve found the nuts, and then the digestive biscuits for the cheesecake base.

'You're lucky,' said Bernice. 'You've got a husband, you've got children, you've got a job. I bet you have a close circle of friends.'

Bernice was still holding the trolley. Neve steered them past the toilet paper and kitchen rolls, the foil and cling film. She put two long orange candles into the trolley and some paper napkins with a pattern of swirly flowers.

'Everybody's life is complicated,' said Neve. 'In its own way.'

'Everyone likes you,' said Bernice. 'I think it's because you're not threatening. You're straightforward.

You've even won over that bald detective. I'm not the same as you. I bet people in the office say I'm cold-hearted and stuck-up.'

'No.' Although they did.

'I never talk like this normally. Not even to people I've known since I was a child. Not to Saul either. It's the shock. It's a bit like being drunk. His murder has loosened my tongue.'

They had reached the checkout.

'I have to go and cook,' said Neve. 'I'm sorry.'

'I can't go back home. My son's staying with my sister tonight and it will just be me in my empty house. What shall I do?'

Neve had a sudden feeling of horror. Bernice couldn't be. Not really. She couldn't be fishing for an invitation to Neve's house. That would be so many kinds of inappropriate.

'Can you call someone?'

'I can't go back there.'

'Or you could stay with them? I'm sure people would be only too glad to help.'

'I don't want people looking at me with that horrible expression. Like they're secretly pleased.'

'I'm sure that's not true.'

'What shall I do?'

Neve simply gave way. She couldn't think of anything else to say, so she heard herself asking, in a weak voice: 'Do you want to come back with me?' She tried to keep her tone neutral. Perhaps Bernice would refuse.

'Could I?'

'What?'

'Then for an evening at least I don't have to be in my own life. I don't have to be me. I would like that.' Bernice let go of the trolley at last and straightened up. She patted her hair. 'If you're sure.' She didn't wait for Neve to respond. 'Thank you. Let me buy some wine. Or would you prefer a bottle of gin? Yes, let's have gin.'

They walked back, Neve pushing her bike, shopping bags swinging from its handlebars and every so often getting snarled up in the spokes. Bernice barely said anything, which Neve was glad about. She was trying to decide if Bernice had some kind of secret plan. When they arrived at the house, she was just getting the key out of her backpack when the front door swung open and Mabel staggered out clutching two splitting bin bags.

'This is my daughter Mabel,' said Neve. 'Mabel. This is Bernice.'

Mabel grunted, and let the bags fall to the ground by the dustbins. She had tied a bright scarf round her hair.

'Bernice Stevenson,' added Neve.

Mabel gave a small jerk, like someone had given her an electric shock.

'Hello,' said Bernice, holding out a thin hand. Mabel shook it slowly, a little frown on her face, then retreated back inside and up the stairs. They heard the door slam.

'She's getting ready to go to university. Come in. I'll make tea.'

She propped her bike up in the hall, took the shopping into the kitchen. Fletcher was in the garden, gazing down at the pile of glass frames. Neve put on the kettle and Bernice sat at the table, not removing her suede jacket. She was gazing around her and Neve tried to see the kitchen through her eyes. Everything was shabby, in need of paint and attention. There were cobwebs in all the corners, one light bulb was gone, the window frames were beginning to rot. And it was, she realised, all very cluttered. She had stopped really seeing how many *things* there were on all the surfaces – not just the ones that should be there, like candlesticks, the coffee grinder, the food mixer and scales, the bread bin and the pot of dying basil, but the ones that had drifted here and never been taken away: empty jars, a hairbrush, a Frisbee, half a bag of rice, a broken plate that she intended to mend with superglue (she had forgotten once again to buy superglue), old postcards, a bicycle pump, a random collection of paperbacks, a paint tray, single socks waiting for their partner to reappear, a radio that no longer worked, swimming goggles, empty wine bottles, a torch that needed new batteries.

Fletcher came in, spreading mud from the garden over the tiles.

'This is Bernice Stevenson,' said Neve. She watched him as the realisation of who Bernice was gathered on his face. He took her hand and told her how very sorry he was while his eyes darted round the kitchen like he was looking for a getaway. Bernice nodded stiffly at him and rummaged in her complicated bag for a tissue that she blew her nose on.

'Connor's at Elias's house,' he said. 'I said Elias could stay here tonight; that's OK isn't it?'

Neve nodded helplessly. There was the sound of footsteps coming down the stairs, things being dropped heavily. Mabel, she thought.

'I thought I'd have a go at the greenhouse before cooking,' Fletcher said. 'Neve's always nagging at me to do it,' he added to Bernice.

'I don't nag, I politely ask,' said Neve, spoiling it by adding, 'over and over again.'

'Whatever. Do you know if there are any chargers for the electric drill in that bag of wires? I haven't used it for ages.'

Bag of wires. Hammer. Murder weapon. Neve sprang into the centre of the kitchen.

'Wait!' she said. 'Make tea! Look after Bernice for one moment. I just have to see Rory. Hang on. Something to do.'

She whisked into the little back room and pushed her hand into the bag. As she grasped the hammer, she thought how perhaps the murderer's fingerprints were on it – and her fingerprints of course. And Mabel's. She looked around for a bag of some kind but there were only the string ones, so she thrust the hammer under her shirt and hurried through the kitchen holding it in place like she had a bad stomach ache, past Fletcher and Bernice, and up the stairs, two at a time. Now where? She went into her room and pulled out the present box and inserted the hammer deep inside, covering it with a shirt that she pulled from its hanger, and then pushing it to the back of the wardrobe. She'd think of a better place later.

Mabel poked her head out of her bedroom door. 'What's she doing here?'

'I couldn't help it.'

'Are you insane?'

'Mabel, we need to—'

'Mum?' came Rory's voice from the floor above.

Her uncomplaining, reclusive, silent son. She went up the stairs and found him sitting on his bed.

'How are you?'

'All right.'

'Have you been outside at all?'

'No.'

'You're going to cook with me, right?'

He brightened. 'Yes. What are we going to make?'

'Your father's doing his cheesecake. Do you want to make the baba ganoush? You have to set fire to aubergines.'

'Cool.'

'And tomorrow we can go for a bike ride.'

'Really?'

'Yes.'

They went downstairs together. Neve introduced him to Bernice, who was drinking tea, still perched on the edge of the chair.

'Rory and I are going to cook dinner,' said Neve.

'I think I need to have a lie down,' said Bernice. She

stood, looking about her as if a couch would magically appear.

'Of course. Do you need a bed?'

'Oh no, a sofa will do.'

So Neve took her through to the living room and Bernice set her shiny bag on the ground, took off her immaculate suede jacket, pulled off her shiny shoes and laid herself down on the baggy sofa that Connor had drawn over in indelible pink ink the day after they had bought it. She closed her eyes, and her face looked suddenly gaunt and old. Neve crept from the room, closing the door softly behind her.

Neve and Rory cooked together. Neve made a spicy, garlicky marinade for the fish and carved the squash into thin wedges, grating ginger over the top. She made a yoghurt and lime sauce to go with it, and soaked rice in a pan so it would cook quickly. Rory scorched aubergines, setting off the blood-curdling shriek of the smoke alarm. He painstakingly mashed their flesh with tahini and scooped seeds out of the pomegranate, splattering himself with red liquid as he did so. Out in the garden, they could see Fletcher struggling with the greenhouse, like a pantomime of frustration and mishap.

Connor and Elias arrived back, throbbing with energy. Sarah nodded at them.

'Good luck,' she said. 'Rather you than me. And thanks. I've got the evening to myself and now I've just got to think of something to do with it. Probably I'll just go to bed early. The exciting life of a single mother.'

She left. The boys charged upstairs. Neve washed the pots and pans. She was hot and sticky, hollow with hunger but nauseous with fear. Her dead lover's wife was asleep on her sofa. Her daughter was upstairs throwing away the entire contents of her room, having removed vital evidence from the murder scene that she herself had also thoroughly cleaned. Her lawyer friend had told her that she and Mabel could go to prison for three years for what they had done. The detective in charge of the murder inquiry was interested in her in some way that she couldn't put her finger on. The murder weapon was in her wardrobe. A birthday present to her from Saul was going to arrive in Saul's flat. And they were about to have a dinner party.

At just after six, Fletcher took over in the kitchen. Neve was very familiar with his air of single-minded purpose as he laid out all the ingredients and rolled up his sleeves, then opened the cookery book to minutely study it as if this was the first time he had ever seen it.

'You can have a shower,' he said. Neve was still in her muddy gardening clothes and her hair needed washing.

She put her head round the living room door to see Bernice fast asleep, then went upstairs and ran a bath. She lay in it for a long time, listening to the sounds of the house. She heard Connor come in with Elias, heard Mabel hurling more bags down the stairs, heard the radio.

When she finally came downstairs, dressed in a long grey shirt dress whose belt she couldn't find, hair still damp, she met Bernice emerging from the living room with newly applied make-up. Her mask was back on.

'Can I borrow a clean shirt?' Bernice asked. 'I feel a bit grubby.

'Of course.'

'Perhaps you can show me your selection.'

'I haven't got anything very smart,' said Neve. And then she thought: the hammer. In the wardrobe.

'Wait one moment,' she said. 'Just a minute. Less.' She sped back up the stairs, fished out the hammer, pushed it into the laundry basket, and stood for a moment, irresolute. Where was safe?

A tree is best hid in a forest she thought; a book is best hid in a library.

She covered the hammer with the throw on their bed and went downstairs again, past Bernice, into the scullery. She opened the toolbox and laid the hammer on top, closed the lid. Her breath was coming in shallow gasps.

'Come and choose,' she said to Bernice, going out into the hall again.

'I've changed my mind. I just need some of that gin,' said Bernice. She fished in her bag and squirted herself with perfume.

Music was thundering from Mabel's room. The two women went into the kitchen just as a football, punted energetically by Connor, span towards the large window and shattered it, spraying glass everywhere. Fletcher, shaving curls of white chocolate on to his cheesecake, swore loudly and picked a shard of glass from his concoction. The guinea pig pressed its earnest face against the wire. The doorbell rang.

Tamsin was the first to arrive.

'You look beautiful,' said Neve, hugging her.

And she did: tall and strong, wearing a tight-fitting blue dress, her dark hair piled on her head. Earrings swung in her lobes.

'Really?' Tamsin grimaced, suddenly awkward. 'Not too much?'

'Not at all. Exactly right.'

Fletcher made four gin and tonics and then Mabel came in. She had looked like a twelve-year-old during the day, but now she seemed at least ten years older, a woman. She had put on skinny jeans, a white blouse that belonged to Neve and high-heeled ankle boots. She was discreetly made up, and hair was hung softly round her face. Neve stared at her daughter. She looked so soft and clean and graceful, like a candle flame. The memory of their terrible morning filled her so that for a moment she couldn't speak. Mabel cast her a demure glance. Her performed placidity was almost worse than her rage. Neve thought of the morning's conversation. She repeated the words that Mabel had said to her towards the end: that it hadn't been her. She hadn't killed Saul. But she had said it in such an uninflected way, like she was performing a role. It had happened so often before, Mabel saying things that weren't true. And Neve knew they weren't true. And Mabel knew Neve knew. What about now?

'Can I have a gin as well?' Mabel asked, and then when Neve made a face at Fletcher: 'I know what that means.'

'What?'

'That expression. It means give Mabel a gin and tonic with almost no gin in it.'

'Of course it doesn't,' said Neve. 'Anyway, there wasn't any expression.' Both statements were lies.

Neve went to the kitchen to get something to go with the drinks. Tamsin followed her.

'What happened?' she asked, gesturing at the plastic that was taped over the broken window.

'Connor broke it. Crisps or olives?'

'How many people are coming?'

Neve did the mental arithmetic. Tamsin and Bernice and Jackie Cornfield and Will Ziegler and Mabel and Fletcher.

'Six,' she said. 'And me of course. Seven. I ought to warn you: there's someone rather unexpected here who—'

'That reminds me,' Tamsin interrupted, 'I hope you don't mind. I was talking to Renata and she might pop round. So that makes eight.'

'Renata?' said Neve, her mind racing. She needed to call her at once and tell her she absolutely mustn't come.

'I think we all need to stick together at a time like this.'

'Yes, of course.'

'So crisps *and* olives would probably be a good idea.'

Neve took a carton of olives from the fridge. She tore

open two different bags of crisps and emptied them into bowls. Tamsin took one from the bowl and put it in her mouth.

'I remember that Will Ziegler from college,' she said. 'I had a feeling that we were going to get together, but it never quite happened.'

'I had no idea.'

'But I wouldn't mind if you sat me next to him at dinner.'

'There's nothing formal about this,' said Neve. 'Just sit yourself wherever you want.'

She picked up her mobile, went into the hall with it, found Renata's number and rang. It went to voicemail. She tried the landline: no reply. She sent a text: *Bernice is here. Don't come!*

There was a ring at the door and when Neve and Tamsin returned to the living room Jackie and Will were standing there. Jackie was wearing a voluminous orange garment and holding out an extravagant bunch of flowers that almost hid her face; Will had two bottles of wine.

'We went to the wrong house,' said Jackie, as if it was a hilarious joke.

'Well, you're here now.'

'This tiny man opened the door. He practically only came up to my waist. He looked like a garden gnome, didn't he, Will?'

She clapped Will on the shoulder. Will nodded, shrugged at Neve. He'd shaved and put on a crisp white shirt. Suddenly she could imagine him running a company, living in a big house in the countryside with his wife and his rescue dogs.

Bernice came down the stairs, gripping the banisters as if she might tumble. From upstairs Neve could hear sounds of a computer game.

'I got white and red,' Will said. 'I didn't know what you were serving.'

Fletcher distributed gin and tonics all round. Neve looked at hers a little warily. She still had barely eaten or slept and would have to pace herself. When she introduced Bernice to everyone, Tamsin was visibly shocked.

'Oh God,' she said. 'I didn't realise. I'm so, so sorry. I can't even begin to think what to say.'

'Then don't say anything,' Bernice replied. Her tone was sarcastic, almost venomous. Neve heard Tamsin give a small gasp. 'I don't mean to be rude,' she continued. 'I've never been a grieving widow before. I'm not sure how to behave. Neve has been good to me though.'

Neve took a gulp of her drink. Her cheeks were burning. Hot flush, she thought. Hot flush of shame.

'It's the least I could do,' she said.

She excused herself saying she needed to check the food. She went upstairs with some pizza that she'd put in the oven for the boys, who were all clustered round the TV screen in Connor's room, playing some game that they couldn't even look up from. She put the pizza on the little desk, knowing it would soon be daubed around the room.

'I'll save you some baba ganoush,' she said to Rory.

When she returned to the living room, she saw them

all clustered in a group. Bernice was talking with that same air of brittle control that might split apart at any moment. Jackie and Will were looking at her with expressions of both sympathy and fascination. Neve thought to herself that they were getting more than they bargained for out of their visit to London. And she also thought of a saying she had read somewhere that there is something in the misfortunes of others that doesn't displease us. That was maybe putting it a bit strongly but they would certainly have something to tell people about when they went back to Newcastle and to Bristol.

There was another ring at the door and Renata raced into the room in a state of excited disarray. She hugged Neve and then Tamsin. Fletcher poured her a drink, though Neve didn't think she needed one. Suddenly it felt more like the hum and buzz of a party rather than the little evening meal she had had in mind. Now Fletcher was topping up the gin and tonics from a jug.

'I'm so sorry for barging in like this,' said Renata to Neve. 'I couldn't face an evening alone.'

'Isn't Charlie there?'

'Yes, Charlie is there.' The door rang. 'That'll be Gary.' Renata noticed Neve's expression. 'Sorry. I was about to say. I was talking to him and mentioned this and I assumed he would be here. So I said he should come along. Is that all right?'

'What if I said it wasn't?'

Renata nudged Neve on the shoulder playfully. 'It's always all right,' she said. 'You're the rock we all cling to.'

'You'd better let him in,' Neve said. She gave up on averting disaster. It was going to happen anyway.

Gary came in clutching a bottle of wine that he handed to Neve and then hugged her.

'You forgot to invite me,' he said with a smile that wasn't entirely warm.

'Shut up,' said Renata. 'You were invited by someone who wasn't invited either, so stop sulking. Anyway, Neve probably assumed you'd be with Jane on a Saturday evening. You usually are.'

Gary shrugged. 'Well, I'm not,' he said. 'I'm here.'

'How is she?'

'How do you think? Not good.'

Renata's eyes immediately filled with tears. She put a hand on his shoulder, looked around and then spoke to Neve in a hiss. 'Oh Christ. Is that—?'

'I sent you a text telling you not to come.'

'I can't face her,' said Renata. 'If I'd known, I would never have come. What shall I do? It's too late now, isn't it? I can't leave. I'll just have to stay away from her. Oh God.' Tears stood in her eyes.

Neve thought that actually it would be a good idea if Renata did leave, so she didn't answer. She saw Mabel picking up the jug of gin and tonics where Fletcher had put it down and starting to fill her glass. She moved into the room and Jackie drifted into her view, coming to a halt in front of her.

'So. What have you been doing in London?' Neve asked her.

'So much. I haven't stopped. I can't even remember

207

where I was today. It's just a blur.' She gave a cheerful laugh.

'You can just look on your phone,' said Will, over-hearing and turning towards them. 'It'll show where you've been today.'

Neve turned away, sweat prickling on her skin. Her phone could give away her movements. Did that mean if she threw her phone away, then she would be all right, or was it stored somewhere? She took another gulp of her gin. She was going to be caught, she thought. It was just a matter of time.

'I think we can all sit down now,' she said loudly. 'I'll bring the food out. Just seat yourselves.'

When she got to the kitchen, she was horribly tempted to keep on going, leave the house and not come back. Perhaps taking the guinea pig with her.

She and Fletcher brought the food through and placed it on the table to theatrical gasps and cries of admiration. Neve sat down and saw that Mabel had sat herself on Will's left. Tamsin was on his right. Neve sat at the end of the table by Tamsin. Bernice was on her other side then Renata, Jackie and Fletcher at the far end of the table. Then Gary came in carrying a chair from the kitchen and inserted himself between Renata and Jackie. Neve looked at the various combinations with some alarm. Will was leaning down towards Mabel who was saying something that Neve couldn't make out. More obviously worrying was that Bernice and Renata were sitting next to each other.

Wine was poured, food spooned out, compliments made.

'This is just great,' said Jackie. 'I can't believe you've done all this. If it was me, I would have just sent out for a takeaway.'

There was the ringing sound of metal clinking on a wine glass. Neve saw with a sinking feeling that Fletcher was going to say something. She felt that there had been enough speeches that week.

'Look,' he said. 'I don't want to be formal about this. Obviously it's great to have you all here. This was all a bit unexpected, but it's the sort of thing we should do more often. It's the sort of thing Neve and I *used* to do. And it's my fault we stopped, because I'm—' He stopped, looked momentarily bewildered. 'Anyway, that's not what I wanted to say. I know this has been a strange and difficult week. But for someone here, Bernice' – he gestured towards her with his wine glass – 'it's been terrible in a way we can't begin to imagine. I'm not going to make a toast or anything like that. I just think we should acknowledge it and hope that an evening like this can be some sort of comfort.'

He looked towards Neve for approval. She gave him a small nod.

There was a murmur of sympathy when he had finished and then an awkward silence, as if people weren't quite sure whether it was decent to continue their normal conversations. Jackie Cornfield was the first to speak.

'I suppose friends are everything at a time like this.'

'I'm a stranger here,' said Bernice. Neve realised that Bernice was on her way to being very drunk, but being drunk in her case meant being more tightly wound up than ever, like a coil that's about to spring horribly free. 'Perhaps I'm a stranger to my friends. Perhaps everyone is a stranger in the end.'

'Hear, hear,' said Will and then looked startled.

'You should see me with my cat,' Jackie said cheerfully. Nobody knew what to say to that.

Another pause. The guests were hesitant to change the subject. It felt disrespectful.

'The rest of you are old friends, aren't you?' asked Bernice.

'Really old friends,' said Jackie. 'And getting older.'

'Remember that weekend?' said Will.

'What weekend?' said Tamsin. 'There were lots of weekends.'

'*The* weekend,' said Gary, a slow smile spreading across his face. 'It was when we went to that house in the country. It was owned by someone's friend. Where was it?'

'It was my friend,' said Jackie. 'Or actually, it belonged to her parents. It was a place outside York.' She started laughing and then covered her mouth. 'Actually it wasn't funny. They had to bring painters in and builders. I didn't realise smoke could do so much damage. They never forgave me.'

'What happened?' asked Bernice.

'It was nothing,' said Jackie. 'We made a fire in the fireplace and it spread a bit.'

'I only remember it in flashes,' said Gary. 'I remember Fletcher letting off fireworks and I remember that they had a pool and at about four in the morning we all took our clothes off and jumped in.'

'Oh God, I remember,' said Renata and took a gulp of wine. She pointed across the table at Will. 'Was that where you and me had our thing?'

Will shook his head and smiled, but he looked slightly upset at her casualness. 'Our thing was earlier,' he said. 'In our second year.'

'I get confused,' said Renata. 'I had a thing with almost everyone.'

Neve looked nervously over at Mabel. She hadn't touched her plate, but she had finished her wine.

'I remember what people were wearing,' said Jackie. 'Renata had a leather jacket with zips.'

'I remember that,' said Renata. 'I wish I still had it.'

'And Neve had an embroidered sort of cap. She always wore hats.'

'I've still got it somewhere,' said Neve. 'It's hard to wear hats when you bike everywhere.'

'Hang on,' said Gary, 'the last thing I remember was finding their drinks cabinet and working our way through all the weird bottles at the back that they'd brought home from holiday.'

'That was when your parents got together,' said Renata animatedly to Mabel, who stared at her stonily.

'Yeah, so though it didn't feel like it at the time, it was the beginning of the end,' said Gary. 'People settling down.'

'I hate that expression,' said Jackie.

Neve did remember it, stumbling into a strange bedroom, their hands on each other, a sense of coming home at last: for why had she not known before that it was always going to be Fletcher that she ended up with? What had happened to them, she wondered; what had happened to Fletcher, who would never let off fireworks now or jump into a pool naked?

'Someone opened the door on you,' said Renata. 'Do you remember? It was you, wasn't it, Gary?'

'Not me. I think it was Will.'

'Definitely not me,' said Will. 'It was Jackie.'

'Oh God, I can't remember any of that,' said Jackie. 'Maybe I was too drunk. I remember everyone roaring with laughter,' she added.

Mabel was staring at each of them in turn, wrinkling up her nose slightly.

Neve heard the others talking and laughing about that party of long ago. Yes, she thought to herself, there had been something wonderful about it, a dream of laughter and joy and possibility. She remembered someone telling her – Gary, she thought, his arm in hers – that she was kind and he was glad to have her as a friend. She remembered dancing with Renata and Tamsin, holding hands in a circle and smiling until her jaw ached. She remembered cooking pasta at three in the morning. She remembered thinking she would remember these days forever. But there had also been the following morning, grey and drizzling, everyone tired and hungover. She had an image of being in the back of a car being driven back, leaning on Fletcher's shoulder. She glanced at Bernice.

'Sorry,' she said. 'You must feel like you've wandered into a college reunion.'

'That's all right.'

'We're all feeling awkward,' said Tamsin. 'We don't know whether to talk about Saul or not talk about him.'

'I don't mind talking about it,' she said. 'It's not as if I'm not thinking about it. My husband being dead, that is. Killed. What should I be thinking about?'

There was a silence as people decided how to respond.

'So, well, what have you actually been doing?' asked Will awkwardly. 'Have you been spending time with the police? I don't know if it's all right to ask a question like that.'

'You don't want to hear about my troubles.'

'We'd love to hear you talk about your troubles,' said Jackie.

Neve silently cursed her.

'When they first came to see me,' Bernice began, 'I didn't even feel upset.' She looked from face to face. 'I still don't really, not properly. It's so – ridiculous. So melodramatic.'

Neve looked at Bernice with a sort of fascination.

'I always thought that Saul had had, was having, an affair. I'm sorry, is that the wrong thing for a grieving widow to say? Am I not meant to speak ill of the dead?'

'No, that's fine,' said Jackie soothingly. 'You must say *exactly* what you want to say.'

Bernice took a large gulp of wine. Neve grimaced at

Fletcher to try to stop him but he didn't seem to notice and leaned across and refilled her glass.

'The police were certainly interested by that,' said Bernice. 'Who's the most likely person to kill an unfaithful husband?'

'But surely they couldn't think that?' said Jackie.

'I don't know what they think,' said Bernice. 'But this detective, this Hitching person. Detective Chief Inspector Hitching, he was talking to me like a friend. I don't know whether he's trying to lull me' – she took another large gulp of wine – 'into a sense of security. I'll tell you what he told me.' She looked around the table. 'I'm talking too much. You probably don't want to hear about this?'

There were murmurs of reassurance from around the table. Neve tried to think of some way of bringing this to a halt but she couldn't think of any.

'What Hitching told me is that the murder shows every sign of being sudden and violent and unexpected.'

'How do they know?' asked Tamsin.

'He said that Saul hadn't tried to defend himself. So it all happened very quickly, but then the whole murder scene had been tidied up. Not just that but the flat had been tidied up. Cleaned from top to bottom. It was apparently done with a hammer. But the hammer wasn't there.'

'How do they know it was done with a hammer then?' asked Gary.

'They took me to the flat,' said Bernice. 'I hardly ever went there. But I helped buy things for it when we first bought it. I remember a hammer because I used it for hanging pictures. It was kept in a tool drawer. It wasn't there.'

'It's so terrible for you,' said Will.

'Does anyone want a second helping?' asked Neve.

As she spoke the words, they immediately sounded crass and unfeeling but they actually came as a relief. Everyone said how wonderful the food was and that they couldn't manage another mouthful.

'Well, you'll have to,' said Fletcher, 'because I've made cheesecake. I hardly ever cook and when I do I have to talk about it a great deal and people have to make a huge fuss of me.'

They gathered up the plates and Fletcher came in with his cheesecake and a couple of bottles of sweet wine from the back of the drinks cupboard. The cheesecake disappeared in a matter of minutes, to Fletcher's visible satisfaction. The sweet wine was drunk so quickly that Fletcher had to bring two more bottles of wine along with a bottle of whisky and some tumblers.

Neve had tried to go easy on the wine but she felt in a state of shock and poured herself some whisky. Gary left his seat and came round to her end of the table and leaned down between her and Tamsin.

'Having a good evening?' he said with a smile.

'I'm the host,' said Neve. 'You're only as happy as your least happy guest.'

'Everybody seems pretty happy. I'm happy.'

Neve thought he seemed drunk.

'But this is what you do, isn't it?' he continued.

'What do I do?'

'You bring people together. Like this.'

Neve felt like saying that the really unexpected, not to say uninvited, person at the table was Gary himself. He leaned in even closer so that she could smell the alcohol in his breath.

'I didn't expect ... you know.' He nodded towards Bernice, who was only a couple of feet away. But Neve saw that she was bent towards Renata and Jackie. The conversations at the table had split into groups.

'She needs help,' Neve said to Gary.

'And she turned to you. It was like the merger.'

Neve was bemused. 'In what way was it like the merger?'

'We were worried we were going to lose our jobs. You just seemed fine about it all. But I'm glad that she's turning to you.'

'She's not turning to me,' Neve said in a whisper.

When the doorbell rang, Neve wondered if she had forgotten someone. As she got up, she asked if anyone was expecting an Uber but nobody was. She opened the door to find Charlie standing there, unsmiling.

'I've come to collect Renata.'

'Come and join us,' said Neve. 'Have a drink.'

'I don't think that will be possible.'

They came into the room as Fletcher was entering from the kitchen with a hastily improvised cheese board, some crackers that Neve knew were stale, and a bottle of red wine. He put them down on the table and turned to Charlie.

'Hey, man,' he said and approached him, holding

his hand out, but Charlie stepped aside slightly to avoid him.

'I thought you were just popping over for a drink,' he said to Renata.

'Did you?' said Renata. 'I did actually have a drink but I was invited to stay for dinner. So I did.'

'You should have said.'

By now all conversation had ceased and everyone had turned to look at Charlie.

'We need to support each other,' said Renata. 'This is Bernice Stevenson. Saul's widow. She was telling us about what's happened. About her difficult time with the police.'

'Please . . .' said Neve, feebly trying to intervene.

Charlie interrupted her, speaking very slowly and clearly. 'Did you tell them about your own difficult time with the police?'

There was a silence.

'What difficult time?' asked Bernice.

'She just had to clarify a few things,' said Neve.

'She can speak for herself,' said Charlie. 'It was about telling the police that she had been to your husband's flat after she'd told them that she hadn't been to it.'

Bernice looked round at Renata, then at Neve. She frowned, licked her lips several times. Her face became stiff, like it was made of china or hard plastic. She looked back at Renata once more. 'It was you,' she said slowly. 'It was you.'

There was a silence so thick that Neve could almost taste it.

'You and Saul.'

Neve, looking at Bernice's expression, realised that Bernice had had no idea.

Renata stood up very suddenly so that her chair fell back with a clatter on the wooden floor. She was still holding her whisky glass.

'You fucker,' she said to Charlie. 'You fucking fucker.'

She ran out of the room and Charlie ran after her. There was a sound of tramping feet and shouting and then a smashing of glass. Everyone at the table was just looking at one another. Nobody spoke and nobody moved. At last, Renata came back in. She looked puzzled.

'I don't know,' she said. 'I think I've . . .'

She held up her hand. Neve thought she was holding ribbons and then saw it was blood. She jumped up and ran towards Renata. She looked at the hand. She saw not just blood but the whiteness of exposed flesh and stringy, sinewy things. It was really deep. She took the hand in hers, feeling a sharp jab of pain and saw that a small shard of glass was now embedded in the heel of her own hand. Blood was bubbling up.

'I'm getting her out of here,' said a voice behind her.

She looked round. It was Charlie, with his hand on Renata's shoulder.

'No,' Neve said.

Now Connor and Elias were standing in the doorway, round-eyed and fascinated, befuddled with sleep.

'Come on,' said Charlie.

'She needs an ambulance.'

'We can deal with this.'

'No.' Fletcher pushed Charlie back, away from Renata. 'You need to get away from her.'

It looked for a moment as if there might be an actual fight.

'Out,' said Fletcher.

There was blood everywhere. Fletcher called the emergency service. Jackie tied her long, sequinned scarf very tightly round and round the bubbling wound. Will told Renata to hold her arm up and, when she didn't do anything, lifted it up himself. Tamsin had her arm wrapped around Renata and was saying that help would come soon. Fletcher noticed that Neve was also bleeding and shouted for someone to get plasters from the bathroom. Gary pulled tissues from his pocket and dabbed at the cut. Neve noticed he looked slightly green. Mabel, crouched in a chair and gazing at the scene, no longer looked self-possessed and womanly but like a frightened child again. Bernice said and did nothing; she sat still and upright in her chair, occasionally lifting her glass to her mouth with a mechanical gesture. It was like she was watching a play.

Renata's face had a ghastly pallor and her eyes were glassy. 'Am I going to die?' she asked. 'I'm too young.'

'You're not going to die,' said Neve.

She looked towards Bernice. 'You might want to go home,' she said. 'I'll call you later.'

Bernice stared at Neve as if she was talking in a foreign language. She lifted her glass, found it empty, and reached out for someone else's.

Neve put on a jacket that belonged to Fletcher, picked up her backpack and went with Renata in the ambulance, everyone gathering at the door to see them off.

'Sorry to leave you with all this,' she said to Fletcher. 'Can you get the boys back to bed?'

He nodded.

'Ring me,' he said.

'Yes. Fletcher.'

'What?'

'I don't know. Just, sorry.'

'For what?'

'All of this.'

'Oh that,' he said. His smile didn't look like a smile.

The Accident and Emergency department was heaving. It was a Saturday night after all. There was a drunk man who was claiming loudly and often to have been bitten by a fox. There were teenage girls and boys with head wounds and twisted ankles and strange rashes. There was a man walking backwards and forwards, shouting unintelligible things at no one in particular. An old woman, sitting on a chair at the front with a grey face, was coughing so hard Neve thought she would break a rib.

But they were whisked past all of these people, into a cubicle with torn green curtains. Renata lay on the stretcher with her eyes half closed. They'd bandaged her wrist in the ambulance and it lay beside her like a strange animal.

'I'll wait outside,' said Neve.

Renata reached out her uninjured hand and held Neve's wrist. 'Do you promise you'll still be here?'

'I promise.'

'What am I going to do?'

'We'll talk after. Now you're going to have your wound seen to.'

Neve rang Fletcher, who was still up, dealing with the wreckage of the evening. He told her that Bernice had gone soon after the ambulance left, but Tamsin, Will and Jackie had stayed on, drinking tea and going over what had happened. 'It was quite jolly,' he said.

'Jolly?'

'You know, Blitz spirit.' There was a slight pause. 'Did you know?' he asked.

'Know?'

'About Renata and Saul Stevenson.'

'She told me yesterday evening.'

'That's what you were talking about outside the pub.'

'Yes.'

'You should have told me.'

'It was a secret.'

'We don't have secrets like that, do we?'

'No,' she said.

She went into the waiting room, where she sat for a long time among the churn of people who turned up through the small hours. Some of them seemed barely injured – one young man had a cut finger that he held solemnly in front of him, wrapped in a sheet of tissue paper. Some looked remarkably ill, grey and thin and defeated. A man in unbuttoned pyjamas and walking boots rocked on his chair a few seats from Neve. A middle-aged woman was sitting alone with a violent black eye.

The evening was now a nasty blur in which a few moments stood out clearly. What she mostly saw when she tried to recall what had happened were the faces: Bernice's snarling fury as she had shouted at Renata; Renata's expression of meek bewilderment as blood streamed from her wrist; Charlie's look of stony hatred. And then Mabel of course, always Mabel – smiling at Will, staring at Bernice, glancing placidly at Neve through the shining fall of her hair, demure and unsafe.

Neve went into the Ladies where she washed her hands and face. She was very cold, and she felt dry and hollow with exhaustion. There was blood on her grey dress and a streak of blood on her neck. It was two in the morning and the night seemed endless.

When Renata finally appeared it was well past four. Her arm was thickly bandaged and in a sling; her face was smeared with make-up and tears.

'They say I can go home.'

'That's good.'

'It's not good at all. How can I go home? You saw Charlie.'

Neve nodded.

'He hates me. He *loathes* me.'

'He had no idea?'

'I don't know. I don't know anything anymore. I can't

face him right now though. I'm too—' She stopped and her face crumpled. 'I'm scared, Neve.'

'I tell you what – let's find somewhere to sit and I'll get us some tea.'

Renata nodded. She was shivering. Neve put an arm round her and steered them down a corridor, through several doors and into the Reception area. Renata collapsed on a chair and Neve went to the vending machine near the lifts. She had enough coins for two cups of tea and a packet of ginger biscuits.

'Get that down you,' she said to Renata.

They sat for several minutes in silence, sipping at milky tea and eating biscuits.

'Does it hurt?' asked Neve.

Renata shook her head.

'Do you want to talk about what happened?'

Renata crouched over her tea. 'I don't even know why I did it,' she said in a low voice. 'I knew it was stupid. I knew Saul wasn't in love with me or anything. But he made me feel . . .' She took a shuddering breath. 'I don't know, he made me feel young again, and desirable. Does that sound horribly vain and facile?'

'No,' said Neve softly.

'And then he had all the power, didn't he? God, I can't believe I was such an idiot.'

'Go on.'

'He was the boss. So confident, so sure of his place in the world. In a way he represented everything I don't like, *we* don't like. The establishment, that complacency. He was the kind of man who always gets what he wants – and for a few weeks he wanted me. He even gave me some gold earrings – those ones you said looked nice – as a present, from that beautiful shop in Covent Garden, the one whose window we stare into sometimes.'

Neve nodded dully. She knew the shop.

'And then suddenly he didn't want me anymore. He fell in love with someone else – though he was kind enough to say it was because he needed to save his marriage.'

Neve didn't speak.

'I guess he thought I was fun. That's all there was to it.' Renata gave a small grimace, and added, 'All there was to *me*. It was like I had no agency at all; I barely made a choice. I just went along with it. And then he left. What was I doing?'

'I suppose it was about you and Charlie.'

'Of course it was. I'm not making an excuse for myself, but we'd got stuck in such a routine.' She took a gulp of tea and wiped the back of her hand across her face, looking so woebegone, thought Neve, like a cartoon of desolation. 'We took each other for granted. Sometimes we could go for days without really talking to each other – just things like, pass the salt, have you put the bins out, there's a bill to pay, where are the keys ...'

'Could you talk about that with Charlie?'

'Maybe I could have before I went and had a stupid fling with a married man. Now he's too angry and he feels wronged.' She sniffed. 'Well, he has been wronged. I'm the wicked woman. He won't forgive me. Or maybe he will – *forgive me*, I mean. For the rest of our marriage, he'll be on the moral high ground because he forgave me when I betrayed him. He'll hold it against me.'

'That's not forgiveness. That's revenge.'

'So what shall I do?'

'What do you want to do?'

'I want to go to bed for a year and not have to think about it.'

Neve knew that as Renata's friend, she should invite her to stay with them for as long as she wanted. But as Mabel's mother, Fletcher's wife, Saul's other lover, and as the woman who'd tampered with evidence and was now in all sorts of trouble, she knew she mustn't. She held her tongue.

'So what happens now?' she asked.

'I have to go home.'

'Do you want me to come with you?'

'I've got to do this on my own. What time is it?'

'Nearly five.'

'So it's Sunday.'

'Yes, it's Sunday.'

# 5

# THE GARDEN PARTY

It was still dark when Neve put Renata in a taxi. A faint drizzle hung in the air.

Now what? She began to walk, not sure which direction she was going in and wishing she was wearing her walking boots. She needed to go home but home felt immensely far off, like a place that she had left long ago. They would all be in bed, fast asleep. She knew how they each slept, the position they lay in and the way their faces looked when they dreamed.

She was tired to her bones, but thoughts spun through her, febrile and disconnected. She suddenly remembered that Whisky hadn't been fed. And she needed to think about Rory's birthday: perhaps they should all go to the Natural History Museum together, which was his favourite place. But of course, Mabel was supposed to be gone by then. Was that even possible now?

The sky had become paler; the drizzle thickened. Neve realised that she was walking away from home, rather than towards it. Ahead of her lay the marshes. She slowed to an aimless drift. She was remembering what Renata had said about Saul: how he was a man who was used to getting what he wanted. Neve was sure there had been several women before the two of them; he was a serially unfaithful man. And she knew there would have been others after her. She had thought of their affair as a joyful escape from the distress of her life, but now it seemed tawdry. Saul, she thought, with his irony and elegance and laughter, Saul who had looked at her as if she was the most beautiful woman in the world, was also tawdry, sleazy. And she'd gone along with it. Neve the mother, Neve the wife, Neve the worker and the friend, Neve who everyone thought was so straightforward and trustworthy. For a moment she let herself imagine everyone's reactions when the fragile secret split apart and they heard what she had done. The disbelief and the glee: Neve Connolly! Who would ever have guessed?

She came to a halt. The hem of her dress was wet and her shoes muddy. Rain dripped down her face. A heron was sitting on a post a few yards away, like a creature carved in stone. If she went to the police, they'd charge Mabel too; they'd put her in prison. If she didn't go to the police they'd come to her, sooner or later, and the longer she waited the worse it would be. Her secret was like a monstrous thing, growing bloated in the dark. She thought of Hitching's unblinking eyes as he watched her. What did he know? About her. About Mabel.

The heron opened its wings, then slowly took off, batting its way impossibly upwards. She followed its flight. A thought dropped like a pebble into her mind and she stood quite still and waited for the ripples. Something about Bernice. What? Something Bernice had said. It was no good. She let it go and continued walking.

She looked at her watch and saw it was just past seven. If it was a weekday, their radio alarm would be going off, the working day beginning. And at this thought, Neve felt that she'd been violently prodded with an electric rod. The alarm. Yes, that was it. She knew now what she had been searching for, and for a few seconds she let the fact of it fall through her, changing everything it touched.

Yesterday, in the supermarket, Bernice had told her about the last morning of Saul's life, and about the sex – the good sex – they had had before Saul rushed off to catch his train to London. That's what Neve had remembered every time she had replayed the conversation in her mind: immediately before coming to meet her, Saul had made love to his wife. What had dominated her thoughts had been the picture of Saul naked with Bernice, entangled with her, just hours after he had been naked with Neve, entangled in Neve.

She could still remember it. She could almost smell it. And it had obscured the real importance of what Bernice had been saying.

Bernice had given her a timeline of their last hour. She had said that their radio alarm went off just before seven, Saul went downstairs to make tea and then returned to the bedroom with it. They had had an argument about a fundraising dinner – and then, unexpectedly, they had kissed each other, Saul had taken off his clothes and they had made love.

Then – Neve pressed her fingers to her temples, concentrating – Bernice had said that the radio was on and that she heard the half-past-seven news. It was only when the alarm on Saul's mobile went off downstairs that he had hurriedly got dressed once more and hastened from the room.

Neve had also heard the news at half past seven on that morning. It had been precisely at that moment that the text had arrived. *I'm free until midday. Come as soon as you can.*

At half past seven, Saul had been in bed with his wife. His mobile was downstairs. He couldn't have sent the text.

But he had to have done. Who else would have sent her that message? She made an effort that felt physical to wrench the new knowledge this way and that to make it fit with the old narrative she had constructed in her mind.

She couldn't. Saul had not sent the text.

There'd been no caller ID, but that hadn't seemed odd at the time: they had never phoned or texted each other, and anyway Bernice had made it clear that he had had several mobiles.

But if it wasn't Saul, then that meant – what did it mean? She felt dizzy and slightly sick. Her breath was coming in shallow gasps. Saul had told her, told Bernice, told colleagues at work, that he was going to the conference that morning. He hadn't planned to be at the flat. Presumably he had dropped in to pick something up. Nobody knew he was going to be there. Nobody at all.

Neve made herself concentrate. Someone who was not Saul had sent her a text telling her to come at once. Why on earth would they do that?

There was an obvious answer, but it was farcical, nonsensical. She searched for another and couldn't find it. Her legs shook and her stomach felt liquid. There was a nasty, metallic taste in her mouth. She clutched at her stomach and let out a moan.

A man walked towards her dragging several branches behind him. He had long white hair and a patchy beard, and he looked old and grubby and melancholy. He stopped in front of Neve and said in a voice that was like a rumble coming from somewhere deep in his chest: 'Can I help?'

She stared wildly at him. He was like a figure from a fever dream.

'No. Nobody can.'

'My boat is up there.' He jerked his head. 'Come and have tea. Out of the rain.'

Without waiting for an answer, he picked up the branches and walked away from her. In a daze, she followed him until they reached a small boat whose roof was piled with wood, and dying plants in their pots. Everything looked neglected. The windows were narrow smeared slits of glass. What was she thinking? She couldn't go into that narrow, dank space with this man who looked like he hadn't had a bath in decades and who might be a bit mad.

'Sorry,' she said. 'I need to get home.'

'Home?'

'To my family.'

'I thought you were alone,' he said and at that, she felt tears starting.

'Thank you for being kind.'

She turned and walked away from him and made herself breathe slowly, in and out, in and out, willing herself to be calm. She let the revelation settle until it was heavy inside her, and then said it out loud to make it real.

'It wasn't meant to be Saul. It was meant to be me.'

Killing Saul had been a mistake. Whoever killed Saul had been expecting Neve.

It felt like a moment of terrible clarity in a dense, dense fog.

What had this person wanted with Neve? And why the flat? Nobody knew about the flat.

Almost nobody.

She knew. Bernice knew. Renata knew. Mabel knew.

Neve walked towards her house very slowly. Every step was an effort, and she felt like an old woman shuffling along in the blustery rain. When she looked at her watch, she saw it was past eight. She didn't know what to do next, where to go, how to continue.

She stopped at the family-run Portuguese deli where she always bought cheese and coffee beans and spices, and sat down at one of the little tables in the corner, next to the shelves of mangoes and plums. When the owner came over, a burly man in a tiny apron, he tutted at her.

'Neve! You're all wet.'

'Hello, Erico.' She smiled at him, wanting to weep. 'I got caught in the rain. Can I have some coffee?'

'And a pastry?'

'Just coffee,' she said. 'I'll buy breakfast to take home to the family when I leave.'

She opened her sodden backpack and pulled out a pen. Reaching across, she took a brown paper bag from the shelf and straightened it out on the table in front of her. She stared at the paper bag and then out of the streaming window. How long had she been awake? How many hours had she slept in the last four days? But if she lay down on her bed and closed her sore, gritty eyes, she knew she wouldn't sleep.

'Coffee,' said Erico, placing a mug beside her. 'Hot milk on the side. And here.' He handed her a small towel. 'For your hair. Or you will be ill.'

'Thank you. That's kind.'

'If you don't mind me saying, you look a bit tired.'

'The morning after,' Neve said.

'And that bruise.'

'I know. It's turning yellow.'

She poured the steaming milk into the coffee then took a sip. Oh, that was good. She let the warmth of it comfort her. Her mobile buzzed: it was her mother and she declined the call. Then she picked up her pen. She frowned at the absurdity, the enormity, of the question she had to ask: who would want to confront and punish Neve for her affair with Saul? That was the person who had killed him.

*Bernice*, she wrote at the top – partly because that was easy; it would be the answer that cost her least. If Bernice knew that she was having an affair with Saul, she might very well want her dead – or Saul. And her steeliness and her control made it imaginable that she could plan it in advance, carry it out without faltering. Neve pinched the bridge of her nose between her thumb and forefinger for a moment, trying to work out the implications. Thoughts swam up from the murk of her mind. She wrote *Text????* next to the name. If Bernice had sent that early morning text to Neve, she could have made up the story about her and Saul making love at the exact time it was sent, in order to cover herself, or even to goad Neve. She could have sent it from any-where. From the flat itself.

She thought back to the previous evening, when Bernice had learned about Renata. Neve felt sure that it had come as a surprise – and yet Bernice had known Saul was having an affair and she had implied that she suspected someone in particular. Neve remembered Bernice putting a hand on her arm, remembered the way she cast her those assessing glances. Did she know?

Had she contacted Neve and told her about that last morning with Saul and come to her house because she didn't know where else to turn – or because she had known all along and had lured her to the flat, but then come face to face with her husband instead?

She realised that there was another person who knew about the flat and who had particular reasons to resent Neve. She wrote it down.

*Katie.*

Neve finished her coffee. She went to the counter and asked Erico for another and then returned to her seat and her brown paper bag of lists. She hesitated then wrote firmly: *Renata.* She stared at the name. Her closest friend, her exuberant, outspoken, needy ally. Even suspecting her felt like a form of gross betrayal.

She made herself consider it. If Renata had been dumped by Saul for Neve, and if Renata knew that to be the case, and if she was smitten with Saul – then it was at least possible. She could have texted Neve from some pay-as-you go phone, then waited for her in the flat. Maybe she still had a key. And then of course, Saul had turned up instead.

The coffee arrived and she paused to drink some. Her feet were wet and her hair was damp and she felt shivery. Out of nowhere, she heard Gary's voice from last night: *this is what you do, isn't it?* What had he said next? *It was like the merger. We were worried we were going to lose our jobs. You just seemed fine about it all.* He'd seemed resentful of her, just as he had often seemed angry over the past weeks and

234

months. Angry with the company, the management, anyone with money or security or luck. He was badly in debt, his partner was dying of MS, the world seemed against him and the future bleak. If he'd discovered she was sleeping with the enemy his anger could have got out of hand.

She thought of him as a young man, small and quick-witted and full of energy; she thought of him now, thin-skinned and battered by life. She wrote: *Gary*.

Then, slowly, her pen like a knife scoring letters in a rough wall, she made herself write the next name. *Fletcher*. If Fletcher knew about her affair with Saul, her betrayal of him, then he would be full of rage and also of humiliation. And Neve knew how humiliated he already felt by his lack of work and the fact that she was the main earner.

Tears pricked in her eyes. For he was *Fletcher*, her life partner, the man she had got together with over the crazy weekend they'd all been remembering the night before. He was the father of her children. He loved her. She swallowed hard. There was a jab of pain in her throat and her eyes throbbed. Didn't he love her? Or did he hate her because she'd been fucking her boss while he'd been sitting in his study failing to make his art and brooding on failure?

Then with a rush of relief, a thought struck her. He'd been there when she received that text so he couldn't have sent it. But the relief was short lived, because as she pictured him that morning, sitting in the kitchen with a plate of toast and marmalade in front of him, she remembered that he'd been fiddling with something on his mobile. Or *a* mobile; the text had come from an unknown number. He could have sent it to her while sitting a few feet from her.

She looked at the grim list. *Bernice, Renata, Gary, Fletcher:* a woman she barely knew but had injured, two of her closest friends, her husband. As an afterthought she added *Charlie,* just because of the look of naked hatred she had seen on his face.

She needed to find out what they had all been doing on the morning Saul had been killed, she thought, and scribbled a note down on the creased brown paper.

The deli was filling up with people. Neve stood up, pushed the paper into her pocket and left the money for the coffee on the table. She got a basket from the entrance and put several still-warm croissants and cinnamon buns into it, then two mangoes and some blueberries. She got some milk, in case they'd run out, and twelve eggs. She paid for them, waved goodbye to Erico, then stopped at the door and took out the list, because of course there was a name she had left off it. She fished in her backpack for the pen. Her fingers felt thick and clumsy; the letters she formed seemed far off, something seen through the wrong end of a telescope.

*Mabel,* she wrote.

And that changed everything. If it was any of the others, even Fletcher, they needed to be discovered and punished. But Mabel was her daughter.

\*

The rain had stopped. There were streaks of blue in the sky. Leaves were falling from the plane trees on her road.

She opened the front door and stepped inside, at once smelling the sweet reek of alcohol. The floor was sticky underfoot. Nobody was downstairs. Almost certainly they were all still asleep. As she passed the sitting room, she saw Tamsin was sprawled on the sofa, fully dressed but with a blanket spread over her. Her mouth was open and her hair undone. Neve paused a few seconds and watched her. At least she wasn't on the list.

There were empty wine glasses on the surfaces and bowls with a few olives still in them. Neve went into the kitchen, where a plastic bag flapped over the hole left by Connor's football. Fletcher had obviously made an attempt to clear up. The dishwasher was full of clean plates and glasses and a few pans were stacked beside the sink. Neve took off the old jacket and rolled up her sleeves. She opened the windows to let a breeze blow through the stale air. She emptied the dishwasher and filled it again with the rest of the dirty dishes, scraping remains of food into the bin and creeping into the living room to retrieve the glasses. She put the empty bottles in the recycling. She swept the floor, not wanting to use the vacuum cleaner in case it woke anyone. She sprayed and scrubbed the surfaces. She wiped the table and then rubbed wood polish into it. She put all the drying-up cloths into the washing machine. There was a bloody tissue on one of the chairs from where she'd cut her hand. She looked at the wound and saw it was still slightly bleeding. She looked down at her grey dress and saw the blood that was smeared over it. Renata's blood. She felt slightly sick.

She made herself some tea and then she remembered the guinea pig. She went outside and squatted by his hutch and Whisky appeared and squeaked at her in an inquisitive fashion. She hadn't cleaned the hutch out for days. She took some of the dirty straw out, then pushed in bundles of clean straw. She heaped the bowl with food, and refilled the water bottle. That would have to do for now. For a few minutes she stood in the garden with her cooling tea and watched him busily eat. She looked back at the house and as she did so the curtains in Rory's room were drawn back and she saw his face appear, like a pale smudge. He saw her and waved, pressing his nose to the glass so it squashed, and she waved back cheerily. How would she get through this day?

Rory sat at the kitchen table scooping cornflakes into his mouth.

'Where shall we bike?' he asked and Neve had to pretend she'd remembered.

'I'll have a think,' she said.

She had a shower, dressed while Fletcher gently snored, threw her dress in the wastepaper basket because she never wanted to touch it again, and then came downstairs to put the pastries in the oven and boil water for coffee. Tamsin shuffled blearily into the room.

'I don't feel quite the ticket,' she said. 'What time did you get home?'

'An hour or so ago.'

'Is Renata OK?'

'Well, her hand is.'

'What a night,' said Tamsin. 'You certainly know how to throw a party.'

'It was a one-off,' said Neve.

'Did you see Charlie's face?'

'Yes.

'Did you know?'

Neve hesitated a beat too long and Tamsin's face turned to one of wounded surprise.

'She told you and not me,' she said. 'Why?'

'She only told me a couple of days ago,' said Neve.

'Still,' said Tamsin. 'It makes me feel a bit on the sidelines. I suppose I shouldn't be surprised.'

'What do you mean?'

'Oh you know – you're always the one people turn to for comfort.'

'That's not true at all.'

Connor and Elias stampeded into the room. Neve chopped the fruit into a bowl, put yoghurt on the table, laid out breakfast things and made coffee. When Fletcher appeared, he put an arm round her shoulder. His face was still puffy from sleep.

'Good morning.'

'Hi.'

'All right?' he asked.

'Yes.'

'You must be exhausted.'

'I will be later,' she said. 'I seem to have got a second wind.'

'That was some dinner,' he said. He seemed, she thought, almost proud of it.

'How was Mabel after I left?'

'Mabel can speak, you know,' said Mabel, stepping into the room. She was wrapped in a large dressing gown. She looked at Neve with an expression that was hard to read, then poured boiling water over a teabag and sat next to Tamsin, sipping it and staring out at the garden.

There was a ringing at the door, then an emphatic knock. Neve groaned.

'Who can that be? I can't face anyone today.'

'They're early,' said Mabel, as Fletcher went to answer.

'Who?'

'Will and Gary are coming to put up our greenhouse.'

'You're joking.'

'I'm not.'

'I hope Jane doesn't mind,' said Neve.

'I think that Jackie woman might come as well,' continued Mabel. 'She was certainly keen about the idea when she left last night. But then, she was rather tipsy, along with the rest of you.' There was a note of derision in her voice that made Neve wince.

'Oh, she'll come,' said Tamsin bitterly. 'She's one of those people who are endlessly enthusiastic about absolutely everything. The party can continue.' She tore a piece off her croissant and pushed it into her mouth.

And then Gary, Will and Jackie were in the room, making it suddenly feel small and crowded. Neve turned her back on them and busied herself with making more coffee, putting slices of bread in the toaster because no, as it happened, they hadn't had any breakfast yet, and yes, they were quite hungry. They made a motley tribe. Jackie was dressed in a long, multi-coloured kaftan that looked like a tent, one that would let in rain at a festival, and one of the stems of Gary's glasses had snapped so every time he moved his head they slipped down his nose. Will had shaved, but badly; there were small patches of stubble on his cheek. There was an air of relaxed intimacy in the room. After last night everyone, thought Neve, felt thoroughly at home here. The greenhouse was just an excuse.

She put the toast on the table and sliced more bread. She needed to speak to Mabel, but Mabel obviously didn't want to speak to her. She needed to lie down on her bed and close her eyes and think. She needed to make a plan. But she was so tired. It was like the tiredness she had felt when her children were tiny and she had seen the world through a film of grease, everything wavering in front of her, nothing holding its shape. She had fallen asleep at the wheel of the car at a traffic lights, the three of them asleep behind her; she'd fallen asleep singing them to sleep; she'd fallen asleep in meetings. Perhaps she could fall asleep now, she thought, standing up like a horse does. Just to shut out the world for a while.

Behind her, people were chomping toast and

slurping coffee and talking over each other. Tamsin was announcing rather solemnly that Charlie had always been mistrustful of Renata because of her rackety past. Into a sudden pocket of silence, she heard Fletcher saying something about secrets and she stiffened. He was telling everyone that he and Neve didn't even know each other's passwords for their mobile phones.

'Because you want to keep things from each other?' asked Jackie.

'Just the opposite. We trust each other, and so we respect each other's privacy. Once you start suspecting another person, where do you end?'

'It's true,' said Will. 'You can only prove someone is guilty, never that they're innocent.'

Neve turned, drying her hands on a towel. She saw Mabel's bright and mocking gaze. There was a scream lodged in the back of her throat and if she didn't get out of here soon it would escape and rip through this cosy little gathering.

'Shall we go on that bike ride?' she said to Rory and his face opened up in pleasure. 'Back in an hour or so,' she added to the rest of them. 'If you're still here.'

'Oh, I think it will take most of the day to get that greenhouse up,' said Fletcher. 'Are there things for lunch?'

Neve had to choose between two options, both unpalatable. Cycle with Rory on the road, with the cars and the lorries and the buses, or along the River Lea, with its pedestrians and cyclists and, of course, the River

Lea with no safety barrier. Rory loved cycling but he was dreamy and also uncoordinated, and the combination was alarming. He would get lost in a thought, drift across a busy road, not see a junction, a van, a pothole, a traffic light. Cycling into the river would be bad but cycling in front of a cement lorry would be far, far worse. So once she had made him put his helmet on, they set off through residential streets and turned north on the towpath, Rory taking the lead.

They had done this ride before and it had always been a sort of solace to her, a miraculous escape in a world of quiet and greenness, water and birdsong, in the middle of London. As they cycled along, Neve called Rory's attention to a cormorant flexing its wings and then instantly regretted it. As he looked round, he swerved towards the water and she shouted a warning to him. They halted by the boathouses as a crew of young women carried a boat across the path. Rory stood astride his bike fascinated as they lowered it into the water.

All the time, Neve was aware of herself as two people. One of them was dutifully pointing out a swan followed by a line of cygnets, shouting out warnings to give way to pedestrians. The second was thinking about events elsewhere. What was happening at home? What were the police doing? Above all, was there someone out there? She couldn't keep the thought away, as if she were prodding at a loose filling with her tongue. Could it be a stranger, someone she didn't know? Or could it really be someone she knew, someone on her list? She couldn't decide which possibility frightened her more – but then the names she had written down went through her head – *Bernice, Renata, Gary, Charlie, Fletcher, Mabel* – and she knew which was infinitely more terrifying.

They passed runners, dog walkers, rowers. When they reached Tottenham Hale, Neve looked at her watch. They had been going for almost half an hour. That would have to be enough. She called on Rory to stop. He looked round and she said it was time to go back.

'We've only just started.' His face showed a look of disappointment that wrung her heart.

'I'll tell you what,' she said. 'One day we'll get the whole family together, we'll borrow a couple of bikes and we'll cycle by the river like this and we'll go on and on until we get to the countryside. How does that sound?'

'What? And Mabel?' said Rory dubiously.

That simple question hit Neve like a punch. The world in which Neve and Mabel did simple, happy, normal things like go on bike rides on summer days felt unimaginably distant.

'We'll see. You're doing very well,' she said to the back of Rory's head as he cycled ahead of her. He did genuinely seem to be swaying less. He didn't reply. She didn't even know if he had heard her. She sank into a sort of trance, cycling automatically, unaware of her surroundings. She wasn't tired though, or not in the way that she had been earlier. She was in no danger of drifting off to sleep on her bike. Instead she felt a steely clarity. She started forming a plan. She would go and talk to the people on her list. She would find out where they had been that morning.

Neve had never paid particular attention to what other people thought of her. If she had considered the matter at all – and she was considering it now, while bumping along the towpath behind the thin figure of her son – she had imagined that people quite liked her. She was someone they turned to for help. They wanted to be her friend. They desired her, a few of them. They confided in her, even when she didn't want them to. Now she saw herself as someone who could be hated and it was a strange sensation. It was as if the sun had come up in a different place and it made the landscape look completely different, darker and bleaker than the one she thought she had been living in.

She had not thought obsessively of herself either, but she had, she supposed, considered herself a basically decent person. In this chilly new light she could be seen quite differently: as an adulterer, a liar, a bad friend, a disloyal colleague. She had broken her vows. Well, she hadn't actually made any vows: when she married Fletcher, she had signed a form in Hackney Town Hall and made – what was it? – a solemn declaration of intent. But in her heart she had made a vow, and she had broken it.

So she would talk to people. She would try to find out where they had been, what they knew and what they suspected.

Just then, two further ideas struck her at exactly the same time. She already knew, or believed, that there was a man or a woman out there somewhere who knew about her, who hated her but had killed Saul instead. Now she was suddenly aware that this man or woman was still out there, in the world, right now, walking around or sitting down or drinking a cup of coffee. And still feeling whatever they were feeling. Except that now they had killed someone.

Her second thought was that if, in talking to people, she actually found something out, if she found out who the person was, what then? What could she do with that knowledge? These two thoughts seemed to flash in her mind alternately, one and then the other.

There was a sudden scraping sound and she pulled on her brakes but even so she nearly collided with Rory, who had suddenly stopped.

'Careful,' she said. 'I almost ran into you.'

He looked at her with a solemn expression. 'Where are we?' he said.

She looked round. She realised that, in her daze, she had led Rory well past the point where they had joined the river. They were almost at Hackney Wick.

'Are we lost?' he said.

'Of course we're not lost. We're just cycling along the river. We're going back another way.'

They followed the path and then turned west on to the Regent's Canal and headed towards home through Victoria Park. It was becoming a beautiful day now. Footballs were being kicked, Frisbees thrown, in another happier world that Neve felt she was looking at as if through glass. They left the park on the opposite side and there was a last perilous few minutes of Neve watching Rory weave through traffic.

As Neve pushed her bike into the hall past the great mountain of bin bags that Mabel had piled up outside the front door, she couldn't hear anything. She felt a sudden faint hope that everyone had gone. She could have some time alone. She could sleep. Think. But then she heard a loud shout from outside and a merry peal of laughter. Rory ran up the stairs and she walked through to the kitchen.

Mabel was sitting at the table with a boy Neve didn't recognise. He was very tall, very pale, with long dark hair. He was dressed entirely in black and he was leaning back on his chair, which was creaking slightly as if it were about to break.

'Hey,' Neve said. She was having to make an enormous effort not to run outside.

They looked round at her with slightly blurry expressions. Neve detected a familiar smell from them and felt a flash of anger: if they were going to smoke weed on a Sunday morning, they could at least have made an attempt to disguise it.

'Hello,' she said to the boy.

'This is Louis,' said Mabel.

'Oh,' said Neve. '*Bonjour.*'

'Oh for God's sake. Louis isn't a French name.'

'It is actually.'

'Louis's completely English.'

'*Half*-English,' said Louis.

'What's the other half?' said Neve.

'German.'

'Good.'

'Why?' asked Mabel.

'It's good to have somewhere to escape to. If you need to escape. Where's everyone else?'

'In the garden.'

Neve started to head for the garden and then turned.

'We should talk,' she said in a low voice.

Mabel looked at her mother with a challenging expression. 'If you want to say something, then say something.'

One of the things that Neve wanted to say to Mabel was that this was a time for keeping a clear head but she didn't.

'Later,' she said and walked through the kitchen and out into the garden.

She felt like she was arriving at a party in her own home. But it wasn't *a* party. It was just last night's party still going on. In fact the party seemed to have begun days before and just moved from place to place with occasional breaks. At the far end, in the corner, Fletcher and Will were standing amidst the unassembled pieces of the greenhouse. Next to them was a woman in jeans and a white sweater that emphasised her breasts and her slim, strong figure. Just the sight of her made Neve feel tired and old and bedraggled. She wondered who the woman was and then realised that of course it was Elias's mother, Sarah. Neve realised that her brain wasn't working very well. She was having difficulty recognising a woman she had met multiple times at the school gate. She had even been to her house on several occasions to collect Connor. She needed to be careful.

Connor and Elias were doing something with trowels in a flower bed. Gary was standing by Whisky's hutch with Jackie, leaning towards her and gesticulating. She was large and made of curves, he was small and made of straight lines and uncomfortable angles. Neve heard him say something about the Levellers. Jackie looked bemused.

'They wore sprigs of rosemary in their hats to identify them, and sea-green ribbons,' he said.

Tamsin was sitting alone at the wooden table. On it was a half-full cafetière and several mugs and tumblers and an empty jug. Neve sat beside her. Tamsin was sipping from a glass of what looked like tomato juice.

'Fletcher fixed me a Bloody Mary,' said Tamsin. 'Hair of the dog. Do you want to join me?'

Neve shuddered at the thought of alcohol. She poured herself a mug of lukewarm coffee.

'I'm a bit surprised,' said Neve. 'I think of you more as coconut water and a five-mile run before breakfast kind of person.'

'Well, it's Sunday. You're allowed to have one day off.'

They looked across at the progress with the greenhouse. Will seemed to be doing most of the work.

Sarah walked across to them. She bent down and kissed Neve on both cheeks. Neve saw that she had beautifully clear skin, lightly tanned, as if she had spent time in the open air. She had a clean smell, lavender, roses, sandalwood, whereas she, Neve, smelt of sweat and fear.

'Join us,' she said. 'It feels wonderfully gendered. The women sitting drinking coffee while the men assemble things.'

Sarah laughed and said she wished she could but she and Elias had a lunch to go to. She dragged a protesting Elias away. Neve saw he had several fat worms in his free hand.

When they were gone, Tamsin looked at Neve. 'You attract people,' she said. She wasn't smiling.

'I don't.'

'Wherever you are, people want to be with you. It's like this party. Perhaps nobody is ever going to leave.'

'The party will end at some point,' said Neve warily. 'Not that there's any hurry.'

Tamsin drained her Bloody Mary. 'You're the breadwinner now, aren't you?'

'I wouldn't put it like that.'

'Men find it difficult. They go along with it, of course. Usually there isn't an alternative. And it's convenient. The woman earns most of the money and she still does the majority of the housework and the cooking. But even so, they still resent it. It's not just that they need to succeed. They need to be seen to succeed.'

Neve knew that Tamsin, aided by the Bloody Mary, was mainly talking about herself and her own experience but she still felt that she had to respond.

'That's not true of Fletcher, any of it. He's always done his share with the house and the children.' She thought of all the evenings she hadn't been at home. 'More than his share, sometimes. He's had difficult times. We all have. But he's been good about it. Mostly.'

'That's nice,' said Tamsin. 'You've stayed in an office job so that Fletcher can follow his dream. Good for you. And lucky him.'

Neve looked across at Fletcher and Will. They had assembled the frame of the front of the greenhouse and were trying to attach it to the frame of one side. It was strange to see him doing the sort of thing that English men were meant to do on Sunday mornings. Was he really following his dream? It didn't feel like it, most of the time.

'This week,' Neve began slowly. 'It's made me think about things.'

'What things?'

Neve looked at Tamsin's face and saw at the same time the slightly awkward, funny, self-mocking young woman she'd met at college and the lines at the edges of the eyes and the mouth, the loose skin around the neck.

'I always thought there was nobody like us,' said Neve. 'We weren't just friends and comrades. We were almost family.'

'And you know how people feel about their family.' Tamsin gave a snort.

'I wonder if some people might feel cross with me about the merger.'

'Why would they feel that?'

'They might feel I'd betrayed the spirit of what we had together.'

'When you say *some people*—'

'What do *you* feel?'

'Let's be honest, it wasn't really a merger. That's like saying a hyena is having a merger with a lion.'

'We weren't exactly killed and eaten.'

'Tell Gary that,' said Tamsin, pulling a face. 'My own opinion is that if we hadn't ...' She hesitated. 'Merged – let's say merged – our company wouldn't have survived. And in my current state of abandonment, that wouldn't be a good thing. So it would be ungrateful of me to complain too loudly.'

Neve didn't think this was an especially warm endorsement. 'Wait,' she said.

She went into the kitchen and returned with two bottles of pale ale from the fridge. She walked across to the two men. They looked round at her and both grinned. Tamsin joined them.

'I hope you know what you're doing,' she said. She was looking at Will, but he didn't seem to notice her.

'Hang on,' said Fletcher.

Fletcher and Will gasped instructions to each other as Will inserted a bolt connecting the two parts and then secured it with a nut. They stood back, contemplating their work. Neve handed them the two bottles and they both took a drink.

'You look like real workers,' said Tamsin.

'We've got about three-quarters of it to go,' said Will.

'It's the manual's fault,' said Fletcher. 'It's like doing a jigsaw without a picture to go by.'

'No problem,' said Tamsin. 'The rest of us will just have to stay here, eating and drinking until the greenhouse is completed and full of pots.'

Fletcher laughed. 'You and Neve must be getting sick of the sight of each other.'

'What do you mean?'

Neve had a sudden sense of what might be coming and she felt as if the ground under her feet had suddenly tipped.

'You're seeing more of her than I am,' Fletcher said.

'I'm just glad she's here while you two are working,' Neve said desperately. 'I was just saying it feels very gendered. We were saying that, weren't we?'

'We're all spending time together,' said Tamsin. 'These last few days have been like a party that never stops.'

'I know,' said Fletcher. 'And they came after the two of you had just spent that long evening together.'

'What?'

'More ale?' asked Neve. 'More coffee?'

Jackie and Gary were coming towards them now; Jackie had a yellow leaf in her hair.

'That's . . .' Fletcher paused, working it out. 'Six days on the trot together, at work as well. And before that, all those other evenings when she was round at yours. You must have run out of things to say to each other.'

Was this going to be it? Was this going to be the stupid thing that brought everything down? She made herself look at the remaining pieces of the greenhouse as if she found them interesting, the strips of metal, the sheets of glass leaning against the garden wall ready to be mounted. Meanwhile, she waited for Tamsin to speak, waited for her to tell Fletcher that his wife hadn't been round that evening. She seemed to be taking a long time. How could they all bear this silence? Then she felt Tamsin's hand grasping her arm.

'You know me and Neve,' she said. 'We never run out of things to talk about.'

Neve had to get away. It felt physically impossible to continue standing there with Fletcher and Tamsin looking at her. She said she would go in and make more tea and coffee for everyone.

'I think lunch would be good,' said Fletcher. 'It's past two. There must be bits and pieces.'

'Gary's been telling me about Charles the First's execution,' said Jackie brightly. 'In great detail. He seems to think the king was asking for it.'

'This is going to take the rest of the day at least,' continued Fletcher. 'The least we can do is feed people.'

Neve turned to go. Her eye fell on something and she stiffened. It was the toolbox. Of course. They were putting up a greenhouse so they needed tools. The lid was shut. She took a few cautious steps forward, as if it might explode. Lifted the lid. The hammer wasn't there.

'Looking for something?' asked Fletcher.

'I thought I'd hang that picture up in the kitchen,' she said weakly. 'I've been meaning to for months. Do you have a hammer?'

'Here.' He handed across a hammer. Small, with a forked head. Not the right one. Not the one that had cracked open Saul's skull.

She took it. 'Thanks,' she said.

She went inside, into the quiet of the house. Mabel and Louis were still at the table, but now Neve's sewing basket was in front of them.

'What's that for?'

'Louis needs another piercing in his ear.'

'Don't be daft!'

'It's OK. We'll use a potato,' said Louis.

'What?'

'A potato. To stab the needle into,' said Mabel slowly, as if she was talking to a very small and very stupid child.

'You're stoned.'

'So?'

Neve left them and dragged herself upstairs, just to be somewhere nobody else was. Her head was thudding. Mabel's bedroom door was open and she couldn't stop herself from glancing inside. It was completely bare. It had been like a Gothic horror story and now it was like a nun's cell. Very quietly, she went inside. There were no pictures or posters on the wall, just marks from where they had been, and even the mirror was gone. She opened the wardrobe and saw it was largely empty, metal hangers in a row. She went into her and Fletcher's room, glowing in the afternoon sun, and sat on the side of the unmade bed. She thought about taking off her shoes and lying down. The pillow looked so soft and fat.

The doorbell rang, then rang again. With an immense effort, Neve stood up. Who else could be coming to this madhouse? She slowly descended the stairs, hearing a yell from the kitchen as she did so.

Renata stood outside, her hand and arm in its great white shroud. She was wearing clean clothes but her face was still smudged and her hair a mess. There was a streak of dried blood on her neck.

'Come on in,' said Neve.

'Oh dear,' Renata said. 'Oh dear.'

Neve led her through to the kitchen, where Louis was dabbing at his ear with a piece of kitchen roll. Mabel had gone into the garden and was talking to Will, her face turned up towards him, her arms dangling by her side. She looked so sweet, thought Neve; anxiety darted through her.

'Sit,' she said to Renata. 'I'm making everyone something to eat.'

There was some bread left, and a couple of half-baked baguettes; sour cream, a few cherry tomatoes, a knob of fresh ginger, butter, a bag of spinach, some parsley. It was hard to make a meal out of that. She thought of all the vegetables in the allotment waiting to be harvested. There were the eggs she had bought that morning though.

'Scrambled eggs?' she said to Renata, but Renata was gone, and so was Louis. Neve looked out into the garden, and saw everyone gathered there, standing around the rudimentary beginnings of the greenhouse in the sunshine. People were laughing. Gary had his arm around Renata – and even she was smiling, leaning against his shoulder with her floppy mass of hair gleaming.

Suddenly Will crouched down, put his head on the ground, then eased himself up into a headstand. Everyone was applauding. He lowered himself, stood up and bowed. Yes, of course Neve remembered him; she remembered all of them when they were young and foolish and eager for their future to begin. Now Tamsin stepped forward into a clear space, lowered herself, stretched her body into a plank and was doing swift and perfect press-ups. She stopped, collapsed on the grass and lay there, smiling. Fletcher was saying something to her and Neve hoped with a small lurch of pity that he wouldn't try any gymnastics; he'd never been the sporty type.

But why hadn't Tamsin blown her cover? What did she know; what had she guessed?

Neve melted a generous amount of butter into a pan, cracked in all twelve eggs, added salt and plenty of black pepper. She stirred the thickening mixture, still looking out at the garden. It looked such fun, so companionable: a gathering of old friends on a warm Sunday afternoon in September, backlit by the sun. Connor did a crooked cartwheel, then another. His face was muddy and flushed with excitement. He'd be impossible this evening. Neve turned the heat down low while she cut bread and put the slices in the toaster. The baguettes in the oven were nearly ready. She checked the eggs and got plates from the cupboard.

In the garden, Mabel was standing between Will and Louis, pointing at something. Neve stared at her: her daughter, her firstborn, her tormentor and protector. Her beloved child.

At any moment, this golden picture could crack and shatter into a thousand pieces.

Suddenly she stiffened: the door to Whisky's hutch was slightly open. She yanked open the back door.

'Where's Whisky?' she called.

Everyone turned towards her and then to the cage. Neve ran out and knelt down. There was no sign of the guinea pig. She made a clicking sound, calling him, and waited for his inquisitive face to appear out of the hay. Nothing. She pushed her hand into the hay and felt for him. He wasn't there.

She stood up. Everyone had gathered round. Unsupported, the frame of the greenhouse swayed.

'He'll be somewhere in the garden,' she said. 'This big.' She showed them with her hands. 'Dirty white colour with black patches.'

'Why did you call him Whisky then?' asked Jackie. Neve ignored her.

They all fanned out round the garden, stooping down to look under bushes, rustling in the fallen leaves.

'He's there,' said Louis after several minutes. His voice was low and excited. He gestured towards the compost bin. The snug little body of Whisky was inserted behind it, half covered in dry leaves.

The group made a semicircle around the bin. Fletcher cautiously crept forward, holding out his hand, murmuring encouragement. Very slowly, he lowered his hand. Whisky shot out the other side at a surprising speed, through Gary's legs, and halfway across the lawn.

'He mustn't get into another garden,' said Neve. It seemed like a matter of life and death that the little animal should be captured and returned to safety.

Once again they made a circle around the guinea pig, all crouching and ready to make a grab. Whisky made a run for it, Neve launched herself and felt his coarse hair under her hand but then he was gone and she was tumbling on to the lawn, and there was someone else almost on top of her. She felt the weight of them, heard them panting, and saw just ahead two arms stretched out and two large hands holding the little creature.

'Got him,' cried Will triumphantly, clambering to his feet and holding Whisky against his chest. 'Sorry about that,' he said cheerfully to Neve.

Neve lay on the ground, her bruised cheek on the cool damp grass, which was muddy from all the football that Connor and Elias had been playing. She looked up at everyone. It felt to her that she was lying at the bottom of a deep hole, staring up at the faces far above her. She started to laugh, a weak, watery, helpless sound. She realised she was crying.

A slight figure detached itself from the huddle and came and squatted beside her.

'What are you doing?' said Mabel hotly into her ear. 'Get up! Fuck it, stand up!'

Neve gave a groan and closed her eyes.

'Well, well,' said a soft, low voice above her. 'I seem to have interrupted some kind of garden party.'

Neve looked up, into Hitching's face. He loomed above everyone else, like a solid wall. Will, standing beside him, still clutching Whisky, looked small. Gary was positively miniature. Hitching was dressed in black trousers and a dark shirt and was holding a briefcase. His skull shone.

'Detective,' she said.

Mabel clutched at her hand so tightly that Neve could feel her wedding ring bite into her fingers.

*It's come*, she thought. *This is it.*

'Your son let me in. Rory, is that right? Quite a gathering.' Hitching gave a chuckle.

'We're putting up a greenhouse,' said Fletcher. He came forward and held out a hand to Neve who took it and got to her feet. She gazed around desperately for the hammer, which must surely be lying on the grass somewhere.

'Tricky business. I know to my cost.'

'Yes.'

'Is it me you've come to see?' asked Renata. She was standing beside Will; her bandaged arm, held in a sling, looked curiously like the muddy white of Whisky against Will's chest.

'Not today,' said Hitching. He took in her bandaged hand. 'I'm sorry to see that you're injured.'

'A stupid accident.' Renata's voice wobbled.

'It's Mrs Connolly I've come to see,' said Hitching.

'Ms.'

'Ms.'

'Why can't this wait? It's Sunday,' said Tamsin. Her cheeks were flushed. There was another Bloody Mary in her fist.

'That's what my wife has been saying,' said Hitching genially. 'This won't take long.'

Neve nodded. 'Why don't you all go inside,' she said to the group. 'Make tea.'

'There's something burnt on the stove,' said Hitching. 'I turned the flame off but I think it's ruined.'

Her scrambled eggs. Neve shrugged. 'It doesn't matter.' She looked towards Mabel. 'Make everyone tea and I'll be in soon.'

'I hear you had quite a party last night,' said Hitching once they were alone and sitting at the little table at the end of the garden, underneath the pear tree.

'Who told you that?'

'Mrs Stevenson.'

'It got a bit out of hand,' said Neve dully. She just wanted him to get it over with. She had lied and she had done that great clean-up largely to protect Mabel from the knowledge of her affair. For a moment it occurred to her that Mabel knew about it and so she could simply be done with this farce and tell Hitching everything. But no. Mabel was involved now. She had removed the hammer. She had lied to the police.

'Sounds like fun,' said Hitching cheerily.

'I suppose you know that Bernice found out about Renata and her husband.'

'She mentioned it,' he said. 'These things usually come out in the end. But that's not what I'm here about.' He picked up his briefcase and put it on the table between them. 'I've something to show you,' he said.

His manner had become more formal. Neve forced herself to meet his gaze and hold it.

'What is it?'

'Mrs Stevenson called me this morning to say that something had been pushed through her letter box. She couldn't tell me the time. She was a bit the worse for wear after your little party.'

Hitching clicked open the lock on his case. He dipped his hand into it and drew out a blue folder in a plastic bag.

'You recognise this?'

'No.'

'You should do. It's your folder. The one that went missing.'

'It's not my folder. I've never seen it. I didn't even know it existed.'

'Well, this file you've never seen was delivered to Mrs Stevenson's house. Curious, don't you think?'

'Yes.'

'Do you have any explanation?'

'No.'

Hitching looked at Neve as though he was disappointed in her or perhaps, she thought, like he pitied her. He ran his hand delicately across his pale skull.

'Is that all?' asked Neve at last.

Hitching once more dipped his hand into the case. This time he drew out a much smaller packet, also in a plastic bag. It looked like a simple glossy white card until he turned it over.

'This was inside the folder,' he said and handed it across.

She recognised it instantly. It was a photograph of her, her hair cut shorter than it was now and blowing in the wind. She was turning towards the person taking the picture, smiling. Towards Fletcher.

She looked up and saw Hitching's dark, watching eyes. 'Oh,' she said. Was that her voice? 'How strange.'

She lifted both hands in a cartoonish gesture of puzzlement. They floated in the air like they didn't belong to her; she saw that they were shaking. Her legs were trembling underneath the table.

'Again, have you any explanation?' asked Hitching.

'No.' She should say something else. What would an innocently surprised person say? 'It's not a very good picture,' she said, horrified even as she spoke the inane words.

'Why would there be a photo of you in the folder?'

'To identify me, I suppose.'

'No one else had one.'

Oh.' Neve paused. 'Oh,' she repeated after a few seconds.

'It's not a very formal photo, is it?'

'No.'

'You look as if you're standing on top of a mountain.'

She had been. Several years ago, she and Fletcher had gone to the Lake District for a long weekend while their children were looked after by Renata and Charlie. It had been just before all their troubles started. They had walked miles every day, up the great peaks, into fog and clouds, pushing themselves until their legs ached and their faces were rubbed raw by the wind.

'Great Gable,' she said.

'So why would this holiday snap be in Saul Stevenson's possession?'

'I've no idea.'

'Did you give it to him?'

Again, she made herself look into Hitching's dark, fixed eyes. She could feel all the muscles in her face quivering. 'No,' she said.

There was a long silence.

'Is there anything else you'd like to tell me?' asked Hitching in a surprisingly gentle tone.

'I can't think of anything.'

'Anything that might have slipped your mind?'

'If I think of anything, of course I'll tell you.'

'That would be helpful.'

She handed him the photo and he slid it into the case. Then he picked up the folder and turned it over.

'Do you know what that is?' he said, tapping his finger on a rusty smear across the top.

'No.'

'I don't either. Yet. But it looks like it might be blood.'

'Whose blood?'

He frowned.

'I just told you. We don't even know if it is blood.' He put the folder into the case and then clicked it shut. 'We'll know by tomorrow.'

Neve ushered him out, through the kitchen full of people and the smell of cannabis and burnt toast and ruined eggs, to the front door. Fletcher accompanied them.

'What did he want?' he asked after Neve closed the door.

'Not much. They've found my personnel file that had gone missing.'

'So?' he asked, a furrow between his eyes.

'He just wanted to keep me informed,' said Neve. 'To clarify things. He doesn't seem to delegate anything.' Was she gabbling? 'Like I said, nothing.'

Fletcher nodded. 'You must be shattered.'

'I am.' Her eyes felt gritty with tiredness. 'Get rid of them.'

'What?'

'Get rid of them.'

'I can't just chuck them out.'

'Ease them out then,' she said. 'Half an hour more of this, and I'll start howling like a wolf.'

'Oh. OK.' He gave her a strange smile. 'Then I'll wash everything up,' he said. 'Leave all of that to me.'

Neve hauled herself up the stairs, into their bedroom. She took off her shoes and lay down. Her brain fizzed and hissed and her body felt itchy. She sat up again. A thought occurred to her and she went to the chest of drawers, pulled open the top one, full of her underwear and rummaged around at the back of it. There it was. She took out a crumpled pack of cigarettes, only four left inside, and one was torn. She pushed her hand in again and found a plastic lighter.

Feeling like a teenager, she went up the next flight of stairs to the landing, opened the little window and squeezed through it on to the small patch of flat roof, covered in moss and dead leaves. She smoked about once every six months and it was always a surreptitious act because Fletcher disapproved, Mabel treated it like a pathetic and yet powerful act of maternal treachery and Rory looked at her as though she was going to die. The last time had been on a beautiful spring night, stars in the sky and a balmy softness in the air; she'd cadged a cigarette from Renata and they'd sat in companionable silence.

She cupped a hand round her lighter, pressing her thumb on the wheel. The little blue flame fluttered and died. She shook the lighter and tried again. She tried not to imagine how ridiculous she looked, crouched in hiding from her children and her husband with a stale cigarette. She wanted not to think; she wanted two inches of time just to sit on this grubby little roof, hidden from view, and do something foolish and unmotherly and trivial.

At last she managed to suck the flame into the tip of the cigarette, feeling the burn in her throat and then a rush of dizziness. She remembered being fourteen, sitting in a circle with a group of friends, and trying to pretend that she was an old hand while the acrid bitterness filled her mouth and she thought she might be sick. Her first boyfriend had told her that it was something you had to persevere with. Neve smiled as she thought of him, stocky and intense; she smiled as she thought of herself then, trying to be grown up. Why had she been in such a hurry to leave childhood behind?

She blew the smoke out and watched as it hung in the air and then dissolved.

Smoking in bed – with whom? She couldn't remember, just the feeling of lying in the darkness in the small hours with the tips of two cigarettes fading and glowing.

Or smoking that mad weekend that seemed somehow like a hinge, swinging her out of a life of reckless, carefree pleasures into one that was more serious: commitment, motherhood, reciprocal and painful love.

She stubbed the cigarette out on the damp moss and left it there. Maybe she'd come up here again in six months' time. Then she slid back through the window again.

She went into the bathroom and cleaned her teeth vigorously then gargled with mouthwash – although Mabel would always be able to tell. She looked out of the window into the garden where the sun was sinking and the sky a soft grey. They were still there, though clearly in the process of leaving. The greenhouse swayed where it stood, a half-skeleton of metal.

Hitching had forgotten to ask a question about the photograph. He had asked what it was. He had asked why it was in the file. What he hadn't asked is where the photograph had come from. If Hitching had asked, Neve would have to have answered. She didn't need to go down to the kitchen to check. Just by the door to the hallway, there was a corkboard with a collage of snapshots. She knew them so well that she could see them if she closed her eyes: there was Fletcher looking almost like a teenager in an old leather jacket holding a month-old Mabel. There were children on their first bikes, on beaches, at Halloween and at Christmas. There was an image of Mabel, about nine years old, sitting in the corner of a sofa reading a book that made Neve almost cry whenever she looked at it, though she had seen it thousands of times.

And there, in that collage, towards the top right, was the picture of Neve on the top of the mountain looking at her husband. She didn't need to go down to the kitchen to check. If Hitching had asked where it had come from, Neve would have pointed to the space on the corkboard. Hitching's next question would have been: how did the picture get from your kitchen into a personnel folder pushed through the letter box of Bernice Stevenson's house?

Neve couldn't answer the question. But she could ask it. Who could have taken it? It felt so confusing and impossible. Perhaps if she waited – for a proper night's sleep, for some peace and quiet – it might become clearer in her mind. But she couldn't wait.

There was only one obvious connection between her house and Bernice's house: Bernice. Hitching only had Bernice's word about the file having been posted through her door. The easiest explanation was that Bernice had removed the photo herself and then fabricated the story as a way of getting the file to Hitching.

There was another scenario, of course. Who could hate you as much as the person closest to you, the person you love?

She walked out on to the landing where she stopped and listened. She could still hear Fletcher rattling around in the kitchen. She would have a few minutes.

She opened the door to Fletcher's office and stepped inside. She didn't know where to begin. Fletcher had a drawing board on one side and on the other, near the window, was his desk. On it were piles of papers, old newspapers, several mugs, a pile of CDs, books, cables. There were several different-sized light bulbs, which he had taken days or weeks ago as a reminder to buy new ones. Neve found the sight of it somehow alarming, as if it represented the bit of Fletcher's interior life that worried her. The chaotic, hopeless side. She felt a disastrous urge to attack it, clear it up, throw most of it away.

In the middle of the desk was his closed laptop.

She would like to have looked at what was on it, at his emails, his search history, just to get some idea of what had been on his mind over the last couple of weeks. But neither of them knew the passwords for each other's phone or computer. They'd said that it represented the last bit of privacy, the last locked door. They kept saying that they should write them down and put them in a sealed envelope, just in case one of them developed dementia or was killed in an accident. But they'd never got around to it.

She pulled open a couple of drawers and saw receipts, instruction manuals, postcards. Where could she even start? Then she saw his desk diary, lying open on the desk. It was at today's date. She turned the pages back slowly one by one. She saw what she expected to see: appointments with clients and friends. She recognised all the friends and most of the clients. There weren't many of them. So far, so boring.

Then she noticed something.

At first she thought it was just a squiggle on the page, as if he had been testing whether his pen was working. But she turned the page back and saw another one, almost identical. Just a little wavy line but it was the same wavy line. She looked at page after page. There were several more. She turned quickly back to earlier in the year, to February, and couldn't find any of the marks. Then she turned back to the present day and worked her way back. The first she got to was a week earlier. She flicked back, checking the days they were on. There were none on weekdays. She checked to see if any of them were on her day off. She couldn't find any. She ought to write them down, she ought to—

'What are you doing?'

She looked round. Fletcher had come in behind her. She looked back at his desk. The coffee cups. She picked them up.

'Since you're doing the washing up,' she said.

'I thought I'd finished.'

'When you think you're finished, you always find another mug.'

He smiled at her, too widely. 'I know it's just an excuse to go through my things,' he said.

'It's what I do.' Neve forced a grin, pretending it was all good fun. 'Whenever I get the chance.'

'Finding my secrets.'

'Everyone has secrets,' she said. She couldn't bear this conversation to continue. It was like he was the enemy.

She went downstairs, feeling like she was in a fever. She felt her face must have gone red and flushed. She heard Fletcher come into the kitchen behind her but she didn't turn round. He was talking and she quickly realised that he wasn't talking to her. He was on the phone and she heard him bring the conversation to a close and then the door to the garden opening and closing. She looked round and saw two things at the same time. Fletcher had gone into the garden and he had left his phone on the kitchen table.

Almost without thinking, she stepped forward and picked it up. She didn't need the password. He'd only just stopped using it. She looked outside. He had walked over to the far side of the garden, joining Mabel, Jackie and Will. She scrolled quickly through his mail: a couple of friends, notifications from Amazon, Russian women wanting to get to know him, a couple of newsletters he subscribed to. Nothing out of the ordinary.

Then she looked at his texts, scrolling down the

names. Her, Mabel, various friends, Charles, work texts, then she saw a name she wasn't expecting.

Sarah.

She clicked on the name. A string of tiny messages: *with you in 10 – tomorrow? – running late – where are you? – miss you.* And lots and lots of *x*'s.

Sarah.

She turned it over in her dull, tired mind. Sarah. So that was the squiggle in the diary. S. It marked their meetings.

Sarah.

Who was Sarah?

And then she knew. Oh. *Sarah.* Elias's mother. Sarah and Fletcher. Fletcher and Sarah.

Very carefully, she replaced the phone on the kitchen table where Fletcher had left it.

She went out into the empty garden and walked backwards and forwards on the lawn, beside the unfinished greenhouse, peering under bushes. The hammer was nowhere to be seen. Whisky's face peered out at her. He cheeped like a canary through the wire.

Renata came blearily into the kitchen, her face creased and puffy from sleep.

'Only me left,' she said.

She didn't ask, but it was clear she was going to stay the night. Neve made sure that Connor and then Rory had baths. She put their dirty clothes into the washing machine and turned it on, then put out their clothes for the following day. She looked into their school bags and saw that Connor hadn't done his homework, and she sat him down at the kitchen table and put his books and pens in front of him. She looked into the fridge and wondered what she could use in their sandwiches tomorrow. Maybe it would just have to be peanut butter. She ordered a Thai takeaway from up the road and Fletcher went to collect it while she made a bed up for Renata.

She didn't know how she was still standing.

Thoughts shimmered in her mind. Sarah. Fletcher. Sarah and Fletcher. The hammer. The folder. The photo. The present that was going to be delivered. Hitching's newly serious manner. Tamsin protecting her. Mabel's false alibi for the morning of Saul's death. She thought about the allotment; everything rotting in the gold autumn light. She thought of her life and it seemed like an avalanche, sliding away down the mountainside, gathering everything up in its roaring descent.

Fletcher arrived back with the takeaway. Neve laid the foil containers out on the table, steam rising from them and the scent of lemongrass and coconut. She put out plates, cutlery, glasses, a jug of water, lit the candles. The sun was low in the sky, the light soft. The boys were in their pyjamas, smelling of soap. Renata had showered and was in Neve's dressing gown, her injured arm tucked inside it in a sling. Mabel had changed into old black leggings and a baggy plum-coloured jumper that also belonged to Neve. She seemed dazed. Everyone was tired and slow and muted.

'What a weekend,' said Fletcher, spooning rice on to his plate.

Neve looked up. 'Yes,' she said.

He looked at her. She knew his face so well; and not well at all.

'Tomorrow we'll be back to normal,' he said.

Mabel leaned towards her, baring her teeth in a not-smile.

'You've been smoking,' she said.

Fletcher cleared the dishes. Renata sat in the garden smoking a cigarette. Neve went upstairs with the boys and made sure they cleaned their teeth. She drew the curtains in both their rooms, pulled back the covers, picked up damp towels from the floor. Mabel put her head in briefly, then withdrew. They were like spies in their own lives, thought Neve, picking up a pair of socks, a curl of orange peel. She saw Connor and Rory into bed, kissed them both on their foreheads, turned off Connor's light and pulled the duvet round him.

Mabel wasn't in her bare room, or anywhere else in the house. Neve went into their bedroom, cleaned her teeth, undressed and climbed into bed. She could hear Fletcher in his study and then his footsteps as he came down the stairs and opened the door. She lay propped on her pillow and watched him as he pulled his clothes off, leaving them scattered on the floor. He was still quite slim but all his weight seemed to have redistributed itself: his legs seemed thinner and he had the beginnings of a middle-aged paunch. His chest was hairier than when they'd first met and there was hair on his back as well. He was pale, soft-looking. When he took his glasses off, his eyes seemed naked.

When had she last looked at him properly? When had he last looked at her? When they had first got together – that wild weekend they'd been remembering at dinner yesterday; the first heady weeks – she had been able to feel him when he came into a room without turning round. Electricity had sparked between them. Sleepless with desire, she had felt alive with energy and hope.

Now they were growing middle-aged together, wrinkles on their skin and grey in their hair, and they barely noticed each other. They didn't go out on dates. They hardly looked up if the other entered the room.

And so she had fallen for Saul, who made her feel desired again. And now she knew about Sarah – though she had no idea if it was a secret flirtation, a fling, or a full-blown affair. She didn't know how long they had been seeing each other or what Fletcher felt about her or if it was still going on. Did it make her guilt less, that he had also deceived her?

He climbed into bed. 'I'm knackered,' he said, turning off his bedside lamp.

Neve just murmured something in response.

'You know what?'

'What?'

'In a couple of days' time,' he said, 'Mabel is supposed to be going to university.'

'I know.'

'Will she?'

'I'm not sure. Maybe not.'

'It's crazy,' he said.

'Which bit?'

'How we don't even dare ask her outright. We probably won't know until the morning arrives if she's leaving.'

He turned and shifted, pulling his pillow under his head, making himself comfortable. His back was towards her.

'Sleep well,' she said.

She turned off her own light and closed her eyes. She was so tired that the room seemed to spin, the bed tip. Her mind hissed with thoughts. Fletcher's breathing deepened.

Saul had died because of her. Someone had meant to kill her, and Saul was just collateral damage. She thought of his dark hair, his bright eyes, his eloquent hands, the way he was carefree, merry; the way he smiled at her and said her name. Neve Jenny Connolly. The poem came to her:

> *Jenny kiss'd me when we met,*
> *Jumping from the chair she sat in;*
> *Time, you thief, who love to get*
> *Sweets into your list, put that in!*
> *Say I'm weary, say I'm sad,*
> *Say that wealth and health have miss'd me,*
> *Say I'm growing old, but add,*
> *Jenny kiss'd me.*

She would never say that poem out loud at parties again. But when she was old herself, she would still remember it, remember him, feel the heat of his desire. Where was it now? Who'd taken it and what were they going to do with it?

She let herself imagine what would have happened if on that Wednesday morning she had simply called the police. They would have arrived; she would have told them the truth – the whole truth, the simple, bare fact of their illicit affair and her discovery of the body. Of course, everyone would have had to learn of her infidelity, but that seemed like a small thing now. She had thought it would destroy Fletcher, and her family, but Fletcher had been having his affair with Sarah all the time.

Then there was Mabel. If Mabel had told her the truth, she had only gone into the flat after Neve to clear away evidence, thinking her mother had killed Saul. If Neve had pressed those three buttons on her mobile, Mabel wouldn't have become involved at all. And she had already known about the adultery.

But if Mabel had gone into the flat before Neve … The thought ticked away in her skull. What then?

Fletcher murmured something and turned slightly. Neve lay with her forearm over her eyes, trying to press herself into deeper darkness. How would she ever sleep, with her mind on fire like this? And she was hot. The menopause, panic, sadness, and the memory of what she had done and what she had lost. That he would never be in the world again. That her daughter was in peril. That her life was a house of cards.

At last she slid from the bed and pulled on an old cotton dressing gown; she crept from the room and went downstairs. The house was full of people sleeping, breathing deeply, dreaming. She went into the kitchen and then out into the garden, which was mysterious in the moonlight.

She looked back at the house. Every window was dark. She thought of her children in their sleep. She pictured Connor, wrapped into a stout, bristle-headed ball, and Rory stretched out, his forearm over his eyes. She'd been so concentrated on Mabel's danger that she had taken her attention off them. They were affected by all of this as well, although they didn't realise it. She felt the impulse to run back into the house and gather them both to her as if they were still babies and she could make everything all right. She sat down on the grass beside Whisky's hutch and called him and after a few moments he pushed his nose out and chirruped at her. Neve picked a few dandelion leaves and pressed them through the wire; he nibbled at them, whiskers twitching.

'What are you doing?'

Neve didn't turn. 'Hello,' she said. 'I couldn't sleep. I think I've gone beyond tiredness. But why are you up?'

Mabel kicked at the scuffed grass. 'That detective . . .' she said.

'He doesn't know anything. That alibi you gave me . . . We have to stick to it now. You came to the allotment with me on Wednesday morning. But don't say anything else like that. OK?'

Mabel shrugged, then nodded.

'It's best to stay as near to the truth as possible. When you lie, you're setting yourself a trap.'

They were criminals, thought Neve, working out how to cover up what had happened. Neither were looking at each other.

'OK.'

'One question. Did you take a file from the flat when you were there?'

Mabel looked puzzled. 'What are you talking about?'

'A file has gone missing. It was in the flat.'

'Well I didn't take it.'

'You're sure.'

'Yes, I'm sure.' She kicked at the grass again.

'Right. Just stay out of all of this from now on. Do nothing, say nothing, leave it to me.'

'I'm quite scared,' said Mabel in a small, flat voice. 'I don't want to go to prison.'

Neve waited, thinking she was about to reveal more, but instead Mabel said, 'Sometimes I feel like some horrible, vicious creature is alive inside me and gnawing its way out with its sharp teeth.'

Neve nodded. 'I know,' she said.

'You won't let me go to prison, will you?'

'No. I promise.' Although how could she make such a promise?

'I'm going to bed now.'

'Me too,' said Neve.

But she stayed outside, staring and staring at nothing; thinking and thinking of nothing, drained, and for this short pinch of time, while everyone else slept and the moon hung like a flag in the sky, she felt oddly peaceful. She sat on the grass and she fell asleep.

She woke up hours later, stiff from the hard ground and cold and damp from dew. She didn't know where she was at first. She heard birds singing, though it was still dark. Everything felt unreal. She even wondered if she was asleep, if this was a dream. She walked across the wet grass and softly into the house, feeling like a ghost, padded up the stairs. In her bedroom she took her clothes off in the dark, just let them fall, and got into the bed. There was a murmur from Fletcher as he felt her weight moving the bed.

# 6

# A Trip to the Country

The next morning, Neve took Rory and Connor to school, and as she left them at the gates, she almost bumped into Sarah. They both laughed as if they were sharing a secret joke, being a woman on a Monday morning at the school gates. Sarah looked fresh-faced, immaculately turned out. She even smelled immaculate, of lemons and pine needles. Her smooth cheeks were flushed. Neve thought she seemed very slightly ill at ease – or perhaps she had been like it for some time but Neve hadn't noticed. She tried to imagine this woman, who presented herself so carefully to the world, with Fletcher. Her Fletcher, anxious, gloomy, clever, creative, kind.

'Good to see you,' she said, forcing a smile.

'You too. Recovered from your mad weekend?'

'Not entirely. Can I have a word?'

'I'm in a bit of a rush,' said Sarah. 'I need to get to work.'

'So do I, but I can walk with you.'

They walked in silence for a couple of minutes. The sky was overcast, promising rain. The air smelled of autumn, leaves were turning. Neve looked across at Sarah. She was several inches shorter than Neve. She wasn't exactly beautiful, but there was something about her that was composed and pleasing. She and Neve weren't friends – Neve didn't even know what her job was; something financial or managerial – but they had always been friendly and supportive of each other: two mothers trying to do the best they could. And Connor and Elias were as thick as thieves.

'Hang on,' said Neve suddenly. 'Can we stop walking for a moment?'

They stopped and Sarah looked at Neve warily. 'What?' she asked.

'I don't know how to say this.'

Sarah waited. She put up her hand – no wedding ring, manicured, and nails painted a mushroom-pink colour – to her face for a moment, her hair. The air between them was thick with tension.

'There is something I need to ask you.'

Sarah's eyes flickered. She licked her lips. 'What?'

'Does Fletcher want to leave?'

'Leave? Leave what?'

'I'm not going to shout at you. I'm not going to cry. I'm not going to make a scene. I just want to know: is Fletcher planning to leave?'

'Leave?' Sarah repeated the word as if it was a foreign language. Her voice was scratchy.

'Us. Me. The children.'

Sarah's face was suddenly pale except for little flecks of pink. 'What did he tell you?'

'Just answer.'

'I don't know,' said Sarah very slowly. 'I don't think so.'

'Does he hate me? Is he angry with me?'

'Don't,' said Sarah. 'Not like this. I'm not comfortable with this.'

'It's not exactly a comfortable situation. Please, just tell me.'

'You have to believe that I never meant—'

Neve held up her hand. 'No,' she said. 'I don't want to hear why you did what you did, or anything like that. I want to know how Fletcher seems to you.'

Sarah looked at her in puzzlement. 'How he *seems*?'

'What's his mood? Guilty? Happy? Angry?'

Sarah shook her head. 'He's not happy, that's for sure. And I don't think he's angry. He's a bit down. I don't know. Maybe he's resentful.'

'Resentful? What of?'

'You're the successful one. You've got the job. The friends. Everything's fine with you and everyone likes you.'

That almost made Neve smile, except that just then she didn't feel like she'd ever smile at anything ever again.

'You've always been nice to me,' said Sarah. 'I don't want you to hate me. Women always blame the other woman.'

Neve looked at her hard and saw the blood rising in Sarah's smooth cheeks.

'I don't hate you,' she said. 'I don't blame you. I just—'

She stopped. Everything was wrong: years of Mabel on the edge, her betrayal of Fletcher, Fletcher's betrayal of her, Saul's murder and her cover-up and now the whole world careering out of control. And here she was, talking to her husband's lover calmly, as if it was a bureaucratic obstacle. Because the truth was that she didn't care. She knew that one day she would. Soon enough she would feel jealous and she would feel wretched and she would feel sad. But it was like a pain that stood to one side, waiting for its time. Now, she could only think of Hitching with his folder, Mabel with her terrified face, the abyss yawning in front of her.

'Is it still going on?' she asked. 'You and Fletcher?'

Sarah's eyes filled with tears. A single drop rolled down her cheek, then another.

'I don't know,' she said. 'Yesterday, in your garden, he said we needed to talk.' She swallowed hard. 'I don't think I can discuss it with you though. Like this.'

'Is he in love with you?'

Sarah looked around desperately as if she were worried about being overheard.

'Shouldn't we go somewhere? Have a coffee.'

'I don't have time for anything like that. I've got things to do.'

'All right,' said Sarah, taking a deep breath. 'I don't know if he's in love with me and I don't know if I'm in love with him. I was so lonely and miserable and he saved me. Or that's how it felt. He noticed me. I felt good about myself again. Though terrible as well,' she added hastily.

Neve nodded.

'And as for Fletch,' Sarah continued, looking past Neve, into the plane tree whose leaves were yellow and red and brown (*Fletch!* thought Neve savagely. *Nobody calls him Fletch. It makes him sound like a dog*), 'I don't know. Sometimes, he seemed ...' She swallowed hard. 'This will come out wrong. He once said that he felt like he'd been drowning and now he could breathe again.'

Once more, Neve remembered being with Saul, lying with him in that dark little room, and hearing herself gasping, like a person coming up for air.

'I see,' she said.

'I never meant to hurt you.'

'Has he done this before?'

'I don't know if he's done things ...' Sarah paused as if she couldn't quite say the words. 'Like this before. And I don't get it. Why are you being so calm? Why aren't you shouting at me or crying or attacking me? That would be better than this.'

'Has he said anything about me?'

'I'm sorry,' said Sarah, blinking quickly several times, as if she had something in her eye. 'I don't know. I don't think so. I mean ...' She stuttered to a halt.

Neve wanted to ask: *does he love you enough to want to kill me? Does he hate me enough to want to kill me?* What she really wanted to find out was if Fletcher knew about her and Saul.

'Did he ever ...?' How should she say this? 'Did he ever say anything about paying me back or anything?'

'Paying you back?' Sarah wrinkled her nose. 'What do you mean?'

'I don't really mean anything. You said he was resentful of me. Just because of my work and things? Nothing specific?'

'Like what?'

Neve wanted to shake her. 'He didn't think I was having an affair or anything, did he? I mean, because I have lots of friends,' she added lamely. 'He might have felt jealous.'

'I don't know. We didn't talk about things like that. I don't think I was just a way of hurting you, if that's what you mean.' She sounded angry. That was easier for her than guilt. 'It wasn't all about you.'

'Do you still want him?' asked Neve.

Their gazes met, locked.

'You have to know that this isn't the sort of thing I do,' said Sarah. 'This isn't me.'

She was wiping tears away from her eyes now. Neve instinctively put out a hand to touch her and then withdrew it. Without another word she turned around and walked towards home. As she strode quickly along, she thought of what Sarah had said. Fletcher resented her because she had the safe job and he was at home. But Fletcher had always hated being part of any organisation. He hated his creativity being stifled. So the agreement had been that she would be the one who did that sort of work. She would free him to follow his own course. And what had he done? She thought of Sarah, all freshness and curves and ripeness. Just for a moment she imagined them in bed together and then she caught herself. What right did she have even to think such a thing? She thought of herself and Saul. Herself and Saul in bed together. What a farce it all was.

As she opened the front door, Fletcher was standing right in front of her, like a rebuke. She gave a start and at the same time felt a huge pang of regret and shame.

'There's someone here for you,' he said.

Neve walked into the living room. A woman was sitting in an armchair. When she saw Neve, she stood up. She was wearing a grey suit and Neve recognised her immediately. She was the detective who had accompanied Hitching to the office. She took out her identification and showed it to Neve.

'I'm DC Ingram,' she said. 'Hitching wants to talk to you.'

'When he wants to talk to me, he usually just turns up at the house, or at the office.'

'If you'd just come with me. There's a car outside.'

'I was about to go to work.'

'You can phone them in the car.'

'Has something happened?'

Ingram gestured towards the door. 'Please,' she said.

Neve mumbled a few words to Fletcher and then she didn't speak for the next twenty minutes. She sat in the back of the car and looked out of the window without seeing anything as it drove towards Holborn. They drove round the back of the station through a heavily reinforced gate. She got out in a walled car park alongside armoured vans and was led into a small back door, along a corridor and up some grey concrete stairs that looked like a fire escape. They met nobody, saw nobody, though there was a sound of voices. She was led into a room with no windows, no pictures, no decoration, a simple table and three steel and moulded plastic chairs. Ingram placed one of the chairs next to the table and gestured Neve to sit down. Then she left the room. Neve took out her phone. No signal. There was a sound of footsteps and the door opened and Hitching came in, followed by Ingram. He was holding a bundle of folders and something else – Neve couldn't make out what – something electronic. He put both of them on the table.

He sat down opposite her and gave a rueful smile, as if all of this were a joke they were sharing. Neve thought to herself that Hitching was playing the part of a man who was a friend as much as a detective. And herself? What part should she be playing?

'I'm sorry about all of this,' he said. 'Apparently some higher-ups don't approve of me just chatting with witnesses. This probably seems horribly official.'

'That's all right.'

Ingram closed the door. She moved the other chair so that it was on Neve's left side, just out of her eyeline, and sat down. Hitching smiled again.

'We're going to record the interview, if that's all right.'

He took the device – it was like a large phone or a small laptop without the top – and laid it in front of him.

'We used to use cassettes,' he said, with a frown. 'I understood cassettes. Now it's something digital. No idea how it works. But I'm going to switch it on now.' He pressed a button and then leaned over and looked down at the machine. 'At least with cassettes you could see the things going round. I don't even know if it's working. Is it working?'

Ingram got up and walked across, her heels clicking on the linoleum. She leaned over.

'It's working,' she said. 'That red light flashes when it's working.'

Then she walked back to her chair and sat down.

'Right,' said Hitching, raising his voice slightly. 'Present are DCI Alastair Hitching, that's me. DC Louise Ingram. And Ms Neve Connolly. The interview is taking place in IR1 in West Central Station and the day is Monday September the twenty-fourth. So. Where were we?' He looked at Neve and smiled again. 'I should say that despite all the paraphernalia, this is a voluntary interview and you can leave at any time. Also, you've got a right to independent legal advice.'

'Do you think I need independent legal advice?'

'It's not for me to say. I'm just meant to remind you.'

'All right,' said Neve.

'You mean that you're happy to answer questions?'

'I'm not exactly happy. But yes.'

Hitching flicked through the folders. He selected one and opened it in front of him but he didn't look down at it.

'The file,' he said. 'The one that was pushed through Mrs Stevenson's door. The one with your name on it. The one with the stain.'

'Yes, I know the one.'

'It's been tested. It was blood, as we suspected.'

'I don't see how—'

'Do you want to know whose blood?'

Neve felt panic pumping through her. He was going to tell her something she didn't want to hear.

'Whose?' she managed to say.

'It was yours.'

'*My* blood?' Neve felt the room tip slightly. She stared at him and he looked back at her. He wasn't smiling any longer.

'Yes. Have you any thoughts on that?'

Neve had many thoughts. Many thoughts and many questions. The first was: how could they tell it was her blood? Then she remembered: the DNA sample in the office. How could her blood have got on the file? There had been lots of blood in the flat, but none of it was hers. She had cut her thumb that day, but that had been when she was wearing rubber gloves, which she had thrown away. She was sure it couldn't have got on anything. Besides, the file hadn't been in the flat. Or maybe it had and been removed later. Mabel was adamant she hadn't taken it. Mabel . . . she wrenched her thoughts back to the interview. All she knew was that she had to be very, very careful. Keep it short. Act like a normal person.

'I'm totally baffled,' she said. 'That's all I can say.'

'Look at it from my point of view,' said Hitching, leaning back in his chair. 'Whatever I do, it seems that all roads lead to Neve Connolly. Everyone talks to you, confides in you. You know their secrets before I do.'

'That's not true.'

'Bernice Stevenson told you about her suspicions before me. Renata Searle confessed her affair to you. I come round to your house and half the people I want to speak to are there.'

'Hardly.'

'And then, at the murder scene, the personnel files of your colleagues are there but yours is missing. Then yours turns up and not only that, it has a holiday photo of you inside and it has your blood on it. Please, Neve, I'm on your side. But you need to give me something to work with.'

Neve didn't believe for a second that Hitching was on her side.

'I don't know why you're asking me,' she said. 'Why would I even have that file? And if I did have it, how would I get blood on it? And if I did have it and get blood on it, why on earth would I push it through Bernice Stevenson's door?'

'Who suggested that you did?'

There was a long pause.

'Was there anything else on the file?' Neve asked.

'Like what?'

'Like fingerprints.'

Hitching rapped the table. 'Now that is a good question,' he said.

'What's the answer?'

'There were no fingerprints on the file.'

'Apart from Bernice Stevenson's.'

Hitching looked at her sharply. 'Why do you say that?'

'I just assumed,' said Neve. 'A letter is pushed through her door, she picks it up, looks at it.'

'You're right,' said Hitching. 'I meant no fingerprints apart from Mrs Stevenson's.'

'Although her fingerprints might have got on the envelope some other way.'

'What do you mean by that?'

'It was just a comment.'

'You mean that Bernice Stevenson was lying about how she got the file. Are you making an accusation?'

'I was just making a comment.'

Without answering, Hitching took another file and opened it.

'This is your personnel file,' he said. 'I mean a copy of your file. We wouldn't want to get any prints on it by mistake.'

Neve tried to read the writing, even though it was upside down. All she could make out clearly were her details at the top of the page.

'They can't even get my address right,' she said.

'What?'

'It says fifty-seven. We live at seventy-five.'

'It's just a typing error,' he said.

'If they can get that wrong, what else can they get wrong?'

Another slow smile from Hitching. 'You sound like a defence barrister,' he said.

'It's just a comment.'

'Another one of your comments.' He leaned back in his chair and looked up at the ceiling as if he were deep in thought. Then he looked back at Neve. 'I've just been looking at the description of the murder scene and I've got a couple of comments of my own.'

Neve didn't reply. She felt she had already said too much. From now on she would say as little as she could.

'The murder scene was cleaned up,' he said. 'Really cleaned up. Not just around the body. It felt as if everything had been scrubbed. But I've told you that, haven't I?' Neve didn't reply. 'Everything back in its place, all surfaces clear. I wish the woman who cleaned my house did that. I keep saying to her: clean, don't just dust. But there's no telling her. But whoever went over that flat cleaned everything. But there was a funny thing. In the freezer, there was a bottle of gin and two glasses. You know, the kind you have cocktails in.'

Neve hadn't thought to look in the freezer. They had drunk dry martinis out of those glasses once. Afterwards she had felt him, warm between her cold lips. She kept her eyes on Hitching's face.

'It was just a pied-à-terre. Why did he have two glasses?'

Guilty people stayed silent, thought Neve. She had to say something.

'In case someone came round?' she said.

'Such as?'

'His wife?'

'She almost never went to the flat,' he said. 'At least that's what she told me.'

'Someone else then. How would I know?'

That place has always looked to me like somewhere for assignations. Like the one with your friend, Renata. Renata Searle. What do you think about that?'

'You keep asking me for my opinion,' said Neve. 'I don't think anything about it.'

'She said that her affair with Saul Stevenson was over. But these glasses in the freezer suggest something different.'

'No, they don't.'

'Why?'

'They could have been left in the freezer for weeks. Months.'

'There's nothing you've observed about your friend?'

'She only told me about the affair a couple of days ago.'

'Oh, yes, of course. That's what you said.'

'Yes.'

'But was she telling the truth?' He leaned forward slightly. 'Were you?'

'Yes.' Even the truth felt like a lie now.

Hitching nodded slowly, several times, as if he was considering this. The silence grew until Neve thought she would have to scream or throw something, just to break it. She laced her hands in her lap and squeezed them together, feeling her wedding ring biting into her flesh.

'Mr Stevenson's assistant is sure that an affair was still going on.'

'Katie? How would she know?'

'She seems to have known almost everything about his life. It was like her job. And her hobby as well.'

'The affair with Renata?' It came to Neve suddenly that by concealing her own involvement with Saul, she might, horribly, be incriminating Renata. She leaned forward and said urgently: 'I'm sure Renata told the truth. It was over.'

'I didn't say *the* affair, I said *an* affair.'

Neve kept her eyes locked on his face. She couldn't speak, but she mustn't look away.

'The question is,' Hitching said at last, 'how did your blood get on to the folder?'

'I have no idea.'

'No idea? I'm assuming that you don't leave your blood around in different places.'

'It's not just that. I've never seen the file. I didn't even know it existed until a couple of days ago.'

Hitching leaned forward and looked at her more closely. 'You took a bit of a knock, though?'

'What?'

He gestured towards her face.

'I came off my bike. On to my face.'

'Bled a bit?'

'A bit.'
'When was that?'
'Several days ago.'
'Before Mr Stevenson died?'
'Yes.'
'Just before?'
'A few days I think.'
'Not the same day?'
'No.'
'Any witnesses?'
'No. But I came home with bruises and scrapes. My family would remember.'
'Your family?'
'Yes.'
Hitching didn't look impressed.
'Anyway, there's an example of bleeding.'
'It doesn't matter. I've never seen the file.'
'The file in which there was a photo of you.'
Neve nodded.
'You on holiday.' He slid a plastic envelope with the photo inside towards her. There she was once again, laughing, wind blowing her hair. 'Why would that be in there?'
'I don't know.'
'Did you give it to Mr Stevenson?'
'No.' Again, another small piece of truth that was sucked into the swirl of lies.
'I know you've answered this question before but I'm going to ask it again. What was your relationship to Mr Stevenson?'

'I worked with him.'

'Nothing more?'

'No.'

'Did you ever go to his flat?'

Neve's mind scrabbled and went blank. What had she told him before?

'As I told you: I went once,' she said. 'To deliver something.'

'Ah yes. The mysterious delivery. And that was the only time?'

'Yes.'

Between each of her answers Hitching left a long pause. Neve knew she mustn't speak into it, but it was hard not to. The silence was so frightful.

'And there's nothing else you want to tell me?'

'I can't think of anything.'

She was beyond trying to work out how an innocent person would behave and was simply holding to a line that wouldn't open the trap door beneath her feet.

'Remind me,' said Hitching. 'Where were you on the morning of Saul Stevenson's death?'

'At the allotment,' said Neve. She knew what he was going to say next.

'With your daughter?'

'Yes.' Was that the right answer or should she have said that Mabel had been mistaken? Too late now.

'Is there anyone who could corroborate that?'

'I don't think so.'

'It must be a busy time of year for gardeners.'

'It was Wednesday morning.'

'Nobody around?'

'There might well have been. I didn't notice.'

'Let's go back to that photo. Can you think of how it got into the folder?'

'No.'

'When did you last see it yourself?'

'I don't know.'

That was true as well: she didn't know. She had been straining to remember when she had last noticed it on the corkboard.

Then he asked the question she had been waiting for. 'Do you know where it came from?'

'The photo?'

'Yes.' He sat back in the chair and folded his arms. 'Do you know where the photograph was before it mysteriously ended up in the folder?'

'Yes,' said Neve. She had no idea if that was a dangerous admission or one that helped her. She was putting one foot in front of the other and everything else was a blur.

Hitching raised his eyebrows. 'Where?'

'It was on the corkboard in the kitchen, near the door to the hall. There are lots of family photos pinned up there. That was one of them.'

'You're sure?'

'Yes.'

'When did you notice it was missing?'

'Not until you showed it to me. But I think it must have gone recently.'

'Why?'

'I would have seen it wasn't there.'

'Really? Because it was special to you?'

'Because there's a space in the collage of photos.'

'So you're saying that someone took it from the board recently and put it into the folder – on which, don't forget, there is your blood.'

'Yes. And pushed that folder through Bernice's front door.'

'You think you're being framed?'

'I can only tell you what I know.'

He smiled at her. Her skin prickled. 'Indeed.' He waited for a few seconds, considering, then said, 'You chose not to tell me you knew where the photo came from. Why is that?'

'I didn't *choose*. You didn't ask until now.' That sounded wrong. 'I would have told you. I didn't notice at once. And then there were so many questions coming at me.' Neve forced a smile. Her face felt stiff. 'I'm just trying to be as clear as I can about everything.'

Hitching gave a snort. 'You call this being clear?'

'In what way is it not being clear? I've answered all your questions.'

'If "I don't know" is an answer.'

'"I don't know" is an answer if I don't know.'

'Your allotment—'

'We're going around in circles,' said Neve, who felt that at any moment she would simply collapse and blurt out the truth, just to have this over with. 'You said I was free to go at any time, right?'

'That's right.'

'Then I'd like to go. Please.'

Hitching and Ingram exchanged glances and Hitching shrugged.

'Then go.' He leaned over and switched off the recorder and then looked up at her with an expression different from anything she'd seen before.

'Remember, if you're holding anything back, I'll find out.'

Neve went down the stairs, along the corridor, out through the main entrance of the station, into the thin drizzle and roar of traffic. She tried to walk steadily, keeping her back straight. Her legs wobbled and her insides felt scraped out. She thought she might throw up. She reached the road and kept on walking, imagining Hitching and Ingram looking at her out of a window. Breathing made her throat burn. Her eyes felt raw.

When she was sure she was out of sight, she lurched across to a bus stop and sat down there. She put her head in her hands and shut her eyes and waited for the terror to subside. What had she said? Had she said anything that would ambush her? She couldn't remember; all she could remember was Hitching's face and her sense of dread.

At last she stood up and stared around her. Nothing looked familiar. Her own hands, when she held them in front of her, seemed to belong to a stranger. She looked at her watch: it was nearly a quarter past eleven. When she pulled her mobile from her pocket she saw that there was a missed call from Gary and a text from Tamsin asking her where she was.

She made her way slowly to Old Street, feeling she was walking up a steep hill. Her heart was still hammering uncomfortably. People bumped into her, or maybe she bumped into them, unsteady on her feet. Hitching would talk to Mabel about the alibi, she thought – and the thought made her mouth furry with dread. Perhaps she should call Mabel and warn her. She rang Mabel's mobile but it went straight to voicemail. She thought of ringing the landline but she didn't want to talk to Fletcher.

Coming out of the lift, she saw Katie approaching her.

'You're rather late,' she said.

'Dentist,' replied Neve. She put hand to her jaw.

'Problems with your teeth?'

Neve remembered that she had used the same excuse for a couple of her assignations with Saul. She remembered what Hitching had said about Katie: that she was sure an affair had been continuing.

'I have,' she said. Another stupid lie that could be found out.

'Someone told me that Bernice has been staying with you.'

'She came round. She didn't stay.'

'I didn't know you knew her.'

'I don't really. It was just one of those things.'

Neve heard herself talking, a stream of meaningless words issuing from her mouth. She saw Katie looking at her intently, a little crease between her eyes.

301

'I need to get to work,' she said. 'Make up for lost time.'

'How's that brochure coming on?'

'Just a few details,' said Neve. She couldn't even remember what it was she was supposed to be doing.

'Bob was asking.'

'Tell him it's all good.'

'Where have you been?' demanded Tamsin.

'Dentist.' Again, she touched her jaw in a weird reflex. Even her fingers were lying, she thought.

'Again?'

'Dentist is the adult's equivalent of the dog ate my homework,' said Gary. He was wearing a pullover with a zig-zag pattern on it that made Neve's eyes throb.

'Bob was looking for you,' said Tamsin. 'He wants to know about the brochure.'

'I know. Where's Renata?'

'She rang to say she's feeling a bit rough and she's not coming in until this afternoon,' said Gary. 'I think she's still at your house.'

'Oh. Right.'

'I'm going to the printers in a few minutes. You and Tamsin will have to hold the fort.'

Neve turned on her computer. She pulled up her work on the brochure for the pharmaceutical conference and stared at it. It was being held over two days and there were eight keynote speakers. She didn't even know what the difference between a keynote speaker and any old speaker was. There was an image of the face of each of them: two women and six men and they were all smiling and seemed to have very white teeth. Again she touched her jaw. She stared at the words: 'digital health ecosystem', 'genomics', 'healthcare big data', 'augmented reality in healthcare solutions' ... She experimented with the font, returned it to what she'd already selected, changed an awkward line break, sighed heavily.

'I'm off,' said Gary, taking his ratty old jacket from the back of the chair.

'How about lunch,' said Tamsin as soon as he'd left.

'It's a bit early,' said Neve. 'I've only been here about half an hour. And the brochure's running out of time.'

'Yes, but you look a bit peaky. Let's go to that salad bar.'

Neve had an aubergine and chickpea salad and Tamsin a violently green and gloopy drink made largely of spinach. They sat at a table at the back.

'Are you OK?' asked Tamsin.

'Don't I seem OK?'

'You look a bit tired.'

'The weekend was crazy. I haven't recovered yet.'

Tamsin nodded. She took a mouthful of her drink and when she next spoke there was a froth of green on her lips.

'So what's your secret?' she asked.

Neve felt a jolt go through her. She made a strange noise.

'You and Fletcher,' said Tamsin. 'The last ones standing.'

'Oh.' Neve put the aubergine into her mouth and chewed it very slowly to give herself time. 'I don't know,' she said when she could trust herself to speak. 'All marriage is hard, isn't it?'

'But you two are nice to each other. You don't put each other down or argue with each other.'

'We've not been perfect,' said Neve. Then before she lost her nerve, she said, 'Why did you cover for me?'

'What?'

'When you said to Fletcher that I'd been with you last Tuesday evening.'

'Oh that,' said Tamsin. 'I didn't think you needed an alibi!' She gave a laugh. 'But you're always at everyone's beck and call. Your last few years, everything with Mabel, with Fletcher, and the boys, and all the changes with work – you must need to be on your own sometimes, not telling everyone where you are and not able to be reached by anyone, answerable to no one.'

'I do,' said Neve fervently. 'I do need that.'

'So that's why.'

'Thank you.'

'You're welcome.' She finished her green drink. 'That wasn't actually very nice.'

'Healthy though.'

'I guess.' She waited a few moments. 'Can I ask you something?'

'Sure.'

'Did you ever have an affair or anything like that?'

Tamsin looked at her for a moment then she wiped her mouth on the paper napkin.

304

'We've all done things we wished we hadn't.'

'Does that mean yes?'

'It just means that everyone behaves badly some-times, me included. Everyone has things in their life they're ashamed of.'

'That's true.'

'So what are yours?'

Neve made herself laugh. It sounded horribly fake to her.

'That's not fair,' she said. 'You wouldn't tell me so now I'm not telling you. Anyway,' she looked at her watch. 'We should get back. That brochure isn't going to finish itself.'

Renata came in at two. She was wearing one of Neve's shirts under one of Neve's jackets and when they hugged, Neve could smell that she had sprayed herself with Neve's perfume. Her hair was clean and smelled of Neve's shampoo and her face looked fresher.

'It's amazing the things you can't do when you only have the use of one hand,' she said. 'I have no idea how I'm going to get any work done. Mabel helped me wash. And Will made me brunch.'

'What?'

'Poached eggs.'

'Will?'

'He's back,' said Renata cheerfully. 'And Jackie's back. And a friend of Jackie's, called Frederika I think. Hair in bunches like a ten year old.'

'At my house?'

'Yes.'

She felt a bone-crushing weariness. 'Don't they have jobs?'

'They're going to finish putting up the greenhouse. I think it's become like a challenge. Although Fletcher says they'll have to dismantle some of it first because they've done it wrong.'

'My God,' said Neve. 'They're never going to leave.'

'Do you mind me being there?'

'Of course not, but you're my close friend, almost my family. I hardly know these people.'

'They feel they know you.' Renata's tone was dry. 'They seem thoroughly at home.'

They settled down at their desks. Katie put her head round the door to say that the following afternoon there would be an office meeting for everyone to discuss the changes that would be implemented following Saul's death. That didn't sound good. Neve made desultory adjustments to the brochure. She called Gary, who was still with the printers, to find out when she could get a proof if she sent the material to them by close of day. Fragments of her interview with Hitching kept returning to her, though most of it remained an appalling blank.

Looking up, she saw that Renata was sitting with her chin in her uninjured hand, staring towards the smeared window; she didn't seem able to concentrate on work either. The earrings that Saul had given her were glinting in her lobes.

'Renata?'

'Yes?'

'Where did you say that Saul got your earrings?'

Renata raised a hand and touched one of them.

'I probably shouldn't be wearing them. You know the place: Farfelou, in Covent Garden.'

Neve nodded. She was thinking about the present that Saul had ordered for her and had said would arrive in time for her birthday. Could it be from there?

She did a surreptitious search on her computer for the shop and keyed the number on to her mobile. Then she stood up.

'I'm going to get us all some coffee,' she said. 'The usual?'

They nodded and she left their little room, went down the stairs and out on to the pavement, where the drizzle was turning to rain. She rang the number and a man with a French accent answered.

'I'm ringing on behalf of Saul Stevenson,' Neve said, trying to adopt a professional tone. 'I hope you can help me.'

'Of course.'

'He ordered some jewellery recently,' said Neve. 'It was going to be sent to him. I just wanted to check if it was ready yet.'

'Wait one moment.'

There was a pause. Neve could hear voices in the background.

'It's all done,' said the man at last.

'Done?'

'The engraving, yes.'

'Oh yes. The engraving,' said Neve. She took a deep breath. '"Neve", wasn't it?'

'No,' said the voice and she felt a rush of relief. 'No, it says "Neve Jenny".' Her relief instantly evaporated.

'Of course. Perhaps I could collect it, since I'm in the area.'

'It has already been sent.'

She swallowed hard and tried to iron out the quaver in her voice. 'Would that be to Flat Three, Hilhurst Street?'

'That's right.'

'When was it sent?'

'This morning I believe. So it will arrive very soon. Tomorrow probably. It's a beautiful piece of work. I hope Mr Stevenson is pleased.'

'I'm sure he will be,' said Neve.

She ended the call. A man in a grey-green suit walked towards her. He had dark hair and blue eyes and he was smiling at her. For a moment, it was Saul and joy and relief rose in her like a great bird.

Of course he wasn't Saul. He was nothing like Saul. And anyway, she had seen Saul dead with his skull caved in and his eyes sightless. She had crouched over his body, searching in his pockets. She stood motionless in the gathering rain, feeling it drip down her neck.

The present was coming. *Very soon.* 'Neve Jenny' engraved on a piece of jewellery, because Jenny kissed me when we met.

She went back into the building and bought three

coffees – a flat white, a double espresso and an Americano – and took them back to the office where she sat at her computer and stared at the screen and saw nothing but Hitching's unsmiling face looking back at her.

Neve went to the Ladies and looked at herself in the mirror: circles of exhaustion under her eyes, a fading bruise on her cheek. She touched it gently. Hitching presumably thought she'd got it from Saul, that they had fought and then she had killed him. Her blood was on the folder. Her photo was in the folder. Who had taken it from the corkboard? When? It must have been recently or she would have noticed the space where it used to be.

She thought back over the last few days, then went back to her desk and tore a piece of paper from her pad. She made another list, this time of all the people who had passed through the house since the death:

*Renata*
*Gary*
*Tamsin*
*Bernice*
*Will*
*Jackie*
*Sarah*
*Louis*

She remembered the young man who had been in a struggle with the stuck armchair on the night of

Renata's dreadful party: she couldn't remember his name so just wrote 'Mabel's friend with chair'.

She added Elias and Rory and Connor, though that was clearly ridiculous, then Fletcher and then, with a dragging pen, Mabel. Still Mabel.

Who else? There was Hitching of course – she wrote down his name; then Ingram.

And Charlie had been there – she remembered the look of stony hatred on his face when he came to take Renata away. He would want to kill Saul, or even his own wife – but why her?

She stared at the names until they were like hiero-glyphs on the page. One came into focus. She stood up.

'I've got a few things I should do.'

'Another dentist's appointment?' Tamsin grinned.

'A few tasks.' Neve made a vague gesture.

As she crossed the office she saw Katie sitting at her desk, in the room next to the empty one where Saul used to sit and which still hadn't been cleared. Katie stared at her. Even when Neve nodded in greeting, she didn't smile.

Neve phoned ahead to check and then took the under-ground to Liverpool Street and caught a train. They went every fifteen minutes. She needed to think but as she looked out of the window she lost herself in the sight of north-east London flashing past her, the office buildings and then the Olympic Park and Hackney Marshes and the reservoirs, all the time snaking back-wards and forwards across the Lea River. There were the scrubby, dishevelled edge lands around the North Circular, shopping centres and factories, and then they crossed the M25 and suddenly she was looking at countryside and in what seemed like a few minutes they had arrived at Roydon. She looked at her phone and checked the address. Getting off, she felt like she was in a little country station but was immediately walking through a series of streets that could have been in the suburbs of London. In a way they were. The streets felt deserted. The people who had had breakfast here were in London. They wouldn't be back until dinner time.

Neve checked her phone again. Yes, this was it. Number Twelve, Malden Road. It was a large, detached house, set back from the road, and shielded by a high thick hedge. She looked around. There were similar houses on both sides of the road. Opposite a man was cutting his own hedge, carefully shaping it with an electric cutter. He was wearing an orange helmet with ear protectors and he didn't notice her at first. When he did, he switched off his cutter, laid it down and took off his helmet. His florid puffy face was sweating profusely.

'Are you a journalist?' he said.

'Why do you say that?'

'I've already talked to the police. So I thought you must be a journalist.'

'I'm a friend of Bernice's. Bernice Stevenson.'

The man didn't reply. He wiped his brow with his sleeve. He was breathing heavily.

'What did the police want to know?'

'They wanted to know if I saw anyone hanging around the house opposite.'

'It's what they say about the countryside, isn't it?' said Neve. 'Everybody notices strangers.'

The man shook his head. 'It used to be like that. Now there are deliveries all bloody day, even on Sundays. You lose track.' He frowned. 'Anyway. What's it to you?'

'I just want to reassure Bernice.'

'She's got other things to worry about.'

'Did you know Saul?'

The man shrugged.

'Only to say hello to. He was never around.'

Neve walked back across the road and knocked at the door of Number Twelve. The door was opened not by Bernice but by a young man, almost a boy. He was very thin and pale with straight dark hair. He was wearing black trousers and a blue tee shirt with wavy orange lines across it. His socks were different colours.

'Mum,' he shouted, very loudly and then padded away. Neve stepped into a large entrance hall. Ahead of her was a wide staircase and there were various closed doors. One at the back opened revealing Bernice in dark, well-ironed trousers and a pink ribbed sweater.

'I thought I'd hear from you,' she said.

She turned and led Neve through a large sitting room into an equally large kitchen that occupied a conservatory backing on to a sweeping lawn surrounded by rose bushes and trees. Neve walked to the glass wall and looked out.

'Are they apple trees?'

'And pear trees and one cherry tree. The birds get all the cherries, though.'

A few minutes later, they were sitting at the wooden kitchen table with mugs of coffee. The light through the glass was so bright that Neve wished she'd brought sunglasses.

'It's good of you to see me,' she said.

'I've been to your house, now you've come to mine,' said Bernice. Her glance slid over Neve's face.

'I'm sorry about the other evening,' Neve said.

'That wasn't your fault,' said Bernice. 'I hope you didn't come all this way to apologise.'

'This morning I was interviewed by the police.'

'Because of the file.'

'Because of the file.'

'I read it,' said Bernice. 'I probably shouldn't have. It's like reading someone's mail. You shouldn't do it but it's hard to resist.'

'It can't have been very interesting,' said Neve, trying to adopt a light tone.

'I found it quite interesting. You're eight years younger than me, for one thing. Also, I read Saul's assessment of you, in his own handwriting. It's funny, now that he's dead, it feels completely different reading something he's written. I pictured him sitting there, thinking what word he should use.'

'I can imagine.'

'Yours was favourable, by the way. More than favourable. Glowing. I can remember phrases from it: "a valuable asset", "key member of the team". He was considering promoting you. I thought you'd like to hear that.'

'What I really wanted to talk about was it being pushed through your door. Didn't it seem very odd to you? Someone just coming all the way out to Roydon, just to deliver it. Why not just give it to the police?'

'All the way out to Roydon,' said Bernice with a smile. 'I suppose it does seem as if we're out in the sticks.'

'I didn't mean that.'

'We're not so far out. Did you come on the train?'

'Yes.'

'How long did it take? Half an hour? Forty minutes?'

'About that.'

'Quite. So I should have always known,' said Bernice. 'He bought that bloody flat fifteen years ago because he said it would be a good investment and a good place for him to stay when he had to work late, go to functions. Did he really need to buy a flat in Covent Garden when he could get home in less than an hour? I should have known from the start what it was really for.'

'Did you never stay there?'

'I used to drop my shopping there sometimes. I stayed there once or twice after going to the theatre. It felt like staying in a hotel room. The sheets were always fresh. He never washed the sheets at home but when I stayed in the flat, the sheets were always clean.'

Neve looked away from her, out of the window.

'You know what I think?' said Bernice. 'Saul married someone because she was clever and interesting and not

314

bad-looking and gradually watched her become boring and less good-looking. He even encouraged us to move out here. He said it would be good for me. And he said the schools would be better for Matt. He was wrong about me. He was wrong about Matt as well.'

'I'm sorry.'

'Still, Saul was right about one thing. The flat was a good investment. It's worth more than this house. So that's something.'

Neve left a pause that was long enough to sound sympathetic and so that she could change the subject without seeming callous. Change it *back*.

'I was asking about the file,' she said. 'About why it was delivered here and not straight to the police. Did you notice it being delivered?'

'It was just there on the mat when I came down in the morning. I got up pretty late.' Bernice gave a hollow laugh. 'I was tired after the excitements of your dinner party.'

'So you didn't see anyone deliver it?'

'No. I must have been asleep.'

'You don't have one of those exterior lights that are set off by intruders?'

'I was warned off those,' said Bernice. 'I was told they'd just be set off by cats wandering past.'

'What time did you get to sleep?'

'You sound like Hitching. Questions, questions.' Her tone seemed mocking or maybe Neve was imagining that.

'It's just that it was my folder.'

'I finally went to sleep at about three in the morning.'

'Three. OK.'

'I got an Uber all the way back here. The driver was very happy.'

'And when did you wake up?'

'Half past nine? Maybe a bit earlier?'

'So someone pushed it through your letter box between three and nine?'

'That's right.'

'Was your son here?'

'No. He was with my sister.' Bernice looked at Neve through narrowed eyes. 'You've come to my home. All the way out here, as you put it. You've been interviewed by the police. Why did this happen? Why *your* file?'

'That's why I wanted to talk to you. I've no idea.'

'You asked the question yourself. Why give *your* file to *me* and not to the police?'

Neve hesitated. She spoke carefully. 'Perhaps someone is trying to cause confusion.'

'What kind of confusion?'

'Suspicion?'

'Suspicion of who? What for?'

Neve had come here to ask questions and now she felt that she was the one who was being interrogated.

'I was part of a small company that was taken over. Saul was our boss. Or one of our bosses. There was some bad feeling about it.'

'From you?' said Bernice. 'Did you have bad feelings towards Saul?'

'We'd been independent. We'd been our own bosses. Some people found that difficult to give up.'

'And they blamed Saul?'

'Some people were disappointed. They didn't blame Saul, though. Or I certainly didn't.'

The conversation had become diverted. The issue for Neve wasn't who might have wanted to kill Saul. It was who might have wanted to kill *her*.

'Do you mind if I ask you something personal?' she said.

Bernice gave a sharp laugh. 'It's a bit late to mind that.'

Neve swallowed; her throat felt painful.

'How would you have reacted if you had found out about the affair? I mean, when he was alive.'

Bernice's eyes flickered and she looked around and put a finger to her lips as Matt entered the kitchen, opened the fridge and took out a carton of milk. He took a bowl from the cupboard and poured some cereal from a packet and added the milk and started to eat it, standing up.

'This is Neve,' said Bernice. 'She used to work with Saul.'

He inclined his head slightly. Suddenly, with that movement, he reminded Neve of his father. It was like a ghost had wandered past her. At the same time, it occurred to her that he was just a few months younger than Mabel.

'I'm so very sorry about your father,' she said. 'It's a terrible, terrible thing.'

Matt took some time to swallow his mouthful. 'That's all right,' he said.

Neve stood up. 'I should go.'

Bernice followed her to the front door. They shook hands.

'Is there something you're not telling me?' Bernice said.

'How do you mean?'

'That photo of you inside the folder.'

'Oh.'

'It was nice. You looked happy.'

Neve looked across at Bernice. She had cut her hand at that wretched dinner party, she thought: that was where the blood had come from. Bernice had been there; everyone had been there.

'I was happy,' she said.

'Funny it was in your file though.'

'Yes. Funny.'

Neve walked back to Roydon station. A crowd was flooding out of the entrance, men and women in suits, phones pressed to their ears. Rush hour was beginning, commuters returning home. She thought how most of them did this day in and day out, how Saul used to be among them. She almost expected to see him now, stepping towards her in his sharp suit. He once referred to his 'whistle' with an ironic smile. She had been puzzled and he'd laughed. Whistle and flute. Suit. Rhyming slang. Didn't she know? She said she didn't know and he laughed again and kissed her. She looked up at the departures board; a train to Liverpool Street was due in a few minutes. She turned and left the station.

She didn't know where she was going but her feet took her down a little road with houses petering out, then a sunken land, and suddenly, improbably, she was in countryside. There were blackberries in the hedgerow; beyond it a stubble field. Brown and yellow leaves drifted down from the oak and ash trees. She remembered how as a child she and her brother would try to catch them as they fell: a caught leaf meant a day of happiness.

She heard a sound and at first she thought it was the wind in the trees, but realised it was water, and saw that in the crease between two fields ran a small, brown river. She climbed over a gate and walked across the field to get to it. A bit further down it was shallower and full of eddies, but here it was slow and quite deep, and when she leaned forward to trail her fingers in the water, she found it was cool but not cold. She took her clothes off and laid them on the grass and slid in. Her feet touched the soft muddy bottom and she pushed herself clear, diving under the surface.

She often swam, but usually in swimming pools, counting off the lengths. This was different. This was a release from the self. Just her and the water and the trees and the sky. She swam very slowly against the current, and then she let herself drift with her eyes half closed. She didn't think, but thoughts and images flowed through her.

The photo in the folder that someone had taken from the corkboard in the last few days.

The blood that frantic evening: blood everywhere, Charlie in a foul temper, Bernice glassy-eyed, someone with a roll of kitchen towel. Her own minor cut, and her own blood. Someone tending to it?

The poem she had written out for Saul and hadn't been able to find in the flat. Was that going to be next?

The present, a piece of jewellery engraved with her name, on its way to the flat. A little package, a ticking bomb.

She lay back, looking up at the shifting grey sky. Hammer. Photo. Folder. Blood. Poem. Present. Each of these objects were pieces of evidence that could incriminate her. Taken together, they could be made to look like proof that she had murdered Saul. They had been lovers, she had been at the flat on the morning of his death, she had cleared up the crime scene. Every single thing she had done since then, every lie she had told and every truth she had concealed, would confirm it.

All she could do now, her only hope, was to find out who was the real killer. And then the thought slid into her mind again, clean as a blade: *unless it was Mabel*. If she knew it was Mabel, she would go to prison in her place without hesitation.

She swam back to the bank and scrambled out, shaking off excess water. She felt cold and had difficulty pulling on her clothes. They stuck unpleasantly to her skin. The river looked uninviting now. She was wet and cold and muddy, and the day was darkening.

# 7

# CLOSING TIME

When she reached Liverpool Street, she didn't go straight home. She took the train to King's Cross and a bus, wishing she was on her bike. Gary's flat was above a fruit and veg shop in Crouch End. She realised with a stab of guilt that she hadn't been there for ages; she couldn't remember the last time. Years ago, they all used to gather there quite regularly, drink wine and beer, smoke, play poker, order in takeaways, argue about politics till the early hours. Nowadays Gary spent most of his time with Jane and made it clear Jane didn't want people round, or he went out without her, usually to Neve and Fletcher's house. She couldn't remember the last time she had actually seen Jane, though they used to be quite close.

Gary had said he was going straight home from the printer's, so she assumed he'd be there now. It was nearly six o'clock and there were three messages on her phone from Fletcher, asking what time she'd be back. She didn't want to think about Fletcher, about Fletcher and Sarah. About her and Fletcher. Everything like that had to wait. Even while she was pushing the thought of Fletcher away, she was asking herself if he would visit her in prison, and at the thought of a trial and prison, a terror rose in her so sharp and pure it tasted like hot metal in her mouth and she couldn't move for a moment.

She rang the doorbell and Gary's voice crackled on the little intercom.

'Yes?'

'It's me, Neve.'

'Neve? What are you doing? Is everything all right?'

'Can I come up?'

'I'll come down.'

She waited. The door swung open and Gary was there in a ratty old tee shirt and jogging trousers. He blinked at her.

'Can I come in for a minute?'

'What's up?'

'Does anything have to be up? I was near and so I thought I'd come and see you. It's been ages.'

He didn't reply, just stared at her with a strange expression.

'I'm sorry,' said Neve. 'I know I should have come before now, I know you've been having a hard time, but I wasn't sure if Jane wanted visitors and then everything with Mabel, and now all that's been happening . . .' She trailed off. Gary still didn't move.

'A cup of tea, maybe,' said Neve.

'We could go to the place on the corner,' said Gary.

'Is Jane in bed?'

'No.'

'Then let me at least say hello.'

'It's a bit of a tip.'

'Since when has that mattered to me?'

Neve went up the steep stairs whose threadbare carpet had been there when Gary moved in over twenty years ago. Gary followed her slowly, muttering something under his breath. The door to the flat stood open and she went into the main room. Stopped dead.

'Don't say I didn't warn you,' said Gary behind her.

It wasn't just that it was a mess. It was squalid. And Neve had three children. She was used to squalor but this was different. Just seeing it made Neve depressed. All the mugs and glasses on the surfaces were dirty, some furred with mould. There were takeaway containers everywhere, empty wine bottles, half-crushed beer cans. Dirty clothes. The air was foetid. Neve went over to the window and opened it wide. She turned to Gary.

'We all want to help,' she said.

'Oh, fuck off, Neve.'

'Where's Jane?'

He didn't answer. She went to the kitchen and opened the door, flinching at the state of it. She went to the main bedroom and looked inside. The sheets were in a knot in the middle of the bed and there was a wine bottle lying on the beige carpet in the centre of a red stain. No Jane. Nor in the second bedroom.

'What's going on?' she asked.

Gary shrugged.

'Gary. Please.'

'Nothing.'

'Where's Jane?'

'She left.'

'Left,' repeated Neve stupidly.

'Why not?' asked Gary. He shrugged his bony shoulders. His face looked very thin and his mouth was working.

'Is she in hospital?'

'She's with her parents.'

'I don't understand.'

'It's very simple. Jane. Has. Left. Me.'

'Why?'

'Because I'm up to my ears in debt. Because I can't cope with anything any longer. Because I'm depressed and grumpy and a miserable git. Because this isn't a very nice place to spend the last days of your life. Because it's over.'

'But you've looked after her for years.'

'Well, now her parents are looking after her.'

'When did this happen?'

'May.'

'May! Why didn't you say anything?'

He kicked a beer can out of his way. 'I was ashamed.'

'Oh, Gary—'

'Don't.' He stepped back. 'Don't go pitying me. That's exactly what I mean. I can't bear that.'

'I'm not—'

'You with your big house and your three children and your adoring husband and everyone saying, oh Neve's so lovely, so motherly and comforting, Neve will understand, let's tell Neve.'

She felt like someone had hit her hard in her stomach.

'I didn't mean it to come out like that.'

'It doesn't matter.'

'It does. I know how it's been with Mabel, but oh Christ, I don't know what to do.' He glared at her. 'I literally do not know what to do next.'

Tears began to roll down his face, into his untrimmed beard. Neve looked at him: a small, scruffy, humiliated man helpless in the wreckage of his life. She took his hand and held it.

'I'm going to make us that tea,' she said.

'Very English of you.'

She filled the kettle. Waiting for it to boil, she sent a text to Mabel, asking her where she was.

She thought: *he is furious with the world; he's resentful of me; he's in debt; he's been lying to us for months; he lives alone and so his alibi is false; he could have taken the photo and the blood-soaked tissue; he could have taken the hammer.*

She thought: *he's my dear friend. If I can't trust him, I can't trust anyone.*

She thought: *I can't trust anyone.*

Her mobile rang; it was Mabel but at first Neve couldn't work out what she was saying because she was sobbing and gasping and her words made no sense.

'Slow down,' she said, turning her back on Gary. 'Take some deep breaths and then tell me. What is it?'

'He came and saw me.'

'Who?'

'That detective. He asked about my alibi. I told him what you said. And he asked me what we've got there at the moment. I don't know. I said potatoes or something and then just I couldn't speak. He was so creepy. He kept smiling at me and not talking and waiting for me to say something stupid.'

'OK,' said Neve carefully.

'And he's so big,' wailed Mabel.

'He's gone now. It's over.'

'You don't understand.'

'Tell me.'

'He thinks it was me. He thinks I killed him.'

The room swam slowly around Neve. She picked her way over the debris on the kitchen floor, past Gary, and out on to the landing. She closed the kitchen door.

'What makes you say that?' she managed to ask.

'I know he does. I could tell. He thinks you're covering up for me. He kept talking about you being such a protective mother, things like that. He knows I've had a hard time. How does he know? Did you tell him?'

'Of course not. Listen to me, Mabel. He doesn't know anything.'

'He thinks it was me.' Mabel's voice was rising again.

'He's trying to rattle you.'

'What shall we do?'

'If he really suspects you, then I'll tell him everything and we'll just have to face the consequences,' said Neve.

'No. Don't you see? If you do that, he'll know I've told you he suspects me, and he'll think you're just making up a story to cover up for me. It will only make him more sure. It'll make everything even worse.'

Mabel was crying again.

'No,' said Neve. 'Stop that. It's going to be all right.'

'Do you promise?' Mabel spoke like a small child.

'I promise,' she said and her voice was firm, even though she knew the promise was meaningless.

'Are you back soon?'

'Half an hour,' she said. 'No more.' And she ended the call.

'Everything OK?' Gary was behind her.

'I'm going to have to postpone that tea. I need to go.'

He shrugged. 'Of course. Your busy life.'

'It's Mabel,' she said uselessly. 'But we need to talk this through properly. And let's make a date for us to clear up your flat together.'

'Sure.' The anguish had gone out of him, and what was left felt worse: he seemed parched and hollowed out and disconnected.

She wanted to hug him but he had become untouchable.

She had to take two buses to get home. On the second, staring out at Clissold Park, a thought came to her.

Whoever had killed Saul had sent her a text and then they had let themselves into his flat to wait for her. The door hadn't been forced, so they must either have gone prepared to break in but had found Saul, who wasn't supposed to be there, or they'd had a key. The second of these scenarios made more sense: it would have been too much of a risk to break in; there were people who lived above and below. How did the killer have a key to the flat?

She knew. They had taken it from her.

Shortly before Saul's death, her old backpack had been stolen when she was in a crowded café. Her key had been inside the wallet. Saul had had another one cut for her and she hadn't thought about it again, just put it down to a random thief and her own carelessness.

She was certain that whoever had killed Saul had taken her bag. When was that? She couldn't remember the date but she'd be able to find out because she'd reported her cards missing. In any case, it was in the days leading up to Saul's death.

Fletcher wouldn't have stolen her backpack, she thought. He had no need. It was there in the house every day. But who'd been with her in the café? She thought that Renata and Tamsin had been. What about Gary? She didn't think so but she couldn't remember. But if they'd taken it, where would they have hidden it? But anyone walking past could have unslung it from the back of the chair.

As she looked back over the past days, it felt like everything was tainted, everything was conspiring against her. There were no accidents. She even started to replay her bike accident in her mind, like she was running a film sequence over and over. That shape that had emerged from the edge of her vision, pushing her off her bike, leaving her with cuts and bruises and her grazed and swollen face – was it the hopeless, chaotic drunk person she had imagined or was it deliberate? An attempt to harm her, to kill her? She remembered a lorry rumbling past a few inches from her as she lay in the road. Was it the same person who had stolen her key, sent her the text, killed Saul, taken the photo from her corkboard, who had pushed the blood-smeared folder through Bernice's letterbox, who had taken the hammer from the garden? Someone watching her, tracking her; someone making plans and yet out of control as well, consumed by hatred. Hatred for her. Who would hate her this much?

Neve knew it had to be someone close to her, intimate with her life, perhaps someone who knew that the best way to destroy her was to destroy her daughter as well.

Even as she was thinking this, a few minutes from home, another thought, ghostly and fleeting, snagged at her and then was gone. Like a dream you forget on waking, Neve couldn't recover it. It slid from her mind leaving no trace, just the sense of missing something crucial.

As she was putting the key in the front door and starting to turn it, Mabel opened the door. It was like she had been waiting for her to arrive.

'Where have you been?' Mabel said.

'I went to see Bernice Stevenson.'

'I thought she lived out of London somewhere.'

'I went out to her house. On the train.'

'What for? Is something happening?'

Neve leaned close in to her daughter. She put her arm round her shoulders. She was so thin. She could feel her shoulder blades. Mabel let her hand rest there for a few seconds then stepped away from her. Neve saw how wrung out she looked. She spoke to her in a soft voice as if she feared being overheard.

'You're going to be all right,' she said and her voice was firm. 'I'll make sure of that.'

'How can you?' said Mabel. 'How can you possibly?'

Neve looked out of the back window. Will was bent down over one of the flower beds.

'Why is he still here?' said Neve. 'Does nobody ever leave this house?'

'I think he's doing some weeding.'

'Who said he could do weeding? Weeding is what I do to relax.'

'Renata's with him as well,' said Mabel. 'She's behaving a bit oddly.'

'Oddly how?'

'Giggly. A bit, well, flirty.'

Neve walked through to the kitchen and out into the garden. Will was tugging at a plant. Neve wasn't entirely sure it was a weed. Renata was standing beside him. She had changed out of Neve's clothes that she'd been wearing at work and was now wearing the tee shirt Neve had retrieved from Saul's flat, Neve's leather jacket and Neve's favourite jeans, the legs rolled up with Fletcher's only tie acting as a belt.

'Hello,' she said gaily. Mabel was right: there was something askew about her, a hectic, jangled quality. 'I'm being the assistant gardener.'

'Hey,' said Neve warily. Will looked round at her. 'I thought you had work.'

'I'm my own boss,' he said cheerfully. 'I'm enjoying myself.'

'You shouldn't do this. You really shouldn't.' It was hard to remain calm.

'It's my way of relaxing.'

Neve stifled the impulse to say that there was no need for him to relax or sit around in her house at all. That maybe it was time for him to go back to his own home. But she didn't say it.

He stood up and brushed the soil from his hands. 'There,' he said with satisfaction.

'This is very kind of you, Will.' Neve tried to keep her voice even. 'Though I think that weed you're pulling up might be a plant I bought a few months ago.'

She went upstairs to check on Rory and Connor: Rory was reading and Connor was playing a computer game. She passed the bathroom and saw the door was shut; there were sounds of water running and she frowned.

'Who's in the bath?' she said to Fletcher as she came into the kitchen.

'Oh, that's Jackie.'

'Jackie!'

'She and Will came together and she said her friend's boiler was playing up so she hadn't had a shower for ages.'

'Jackie is in our bath?'

'Yes.' He made a mock-apologetic face. 'Sorry.'

She made tea, and they went out to the garden with it.

'I've never been good with the garden,' said Fletcher. 'I've just never been interested in it, that's my problem.'

'I love competent men,' said Renata. 'Charlie isn't competent. Not competent at all.'

Neve wondered if she was drunk again, or perhaps the drunkenness had never gone away.

Will looked at her and smiled and she smiled back at him.

'I don't know about competence. But if you see a weed, you want to pull it up, get rid of it.'

'Unless it's a plant,' said Neve.

'I'd probably have been better off if I'd trained as a plumber,' said Fletcher glumly. 'I think the world could do without another failed artist but it can always do with someone who knows how to fix a leaking pipe.'

'You're not a failed artist,' said Neve. 'And I don't think you should have trained as a plumber.'

Fletcher was just starting to explain that this was just snobbery but then Neve's phone rang and when she saw who was calling, she walked inside before answering.

'Can you talk?' said Sarah.

Neve looked at Will, Renata and Fletcher in the garden. Fletcher seemed to sense her attention and smiled at her and she smiled back.

'It's not the best time.'

'It's important. I'll be really quick.'

Jackie walked into the kitchen, gave Neve an exuberant wave, put her finger to her lips, then picked up
Neve's mug of tea and sailed out into the garden.

'That's all right,' Neve said.

'I've been plucking up courage to ring you. I
wanted to talk to you in person but I thought it would
be awkward.'

Neve started to speak but Sarah interrupted.

'Let me just say what I rang to say and then you can
reply and say anything you want.' Neve could hear
Sarah take a breath. 'I'm so, so sorry about what we
did. What I did. If I've hurt you – no, that's wrong.
I know I've hurt you. I'm going to break it off with
Fletcher.' There was a pause. Neve wasn't sure whether
she needed to reply to this. What was she meant to do?
Congratulate her? So she said nothing. 'That doesn't
sound right,' Sarah continued. 'That sounds like there's
something big to break off. It was all just a mess. I just
wanted to be noticed by someone. And Fletcher's been
in a bad place but he's devoted to you.'

Neve thought of several replies she could make and
didn't say any of them aloud. Who was she to be angry?
Maybe some vengeful God somewhere was giving her
some deserved punishment.

'You don't need to justify yourself to me,' Neve said.
'I don't blame you.'

'But you shouldn't blame Fletcher either. He's already
tried to end it with me twice but I persuaded him it

wasn't doing anybody any harm. And I believed that, kind of. The thing is, Neve, he loves you. He was clear about that all the time. I always knew I was just a way of getting him through a rough patch. He thought you didn't care about him anymore or respect him. And then everything you've both been through with Mabel—'

'Don't bring Mabel into this.'

'Sorry. I'm sorry.'

Neve took a breath. 'Thank you,' she said in as a calm tone as she could manage. 'It must have taken a lot for you to call like this. And I'm not angry with you.'

'Really?' The word ended on a small sob.

'Really. But I need to go now. We can talk later.'

She ended the call and tried to collect herself by going round the kitchen, collecting cups and glasses and putting them in the dishwasher. She wiped the kitchen table. Another deep breath. She was ready to face the world. She walked back into the garden.

'Everything all right?' said Fletcher.

'Fine.'

'Who was it?'

Neve shrugged. 'It was nothing.'

There was a familiar pinging sound and Fletcher took his phone from his pocket and looked at it and took a few steps away. Neve followed him with her gaze, paying no attention to what Will was saying about options for the garden or what Renata was saying about Charlie or what Jackie was saying about men in general. He was reading a text and she knew the text he was reading. He had turned so that his back was to her but she could recognise his shock even from his hunched posture. He stood there for several minutes, far longer than it would take to read what he had to read. Finally he put his phone in his pocket and walked back to join them. His face was pale and set. He nodded as Will spoke and looked at him, but Neve could see that he wasn't hearing anything, wasn't seeing anything.

She gave him a nudge. He turned to her as if she had woken him up.

'OK?' she said. Her husband had just been told by the woman he had been having an affair with that it was over, and all she could feel was a kind of exhausted pity. He seemed so defeated.

He just looked at her as if he couldn't understand what she was saying.

'Gin,' he said finally.

'What?'

He looked at Jackie, Will and Renata. 'I think we should have a gin and tonic.'

'Well,' began Will. 'I really think I've had enough drink over the past few days to—'

'Great,' said Renata.

'I'm on,' said Jackie.

Fletcher looked at Neve.

'A small one,' she said. 'A really, really small one.'

Fletcher went into the kitchen and Renata turned to Neve.

'Can I borrow a jumper of yours? I'm getting a bit chilly.'

'Sure.'

'I'll get it. I know where all your clothes are.'

Alone, Jackie, Neve and Will were silent for a while. Neve didn't want to talk about anything; she just wanted them gone. Will looked at her with an expression of concern.

'Are you all right?' he said.

'In what sense?'

'You look tired. Stressed. I feel bad about still being here. You've had people in the house non-stop.'

'No,' said Neve wearily. 'That's been good.'

'Look who's here,' said Fletcher.

She looked round. Fletcher was holding a tray with five glasses on it. Behind him, Hitching filled the doorway. He smiled at Neve as though nothing had happened that morning at the police station. She stared back at him, her stomach dropping away.

'You're going to say, we must stop meeting like this.'

'No,' said Neve. 'I wasn't.'

'I thought I'd just drop by.'

'I was going to offer you a gin and tonic,' said Fletcher. 'But whenever you do that, police always say: not while I'm on duty.'

'But I'm not on duty,' said Hitching. 'Not really. I'm on my way home.'

'Does that mean you'd like one?'

'It does. It looks like your party is still going on.'

'Excellent,' said Fletcher. 'Take this one.' He handed Hitching his own drink and went back inside.

Renata pranced into the garden in a jumper that was far too large for her and did a comic double take.

'Why are you here?' she asked, then picked up her glass and took two large mouthfuls of gin.

'A few loose ends,' said Hitching.

'I don't like the sound of that.' And she walked back into the kitchen, holding her glass in both hands as though it was a chalice. Jackie patted Neve on the head like she was a stray dog and followed.

Neve introduced Will to Hitching as an old college friend.

'College, eh?' said Hitching. 'So what was Neve like as a teenager?'

Will frowned, as if he were trying to remember. 'She knew how to have fun,' he said.

'I bet she did,' said Hitching. 'I bet you could tell some stories.'

'I hope he won't,' said Neve.

'She was nice,' said Will.

'Still is, I hope,' said Hitching with a smile that sent a shudder through Neve.

'She always included everyone,' continued Will.

'Well, I can see she still does that. Every time I come here, the house is full of people.'

Fletcher re-emerged from the house with his gin and tonic. Hitching nodded at Neve.

'Can I have a word?'

'I thought you were off duty.'

'Just a word.'

The two of them walked down the garden and stood next to the finished greenhouse. He contemplated it.

'Nice,' he said. 'What are you going to grow in it?'

'I don't know. Something I don't grow in my allotment. Tomatoes maybe. Or chillis.'

'Chillis? Here in England?'

'They're not hard.'

Hitching took a sip of his drink and Neve saw that
he had already finished it. He took the lemon from the
bottom of the glass and ate it in two bites, peel and all.

'Do you want another one?'

'I talked to Katie Rouse,' he said, ignoring her question. 'Saul Stevenson's assistant.'

'Yes, I know Katie.'

'I was going to say his secretary but you're not really
allowed to call anyone a secretary anymore.'

'She's not a secretary.'

'Indeed,' said Hitching. 'She wasn't typing his letters. She was more the keeper of his diary, arranging
his affairs.'

Neve felt a growing dread. What was coming?

'She asked to see me. She knew I had been asking
people in the office if they had ever gone to his flat. She
had never gone there. Not once. Did you know that?'

'No.'

'She'd heard that you had delivered a package there.
She wanted me to know that she was surprised by
that. Very.'

He looked at her, obviously waiting for an answer,
so she gave the simplest one she could think of.

'Why?'

'She said that if he had needed something delivered
to his flat, it would have been sent by messenger, or

he would have asked her to take it. She thought it was highly unlikely he would have asked anyone else.' He paused but Neve didn't answer. 'Do you have a comment?'

'I don't know what to say,' said Neve, cursing herself inwardly for having told this unnecessary lie. 'He asked me to take him this package and I took it.'

'How did he ask you?'

'I think he phoned me.'

'Where was the package?'

Neve desperately tried to think of something that couldn't be checked. 'I think it was on his desk.'

'Why do you think he asked you and not Ms Rouse?'

'I don't know. Maybe she was away. But I don't know.'

'Why would he choose you?'

'I've no idea. He knew I rode a bike, so perhaps he assumed it would be easy for me to do it.'

Hitching looked down at his glass again, then looked up at her. 'How did he know you rode a bike?'

'He just knew. Most people know. I think we met once when I was locking it up. Or unlocking it.'

Hitching looked over Neve's head with a distant expression for a long time, a minute or more. Finally he shook his head.

'Chillis,' he said. 'Who'd have thought it.'

'I haven't grown them yet.'

'I've visited your allotment.'

'Oh.' The syllable was a hoarse croak.

'One of your neighbours pointed it out to me. We agreed that it's a bit in need of attention.'

'I've been busy. I haven't been back since last Wednesday.'

'Yes, when you were there with your daughter.' He let the silence thicken between them.

'That's right,' said Neve at last.

'It looks like much longer than that. Lots of things need picking. Your chard's gone wild. Your raspberries are going rotten. I ate a few, I have to confess. Very tasty.'

'Things grow quickly at this time of year.'

'Thistles have taken over. Your lettuce has bolted. That's what you say, isn't it? Bolted.'

'Yes. As I say, I've been busy.'

'We've made inquiries there.' He said this vaguely, like it was an afterthought. 'We haven't found anyone yet who saw you that morning. You and your daughter, that is.'

'As I said, I didn't notice anyone, so why would anyone particularly notice me?'

'Your allotment neighbour, he said he thought he was there that day.'

'I didn't see him.'

'He says he hasn't seen you for some weeks.'

'We all go at different times.'

'Indeed.'

Neve took the glass from Hitching's hand.

'I talked to your daughter, by the way,' he said casually.

'She told me.'

'Clever girl.'

'She's better than clever.'

'You mean *very* clever?'

'I mean she's good.'

Hitching gave his smile, the smile that Neve no longer cared for.

'Good,' he said. 'Yes, I like that. Thanks for the drink.'

Neve chopped red peppers, aubergine and shallots into chunks; she poured a small amount of oil over them and put them in the oven. She chopped vine tomatoes and put them in as well. Her hands were trembling. She poured rice into a small pan and covered it with water. She could hear Jackie, Renata and Will in the living room, laughing. Renata's laugh was high and on the verge of cracking into something else.

Fletcher came into the kitchen. His hair needed cutting and his beard trimming. His round glasses were slightly smeared. She felt a wave of such tenderness pass through her she could hardly keep standing.

'Neve,' he said. 'We should talk.'

'Are you all right?'

'There are things I need to tell you.'

There were things he mustn't tell her. He mustn't tell her about his affair with Sarah, because Neve couldn't tell him about her affair with Saul, and so she would be in the unpardonable position of forgiving him for something she too had done. He would be forever in the wrong, she in the right. She mustn't do that to him. She put her hands on his shoulders and their eyes met. He looked so miserable.

'Fletcher,' she said. 'These last few years have been almost unendurable for both of us. I know we've neglected each other, been resentful of each other, angry, or distant, which is even worse. We haven't paid each other enough attention or given each other enough time. Or had *fun*. Or talked. We've just struggled on trying in whatever way we could to keep going, like moles pushing through the soil.'

'But—'

'Whatever's happened in those years isn't your fault and it isn't my fault. It's both of us. We needed to be a bit more understanding of what the other was going through, a bit more vigilant.'

'You really don't understand.'

'I think I do. Look, Mabel's probably going away soon.'

'Is she?'

'I don't know. I don't think she knows. But soon everything will feel different. We'll have time and space and we can think about what the rest of our lives are going to be.'

'Do you want to leave me?'

'That's not what I'm saying. I just think that now is the wrong time to talk about things. It's like a mad house. Renata, Jackie and Will are here – *still* here. Mabel and the boys are here. We're all exhausted.'

Another gale of laughter reached them from the living room.

'Did you give Renata a second gin and tonic?'

'She helped herself to one – rather more gin than tonic.'

The doorbell rang.

'Oh Christ, I cannot have another person in this house,' said Neve. 'Whoever it is, send them away. No, actually, I will.'

She strode towards the front door and yanked it open.

'Oh. Charlie.'

'Is she here?'

'Yes.'

'What the fuck is she playing at? She sleeps with her boss and then she waltzes off to have a never-ending party with you lot.'

'She asked me if she could stay here and I said yes. That's all.'

'Hello, Charlie,' said Renata, and Neve turned to see her propped up in the hallway. 'Meet Will.'

As if on cue, he emerged from the living room.

'Can you come home so we can talk?'

'Will and I were once an item,' said Renata brightly. 'Weren't we, Will, back in the day? Such a long way back. When we were young.'

'I should go,' said Will, who was slack-jawed with embarrassment.

Serve him right for hanging around long after his welcome had expired, thought Neve.

'But then, I slept with lots of gorgeous men,' continued Renata.

Neve knew she should stop her but she couldn't seem to speak. Behind her, Mabel was coming slowly down the stairs.

'So many. Such fun. But it was like musical chairs.

One day, the music stopped and I was with you and you were with me and the rest, as they say, is history.'

'Renata,' Neve managed to say. Mabel had halted on the final step. Fletcher was in the doorway of the kitchen, on his face a look of almost comical disbelief.

'Did I love you?' Renata asked reflectively, genuinely seeming to want an answer. 'Did you love me? Did we *like* each other? And if we did, what happened? That's what I want to know. What do you think, Charlie?'

Charlie's mouth was open. He blinked several times, then lifted his hand and patted his neat hair. All the fight seemed to have gone out of him. Neve almost felt sorry for him.

'Let's have another gin,' said Renata. 'I drink too much. That's so I don't have to think too much. Oh, it rhymes.'

There was a silence and Neve had the terrible feeling she would start laughing at the brutal farce that was unfolding.

'Renata,' she said, at last going to her. 'Please stop. You're saying cruel things you don't mean and you'll regret.'

'Am I? Am I, Charlie?'

But Charlie had gone. Neve ran to the pavement and saw him walking away from the house, head down. She thought of chasing after him, but didn't know what she'd say. She went back in and found Renata sitting on the floor of the hallway, her head in her hands, weeping. Will was crouched beside her, and Jackie was bending over her, cooing.

'I think she's had too much to drink,' Will said apologetically.

'I think you're right.'

'We should go.'

'That would probably be best.'

He stood up.

'I'm sorry if we all stayed too long. I'm going back to Bristol the day after tomorrow, so this is goodbye. Let's not leave it so long next time. It's all been very ...' He hesitated. 'Interesting.'

'Good choice of word,' said Neve. 'I hope it gets less interesting from now on.'

She steered Renata to her bed, where she sat, still weeping steadily while Neve pulled off her shoes, socks, jeans, jumper and tee shirt.

'What have I done?' wailed Renata, lying back on the pillow, her face a smudge of ruined make-up and grief. 'What have I gone and done?' She sat up suddenly, clutching her wild hair. 'I should go and tell him I'm sorry.'

'You should work out what you want first,' said Neve. 'Whether you want to save the marriage or leave it. And you're not going to do that tonight. You need to sleep. Tomorrow everything will be clearer.'

'I don't want it to be clearer. Clearer is horrible.'

'Do you want anything to eat?'

In response, Renata only grimaced.

'I'll bring you tea.'

'He's a bit of a cold fish though.'

'Charlie?'

'Yes.'

'Let's talk about it tomorrow.'

The supper was burnt: yet another ruined meal.

'I don't care what we eat,' said Neve.

'How about cheese and crackers,' suggested Fletcher.

'I'm starving,' said Connor.

'You can have beans on toast then.'

They ate in front of the TV because Neve couldn't bear the thought of trying to talk. Rory had a bowl of cornflakes, Connor beans on toast, Mabel ate a mouthful of cheese and then curled up in the corner of the sofa and closed her eyes.

Neve watched the blue whale on the television screen, its mighty body rising above the waves, and the thought that had briefly twitched in her mind came swimming towards her again. She sat quite still, trying not to concentrate on it because that would only scare it away. And then at last she had it.

She got up and stacked the plates.

'Don't worry,' she said when Fletcher made a move to join her. 'I'll do this and feed Whisky and you can get Rory and Connor upstairs.'

She leaned over Mabel and touched her shoulder. Mabel's eyes flickered open and she stared into Neve's face as if she didn't know who she was.

'Bed,' she said.

'It's only nine o'clock.'

'You were asleep. You're all in.'

In the kitchen, she put the plates in the dishwasher, wiped the surfaces, put the milk and the cheese back in the fridge. Then she went into the garden with the guinea-pig food. Whisky pushed his face out of the straw and stared at her beadily, then came forward and pressed his nose against the wire. Neve opened the door and filled his bowl, checked the water. She stroked the creature's rough little body gently, while her mind worked so hard she felt it might fly apart in a thousand fragments.

Back inside, she said goodnight to the boys, checking they'd cleaned their teeth and that their clothes were ready for the morning. She kissed them both on their foreheads and said that tomorrow night they'd have a proper meal together because it might be Mabel's last evening.

She went softly into Mabel's room and stood for a while looking at her daughter sleeping. She looked so young and defenceless it made Neve's chest ache. She adjusted the duvet and crept out.

Fletcher was in his study. She could see the line of light around its closed door. She went downstairs, pulled on her jacket, slipped the house key into her pocket and went outside. It was dark now, and gusty, with leaves fluttering about her, and she felt a few drops of rain on her cheek. It smelled like autumn.

She walked down the street and knocked on the door of the house. She thought she heard shuffling steps, then the door opened. At first she thought that a child was standing in front of her, but it was a tiny man, very old and very bald, with mottled green eyes. Like a garden gnome who'd stood years in the rain.

'Yes?' His voice crackled like a radio with poor signal.

'I'm sorry,' said Neve. 'I must have the wrong number.'

'I've seen you. On your bike.'

'That's me.'

She shook his hand, said she was sorry to have disturbed him and they must meet properly sometime, and left. Back at home, the house was quiet. She sat at the kitchen table and pressed her fingers against her temples. She knew now. She knew and the knowledge burned into her like a brand.

She knew and her heart lifted in rage and gladness. Because it wasn't Mabel. Of course it wasn't Mabel.

Finally, she did a google search. It didn't take her long to find Alison Ferrimore's number. Alison with eyes of different colours.

'Sorry to ring out of the blue like this,' she said. 'It's Neve Connolly.

There was a pause. She could almost hear the cogs in Alison's brain turning.

'Neve. Wow, Neve. How long has it been?'

'Too long,' said Neve. 'And I'd like to catch up sometime but right now I just need your help with something.'

'My help?'

'I need an address and phone number.'

It took a few minutes for Alison to find it. It had been ages since they'd been in contact, she said.

Neve frowned as she wrote it down.

'I'm not sure this can be right.'

'It's all I've got. Let's meet before we die,' she added.

After the call, Neve made lunch for Rory and Connor for the next morning – bread from the freezer, with the remainder of the cheese and chutney, a biscuit each and an apple. She put both lunch boxes into the fridge and wrote a note for Fletcher. She made sure that their PE kits were hanging from the hook in the scullery.

There was one more thing she needed to do. She went out into the garden with her mobile and called Gary.

'Are you all right?' she said.

'I've been better.'

'I'm very sorry for the way I left.'

'As you said, something came up.'

'And I'm sorry that I haven't been a good enough friend,' she persisted.

Gary grunted.

'In a few days' time,' she said, 'I'd like to come over for the day and we can clear up your flat. It's easier with another person – and then we can go out for supper together, just you and me.'

'You're too busy.'

'No, I'm not. I'd like to. Also, I think you should ask Charlie to help you sort out your debts. I think he'd be glad to help.'

'I don't want people's pity.'

'Don't be daft, Gary. This is what friends do for each other. We help each other.'

After she ended the call, she pulled up Google Maps

on her phone and keyed in a postcode before setting the alarm for 5.30.

All the tiredness had gone from her and she felt alert now. It was as if electricity was running through her, and she didn't know how she would ever sleep. She went through the house in her bare feet, stopping at each bedroom door. The light was off in Fletcher's study and when she went into their room he was propped up against the pillows. Without his glasses, his eyes looked naked.

'Did you go out?' he asked. 'I thought I heard the front door.'

'I needed some fresh air.'

He nodded.

Neve undressed, feeling oddly self-conscious, and climbed into bed beside him. They were both tense, careful not to touch each other. She slid her mobile under her pillow, so he wouldn't be woken by the early alarm, and turned off her lamp. They lay side by side in the darkness. She knew he was awake, and she listened to him breathing softly. At last she reached out and took his hand.

'Goodnight,' she said.

'Neve—'

'Sweet dreams.'

She let go of his hand and he turned from her and before long a little rumbling snore came from him. But Neve lay for a long time, waiting for the morning to come.

# 8

# THE LAST SUPPER

Neve slept fitfully and was awake before the alarm went off, sliding out of bed quietly so as not to wake Fletcher. In the dark, she pulled clothes out of the drawer and put them on, then crept out of the room and down the stairs. Jacket, shoes, backpack, mobile, keys, bike lock.

She wheeled her bike out and shut the door gently. The sun hadn't risen yet but to the east the horizon was beginning to glow. It was cool, fresh after the rain. The wind lifted her hair. There was nobody on the streets, and until she reached Lower Clapton Road, barely any cars. She paused and closed her eyes, surveying the mental map of London in her head. Normally with a long ride of this kind right across the city she would choose a route along a canal or by the river or through parks. But now none of that mattered. The traffic would be light, or as light as it ever got in central

London. She just needed to get there quickly. It was a matter of heading west as directly as possible and then curving slightly to the south.

She set off and turned down Victoria Park Road. From then on, with various twists and turns, it was really just one long road: Hackney Road, Farringdon Road, Oxford Street, along the side of Hyde Park. She saw some early runners, dog walkers and she met a growing number of cyclists coming to work early from the west. Sometimes cycling was a way of thinking, but not this morning. There were too many buses and delivery vans. Anyway, what was there to think about? Not yet. Soon there would be plenty.

Down the hill to the Shepherd's Bush roundabout and straight across and along to Goldhawk Road. The morning rush hour was taking shape but it was all in the other direction. She crossed the river on Chiswick Bridge and pulled into the side of the road and looked at her phone. Yes, she was almost there. She turned left into a residential street and in a couple of minutes she had pulled up in front of Number Thirty-Six, Coleridge Road. The Thames was only a few minutes away in one direction and Kew Gardens a few minutes away in the other, but this was just a quiet street of Victorian ter-raced houses that could have been anywhere in London.

The windows were dark. It looked as if everyone was asleep. She looked at her watch. It was ten to seven. It was a terrible time to call on someone she had never met. She decided to wait until seven. That would be all right. After seven – even one minute past seven – it was all right to make a delivery or come to read the meter. A surprise visit from a stranger might seem odd but she felt that now she was here she had to go through with it.

She stood there on the little front path looking at her watch as the second hand slowly went round. She stared at it. It seemed to be going too slowly. It had almost come to a stop. She blinked. It was still moving.

'Hello?' said a voice. It was more an accusation than a greeting.

Neve looked round. A woman had emerged from next door and was looking over the fence. She was grey-haired, wearing a dressing gown and slippers.

'I saw you through the window,' the woman said. 'Can I help you?'

'I'm calling on Karen,' said Neve, half expecting to be told that no such person had ever lived here. Because of course they lived just outside Bristol, in a village, with two rescue dogs.

'You're not doing much calling while standing in her front garden.'

'I was waiting until seven o'clock.' She looked at her watch. 'It's seven o'clock now.'

'She's not here,' said the woman.

'Is she on holiday?'

'She's in hospital.'

'Has something happened?'

'It must have come early.'

'What?'

'It wasn't due till next week. They went in yesterday afternoon.'

'Due?'

'The baby.'

'I don't understand. I thought they couldn't . . .' Neve trailed off. She didn't know where to start unpicking her confusion. 'Is Will here?'

'I've got to feed Billy while they're away.'

'I'm sorry.' Neve peered at her. 'Did you say *Billy*?'

'I thought you were a friend.'

'Of a friend. Do you know which hospital?'

Half an hour later Neve was walking up the stairs of St Joseph's Hospital in Barnes. A small voice was telling her that it was hideously inappropriate to ambush a woman in a hospital bed who had just given birth. But she ignored the little voice. She'd done enough bad things already. What did another matter?

She told the nurse at the front desk who she was here to see.

'It's not visiting hours,' said the nurse.

'I'll just be a moment. I just want to give my congratulations. Is Karen all right?'

'She's fine.'

'Where is she?'

'Along the right-hand corridor. Room G3. Wash your hands first.'

Neve used the liquid dispenser then pushed the large doors open and turned right. She stepped into room G3. There were four occupied beds. Trying not to be conspicuous, Neve looked at the charts on the end of each bed. Karen Maxwell was in a bed by the window, a window that looked out on a patch of green and beyond, there was even a glimpse of the river.

She looked at the woman in the bed. She was asleep. She had blond hair with a tint of red and pale, almost transparent, skin. Neve looked into the cot beside the bed, down at the fiercely pink little prune face, the scrunched-up fingers. Neve felt a sudden pang. She remembered Mabel and Rory and Connor when they were just born. It felt so long ago and yet it was a memory she could almost smell.

'Who are you?' said a dreamy voice.

'You've got a beautiful baby,' Neve said.

'Yes, I have.'

'Is it a boy or a girl?'

'Agnes,' she said. 'She's called Agnes. Eight and a half pounds.'

'It must have hurt.'

'I can't remember anything about it. Just seeing her for the first time.'

Neve walked to the other side of the bed, pulled a chair over and sat down. Karen turned her head slowly to look at Neve.

'Who are you?'

'I'm called Neve. I'm a friend of Alison Ferrimore.'

'Alison Ferrimore,' she repeated sleepily. 'Ferrimore.' It was like she was rolling the name around in her mouth.

'You look happy,' said Neve.

'Yes. I am happy. I never thought I'd be happy. I never thought I'd have a child. I'm forty years old and I've got a child.' She was still speaking in a dreamy, slurred tone. 'I know I'm old to have a child. When Agnes is my age I'll be eighty.'

'You're not old,' said Neve. She put a hand out and touched Karen's arm. 'I wanted to talk to you. I don't know you but I know your husband.' She stopped. Nothing made sense; she had wandered into the wrong story. 'I think I do,' she added helplessly.

'Michael,' said Karen. 'Michael's nice.'

'I meant Will.'

'You know Will?'

'Yes. But I thought – well, I thought Will was married to you.'

'He was once.' Karen's voice became dreamy. 'Long, long ago,' she said.

'But I don't understand. Has he married again?'

'God, I hope not.'

'When did you separate?'

'Eleven years ago.'

'Oh,' said Neve. 'So you don't live in a village near Bristol with two rescue dogs.'

Karen looked at her and an odd little smile twitched at her mouth. 'No,' she said. 'Is that what he said?'

'Yes.'

'What else?'

'That he ran a company – something to do with logistics and data analysis.'

'He once worked for a shoe company,' said Karen. 'Not for long though. There wasn't much data analysis.'

'And that you two couldn't have children.'

Karen's glance settled on the baby at her side. 'But now I have. I almost feel sorry for him. Almost.'

'So everything's a lie?' asked Neve.

'He has to lie,' said Sarah. 'He always lied. I hope he hasn't hurt you.'

Neve opened her mouth to speak then shut it again. 'It's not me he's hurt,' she said.

'How do you know him?'

'I was at university with him. He was part of a group of people I knew at Newcastle.'

Karen gave a strange little laugh but didn't reply.

'What?' said Neve.

'Oh nothing,' said Karen. 'They gave me all kinds of drugs and I've got a new little daughter and I feel all discom—' She stopped. 'I can't think of what the word is. I lost my thread halfway through saying the word.'

'Newcastle,' said Neve. 'You laughed when I said Newcastle. Is there something funny about the city?'

Karen's expression changed. It seemed to become clearer, more focused.

'Could you help me sit up?'

Neve had to put her arm behind Karen's shoulders to pull her up and put a pillow behind her back. As they were doing so, there was a tiny whimpering sound from the cot.

'I'll do it,' said Neve.

Neve bent down and picked up the little bundle from the cot. The familiar heft of it in her arms gave her a pain deep in her chest. It was almost painful to hand Agnes across to Karen. Agnes was starting to cry. Karen pushed the top of her nightie down and held Agnes to her breast and the crying turned to a gurgling mumble and then stopped. Neve sat back down. There was silence for a moment. When Karen began to speak, it was almost like she was talking to herself.

'I never thought I'd have this,' she said. 'I thought I'd missed it.'

'About Newcastle . . .'

'Maybe that's where it began to go so wrong for him. When he dropped out.'

'What?'

'He had a kind of breakdown and never finished his degree. Didn't you know?'

Neve shook her head slowly. 'No,' she said. 'I didn't. I lost touch with him. I just didn't notice.'

But perhaps it wasn't so odd, she thought. He'd always been on the outside, someone who tagged along, nice enough but not distinctive; never anyone's first choice best friend; never the centre of any group. He'd drifted into her life and then dissolved out of it and she hadn't even realised he had gone.

'Will was angry at Newcastle but Will was angry with everything. He was angry with the places he worked for; they were never good enough for him; they never recognised his talents. He was angry with his family. He was angry with his friends. Everything had gone wrong in his life, wrong from the beginning, and he was so angry. He was angry with me as well, of course. Really angry. Sometimes I thought he might even, well—'

She stopped.

'What?' said Neve. 'What did you think?'

'I don't want to say. Not with Agnes here, even though she can't understand. Have you had children?'

'Three.'

'Oh my God. I feel tired just thinking about it.'

'You said that Newcastle made him angry. Especially angry.'

'He got fixated on it. He said it was where he took the wrong road. It was all right for everybody else except for him. That was always the story of his life. I felt like I was trapped in it and then I got away.'

Neve was thinking frantically, trying to make sense of it. There was another question. She didn't need to ask it. But she asked it anyway.

'Was there anyone in particular?' she asked.

'What do you mean?'

'At university. Was he angry with anyone in particular? Like a girl?'

'He always said it was easier for girls than for boys. They could do what they liked. They just glided through life. And there was one girl he was involved with who he felt really let him down; she led him up the garden path, made him think they would be together. They were all but engaged, he said, and then she humiliated him in front of everyone. Or that was his story.'

'Was she called Renata?'

'Maybe. I don't know. He was still angry about the way she treated him and he took it out on me.'

Neve stood up and gently touched the top of Agnes's head.

'It doesn't matter,' she said. 'As you said, it was a long time ago. You're free of all that and you've got Agnes and you've got Michael and you don't need to think about him.'

Karen smiled.

'No, I don't, do I?'

'What's going on?'

Neve looked round and saw a bleary-looking unshaven man in a grey sweater and blue jeans holding a cup of coffee.

'This is Neve,' said Karen. 'She's a friend. Except I've never met her before.'

'That's true,' said Neve. 'Congratulations.'

'What do you mean?' said the man who Neve realised was Michael.

'I've got to go now. But you've got a beautiful daughter.'

Neve leaned across and kissed Karen's forehead.

'Bye,' she whispered.

'Hats,' said Karen.

'What?'

'Hats. The girl he was meant to be with. She always wore hats. "Fucking hats," he said. She thought she was better than everyone. I wish I'd met her.'

'Thank you,' said Neve and went out, leaving Michael looking baffled.

As she walked down the stairs, she tried to think clearly. She knew. She knew everything. But what should she do?

She took out her phone and called Mabel.

'Don't speak,' Neve said hurriedly. 'Just yes or no. Are you still at home?'

'Yes.'

'Is Will there?'

'Yes.'

'Pretend you're speaking to someone else.'

'I can't today, Louis,' said Mabel in an over-bright voice. 'Sorry!'

'Is Fletcher there too?'

'Yes. Another time,' she added.

'I want you to do exactly what I say. Do you understand?'

'Yes, Louis.'

'Stay there with Fletcher. Don't go out. Especially, do not go out with Will. Whatever happens, whatever he says to you. Do you understand?'

'I do, Louis.' The voice was even brighter and louder.

'You promise?'

'Yes.'

'Make sure Fletcher stays there too. Invite other friends over. Fill the house. I'll be back as soon as I can.'

'Yeah, yeah,' said Mabel sarcastically. 'Whatever you say, Louis.'

Neve felt she was overdoing the Louis-thing a bit. 'I have one more thing to do,' she said, 'and then this will be over.'

She ended the call. She felt breathless. The man who had murdered Saul, who wanted to kill her or put her in prison, was with her husband and her daughter at this very moment. She could picture him, with his boyish charm, his slightly jug ears, his rueful self-deprecation, the toxic anger seething beneath the surface. But Mabel and Fletcher were together.

She just needed to call Hitching and tell him everything and they would be safe. But first, there was the present. The present in the flat.

If she called Hitching, Will would be arrested. Perhaps he would tell them about her and Saul but she could simply deny it. Except that they would go to the flat and find the package and Hitching would know. And then Mabel, who had cleared away evidence and given a false alibi, would still have committed a crime.

She would go to the flat, retrieve the package and then phone the police. One more hour.

She briefly thought of going by taxi but knew in the snarl of rush-hour traffic it would be quicker to cycle. She ran to her bike, unlocked it and set off. She went as fast as she could, hearing the blare of horns, breathing in the exhaust fumes, jolting over potholes that opened up beneath her. Her back was sweaty and her chest ached with the effort.

She pedalled hard up a hill. Will Ziegler. She had suspected her dearest friends, Tamsin, Renata and Gary. She had suspected Fletcher, who she would have said before a week ago she knew intimately and trusted implicitly. And she had suspected Mabel. There had been times when she had felt sure Mabel had killed Saul. But it was Will Ziegler all along. She had never thought about him, had barely remembered him when they met. But he'd thought about her, obsessed over her, felt shamed by her, blamed her for ruining his life. His hatred had grown fat on his bitterness and humiliation and self-pity. Will Ziegler. He had followed her, seen her with Saul – and the thought of him crouched in the shadows watching her as she allowed herself to come alive again, made her feel sick. Was he the one who had pushed her off his bike? He had stolen her bag and found the secret key. He had let himself into Saul's flat to wait for her, perhaps to confront her or blackmail her or kill her, but Saul had arrived instead. Disastrously. Fatally. And then he had set out to frame her and Mabel had been dragged into it. Collateral damage. He had spread distrust through her like a stain.

She cycled through a red light, past queues of barely moving cars. A man leaned out of his window and jabbed his middle finger at her, shouting loud obscenities. So much hatred swirling around. Her legs hurt and sweat ran into her eyes. She would see Will Ziegler arrested. She would see him put behind bars.

She arrived and jumped off her bike, leaning it against the wall outside the building and not bothering to lock it. She felt that every second counted. She punched in the code and ran up the stairs two steps at a time, unslinging her backpack as she went, pulling out her wallet, finding the key. *Let it be there*, she thought, *let it be there*.

She pushed open the door, shut it behind her. There were several envelopes lying on the floor beneath its letter box and she squatted and scrabbled through them. Among the junk mail and flyers was a slim, squashy packet addressed to Mr Saul Stevenson. A staple ripped at her finger as she tore it open. She registered the pain without feeling it and shook out a fold of bubble wrap and thick tissue. She went into the living room and unrolled it and laid the necklace on the table. It was delicate and beautiful, a little scroll of worked gold on a thin chain.

She lifted it to the light and only then could she make out the miniature engraving on the rectangular gold clasp at the back. *Neve Jenny.* Hot tears filled her eyes, ran down her sweaty, grimy face. She wiped them away. Later. She would have time later for grief, for mourning, for shame and guilt and relief. Not yet.

She pulled her mobile out of her pocket.

There was a sound, a faint but unmistakeable click. The breath went out of her and then she felt like she was breathing acrid smoke and there was a roiling liquid in her stomach. If she could only make a call, lift the phone with her thick fingers.

The silence was almost worse than the sound. Nothing but the little gasps that were coming from her. There was no way out except through the front door. She couldn't even jump out of the window. It only opened a few inches. Childproof. Burglarproof.

And there was nowhere to hide in here. The table was pushed against the wall, the cupboards were small.

She heard soft footsteps in the hall. With immense difficulty, she lifted her mobile and pressed on the phone icon, but time wasn't working the way that it should because it took so long for the contacts and numbers to appear on her screen, and then they merged in her vision.

The footsteps came nearer. She couldn't look up because she knew who she'd see. It had all been for nothing.

A shadow fell across her. She lifted her head.

Will was standing in front of her. This was how it ended. All the plans, all the lies and betrayals, all the sleepless nights and desperate plans and frantic improvisations, the countless moments of terror as she had stumbled across the ice floes that melted beneath her, had led to this. She was back where it had begun, back where Saul had unbuttoned her shirt and called her my love, where he had died because he had stumbled into a trap that was meant for her.

She wanted it to be over now, quickly, but it was all so slow. She could see the red veins in his eyes, the knobbly Adam's apple rising and falling. He had cut himself shaving, just below his left ear. He was wearing transparent latex gloves. She remembered how she'd worn gloves too, when she had scrubbed this flat from top to bottom. All for nothing. Worse than nothing. Because now she was going to die and nobody would ever know who had killed her.

He was holding a hammer. *The* hammer. The one she'd last seen in the toolbox in the garden.

He took the phone out of her hand and tossed it away. She heard it fall and skitter across the boards.

She didn't speak. He was looking at her and she was looking at him, as if they were about to kiss each other politely on the cheek in greeting. A tiny corner of her mind was telling her to pretend to be surprised, to pretend she didn't know, as if there was still a way out of this horror story. She thought of her daughter, of the promise she had made Mabel that she would be all right. She saw Will's face. His blank, pale, staring face. It was too late for any of that.

She was looking at him and at the same time, she was trying to look beyond him, towards the hall and the door. If she could run past him, into the hall, get the door open. She pictured the way the lock worked.

But he was holding the hammer and he was blocking her way.

'You'll be caught,' she said.

'How?'

Neve thought of her phone call to Mabel that morning. Mabel would know – but she mustn't tell Will that. He couldn't know.

She thought of pushing past him; her body was poised ready to do it. She took a breath. But he stepped closer.

'I never harmed you,' Neve said softly. Her fingers curled into fists. She had never wanted to kill anyone before.

'You *only* harmed me, Neve. We were meant to be

together. You led me on, and then you started your affair with that loser Fletcher under my nose just so I would see you with him like that. You laughed at me. Everyone did. You destroyed me.'

She realised it with a jolt.

It had been Will who had come into their room on that weekend long ago. Looking for Neve and finding her making love to someone else.

'I never laughed at you,' she said softly. 'I never laughed at anyone.'

'It was meant to be me. I knew that. You knew that. Don't pretend you didn't know that it was meant to be me.'

There was a noise outside in the hall. Neither of them paid any attention.

'I didn't know,' said Neve.

'Of course you knew. Are you saying I'm so stupid, so completely pitiful, that my whole life got wrecked over something that you didn't even realise was going on?'

'Will. Please. Put the hammer down and we can talk.'

'You pretend to be so kind,' said Will. 'You make people think you love them.'

'I'm sorry,' she said helplessly. 'I'm sorry I hurt you.'

'I heard your marriage with Fletcher was in trouble. I came to find you, I was going to forgive you, to give you a second chance and say we could start again. But I saw you with your boss. You looked at him the way you should have looked at me. You kissed him.'

So he thought she had done it to him all over again.

'You never told me, Will. If you had only told me

what you felt.' Her voice cracked but she went on. 'Now that I know,' she said, 'everything can be different between us.'

She heard her craven voice and cringed. But for a moment he looked uncertain. He lifted a hand, the one without the hammer in it, and touched her hair. Before she could stop herself, she flinched. It was the tiniest movement, but it was enough.

'You were so lucky,' he said. 'Always lucky.'

'I wasn't.'

'Now, you'll know what it's been like to be me. For a moment. Before you die.'

Neve thought of Fletcher and Mabel, in the house together. Perhaps Fletcher was in his studio, sitting in front of a canvas. And perhaps Mabel was packing for university. She hadn't fed Whisky this morning. Who'd remember, once she was gone? Who'd go on bike rides with Rory and cook with him? Who'd make sure that Connor did his homework and cleaned his teeth and didn't play computer games long into the night? Who would see them all into adulthood, all along the bumpy way? They were too young. How would they all cope without her?

'And that daughter of yours—'

Neve's arm went up. With a strength she didn't know she possessed, she hit Will in the face and she kicked him hard in the shin. She ran past him, into the hall, got to the door, her fingers on the latch, trying to open it. For an agonising moment, she thought she felt it give. Then something smashed into her and she fell, her face hitting the wooden floor. She was being dragged backwards by her legs. Her arm was at an odd angle, her body bumped against a chair leg. It was strangely quiet, neither of them saying anything, just the noise of breathing, hers and his. She should cry out, she thought, but she didn't cry out.

She could see him above her, but the sun coming in through the window made him into a dark silhouette. *It's still quite early*, she thought: *the day is only just beginning; Tamsin and Renata and Gary will be arriving at work. When will anyone know? How long will I lie here? Like Saul lay here.*

The hammer in Will's hand lifted. She was going to be killed with the same hammer that had been used to murder Saul. She kicked and found a leg, heard a grunt.

And then all of a sudden, a shape streaked through her vision, and she heard a yell. It took only a second, but as in slow motion, Neve saw Mabel standing there, she saw the swing of her left hand, she saw that her daughter was wearing Neve's favourite tee shirt, the one that only a week ago she had retrieved from this flat, she saw her daughter's pale face.

Will staggered backwards, recovered and lifted the hammer high above him. He lunged towards her, and Neve pushed herself into a slithering dive and caught one ankle. He half tripped, his momentum carrying him forward, the hammer clattering from his hand, his body doing a weird, unbalanced dance, arms flailing until he fell. She heard his head crack against the corner of the table, like a gun going off, and then she heard it hit the floor, bounce and hit it again. She heard his breath exhale in a roar, like a train coming out of a tunnel. Then there was silence and for a few moments, nobody moved. Neve lay spreadeagled on the floor and Mabel stood beside her gasping for breath. Neve saw what Mabel was holding, what she had struck Will with: Saul's stone trophy.

Neve scrambled to her feet, a leg giving way beneath her, pain coursing through her, though she couldn't tell where it was coming from. It was hard to focus. She felt like she was under a stormy sea. But she could see Mabel. Only Mabel. She looked utterly bewildered.

Neve stood and Mabel clung to her, her body small and soft in Neve's arms. Neve could feel her shaking. She could smell her musky hair and the fear on her skin.

'Wait,' she said. 'My darling love. Wait.'

She knelt beside Will. His eyes were open and he looked past her. Blood pooled out from his cracked skull, so much blood and Neve was kneeling in it; it seemed to wash around her. Uselessly, she put her head to his chest and could hear no heartbeat. She put her thumb against the pulse on his wrist to feel for the tick of a pulse. Nothing. She pumped her fists uselessly up and down on his chest, pausing every so often. Then she stopped.

Mabel's voice quavered; she pressed both hands against her stomach and bent over slightly. 'You're sure?'

'Quite sure.'

'Did I do that?'

'No. He did. But you saved me.'

'Mummy?'

'You saved my life.'

'I knew when you said on the phone that you had one thing left to do,' said Mabel in a small, high voice. 'I just knew you'd come here. I had this terrible feeling about everything. I thought I wouldn't be in time.' She gave a single, harsh sob.

'But you were,' said Neve softly.

'If the door hadn't been open—'

'It was open.'

She stood up. Will's blood was on her jeans and on her hands and on the soles of her shoes.

'I want to hug you and comfort you and take you home, but I can't touch you again.'

'What?'

The two of them looked at each other, panting. Neve was thinking desperately. Was there any way out of this?

'Do you have your mobile on you?' she said.

'No.'

'Good. That's good. Was Fletcher there when you left?'

'In his room, yes.'

She looked at Mabel as she stood there, her hands still against her stomach and her face wet with tears.

'You have to go back home as quickly as you can; take the side roads to the underground. On your way back, buy yourself a new pair of trainers and dump those in a bin somewhere. There might be blood on them. Pack clothes for uni – and that's what you've been doing, all morning, all right? Make sure Fletcher knows you're there. Have coffee together. If I know him, he'll think you've been at home all along. And your mobile will confirm that.'

'I don't understand.'

'But you'll do all that? Mabel?'

'Yes.'

'One more thing. This is very important.'

'What?'

Neve took her purse from her bag, extracted two twenty-pound notes and handed them to Mabel.

'Go round the corner to a booth and buy a pay-as-you go phone. Walk about five minutes up the road and send me a text. The text should say, "Come to Saul's flat." That's all. Then switch it off and throw it away. Have you got that?'

'What do you mean?' said Mabel. 'What are you talking about?'

'Listen. This is important. Did you hear what I said?'

'Yes.'

'Say the words back to me.'

'Come to Saul's flat.'

'That's right. You need to do it very, very quickly. As quickly as you can.'

Mabel nodded slowly. She looked dazed, as if she had just clambered out of the wreckage of an accident.

'How can you do this? Someone's died. He's lying there in front of us and you're thinking all of this.'

'You haven't touched Will, but have a shower anyway, put your clothes in the wash along with some of the boys' stuff.'

'What are you going to do?'

'You don't need to worry about that. It's over.'

'But I—'

'Go, Mabel. You need to hurry.'

'I want you to come as well. You're hurt. You look terrible.'

'I'm fine and I'll come as soon as I can.' She looked into her daughter's frightened face. 'You're safe from harm,' she said very softly. 'Go.'

Mabel left and Neve stood by Will's body. Her left arm throbbed painfully and she remembered being dragged along the floor with it wedged under her body. Her face throbbed as well. She could feel her brain working, thoughts clicking into place. She retrieved her mobile from where it was lying in a corner of the room and checked she still had the key to the flat. She left, shutting the door behind her, and found her unlocked bike still leaned against the wall. She pedalled furiously away, not caring in which direction, and braked to a halt as soon as she heard her mobile ping.

Mabel had done it. She had sent the message.

She had no idea if the police would be able to tell where she had been when she received it but at least she wasn't in the flat.

She cycled back, keeping her head down, locking her bike this time, punching in the code. She was about to go in when she remembered something and rubbed at the buttons with her sleeve. Then she firmly pressed the intercom with her index finger, held it there, released it. Then she ran back up the stairs. She looked at her watch when she got to the door of the flat and had to check it was still working: it was not yet ten o'clock. The morning sun was still low in the sky.

Inside, she took off her backpack and her jacket and put them by the front door. She rolled up her sleeves and began.

She filled the sink with hot soapy water and found the disinfectant spray. What would Mabel have touched? She began with the door, outside and then in. Then she picked up the trophy and plunged it into the water and scrubbed at it with the scouring pad, top to bottom, dried it, and held it tightly, pressing her fingers on to it.

She wiped the walls, which Mabel might have stumbled against, the surfaces she might have touched, the edge of the table.

Once that was done, she turned to the body. The hammer was on the floor near it. She picked it up and put that into the soapy water as well, scrubbed it violently, sprayed disinfectant on to it, dried it, and laid it back beside the body. He was wearing gloves, so it wouldn't seem strange that there were no prints on it.

What else? She made herself concentrate. What if he had taken photos of her? She went to the kitchen and pulled on the rubber gloves she knew were under the sink, and then knelt beside the body, in the pool of blood, and patted at the pockets until she found Will's mobile. She pulled it out. But she couldn't open it because it asked for a password and she didn't have that. She would just have to pray that Will hadn't been stupid enough to have anything incriminating on his phone. She was about to slide it back into his pocket when it began to ring, and she saw that the caller was Fletcher. Feeling sick, she waited for it to stop, then put it back in the pocket.

What else? The poem, she thought – where was that little poem she had written on a card and given to Saul? She needed to check Will didn't have it on him. Once again, she patted his pockets. His eyes stared past her. She found his wallet and opening it, shook out its contents. Nothing. She pushed her fingers into all the pockets of his trousers, having to reach under his body to do so. Her fingers, clumsy in the rubber gloves, found a card. She pulled it out and there it was: *Jenny kiss'd me when we met* ... She put it into the soapy water and watched the ink dissolve. Then she picked up the mushy remains of the paper, tore it into tiny bits and flushed it down the lavatory. She saw herself in the mirror and almost didn't recognise herself. She had a fresh bruise on her face, running all the way down one cheek and eclipsing the old one, and an ugly gash under one ear. Blood was running down her neck. She looked down at her trousers, which were wet with blood – his, this time.

Was there anything she was missing, something that could betray her? The key to the flat, she thought. She got it out of her wallet and washed it thoroughly as well, then frowned. She'd had the idea of taking it out of the flat and dropping it into a bin, but then she wouldn't be able to get back in again; it was too risky to go out and just leave the door on the latch. Eventually, she slid it into Will's jacket pocket. She peeled off the rubber gloves. Would they retain traces of her? Fingerprints? She turned them inside out and then ran very hot water over them and rubbed them with a wire-wool brush. That would have to do. Holding them between the tips of her fingers, she put them under the sink again, pulled the plug to let out the water. She looked at her watch. It was nearly half past ten.

She took out her mobile but then she saw the little packet on the table, torn open, and the coil of gold beside it. The necklace. She pulled her sleeve down over her hand and inspected the envelope to make sure there was nothing incriminating inside, then simply laid it with all the other junk mail on the floor beneath the letter box. The little necklace she put around her neck.

As she did so, she thought of the man who had given it to her. Once, as they were lying in the dark, Saul had told her how he had first noticed her, how he had watched her when she couldn't see him, how just the sight of her had excited him. And then she looked down at the body on the floor – the second body on the floor. All these years he had been thinking about her, blaming her for things she knew nothing about. He had followed her, planned about her, tried to destroy her life. And all the time she had been unaware. What had set it off? Was it the wrong kind of look, years ago in Newcastle, in some forgotten party? Was it a dismissive word? Or was it just his own fantasy about who she was? It was like being loved, in a way, the great mystery of love and desire and hatred.

A final thought occurred to her. Her hands were too clean. She knelt once more beside Will and put both hands on his body, lifted them off and looked at them. Now she was marked by his clothes and his blood.

She made the call.

She began to feel very cold and she also felt like her mind was working slowly. It was hard to think at a time when she urgently needed to think. Was this what it was like to be in shock? She vaguely remembered reading about people lost in the snow up on mountains and they would become unable to think and in the end they would just lie down and go to sleep and quietly die. Except that then they suddenly felt warm instead of cold.

Neve's mind was starting to drift and she knew that it mustn't. These would be the crucial minutes. It would just take one mistake. She must be composed. She must remember.

She walked away from the body and into the hall. She knelt on the bare boards and pressed her head against her knees. Her bloodstained fingers were tingling and her lips were very dry. She closed her eyes because the light was hurting them. It felt like hours but it was barely fifteen minutes when there was a harsh ringing sound from just a few feet away. She scrambled to her feet, took a deep breath and pressed the button next to the front door with the back of her hand so that she wouldn't get blood on it. Though of course that didn't matter; the blood was meant to be there. Think, she told herself: *think*.

A voice crackled from the speaker and she buzzed him in. She opened the door of the flat and heard footsteps. Hitching appeared.

'What's up?' he said.

Neve held up her hands, smeared with Will's blood. Hitching's eyes widened in shock and alarm.

'He tried to kill me,' she said. It sounded strange, wrong, the words coming from very far away. 'He tried to kill me,' she repeated. Her voice came out low and cracked.

Hitching's mouth opened in surprise that was almost comical.

'What? Who tried to kill you?'

'He's in there.'

Hitching pushed past her. She heard his footsteps clattering on the wooden floor. She followed and found him leaning down over Will's vacant face. He looked up at her.

'Did you call an ambulance?'

'I called *you*.'

'Why the hell not?' He took his phone out. 'Don't touch anything,' he said. 'Nothing at all.'

He turned away from her but she could hear him calling for an ambulance and then for police. When he was finished he looked back down at the body and then up at Neve. His face looked chalky with shock.

'Why the hell didn't you call an ambulance?' he repeated.

'He was dead.' It occurred to her somewhere in the sluggish murk of her mind that of course she should have called an ambulance after she had phoned Hitching. It would have been the obvious thing to do. 'I don't know,' she said. 'I don't know why I didn't. I just – I called you. It was all I could think to do.'

'Was he dead when you found him?'

Neve took a deep breath, which hurt her chest, like something was ripping. This was the beginning.

'He tried to kill me,' she said.

Hitching seemed almost physically stunned. 'You mean, you killed him?'

Neve shook her head slowly, too many times. Pain swung around in her skull. 'No. I tried to defend myself. He had a hammer and he was going to hit me but I picked up the stone block from the windowsill and hit him and he staggered and ran at me and fell and hit his head on the table.' She remembered the crack. 'It was so loud,' she said. 'Then he hit it on the floor and there was another crack. I tried to help but he died.'

Hitching kept looking between the body and Neve. 'Who is it?'

'You've met him. It's Will Ziegler.'

Hitching rubbed his bald head with one hand, massaging it.

'I've got so many questions,' he said. 'I've got so many that I don't know which one to ask first.' His face was contorted in concentration. 'But here's one. Why were you here?'

'I got a text.'

'What text?'

Neve took out her phone and unlocked and handed it to Hitching but he shook his head and stepped back.

'I don't want to touch it,' he said. 'Put it down on the table.'

Neve did as she was told and Hitching looked down at it.

'*Come to Saul's flat,*' he read aloud. 'What was that about?'

Neve was trying to remember the right answer when she heard sirens. They both looked out of the window. The little street was suddenly full. There were two ambulances and three police cars and then a fourth, skewed across the road, up on the pavement. Neve saw uniforms, green and blue. A minute later the room was full of them. Will's body was surrounded. She could no longer see it.

Hitching remained close to Neve, as if he were protecting her.

'Is there a bathroom here?'

She was about to point it out and then stopped herself. The story was that she had only ever come here to make a delivery.

'There must be,' she said.

Hitching pointed to a young woman in uniform standing beside him.

'My colleague is going to accompany you to the bathroom. You're going to take off your . . .' He waved his hands vaguely. 'Outer garments. We have clothes for you to wear.'

'My clothes?' said Neve. 'Why?'

'Someone has died,' said Hitching. 'You say you were here at the time and that he attacked you. One thing more. Do not wash your hands.' He looked at the officer. 'Make sure of that.'

In the bathroom that she knew so well, the bathroom she had cleaned out, in front of the young police officer, Neve took her clothes off and put on instead brown corduroy trousers and a thin sweater that were slightly too large for her and flat shoes that were slightly too small. She didn't want to think of where the police had got them.

When she emerged from the bathroom, everything looked different. The paramedics had gone. They had been replaced by white-suited scene-of-crime investigators. One of them took Neve by each hand and scraped under nails. She also dabbed at the blood on Neve's hand with cotton wool and placed it in a transparent bag.

All the time, Hitching was watching her with an almost hungry expression. When the investigator was finished, he approached Neve.

'How are you feeling?'

'Strange. I'm feeling strange.'

That at least was the truth. And everything could be true except the central thing, she told herself. She must remember when to lie, that was all. Remember the traps.

'Of course, you are. If you need anything—'

'I'm all right.'

'There's a room along the corridor. It's quieter. I thought we could go there, get away from everything.' He paused. 'Have a preliminary chat.'

She nodded.

'A colleague will join us.'

Hitching called across to a woman who was standing in a group. She turned and walked over to them.

'This is Detective Chief Inspector Celia Ryman,' said Hitching.

Celia Ryman had short hair and a pale angular face and narrow eyes, like the eyes of a cat. She was dressed in an amber shirt and dark trousers. As they shook hands, Neve felt she was the sort of person she could be friends with. She also felt she needed to be careful with her.

They went into the room that Neve knew as Saul's office. She sat on the little sofa. She was shivering through her old body as if she was cold. Hitching pushed the office chair into one corner and Ryman sat on it. Hitching stood, half leaning on the desk that was under a window facing the street. He looked at Ryman.

'Let me bring you up to speed,' he said. 'Neve Connolly says she was summoned to the flat by text, that she was attacked. She fought back in self-defence. Will Ziegler fell, hit his head and died almost immediately.' He turned to Neve. 'Is that right?'

'Yes.'

'As I said, this is just a chat to sort things out.' He gave his familiar smile. 'You know this as well as I do

382

by now, but you may want to talk to a lawyer. You may want to make this more formal.'

'I don't need a lawyer. I'll tell you anything you want to know.'

He turned his head, looking out of the window. Neve could see that the ambulances were gone but the police cars were still there, blocking the street. He turned back to her.

'Doesn't all this seem a bit ironic?'

'Not really.'

'It seems ironic to me.' He looked at Ryman. 'Over the last few days, I've been saying that all roads lead to Neve Connolly and now here we are back at the murder scene, and here she is, where she's never been before—'

'That's not true,' said Neve quickly. 'I was here once before.'

'Sorry, I forgot. Where she's been once before. Along with the dead body of a man who didn't know the murder victim but is an old friend of hers. That seems ... well, maybe ironic isn't the right word. Peculiar might be a better word.'

Neve didn't speak.

'So to begin at the beginning: why were you here?' Hitching asked.

'I got a text. I showed it to you. It said, "Come to Saul's flat".'

'Who from?'

'It didn't say.' Her voice wobbled. But it was all right to seem distressed and scared, she told herself. A man had just died in front of her.

'And you just came here?'

'Yes.'

'Why didn't you call the police?'

'I assumed it was from Bernice.'

'Why?'

'She owns it now. She has the key. I just assumed.' She rubbed the side of her face, which felt a bit rubbery. 'I don't know why,' she said. 'I just – just didn't think.'

'Where were you when you received the text?'

'On my bike.'

'Where?'

Neve's mind raced. She was trying to remember where her dash from the flat had taken her.

'Holborn. Towards Farringdon,' she said.

'So you got the text and biked to the flat.'

'Yes.'

'Then what happened?'

'It was a blur,' said Neve. 'He opened the door—'

'Hang on, you had to get in the main entrance first.'

'Yes. I pressed the buzzer and the door opened for me.'

'No words?'

'No.'

'Go on.'

'I knocked on the door and he opened it and then shut it behind me. It was Will. I knew it was all wrong. He was holding a hammer in his hand and he was wearing gloves. I tried to get the door open again but he dragged me, he hit me.' She touched the side of her face delicately.

'Another bruise,' said Hitching with what was almost a sneer.

'And he shouted at me, horrible stuff, then he—'
Neve stopped.

'Go on.'

'He lifted the hammer. I thought I was going to die.'

'What did you do?'

'I picked up this stone thing that was on the window-sill and I swung it at him. He made a lunge, a kind of running lurch. Then he tripped and fell.'

'That was when you didn't call the ambulance?'

'I just saw his open eyes staring up. There was blood everywhere. I pumped on his chest, but he was obviously dead. I called you. I'm sorry.'

'You said he shouted at you. What did he say?'

'He was shouting about Renata. He said he had punished Saul because of Renata.'

Hitching looked at Ryman and then back at Neve.

'Hang on. You're saying that Saul Stevenson was killed by your friend, William Ziegler?'

'He wasn't really my friend.'

'For someone who wasn't your friend, he seems to have spent a lot of time in your house.'

'I can't always choose who's in my house.'

'Yes,' said Hitching. 'I know the feeling. So you're saying that all this was done because he was fixated on your friend, Renata.'

'That's not what I'm saying. It's what he was saying.'

'Is there anyone else who can corroborate this?'

'Will's ex-wife. She told me.'

'Did she now?'

'Yes.'

'When?'

'This morning; that's where I was biking back from. I went to see her. She was in hospital. She's just had a baby.'

Hot tears suddenly filled Neve's eyes and coursed down her face. She was thinking of that helpless little creature with her pink face and tiny fingers; she was thinking of Mabel and Rory and Connor when they were little.

'Sorry,' she said. 'Sorry.'

'Take your time.'

'She told me about Will. What he was like.'

'There's something that puzzles me. He's fixated on Renata, so he kills Saul. All right, they had an affair. That makes a bizarre kind of sense. But why attack you? What are you doing in this story of yours?'

'I'd found out about him, or half found out.'

'Been playing the detective, have you?'

'It was when I saw the wrong address in my file.'

Hitching leaned forward. 'Explain.'

'I remembered the first time he came to the house, he and Jackie—'

'Jackie?'

'Another friend from university. They went to the wrong address. They described the man who opened the door. So when I saw the wrong address, I remembered that, and I went to Number Seventy-Five, the address in the folder. And the same man answered. That meant Will must have looked in my file. Do you see?'

Hitching nodded.

'Then,' continued Neve, 'he very clearly said that he had only just arrived in London. But Karen said he'd been here for weeks. I found out about his obsession with Renata.'

'Did he know you'd found out?'

'He must have done.'

'How?'

'I don't know.' It was all right not to know, Neve told herself. 'My manner, maybe.'

'But you only saw his ex-wife this morning, am I right?'

'I found out about the house number before. And maybe Karen contacted him. I don't know.'

He frowned at her and waited but Neve said nothing.

'And you found out all of this as he attacked you?'

'Yes. In a confused way.'

'In a confused way. But the message got across.'

'Yes.'

'It seems like he was shouting quite a lot while he tried to kill you. It sounds like he was delivering quite a lot of information.'

'He was angry,' said Neve. 'Hysterical.'

'It sounds like you were lucky.'

'In what way?'

'Against a big strong man like that.'

'I did what I could. If he hadn't tripped—'

'Celia?' said Hitching, glancing at his colleague. 'Anything to add?'

Neve was panting. She felt like she had been running. She glanced across at Celia Ryman who was looking back at her, entirely impassive. She found it unnerving. The account she had given to Hitching felt like a rickety, jerry-built contraption held together with bits of old string and tape. The slightest tug in the right place would pull the whole thing apart and bring it clattering to the ground.

When Ryman spoke, Neve suddenly realised she hadn't heard her voice before. It was unexpectedly low, husky.

'Why here?' she said.

'How do you mean?'

'Why would Ziegler want to meet you at the murder scene? What was the point in taking such a risk?'

'I don't know,' said Neve. It didn't feel enough. She had to think of something else. 'Maybe he wanted to get me somewhere isolated.'

Ryman's expression was unchanged. Neve had no idea whether she was convinced or unconvinced, whether she might have given herself away.

'You said you talked to Ziegler's ex-wife. Why did you do that?'

'I became suspicious.'

'If you were suspicious, why didn't you call the police?'

'I should have done. I see that now. But I didn't know anything. I was worried and I wanted to find out more before I said anything. When I talked to his ex-wife and found out about him, I was going to call the police. But then I got the text.'

Ryman gave a smile, a compassionate smile. A part

of Neve wanted to rush forward and hug her and get consolation from her. And another part felt wary of her, warier than at any other moment in the previous few days.

'I can barely imagine what you must be going through,' said Ryman. 'But can you help me out?'

'I'm trying.'

'Yes, of course, but bear with me. Correct me if I'm wrong, but what you're suggesting is the following. William Ziegler believes you're on his trail and decides the only solution is to kill you. He sends you a text. His phone was found on his body and no texts have been sent from it today. So it must have been another phone, which he then disposes of. He decides not only to kill you but to kill you at the scene of his previous murder. And then what?'

'I don't understand the question,' Neve said.

'I don't understand it either,' said Hitching.

Ryman gave him a sharp look. 'I was just saying that it seems like a perverse plan to me.'

'I'm sorry,' said Neve, trying to keep her voice steady. 'Somebody just tried to kill me. I don't know why he did everything he did. I don't know how murderers think.'

'Our problem is that so much of it depends on what he said to you. Or what you *say* he said to you.'

With an iciness that almost shocked her, Neve decided it was time to seem angry and upset.

'What does it matter?' she said in a raised voice. 'This had nothing to do with me until I walked into this flat. I was just trying to help. I know I was foolish; I know I was reckless.' Her voice became louder; she wasn't acting any longer. 'But he tried to kill me, he was going to kill me, and if he hadn't fallen and hit his head it'd be my body lying on the floor.'

She stopped herself. She mustn't say too much. She would say the wrong thing, give herself away.

'I didn't mean to shout,' she said. 'I'm sorry. But you can talk to his ex-wife about his obsession with Renata. You can check on his movements, how he lied about where he was. Check everything I've said.'

'Oh, we will,' said Ryman.

Neve looked from her to Hitching. He had his arms crossed. He seemed thoughtful and dissatisfied. He was shaking his head slowly and when he spoke, Neve wasn't clear whether he was asking a question or thinking aloud.

'So it was Ziegler who pushed the file through Bernice Stevenson's door?'

'I suppose so.'

'But why your file? Why not Renata's?'

'I don't know.'

'You say he knew you suspected him. But he took the file when he committed the murder. Why would he do that?'

Neve stared blankly at the two detectives.

'I really don't know what to say. I wish I did. I don't know anything else.'

'Your blood on the file,' said Hitching. 'You still can't enlighten us about that?'

Neve tried to think clearly, to work out if what she was about to say helped or harmed her. 'I cut myself when Renata had her accident at our house,' she said slowly. 'Someone mopped it with kitchen towel, I can't remember who. But Will was there then. Maybe that's when it happened.'

'And your photo,' said Hitching. 'The one that was found in the file.'

'He could have taken that at the same time.'

'To incriminate you?'

'I can't think of another reason.'

'Why you?'

'I don't know. I wish I did. I wish I could give you neat answers. You think it's strange, but what do you think I feel?' She stared fiercely at Hitching. 'I was going to be killed. And I've just seen a man die.'

Hitching eased himself off the desk. Saul's desk. He sighed. 'Walk us through it,' he said.

'What?'

'While it's fresh in your mind.'

Neve tried to stand up but suddenly her legs wouldn't hold her and she put a hand out to steady herself.

'Careful,' said Ryman.

'Sorry,' said Neve. 'I just . . . I feel a bit odd.'

She led them out of the study and into the hall. Lights had been set up and in their brilliance everything looked harsh and unfamiliar. She walked Hitching and Ryman through the story, and it felt even more fragile. 'This is where he hit me,' she said. She could barely hear her own voice over the beating of her heart.

'This is where I fell.' She pointed. 'He dragged me to about here.' And of course, he had. 'He was shouting things at me.'

They reached the living space, garish now under the lights, the lake of blood thick and dark. She blinked and for a moment couldn't remember what she was supposed to say next.

'I scrambled to my feet here I think, though it's hard to be sure. I can't remember clearly.'

'Don't worry,' said Hitching. 'We'll check everything. Every fingerprint, every drop of blood, every fibre. What do you think they're doing now?' and he nodded towards the figures in white, who were moving in eerie silence through the scene. 'If what you say is accurate, it will be confirmed. If it's not . . .' He let the silence grow between them and then said: 'Go on with your story.'

Neve didn't like the way he emphasised the last word.

'I grabbed the stone and swung it and heard it hit him. I'm not sure where. On the side of his head or his shoulder. And he kind of half fell and staggered a few steps forward through the living room and he tripped. And his head hit the table there.' She pointed. 'And he fell. And his head banged on the floor.'

'Then you called me.'

'Yes.'

'And I arrived about a quarter of an hour later.'

'Yes.'

'What did you do while you waited for me?'

Neve blinked at him. Her mouth was very dry and her stomach felt loose. 'I went into the hall,' she said.

'Away from the body. And I knelt on the floor and I put my head on my knees and I just – I just stayed like that. I don't know how much time passed. I don't know what I was thinking.'

Hitching stared at her. Neve made herself stare back.

'We've put you through enough for the time being,' he said at last.

'Can I go home now?'

'Home?' He gave a bark of laughter. 'You're coming with us to the station. We need to get your formal statement.'

'I've told you everything that happened.'

'Yes, and now you'll tell us again, and this time you'll be recorded and cautioned, and over the next few days and weeks we'll go over it many more times. A man has died.'

'Yes,' said Neve.

'You still don't want a solicitor?'

'I just want to tell you the truth.'

'The truth,' repeated Hitching. 'That would be nice.'

As Neve left the room, she glanced at Celia Ryman who seemed to be looking right through her.

Seven and a half hours later, a police officer drove Neve home. She was still dressed in the drab borrowed clothes. They'd taken her little rucksack too, and they'd taken her phone: she felt a brief throb of fear at the thought that they might find that deleted text that one week ago had started this whole story. She had been allowed to call Fletcher from the station, and she had very briefly told him what she was telling Hitching. He had barely been able to speak when he heard. When he did, it was as though he was caught on a loop of incredulity. 'Will!' he kept saying, and 'Oh my God, are you OK? Oh my God!'

Now she sat in the back of the car and watched London pour past her. She found it hard to believe that this day was real. It lay behind her like a movie she had seen long ago and could only remember in incoherent snatches. The dawn bike ride; the baby's pink and wrinkled face and her dark, old-woman's eyes; the moment when she had heard the flat door open and close and knew that Will was there; Mabel flinging herself across the room with that ecstatic expression on her face; the body on the floor in its pool of blood. So much blood.

At the station she had told her story again, and then again, until every word felt like nonsense, every truth a lie and every lie an absurd transparent concoction. She had sat in a plastic chair and felt Hitching's eyes boring through her. She had drunk glass after glass of water, never enough, and several mugs of tepid milky tea, and she'd taken a bite out of a tuna and mayo sandwich someone had brought her; the plasticky bread had stuck in her teeth and the taste of fish had made her want to heave.

When had she last eaten a proper meal? When had she last slept through the night? She was hollow with hunger and her eyes burned. But she was going home.

As the car approached her road, she told the driver to stop.

'I'll get out here.'

'You're sure?'

He shrugged and pulled over. Neve climbed out. She needed the wind in her face and the feel of the ground beneath her feet. She waited till the car drew away again and then went into the Portuguese deli. Erico was stacking cardboard boxes; his eyes widened when he saw her.

'Your face,' he said.

'Another accident,' said Neve.

'You must stop biking, Neve.'

'Am I in time to buy a few things?'

'Of course.'

'I don't have any money with me. Can I pay you tomorrow?'

He opened his arms in an expansive gesture. 'No hurry.'

Neve picked up a basket. She filled a paper bag with cherry tomatoes, another with courgette flowers, which made her think of her neglected allotment. She took handfuls of peppery salad leaves, several avocados, radishes, some padron peppers which Fletcher loved. There were some late raspberries on offer and she put three punnets of them in the basket. Ricotta cheese, parmesan, tubs of creamy hummus, falafels, pitted olives, a large soft slice of brie, several wafer-thin slices of prosciutto, garlicky flatbreads, salted caramel chocolate, ginger beer and two bottles of good red wine. She remembered Connor and put in a tub of butterscotch ice cream.

Erico carefully packed everything in a big cardboard box, the lighter things on top. He opened the door for her and as she left he said, 'Take care, Neve,' in such a kind voice that Neve almost started to sob in front of him.

She walked home, her arms aching, and she rang the bell. She heard footsteps running and then the door was flung open and Fletcher was there, his face screwed up in anxious solicitude. He took the box and put it on the floor and he hugged her and she felt his beard scratch against her cheek and his fingers press into her skin. She thought that she might break into a hundred pieces. But then Mabel came down the stairs, one step at a time, and Neve moved away from Fletcher and held out her arms. When Mabel stepped into them she whispered, 'It's all right, everything's all right. It's over,' and she felt her daughter's body begin to tremble against hers, or perhaps it was her own body trembling.

'Will Ziegler,' said Fletcher. 'Will fucking Ziegler.'

'I don't want to talk about it,' said Neve. 'Not tonight.'

'But who would have thought—?'

'Not now, Fletcher. I can't.'

He shrugged, nodded, and looked down at the box of provisions. 'Only you would do a food shop after going through such a day. But I'm going to order us a takeaway. You go and have a bath.'

'I don't know. It might be Mabel's last meal before she goes,' said Neve. 'Mabel?'

Mabel gave a sour grimace. 'Why would I stay in this bloody madhouse a day longer than I need to?' she said.

'That's my brave daughter,' said Neve.

Their eyes met. Mabel gave a little nod. A nod of understanding, of complicity.

'So we're going to have a proper meal together,' Neve said. 'Is Renata still here?'

'She's gone back to her house,' said Fletcher. 'Charlie came to collect her. I don't know if that's a good or bad thing.'

'So it's just us five. Just family. That's good.'

Neve took off her borrowed clothes, showered and dressed in a loose, long-sleeved dress. She and Rory cooked together. She showed him how to stuff the courgette flowers with ricotta and grated parmesan, then coat them with a thin batter. He scowled in concentration, his bony shoulders tense as he fried them in batches and then laid them on a plate and drizzled honey across them. Neve cut tomatoes and sliced avocados, shook salad leaves into a bowl, laid the cheese and the prosciutto on a board, put olives in a bowl, heated the flatbreads in the oven. Outside in the garden, where the light was failing and the new greenhouse stood empty, Connor kicked a football to and fro, shouting encouragement to himself, lifting his fist in imagined victory. Fletcher opened the wine and Mabel laid the table.

Neve lit candles, and everyone sat down together. She looked from face to face. Connor was shovelling food into his mouth, his face red from his exertions. Rory picked delicately at the meal, making neat packages on his fork, chewing methodically. He looked contented, thought Neve, and her heart contracted: it took so little. Fletcher still seemed dazed; he kept glancing across at her and opening his mouth to say something, but then meeting her stern gaze and stopping himself.

And Mabel. Mabel was very quiet tonight, but it wasn't the black-hole silence that Neve and Fletcher had come to dread over the years; rather, she was subdued and thoughtful. She seemed very small and very young, thought Neve: surely too young to be leaving home. Was this it, then, the end of Mabel's childhood? She thought of her daughter as a baby, of holding the squashy, sweet-smelling weight of her. She thought of her as a toddler, when if she was hurt or upset Neve could pick her up and comfort her. Going off to school for the first time, with a red school bag almost as big as her. As an eager little girl, wanting to please. As a stormy, ferocious adolescent, lashing out at anyone who tried to help her, almost ruining her own life and the lives of those who loved her.

And now she was leaving home.

Neve raised her glass, put her finger to her lips for silence.

'To our fabulous Mabel,' she said.

Everyone raised their glasses of wine or ginger beer. 'To Mabel.'

Mabel scowled. Neve smiled and smiled. Everything was too much; love was just too much to bear.

*

Fletcher cleared away and Neve went upstairs with Rory and Connor, made sure they cleaned their teeth, made sure their clothes were ready for school tomorrow and their homework was in their bags. She kissed them both on their foreheads, adjusted their duvets, turned off their lights.

She went into Mabel's room. Two cases stood ready on the floor, and a box of books and another of kitchen items. Beside them was the duvet, still in its plastic, and new bed linen and towels. Mabel sat on the bed, plaiting her hair.

'All ready for tomorrow?' Neve asked.

'As ready as I'll ever be.'

'Why don't I come as well?'

'No thanks.'

'Oh. OK.' She tried not to sound hurt.

'You can come and visit me though.'

'I'll miss you.'

'You'll be glad I'm not here,' said Mabel. 'Making your life a misery.' She looked up at her mother. 'Will I be all right?'

Neve sat beside her and put her arms around her.

'Yes,' she said. 'You will be. You are. And whenever you're not, call me. I'll be there.'

'I know.' There was a pause and then she asked: 'What did you do?'

'You don't need to know.'

Mabel nodded. 'I've been so scared.'

'You saved me,' said Neve. 'You saved my life.'

'You saved mine,' said Mabel. 'Lots of times.'

# 9

# LEAVING HOME

Neve pulled up the blinds and the kitchen sprang into life like a theatre set, empty and waiting for the familiar show to begin.

It was ten past seven. She filled a glass with water and drank it slowly, tied her dressing gown more firmly, took a deep breath and turned to face the room. The door opened on cue.

Rory was first, as he always was. He sat at the table, poured himself a large bowl of cornflakes, and ate it with a book propped up in front of him.

Fletcher arrived, his hair still damp from the shower, and made a pot of tea. He emptied the dishwasher while Neve made porridge for Connor and then packed lunches for the boys.

Now Fletcher went to the bottom of the stairs and called for Connor.

Soon Connor was in the room, face still puffy from

sleep, his shoelaces undone, a bit grumpy and spoiling for a fight.

Mabel came in and Fletcher was pouring boiling water over her spiced-ginger teabag and saying something about leaving by nine. He turned the radio on for the seven-thirty news and sat down with his toast and marmalade.

*Family life*, thought Neve – *carrying us all forward.*

She walked with the boys to the school gate, watched them disappear. She saw Sarah in the distance; both women raised their hands in acknowledgement then went in opposite directions.

Back home, Fletcher was loading the car. Mabel came down the stairs, her jacket over her arm. She looked composed but when they hugged goodbye she held on to Neve tightly.

'What will you do today?' she asked.

'Perhaps I'll actually go to the allotment,' said Neve, and Mabel's face broke into a grin.

She got into the car, pulled the door shut, opened the window and leaned out. But she didn't say anything, just looked back as the car pulled away.

Neve was alone in the house and the empty day lay ahead of her.

She called her mother and told her that she thought Rory would like binoculars for his birthday.

She phoned Fletcher's parents and made a date to visit them.

She put the breakfast things into the dishwasher, sprayed the surfaces. She vacuumed downstairs and wiped away stains, all the signs of the previous week when this house had been so full of people. She scrubbed at a stain on the carpet – was that Renata's blood? Her own?

She went into the spare bedroom and stripped the sheets from the bed where Renata had slept, put them into the washing machine. Then into Connor and Rory's rooms, where she opened the curtains, pulled up the duvets, gathered dirty clothes.

In Mabel's room, the wardrobe was full of hangers, the drawers were empty. There were patches on the wall where posters had been stuck, and gaps in the bookshelf. Neve picked up a shirt that Mabel had left in a corner and put her face into its silky folds, breathing in the smell of her daughter. Then she took the sheets off the bed, opened the windows, picked up a mug, went downstairs again.

She opened the fridge and took out the remaining salad leaves from last night and took them into the garden. Sitting on the damp grass beside Whisky's hutch, she called softly. He bustled out of the straw, pressing his snout against the wire mesh.

'Hello,' said Neve. 'Time for your big clean.'

She closed the wire run with the little creature safely inside it and pushed the dandelion leaves through to him. Then she tipped all the straw out of the wooden hutch and dumped it into the compost. She got a basin full of soapy water and some spray and she scrubbed everything thoroughly before laying a thick layer of sawdust on the floor and then filling it up with fresh straw. She washed the bowl and filled it with food; topped up the water bottle, reattached the hutch to the run.

'Do you know,' she said to the guinea pig. 'There was nobody I didn't think could have killed him. I suspected all the people I loved the most and knew the best. My friends, my husband, my beautiful, brave daughter.'

She waited. The sky had darkened and a few large drops of rain fell.

'Saul died because of me,' she told him. 'He just got in the way. It was meant to be me. It was just a stupid, stupid accident.'

The garden was quiet. There was hardly a breath of wind.

'I loved him. I shouldn't have, but I loved him very much. But it's finished,' she said. 'All done. I've come home.'

Because there was no one she could tell. For the rest of her days, she would never be able to talk about what had happened to her over these few weeks in autumn, when she had fallen for a man who would die: what she had done, what she had felt, what she had risked and what she had saved; what she had lost.

Her hidden life. Her secret self. Her terrible days in the sun.

# 10

# BACK IN THE ALLOTMENT

Even though it was a weekday, there were a number of people at work on their allotments, a motley collection, mainly middle-aged, mainly grey-haired. They didn't mingle much, just exchanged the occasional complaint about too little rain or too much rain, or politely praised Jenny's over-wintered broad beans or the fragrant late raspberries grown by an ancient, wrinkled man whose name Neve had never quite caught.

Over the past weeks, Neve had come here whenever she could, often spending hours in the cold and the rain salvaging the last of the potatoes and marrows, pulling up the thicket of weeds and hacking away the thistles, cutting the raspberry cane down to short sticks. Her palms were callused from digging. There was dirt under her nails.

She saw Hitching from a distance picking his way through the patchwork of gardens. He looked incongruous in his grey suit and dark tie. One woman stopped digging and leaned on her spade to look at him as he passed her, giving her a brief nod. Neve wondered what must be happening to his fine leather shoes. But mainly she wondered what he was going to say. She hadn't spoken to him for three weeks. A little more than three weeks. Almost a month. Every time there was a ring at the door, she had thought it might be him. Now he was here. He was alone. Or he seemed to be alone. To get to the allotment, you had to walk along a narrow passage between two houses on Langham Road. There could be police cars waiting for her there. After all, what was she going to do, there in the middle of her allotment with her spade and her wellington boots? Hit him over the head and make a run for it?

When he was still some distance away, their gazes met and he half raised an arm in greeting. There followed an awkward minute when they were too far away to speak and so Neve looked around at her little patch, as if she were assessing it. When she turned round, Hitching was beside her.

'I called at the house,' he said. 'Your husband said you were here.'

'I'm preparing for winter.'

'Looks like it. Lots of digging, I'd imagine.'

'Quite a lot.'

'How was your harvest?'

'Fairly disappointing.'

'How were the courgettes and squash?'

Neve managed a smile. 'They've come and gone. I've

got a few potatoes left. They're rather undemanding. They can just wait under the soil until you're ready for them.'

'But a disappointing year on the whole?'

'Yes.'

'Even though you've spent so much time here.'

Neve looked at Hitching with more attention. Was he still trying to catch her out?

'I wasn't here as much as I wanted when it mattered. I'll do better next year.'

'That's what I always tell myself,' said Hitching. 'It never works.'

'I think I'll do better. Now that my daughter's left home, it will ...' She paused. 'I don't know. It might fill the space.'

'Mabel went to university?'

'She did. In the end.'

'How's it going?'

'She keeps threatening to quit but she's still there. That's something. Nothing will ever be easy for Mabel.'

The two of them stood in silence for a while. Neve surveyed the freshly tilled earth and then looked back at Hitching. His expression had turned more sombre.

'So,' he said, as if he were beginning a prepared statement. 'Me and my colleague Celia Ryman have spent the last few days reviewing the file. This has involved a careful—'

'I'm sorry,' said Neve. 'Could you skip straight to the end of this?'

Hitching looked mildly offended.

'All right.' When he spoke again, it was as if he were

delivering a prepared text. 'After conducting an investigation, it has been concluded that the death of William Ziegler was either an accident or a case of lawful killing and that there is no cause for further action. Every single bit of your story was tested against the evidence at the scene: it was amazing how neatly it fitted, like a perfect machine. Things are usually a lot messier than that.'

Neve kept her gaze on his.

'And, since I imagine you're interested, we have also concluded that Ziegler did indeed murder Saul Stevenson. Even the hammer he used against you was consistent with the injuries to Stevenson. So what do you think of that?'

So what *did* Neve think of that?

At first she thought nothing at all. She felt like the ground was swaying beneath her. She felt like she might faint and fall forward into the mud. It took an immense effort to answer in an even tone: 'I think that's right.'

And it was right. There had been so much deceit, so much obfuscation. She had lied to the police, she had lied to her husband, she had lied to her friends. She had lied to everybody except Mabel.

Almost every part of the police investigation was wrong or misleading, the crucial evidence had been removed or destroyed. Their narrative of events was entirely false.

But after all of that, the conclusions were correct.

Neve thought to herself that it could be seen as comic, except that it wasn't comic at all, not in any way.

'It was good of you to come and tell me,' she

continued. 'I suppose I'll miss you suddenly popping up in my life when I least expect it.'

'I thought you'd like to know,' Hitching said. 'But that wasn't the only reason I came.'

Neve felt a lurch of panic that had become horribly familiar. It was the sense that she might have forgotten something, made a mistake, said the wrong thing.

'We're going out for a drink this evening,' said Hitching. 'Two cases closed. Two results. My boss is a very happy woman. She's very happy and she's very happy with me. But do you know who isn't happy?'

'Me,' said Neve. 'I'm not particularly happy, just at the moment.'

'Apart from you, of course. I know what you've been through. But I was talking about my colleague, Celia. The aforementioned Celia Ryman.'

'Why isn't she happy?'

'She didn't want to close the case.'

'Why?'

Hitching made an expansive gesture. 'Exactly. That's what I said. I said to her, we've cracked two cases. Take the victory, I said. You know what worried her?'

'No, what?'

'The crime scene,' he said. 'I mean the first one. The way the whole flat was cleaned from top to bottom. She didn't understand why Ziegler would have done that.'

'Is this your colleague talking or you talking?'

'A bit of both maybe.'

'So are you saying that the case isn't really closed?'

Hitching shook his head. 'No, it's closed. Signed off

on. Everyone reassigned. There'll be the inquest but that's a done deal.'

'So that's that then.'

'Kind of,' said Hitching. He put his hands in his suit pockets and he took on an almost pleading tone. 'You know, one of the difficult things you learn in my job is that the law isn't about finding out what really happened. It's about building a case, assembling evidence and seeing if it's proved beyond a reasonable doubt. My first boss said to me that some cases you win and some cases you lose, and if you obsess too much about what really happened, it'll drive you mad.'

'You've got the right man,' she said. 'Why are you saying this?'

'That's what I said to Celia. We've got the right man all right. He told you all he'd just arrived in London. Turns out he'd been staying with a friend in Somers Town for almost four weeks.'

'So he was there all along?' said Neve.

'All along. And we talked to the first wife. She confirmed your story. He was an angry man, she says. He had always been fixated on a girl from university, blamed her for everything.'

'Renata,' said Neve, careful not to make it into a question.

'She didn't know the name but it sounds plausible.'

He squared his shoulders slightly, like he was working himself up to say something. 'I want to make it clear, Neve ... Is it OK if I still call you Neve?'

'Sure.'

'Well, Neve, as I say, the case is finished. I'm done with it. I'm already working on something else.' He took a step closer and spoke in a subdued tone as if he were worried about being overheard, even though there was nobody within thirty yards. 'I feel like I'm missing something. Could you tell me what it is?'

'Why? To make you feel better?'

'To make me feel better, yes. And to make you feel better as well, maybe.'

Neve suddenly felt as if she were back in the flat, Saul's body on the floor, back at that moment of decision. She looked into Hitching's dark eyes, his unreadable face. The thought of unburdening herself at last, describing everything she had gone through and confessing her guilt, was so tempting that she could feel the words in her mouth. But Hitching wasn't a priest or a doctor, he was a detective. She didn't trust him. Mustn't trust him.

'I don't know what you mean,' she said coolly. 'Will Ziegler killed Saul Stevenson and tried to kill me and died when he fell. That is the truth; that is your case. I can't say any more than that and I don't know which bit of that is meant to make me feel better.'

His eyes seemed to become even darker in disappointment.

'All right,' he said softly and deliberately. 'I suppose we're done. By the way, you'll get a letter in a day or two. It'll say that you could be offered counselling for what you've gone through. They say it can be helpful, you know, to have someone to tell things to.'

'I'll think about it.'

Hitching nodded. 'See you then. I'll miss dropping in on you.'

'It always made me feel a bit nervous.'

'Nervous?'

'Don't police officers make everyone nervous?'

'You don't need to think of me as a police officer anymore.'

She met his gaze and held it. 'I will always think of you as a police officer,' she said.

He nodded slowly.

'I guess that's that then,' he said.

'I guess it is.'

He turned and made his way back through the allotments. Even from behind, he didn't look like a man who had just been congratulated on a successful case.

When he was out of sight, Neve squatted and with her trowel made a small, deep hole in the earth. She took off the little gold necklace and for a moment held it in the palm of her hand, staring at it. Then she dropped it into the hole and covered it, standing to press down the earth with her foot.

Suddenly she smelled something. She realised it was from a bonfire of branches at the other end of the gardens, the end near the Lea River. It was the reek of autumn, the reek of change, the ending of the year.

She took hold of her spade, put her boot on the top of the blade, pushed it into the dark soft soil and started to dig.

# 11

## TIME, YOU THIEF

He saw her first coming down the stairs that he was going up. She was with a crowd of other people who were talking and laughing, but they were all just a blur. She was quite tall, not thin but not plump either; strong-looking. Her hair was dark and as he drew closer he saw that her eyes were a pale kind of brown, like pond water. She was wearing jeans, a blue tee shirt and white pumps. She was looking straight at him. She smiled. She smiled at him.

Then she was gone.

But he stood still on the stairs and let the people flow past him.

'My name's Will,' he said.

It was a party. He didn't normally go to parties but he'd found out she was going to be at this one. He'd worried she wasn't going to turn up but then there she was, at the end of the room, talking to a thin man with glasses. He made his way towards her. She was wearing a long, high-necked dress and had an over-sized watch on her wrist. And now at last he was next to her. She had a sprinkle of freckles on the bridge of her nose.

'Neve,' she said.

He held out a hand and she took it.

'Join us,' she said and made a space for him in the circle.

He sat beside her on the grass. She introduced him to everyone. Tamsin, Renata, Gary, Alison, Jackie. Other people whose names he quickly forgot.

She was wearing a yellow dress and she had grass in her hair. She held out a punnet of strawberries. He took one and put it in his mouth. Cool and sweet.

Renata was a mistake. Anyway, when it came to it, it wasn't really a betrayal of Neve because he couldn't do it. She didn't seem to mind at all. She laughed and kissed him on the cheek and said it was because they were both drunk and maybe it was just as well. They could be friends instead. She lit a cigarette and said friends were more important than lovers in the end.

He asked her to dance with him and she left the man she was talking to and stood opposite him, lifting her skirt in one hand. She often wore long skirts and dresses, brightly coloured, quite torn and patched up. Her feet were bare. He wasn't a practised dancer but he tried to copy other people and it seemed all right. She was moving to the music and smiling at him. She took his hands and made a complicated twirl.

It was just for a minute.

They were talking about love and fidelity. Gary was against it. He said it was a patriarchal invention to subjugate women and Tamsin didn't know how you could ever want to stay with one person for the rest of your life – or rather, she said gloomily, no one would want to stay with her. Renata said that love was one thing and fidelity was something else.

'It's about making a choice,' said Neve. 'About making a promise. However hard it is.'

Someone said that didn't sound very romantic and Will shook his head.

'No,' he said. 'I agree with Neve.'

In the little café they always went to, they were discussing the weekend they were going to spend in the country. It was Jackie's idea because it was Jackie who knew of a house they could borrow. They were going to take board games and gin. A man called Fletcher, who Will hadn't met before but who was funny and lugubrious at the same time, said he would bring fireworks. Renata said they should dress up in fancy clothes for dinner.

'It sounds fun,' Will said at last.

A silence fell.

Then Neve put a hand on his arm.

'Why don't you come with us,' she said. 'There's room for one more.'

The house was huge and beautiful, with outhouses, a swimming pool, a long lawn and shady wooded spaces. They drew lots for rooms. Will's was a poky box room at the top of the house under the eaves where he thought he could hear mice scuttling and scrabbling. Neve got the nicest room, though she protested to everyone she didn't need it. It was on the ground floor with French windows that opened out on to fruit trees and roses.

'It's far too big for one person,' she said.

Will understood.

They cooked sausages for breakfast. They drank gin and threw a Frisbee. They swam in the pool in the hot afternoon. They dressed up for dinner, ate pies, consumed vast quantities of wine. Gary played the piano, badly, and everyone sang.

Jackie found bottles in the back of a cupboard and mixed everything together into an orange-coloured lethal brew.

They played Scrabble. Fletcher won. He was wearing a shirt belonging to Neve and she was wearing his hat, which was too big for her and slanted over one eye rakishly. When Will looked at her, he felt like he was watching a film or listening to a song.

They made a fire in the old fireplace and when a spark spat out and landed on the rug, Tamsin threw her whisky at it and it exploded into life. Everyone ran round shouting and laughing and pouring water over it.

They went into the garden and danced to the music in their heads.

Jackie took her clothes off and jumped naked into the pool. Everyone followed. Will turned his head so he didn't have to see their gleaming shapes in the water.

There were fireworks, bright petals falling towards them. A half-moon hung above them. Gibbous moon, said Gary, lying on the grass. Even when he was drunk he was pedantic.

'We must always remember this,' said Renata. She started crying.

Will touched Neve's fingers and she smiled at him. Her eyes were bright.

He was going to say something but then she was gone.

Just before dawn, everyone gathered in the kitchen. Jackie plundered the chest freezer and came out with pizza.

But Neve was no longer there. Will knew where she had gone. He made his way towards her room, which was just across the hall. The house was full of creaks and the rattling of old pipes. Neve's door was closed. For a moment he stood in front of it, gathering his courage. Then he turned the handle and pushed.

It swung inwards. A ghost moon hung in the window; its insubstantial light lay over the bed, the puddle of sheets, a tangle of naked legs.

He took a blind step forward and stopped. For a

second he saw Neve's pale face; then she leaned forward and her dark hair fell like a curtain over her and Fletcher, shutting him out.

He stumbled from the room and into the kitchen.

'Neve and Fletcher,' he said. As if there was another fire that needed to be put out.

There were roars of laughter all round him. He looked from face to face. His cheeks burned. Everyone was laughing. Howling with laughter because it was a great big joke. Laughing and laughing, young and happy and hopeful. But not him. He was the joke.

He left the house, went down the lawn, past the pool, into the wood. He was worried that they might come after him but nobody did.

He lay curled up under a tree, nauseous and shivery. The night was over. The sun rose like a terrible red ball that swung through his skull. It was all over and it was only just beginning.

Nicci French is the pseudonym for the writing partnership of journalists Nicci Gerrard and Sean French. The couple are married and live in London and Suffolk. They have written 21 books.

# ALSO BY
# NICCI FRENCH

### DARK SATURDAY
A NOVEL

"Fabulous, unsettling, and riveting."
—Louise Penny

In this electrifying thriller, psychologist Frieda Klein is asked to assess an 18-year-old girl accused of the shocking murder of her family—but is she really a killer, or just another victim?

### SUNDAY SILENCE
A NOVEL

"Complex...intriguing...truly unique."
—Tami Hoag

Gifted psychologist, frequent police consultant— Frieda Klein is many things. And now she's a person of interest in a murder case...because a body has been discovered beneath the floorboards of Frieda's house.

### DAY OF THE DEAD
A NOVEL

"Unforgettable. Psychological dynamite."
—Alan Bradley

A decade ago, psychologist Frieda Klein was sucked into the orbit of Dean Reeve—a killer and psychopath obsessed with Frieda herself. When a series of murders announces his return, Frieda must emerge from the shadows to confront her nemesis. And it's a showdown she might not survive...